FOREVER WASTE

Forever Waste

By

Suzanne Stephenson

Going To Waste

The Beginning

THE WRITER THOUGHT ABOUT HIS memoires. What should he do? Then it struck him. He wouldn't write about his own life, but he would draw from his experiences and the people he had met. He started to tap something out... A gust of wind caught the first page which he had recently printed out...

'In the north country lies a substantial town which spends most of its time minding its own business. You won't hear it mentioned in the media. It does not make the headlines. People just get on with their lives and if anything is wrong the expressions used are, 'Stop grumbling and get on wi' it', or 'if there's summit wrong, thou best try an' fix it'.

The town has an industrial eastern section and a middle class affluent western section. In the middle is the town centre boasting a nineteenth century gothic Town Hall, a market square, a nineteen fifties' police station, a large parish church of Norman origins and a court complex with an interesting Georgian frontage to a nineteen sixties' development at the rear. The railway station and general hospital lie half a mile to the south. Lying to the north of the town is a very large lake which borders the industrial area to the east of town and the golf links on the northwest of town. There are 2 parliamentary constituencies, solid Tory to the west and Labour to the east. There is one borough council where the balance of power is usual held by a minority party or some independents.

The town boasts a grammar school in the west and a large comprehensive in the east. There are several pleasant villages and fine country houses within the borough boundaries and a daily train service to London. The railway also serves to bring waste to the huge waste processing plant to the east of town.'

The page flapped and blew out of the window towards the railway station where Scyathica Wentworth and Steven Hovell arrived one April day.

Scyathica would much rather have found herself with a top newspaper in Fleet Street or at TV studios even in Salford but instead she found herself on the way to our town to work in the local media outlet. Her uncle, a media baron, Lord Coldharbour of Southend was most displeased with her endeavours. After two years with a scurrilous tabloid, he shouted at her, "You and your stupid name. You seem incapable of getting dirt on anyone. People don't want to read about politicians and royals doing the right things, they want shock and dirt." He continued, "So you go and work in local media court reporting and suchlike and perhaps after some hard graft you might turn into a proper journalist. Post covid the world has not got any easier." Before she could say another word the 30-year-old not unattractive victim of the diatribe was told, "Oh, and before you ask me where you will stay, I have spoken to your other uncle… that chap Wentworth who owns the farms… and you can stay with him."

While Scyathica Wentworth was rather disappointed with her move Steven Hovell was excited with his move. It was rather after all, a promotion and an exciting one at that.

Steven was a very timid young man who had hoped to rise through the ranks of the civil service in the Ministry of Justice. Instead, he had spent the last 10 years in a lowly role filing old documents in the basement of the Royal Courts of Justice save during covid lockdowns when he had worked remotely on digital file records. Every time he had tried to climb up the greasy pole something held him back. Mostly he suspected it was his nerves and his mousy presentation. And it certainly did not help him that so many applicants favoured London and the Southeast. One day, however, he had noticed a vacancy for a judge's clerk in a town miles away from London. The online application was not a problem to him. When it came to the video interview, he was amazed how warm and welcoming the Courts' Manager was. He seemed so keen that for once he was less nervous. And now he found himself on the way to his lodgings in Canal Street...

Chapter 1

THE SUN TRIED HARD TO shine on Waste. It managed a feeble glint on Wastewater (pronounced Waast Water by the locals). Steven got off the train hesitantly and clutched his two heavy, battered suitcases close to him. Despite the fact the exit markers were battered and defaced he located the station exit only to see all the locals grab all the taxis. He stood alone for a while. His rain jacket felt inadequate. He thought of going into the dilapidated newsagents' opposite and seeing if they sold a take-away coffee. Its rusted metal sign swung slightly in the breeze making a disconcerting creaking sound. The buildings around him were drab and it was drizzling. After about 10 minutes which seemed an eternity a dented silver estate car with a green sign saying 'Khan cars' pulled up. A smiling face leaned out of the driver's window.

"Want a taxi, mate?"

"Yesss," stuttered Steven in reply. "Can you take me to 3 Canal Street?"

"Thaas a bit crap place innit? Sure you want to go there?" was the surprising response of the driver who got out and flung the cases in the back. The smiling countenance revealed a number of gold teeth and had a considerable amount of 5 o'clock shadow but when it saw Steven's worried look said, "Only joking, mate. You don't look like you're from round 'ere?"

"No. I am starting a new job here. I am lodging in Canal Street. It sounded by its name as if I could go walking in my free time by the canal."

"Naaw, you won't be able to do that, mate," was the answer. "Ain't no canal there. Never has been." The smiling face went on, "I suppose they might 'ave wanted a canal for the waste water from the waste plant once upon a time. But there ain't no canal... I don't know what happens these days to Waste waste waste water... suppose it goes into Wastewater... the lake I mean." The face was chuckling at his own statement and went on with his conversation, "You don't look strong enough to work in the waste plant so I suppose you must be going to work somewhere else?"

"Yesss," stammered Steven, but the face wasn't listening. It kept firing questions but then supplying its own answers. By the end of the journey Steven had a good idea of the layout of the town and what the driver thought of various parts of it. And now he stood outside 3 Canal Street.

The address was an end of terrace 3-storey late Victorian house. There were 6 houses in a row in a very short cul-de-sac opposite what appeared to be a railway siding protected by a rusty, spiked, metal fence. They looked in need of repairs and redecoration, but the gardens were mostly neat and tidy. There were allotments immediately behind the terrace and the narrow cul-de-sac was cobbled. Incongruously, silver satellite dishes were fixed to most of the houses and there were double yellow lines painted on the cobbles. The numbers of the houses ran 1,6,2, 5,4 ,3. There was a wrought iron sign at the entrance of Canal Street: 'No parking by order of Waste D.C. Parking and deliveries to Pither's Yard'.

Steven rang the bell.

After a few minutes a quavery female voice called through the letter box,

"If you're a Jehovah's witness GO AWAY! But if you are mi' new lodger Mr Shovell, come in."

Steven gently pushed open the door. "I'm Steven Hovell," he said.

"Come in. Come in. I'm Annie Beaswick... but most people call me Auntie Bea. I'll get the kettle on."

As Auntie Bea was making a most welcome cup of tea for Steven, Scyathica Wentworth alighted from the next train. She had missed the direct service from London and had had to change trains twice before eventually arriving on the local stopping passenger service run by North Waste Rail. This final leg of the journey had been a nightmare for Scyathica. She had sat tremulously on a somewhat grubby seat clutching her Louis Vuitton case and her laptop bag to her while the out-of-control children opposite seemed to scream for most of the short journey. They all had runny noses and their mother spent most of the time on her mobile phone discussing her frozen food shopping with someone who sounded to be a close family member.

Scyathica's ears were ringing with the cacophony of screams from the children: "I want it, I want it, I want it," 'ee's got it. 'ee pinched it from us... give it back, give it back," "She's just a scrubby elephant." But Scyathica's ears also hurt from the mum's inane chatter: "Oh, I know, yes, Mum I know but I want Kevin to have something special," "I saw this recipe for prawns tombola I thought was really special and you take frozen pizza, frozen prawns, frozen cream, frozen gherkins, frozen mac and cheese, frozen pineapple..." "Yes I know. I know. Well anyway..."

Scyathica paused on the platform and drew breath. The air was cold, and it was drizzling. The other passengers beat her to the awaiting taxis.

After 10 minutes a silver estate car which had seen better days rolled up. It bore the logo 'Khan cars'. A smiling face peered out of the driver's window displaying a row of gold teeth. "Want a taxi, luvvy?"

"Yes, please," replied Scyathica. "Please can you take me to High Cliffe, The Mount...? I think it's off Links Road."

The smiling face smiled even more broadly. "Wow, that's a bit posh, luvvy… are you sure?" Scyathica visibly winced and the smiling face said, "Only joking... Yes, of course."

As Scyathica was whizzed through Waste she barely listened to the running commentary. She hoped her Uncle Sir Hugo Wentworth-Knubb would not mind too much her staying with him. As West Waste's sitting Tory MP she was not sure how he felt about the press. They had been strident about her father's behaviour except outlets owned by her other uncle.

Eventually her taxi was travelling down a rather flat road next to a golf course. She could see a lake glinting beyond it so she realised she must be travelling down Links Road. One or two side roads boasting executive developments could be seen with their identikit modern houses and Range Rover cars or similar in their driveways. They passed first 'The Ridings' and also 'Links Close'. Each house seemed to be some type of plastic neo-Georgian effort in The Ridings and Links Close from what she could glance. Their seemed to be a smaller development of non-descript town houses inserted between The Ridings and Links Close called 'The View' but Scyathica speculated to herself that the main view would be of larger executive homes.

Eventually there were no more side roads and the road appeared to merge with a country lane which had a small road sign saying, 'The Mount'. After passing a small, wooded area the taxi stopped outside some iron gates resplendent with a rusty metal sign saying 'High Cliffe'. The area gently undulated so Scyathica was wondering where the 'mount' or 'cliff' might be found.

The driver tried an intercom at the gates. A plummy voice answered, "I expect you've got my niece... Well, tell her I apologise, but she'll have to come in the farm entrance past the pig farm... gates are broken... Just go 100 yards up the lane and go in where it says 'Knubb Pigs'." So that's what they did.

Scyathica alighted outside a large eighteenth century house which some would have described as looking like a stately home. It was perhaps not as big as the grand houses and some of its guttering clearly needed attention as a few pieces of gutter were hanging from the eaves at eccentric angles. However, the front door gleamed, and the downstairs looked as if the window frames had been freshly painted. She took an intake of breath but then regretted it as she inhaled strong manurial odours which she was sure came from the adjacent pig farm not 100 metres away in the large collection of metal barns.

Her uncle soon ushered her indoors and boomed at her, "I am overjoyed you are staying in the old place... I am just rattling around here ever since Muriel left me... It's just me and Charmaine now..."

Scyathica tried to absorb this, Muriel being his wife, but who was Charmaine? "Yes, Muriel has gone off with her gym... or fitness… instructor. Charmaine comes in each day from Waste to clean and cook… well not weekends when I try to eat out... or when I am in Westminster..." came the answer before she asked the question.

"Sit down, sit down, we will have tea," he boomed on. A girl with purple and green hair and extremely long artificial fingernails also bright green appeared preceded by her artificial eyelashes. She had a tray of teacups, a teapot, a milk jug and a plate of biscuits. "Thanks, Charmaine," said her uncle. She nodded in response. It seemed as if her eyelashes and fingernails left the room ahead of her. Sir Hugo continued talking. Despite his corpulent appearance and very red face he seemed capable of speaking at length without stopping to draw breath or wait for any response. No doubt this attribute assisted him when he was speaking in the House of Commons.

"How's my sister? I think Pandora is better off since that ghastly father of yours left. You can't be blamed for him… but I do blame her for your silly name."

Scyathica winced but thought that maybe her mother was better off without her father.

"Uncle, you know she got my name from Greek mythology, from the legend of Scythians who fought monsters."

Her uncle snorted. "Susan or Sarah would have been better. I doubt if you will be fighting monsters around here."

Fortunately, Pandora had support from a family trust since Davey Scarlett her husband and Scyathica's father was doing all he could to avoid his creditors. Scyathica had long ago adopted the maternal family name 'Wentworth' to distance herself from him and his financial dealings. It had transpired his investment house and hedge fund, 'Scarlett Holdings', had foundations of sand. Somehow, Davey, however, had managed to run away to one of his 3 yachts in the Caribbean. His staff were all left unemployed, and many were left on the verge of bankruptcy. The trouble he was in would have been far greater if it were not for his press baron half-brother Lord Coldharbour who kept most of the story out of his publications. Scyathica had never felt much fondness for her father despite him funding her attendance at the best girls' boarding schools and a stint getting a mediocre degree at the London School of Economics followed by a Masters' degree in something vague from the University of South Kent.

He liked to boast in his best 'mockney', "I started with nuffink... just a market stall in the East End. I built my fortune all on my own, going to the University of 'Ard Knocks." Really, he was a grammar school boy from Chelmsford who inherited a modest fortune from his deceased father's used car business. He rose using his money to make more money but was not too fussy how he did it.

Scyathica stopped thinking about her father as her uncle continued to boom at her,

"Put you on the first floor. It's not falling down, and you'll have your own bathroom. I should avoid the east side of the house don't you know, it's not in great shape. Mind you the West Wing is in even worse shape so don't go there at all... still getting rotten flooring fixed there... I'll give you some keys... You can come and go as you please but don't bring too many men here..."

Scyathica winced but he went on, "I spend a lot of time with the pigs, you know, and also the constituents... Ha, ha... not much difference there. Now what are you doing for transport?"

Scyathica replied, "Gosh, I hadn't given it much thought... in London I always took the Tube."

"Well you're not in ruddy London now. No bloody Tube out here. Hope you have a driving licence?" he said and Scyathica nodded. He continued, "I've got a little old MG round by the pig barns. You can use it while you're here. I've got a couple of Landies and the Bentley, so it is spare. It's a nice little runner, properly looked after..."

Scyathica thanked him profusely. She was relieved now that he had raised the subject of transport because it was something she had not considered. She did, however, hope the MG had not taken on the odour of the 1000 pigs who lived in the Knubb pig barns until they serviced the Knubb bacon factory nearby in Waste.

On the other side of Waste at that time, Auntie Bea happened to be opening a pack of Knubb's Best Bacon to make a bacon sandwich for Steven Hovell. Everyone in the borough of Waste was familiar with Waste's premier bacon and the advertising hoardings saying,

'There's no waste in Knubb's bacon but it's the best bacon in Waste!'

Steven had just finished his second cup of tea and felt more welcome than he had for a long time. However, he jolted back to life from the warmth of his saggy armchair in Auntie Bea's sitting room when she said,

"Now then, how are you going to travel to this new job of yours? The buses are not very good. Since covid the service is non-existent after 6 o'clock. Did you say you were working in town centre at the court?"

Steven was shocked. In London he relied on the Underground. He had never passed his driving test as he was frightened of the London traffic although he had kept up his provisional licence and from time to time made half–hearted efforts to take more driving lessons.

"I don't know... I mean, I thought I could take a bus," he stammered.

Auntie Bea smiled. Beneath her wrinkled countenance of indeterminate gaze was a knowing look.

"One of my old lodgers sold me his old, moped scooter thing for a song when he left for bigger and better things. Nat Cartey became an MP! But I got a good deal off him, and I got Ron from next door to sort it out before you came. I kind of guessed... you being from London..."

Steven stuttered, "Well I suppose I could learn to ride it... I mean… what do you want for it? Is there a helmet?"

While Auntie Bea and Steven sorted out a deal and where he could practice on the scooter at the back of the allotments and while Scyathica unpacked her Louis Vuitton case in the surprisingly chilly bedroom at High Cliffe, another presence sat gloomily in the centre of town. It was Waste Combined Court.

Before long Steven would have to navigate all parts of the court and Scyathica would need to find her way to the public galleries. The Georgian frontage belied the gloomy sixties' rear extensions to the building. It had a very heavy oak door with large metal studs which opened onto a fine Georgian hallway with marbled floor and walls and a domed ceiling from which an elaborate light dangled resplendent with about 30 electric candle bulbs only a third of which were working. There were two handsome portraits of nineteenth century judges in gilt frames. There was a marbled staircase leading to the first floor with black wrought iron bannisters. A small wooden sign just beyond the security arch pointed heaven ward and said, 'Court 1'. Indeed, if one ventured up the marbled staircase one could find one's way to the landing outside Court 1 which was the old oak panelled assize court. Aside from the installation of modern IT, it had not changed much in 100 years.

At the rear of the Georgian entrance hall was an open doorway. It had once been a rear door to the courthouse but now led to the main part of the court complex. There was a broad corridor, a bank of lifts and a further staircase. The broad corridor led to the court offices where there were several Perspex windows for the public to approach. On the first and second floors of the building there were three more courtrooms, three District Judge's Chambers, four Judges' retiring rooms, the advocates' robing rooms and lawyers' consultation room. On the top floor of the building was an overflow Chambers, the Juries' retiring rooms and various overflow offices.

A tired air of neglect pervaded the building. Various areas of paintwork were scuffed. Much of the lighting was gloomy. Furnishings were faded and worn. There was an indefinable background odour, perhaps a little like damp dog. The staff area of the building and Judges' corridors neither escaped the air of neglect nor the faint odour. The car park behind the court from whence staff and judges entered the building and where the prison van came to disgorge its contents was a narrow and inadequate concrete strip. Once it had had a small garden area, but this had gone in order to free up more parking. Occasionally, seagulls who were blown off course from Wastewater would occupy the car park. More often it would be pigeons who would annoy judges and staff by leaving foul droppings on vehicles.

Presiding over this gloomy kingdom were the Recorder of Waste His Honour Judge Oliver Grasby KC and the Courts' Manager Derek Devene. The subjects of this nation of gloom were on the judicial side His Honour Judge Michael Phitt, Her Honour Judge Davina dela Notte, District Judge Eric Ercol, District Judge Cecily Stump and a collection of visiting part-time judiciary. The staff were numerous and included Derek Devene's 'assistant', Team Leader and Office Manager Julie Johnson, the Senior Judge's clerk Julie Jacobs, the Usher Manager Julie James and the bailiff manager James Julius.

Chapter 2

His Honour Judge Oliver Grasby KC eased his bulk out of his battered old Insignia car. Sometimes colleagues were surprised that he did not have a shiny top of the range car but that was not the way he and his wife Annette (pronounced by him 'One-ate') chose to spend their money. Despite the fact she was a High Court Judge sitting between the main Circuit Court in a nearby county town and London their expenses were considerable. They maintained their family home on Links Road and a 1-bedroomed flat in London. Of their 6 children, one was still at boarding school, two were still at university, two lived at home doing he knew not what and one had produced three expensive grandchildren but did not seem to have much in the way of financial support from a son-in-law he regarded as the world's biggest layabout. His ex-wife Prunella showed no inclination to remarry and despite the fact she was forever involved in charitable works always came up with an illness which made her too unwell to do anything remunerative. And now she was probably too old to get a job so that after 31 years he could see no end in sight to supporting her. To add insult to injury she had recently moved into a town house not far from him in the ineptly named road 'The View'.

As he hobbled his was across the concrete car park with a bow-legged walk which was the souvenir of an old rugby injury he mused to himself first that it was a good thing that bitch Prunella and himself had never had children or he would not even be able to afford a decent bottle of claret and second, that last night's claret must have been a bit rough as he was now suffering from indigestion. One of his pleasures was a subscription to an online wine merchant. He was very keen on his Bordeaux wines but also was knowledgeable on South African wines due to five years he had spent in

South Africa in his youth. He hoped he had not been palmed off with an inferior wine.

Even without his wig and robes Oliver was an imposing figure. Despite being somewhat corpulent he compensated for this with his height. He wore small, round, metal-rimmed spectacles and a dusty crumpled pinstripe suit which harboured a faint odour of pipe smoke and cigars he secretly smoked. He sported a small, bristly, grey moustache, and he was topped off by unruly grey and white hair.

He struggled with his large leather bag into the rear of the building only to bump into his immediate colleague Her Honour Judge Davina dela Notte.

"Shall we take the lift?" she barked at him.

Davina dela Notte was an exceptionally tall woman of 51 whose career had risen in meteoric form in recent years. She had long blonde hair which was tied neatly back and had a somewhat bony look to her face. She was tipped by many to go to the High Court bench. Her husband was a City banker who was never seen in Waste. She often referred to her 'super' skiing trips with him and their 'super-dooper' trips together to their house in Tuscany. Oliver knew her husband was called Jerome but had no idea what he looked like and whether Davina ever saw him other than to go on holiday. He knew she had 3 children. Two were adults, both apparently doctors who Davina assured everyone would be top-notch consultants shortly. The youngest was a boy of 12 called Flavio in a homage to Davina's far removed Italian ancestors.

As they entered the lift Davina said, "Flavio rang me last night from his school, I think he was a little homesick. He asked if he could come home again this weekend. But I said 'no' my mind would be on a forthcoming fraud trial. 'Mummy,' he said to me, 'You work far too hard you really ought to have a hobby'."

Oliver shrugged and said, "Maybe you should."

"Oh no," chortled Davina in response, "I'm far too busy looking after the family estates near Waste and in Scotland, as well as my work here!"

Oliver felt sorry for the boy. If his youngest asked if he could come home for the weekend, he would work it out somehow. He felt he had hobbies of sorts, being his wine club and pipe collecting. He hoped Annette hadn't found out about his cigar smoking in the greenhouse or found his secret stash of cigars in the seed drawer. She knew about his pipe smoking since she 'allowed it' on special occasions.

Davina went into her Chambers shortly after they left the lift, but he carried on up the corridor. He paused at the door of the Chambers of His Honour Judge Michael Phitt. It was very slightly ajar. He poked his head into the room and saw his colleague clad in sports' vest and shorts furiously rowing on a rowing machine. The Chambers were very Spartan unlike his own. There was a desk with one folder… presumably today's first case, some shelves with papers neatly placed, a modern desk with laptop on it, a modern matching chair, a rowing machine, some weights and an exercise bike. Oliver assumed Michael's robes were hung in the judicial washroom and that Michael accessed reference works online. There was one picture on the wall which was a grainy photograph of a man called Horace, who Oliver understood to be Michael's late father in his youth. It had a caption 'County cricket captain 1969'.

"Good morning, Michael," said Oliver.

"Is it?" replied Michael looking up but still rowing. "I need to put some extra time in, or I will not be fit for the Fell Marathon next Sunday. I had to throw a birthday party for the twins this weekend. I suppose we couldn't let their eleventh go but Julia had me decorating half the house for it. Not sure that Paris and Twiggy noticed…"

Julia was Michael's house-proud wife who worked as a part-time accountant. They had recently moved into one of the newist neo-Georgian modern executive houses on the Ridings, but house-proud Julia still seemed to find places for him to decorate. Paris and Twiggy were his twin daughters. Both of them showed no inclination to take part in any form of sport. Their interests were girly… make-up and clothes… but also sweets and cakes. He felt Julia indulged them and was sorry to think they both looked fat as butter. Julia didn't want more children and certainly showed no interest in sport. Michael found himself the sole member of his household with a passion for fitness and sports. Sadly, his parents were deceased and his brother Gus who also was keen on sport lived in London where he practiced dentistry in between cycling and long-distance running.

Michael was not keen on engaging in further conversation with Oliver. It would mean he would have to say something about the birthday present Oliver had sent him next week. He had found a present bag on his desk containing a bottle of St Emilion Gran Cru and a box of chocolate truffles. With his fitness regime he preferred to be teetotal and not to eat chocolates and cakes. The accompanying card had a scrawl 'to ease the pain'. He felt sure Oliver was trying to wind him up. Now and again, Oliver would choose a hapless victim to wind-up, usually a colleague. Whilst he had passed the wine to Julia and the chocolates to the girls, Michael was mildly annoyed by the gift and card.

Oliver said some platitude to Michael and then plodded off to his own Chambers. His Chambers could not have been more different. They were dominated by a huge curved antique walnut desk. An enormous wood and leather office chair was behind the desk. Behind the desk and chair were two matching walnut bookcases.

In a corner of the room was a large walnut hat and coat stand from which Oliver's robes dangled together with a spare suit on a hanger, spare shirt and more Judicial paraphernalia. A large wig tin lay at the feet of the hat and coat stand. Under the picture window which looked out onto the car park was a small, battered settee, a small cupboard and a small fridge. On the shelves of one bookcase were many different lawbooks which ranged from the latest Archbold to some veritable antiques. On the desk and the other bookcase papers and folders were strewn in what looked to be no particular order. Somehow the desk also accommodated a laptop and large screen.

On the wall was a faded picture of a South African vineyard with a youth of about nineteen or twenty standing outside an entrance gate. Close scrutiny would reveal it was Oliver as a youngster. Just occasionally there would be a faint South African intonation when he spoke. Not many people were aware that his mother was of South African heritage from a wine growing family. They were not aware of Oliver's South African years or his involvement in the anti-Apartheid movement as a youth.

Out of sight in his cupboard were half a dozen bottles of his favourite claret which he knew was strictly against court service rules. Hidden in a tin which had a sticker saying, 'Spare stationery' and which was secreted under the 'Equal Treatment Judicial Guide' in his desk drawer were 12 of his favourite cigars. On top of his bookcase in a small glass case was a small display of antique tobacco pipes.

Oliver began to sort out his documents for the day. Although everything would be online in Court 1, Oliver liked to have paper copies of anything he deemed particularly important. When he had checked the case list last night, he knew there would be a plea appearance from a particular recidivist, Johnny O'Hanrahan and his wife May Lou O'Hanrahan on charges of burglary, robbery and receiving stolen goods. Both were in custody, and he therefore hoped the prison vans would not be late.

As he was sorting his papers there was a knock at the door. "Enter," Oliver barked.

Derek Devene sidled into the room. A thin man of indeterminate age with lank, mousy hair and an issue with one eye. He and his husband Julian were known as one of Waste's most devoted couples. The unkind queried how he had got the job as Courts' Manager. They usually concluded he ticked the right boxes. He was very much a 'Yes-man' for the senior managers at the Circuit Office. He ticked a couple of the diversity boxes. He was partially sighted sporting a slightly disconcerting glass eye due to a childhood illness when he had lost an eye. The main thing was he had a talent for avoiding offending difficult characters, and he was very diplomatic with his judges.

"Just wanted to tell you, Your Honour, we got you a new permanent judge's clerk. He is coming in on Friday to do some induction work with the other staff and get used to the building. Then I hope after a few days' training he can start with you later next week."

Oliver looked up in response to Derek Devene's statement and replied,

"OK, Devine..." he started but Derek interrupted.

"It's Devene pronounced Deveen not Devine as you know, Your Honour."

Oliver continued, "Okay, Devine. What's the fella called? Where did you get him from? We've needed another clerk for ages."

Derek ignored the deliberate mistake over his name. His Honour Judge Grasby KC did it every time he spoke to him.

"Your Honour, he is called Steven Hovell, and he comes from London. He has worked in admin at the Royal Courts for many years. I think we were lucky to get him. I think he decided to come to us as the job is a jump upwards for him. As you know not everyone wants to come and work in Waste."

"I'll say," said Oliver pulling a face. "Maybe if you were less of a shrinking violet with Circuit Office, we could get more staff and judges, Devine."

Devene ignored the insult. He was good at ignoring such slights, but he replied,

"We also have a Recorder sitting with us for 5 weeks to help with some of the backlog. It's Recorder Aziz Ahmed who was with us last year."

Oliver seemed pleased. "At least he's pretty competent. The trouble is he'll get a permanent appointment next competition if he applies. Then he'll be off to London or Birmingham. Anyway, thank you very much, Devine... If that's it you can go," which he did.

In fact, Derek Devene was on his way to see the District Judges who heard the civil cases and most of the family cases at the court. Serious civil work was mainly sent off to the main Circuit Court. Waste Combined Court had had a vacancy for a senior Civil Circuit Judge for years. The most serious family cases in the borough went to Her Honour Davina dela Notte who doubled up as Designated Family Judge as well as being a Criminal Circuit Judge. The least complicated family cases went to the local lay magistrates. The two District Judges were left with huge caseloads. Part-time Deputy District Judges were brought in to assist since there had been a vacancy for a permanent third District Judge for two years.

As it happened District Judge Cecily Stump and District Judge Eric Ercol were both together in the room which doubled up as a photocopying room and Judges' dining room. Neither of them had Chambers for retiring, separate to the two Chambers, or hearing rooms in which they heard cases. Each hearing room was similar to the other... desk, chair, witness box, no dock and 12 chairs with a bank of tables forming 2 rows so that 6 people could sit on each row. However, just now they were examining their lists over coffee in the dining room.

District Judge Cecily Stump had grey, curly hair and looked older than her 60 years. She always seemed a very jumpy person to Derek Devene. He knew she put on a calm air during hearings because he had seen it, but when not sitting she often looked on the verge of tears. Unmarried, she lived a few miles out of town on the shores of Wastewater and was known as a leading light in the church choir. Her 'gentleman', as she called her partner, who did not live with her, visited monthly. He lived about 50 miles away and was the leading light of a local Morris Dancing group and cider preservation society. They seemed an incongruous mix which was presumably why they didn't live together.

District Judge Eric Ercol was short, fat, pompous and did not take fools gladly. He had a shiny, bald head and prominent and disconcerting mole on the end of his nose. He was in his mid-fifties and his wife Tina was a local solicitor. They had three children, Mostyn who was studying law at university, Sarah who was studying for A levels and Thomas who had just started at the grammar school. They had not moved out to the Links area like many of their professional contemporaries but remained in the town of Waste, living in a large Victorian house just on the boundaries of East and West Waste. His hobbies were gardening, reading local history and home brewing.

Derek Devene cleared his throat. "District Judges... I have some bad news for you which is why I am visiting you in person."

Both District Judges waited for him to continue. "I know you have full lists but unfortunately there is a care case. It seems the magistrates transferred it, but the Legal Advisor forgot to check if there was space in one of your lists. All the lawyers are rolling up now to the building so I can't just take it out..."

Cecily's lip began to quiver. "I've got the possession list," she said.

Eric raised his eyebrows.

"There may be some good news," continued Derek. "I suspect the parents will welcome an adjournment since they can't be in 2 cases at once. They are also due for plea and directions in the Crown Court..."

Eric responded, "Anyone we know and love?"

"Well," said Derek, "I think you may have come across the family before. It's the O'Hanrahan children. The children of Johnny and May Lou. I believe that you did a case last year involving that family?"

"Good God," said Eric. "I had a case involving 6 children who I think were nephews and nieces. I remember it well. The dad Padric caused some security concerns. He somehow got a knuckle-duster into the building. No-one knew how…"

Derek replied, "I remember it. There were all sorts of questions for our security guards... was the arch working and suchlike. Didn't Padric brandish the knuckle-duster in one of your hearings and threaten he would 'get' the social workers?"

"That's right. I sent him straight before a CJ... I think we had a rare visit from an outside judge with time on his hands. Padric got 28 days. As for the children I finished the case on a calmer occasion a few weeks later. Full care orders as I recall." He paused, "I suppose I will have to take the new case then, although it's not very convenient. I already have 8 cases of mums and dads scrapping about their children. How many children are there this time?"

Derek took a folded piece of paper from his pocket which was a print-out of some details.

"Petunia, Pansie, Prince, Paula, Persephone, Pearl, Parker and Patella..."

Eric guffawed. "Patella? Surely not...?"

Derek replied, "I believe so. Changing the subject, we have a new clerk starting with us soon, Steven Hovell. Do you mind if he spends a little time in your court, sir, before I let him loose on His Honour Judge Grasby KC?"

"No problem," said Eric. "I'll get him used to some of our local ways."

District Judge Stump seemed relieved she had not had to take the care case or have the new clerk in her court. Derek was just relieved he had someone to hear the extra case. He returned to the office downstairs only to be assailed by questions from all quarters. As he sighed and started to consider the latest problem, he did at least consider himself lucky to have a core contingent of loyal staff. The three Julies had worked at the court for many years and could be relied upon to do their best. That was one advantage he had in Waste. It was too far from other large centres to draw local people into doing a commute.

The centres of employment were the Waste Processing plant, Knubb Bacon, the council, the local paper and local radio station, the Court and small employers such as solicitors and local garages. It did of course make it rare for outsiders to work in Waste. He felt lucky to have engaged Steven Hovell. He had heard a rumour too that there was a new young female court reporter from London. He wondered if these incomers knew what they had let themselves in for.

Chapter 3

SCYATHICA WENTWORTH PARKED HER UNCLE'S sports car on the yellow lines outside the building the local paper the Waste Telegraph shared with Waste F.M. (known by the locals as Lefty FM). She was not used to driving to work so she hoped it would be alright since she had no idea where to park. As she got out of the car an aged, battered BMW screeched to a halt. She caught sight of what must be a personalised number plate spelling 'BRIECEY' but realised the 'E' was a '4' which had been slightly doctored.

A tall man in his mid-forties jumped out. He sported a ponytail and a sweatshirt with the logo on it 'Simply the best'. He beat her to the door of the building which he preceded to hold open.

"Thank you," said Scyathica hesitantly. "You wouldn't know where the Crime Desk is would you?"

"The Crime Desk... where did you emerge from? If you want to give hot tips on a story then give them to Bricey."

"Bricey? Who is Bricey?" responded Scyathica.

Bricey replied, "Don't you know who I am...? Melvyn Brice... who does the mid-morning show and Saturday 'Footcast'. The main man of Waste FM."

Scyathica shook her head. This was not going well.

"Everyone knows me so you must be that new girl from London. Just go to the basement and you'll see some other junior reporters. If they don't send you on something, mind you move your car at lunchtime before the traffic warden comes round. The traffic warden won't have me cos he's dying to get on the show. That's why I brought the BM with my own number plate today. I've got 3 others you know. This is the one in best nick."

As Bricey showed her how to find the basement stairs he chortled on about his popular shows and his passion for old BMWs. Scyathica just kept nodding and smiled weakly. When she was finally met by her new boss, a no-nonsense lady called Stacey Birch she was relieved that Stacey sat her down with a coffee and went through what her job entailed in a calm and collected fashion. Stacey commented,

"You may occasionally get to do a radio report, so you'll come across that twit Bricey if you do. They have given him the mid-morning show, so he has to report and chat on news when all he really cares about are the Wastrels..."

"The Wastrels?" queried Scyathica.

"Waste Wanderers football club," responded Stacey. "Our local football club which hangs on by its teeth in the bottom reaches of the football league. The team is nicknamed the Wastrels and the supporters the Wasters. They are owned 50/50 between the supporters' trust and the French bloke who has a stake in Waste Waste."

"French bloke?"

Stacey continued, "Yeah, didn't you know the French have a stake in our Waste plant... the bloke's called something like Xavier Didier Le Perte... the unions and our Labour MP don't like him one little bit. Look, I know your uncle is MP for Waste West, but has he filled you in on the local scene?"

"Not really... I thought as Court reporter I would mainly need to know about the court and police, but it sounds as if I need to know a lot more," said Scyathica.

Stacey switched her computer on.

"Okay," she answered, "I'll put up a few pictures on screen and fill you in. Just to start here is a rare picture of Xavier Didier Le Perte. You can see in the box at the stadium the tall thin bloke with the limp hair and what is probably a Gauloise in his mouth. The football supporters don't care for him because he is rarely ever at the club and the view is he only bought a stake to ingratiate himself with the locals. The club was in danger of going bust, so the money was welcome.

"I think he thought he might make a better impression after falling out with the unions at Waste Waste. As you know I hope, the 2 biggest employers in Waste are Waste Waste and Knubb Bacon. I'm not just trying to say good things about your uncle, but he is a popular employer with a reputation for fairness. When Knubb Bacon was going through a rough period rumour has it he mortgaged his own house rather than make redundancies or pay cuts."

Scyathica pondered this might be why part of her uncle's house might need some 'TLC'.

"Now Waste Waste has been considered a dodgy outfit for years. From time to time, we get the odd story about what disgusting or dangerous things may lurk within the waste. But they have been owned by one consortium after another for years. Recently they were acquired by the hedge fund run by that dodgy businessman Davey Scarlett, but it's now been sold on, and I am told Xavier has at least a 50% stake in it. Waste Waste has been trying to change the workers' contracts."

Scyathica winced. Somehow Stacey was not aware her father was the said Davey Scarlett. She supposed Lord Coldharbour would have done his best to bury this piece of information. Stacey put some more pictures up on her screen.

"These two have taken up the workers' cause. The one on the left... and I don't mean it ironically, is Waste East's MP, Nat Cartey. He was convenor for the union at the Waste plant for a while. He's the one in the Karl Marx t-shirt there. He's only been in the town for about 8 years so his rise to being an MP has been meteoric. That's our Nat there and standing with him is his agent who still is very much involved with the unions, Mickey Gasson... Yes, the short, fat, bald one with the tartan shirt."

Stacey put another picture on screen. While she was doing so Scyathica considered Nat Cartey looked oddly familiar.

He looked like her older cousin Nathanial Coldharbour whom she had not seen for about 10 years.

"Here is a picture of the main members of Waste Borough Council. The councillor in the middle with all the chains who is stooping a bit is the Leader of the Council and Mayor of Waste, Norman Ryder aka 'Easy' Ryder. He is not known for making waves and I think got the jobs because he is not at all controversial."

Stacey carried on telling her about the Chief Constable of Waste Police Force, the Police and Crime Commissioner and what she knew of the Judges and the Court. Eventually she showed Scyathica to a workstation and a computer and said,

"Before you do any reporting spend a little time working out who is whom and what is what."

It was not surprising Nat Cartey looked familiar because Nat Cartey harboured several secrets. First, he had not always been called Nat Cartey; he had been born Nathanial Justin Coldharbour. There was a Nat Cartey with whom he had been to the Poly many years ago. Before they both dropped out they had decided it would be a huge laugh to swap IDs for a bit. Nat felt it might aid Nathanial getting a job but after a while Nat had other ideas and disappeared backpacking. Nathanial could not believe his luck. He was able to throw off his public-school background and keep using Nat's birth certificate to show his identity as a 'working man' although just to be on the safe side he also had executed a change of name deed. People put his occasional poshness of voice down to him having come from London. He learned a lot about the local scene while he was lodging at Auntie Bea's and his party were glad of him when he voted from time to time in the House of Commons. He was sure Sir Hugo had no idea who he really was, and he was not sure if his own father had figured things out or not.

He was rarely in touch with Lord Coldharbour. Last time they spoke was 6 months ago when he vaguely mentioned "doing something up north". Still, the allowance from the Trust Fund (obviously not declared amongst his member's interests) kept coming and that kept him in beer and ciggies and meant his MP's salary could be saved up and used to bolster his stock market portfolio. Mickey Gasson had no idea, which was just as well. He wondered if he might have an issue if he ever got to the altar with Mickey's daughter Brittany who at present had 'status' of fiancée. Hopefully he could manage to avoid it until he could figure out a way forward. He might have been more nervous if he had realised his cousin was in town.

Said cousin was wending her way back to High Cliffe through the pig farmyard. She was greeted enthusiastically by Sir Hugo.

"Good day... eh... What? Port, sherry..."

She thanked him.

"Well help yourself... if you want some. There's venison pate and camembert in the fridge don't you know... plenty of smoked salmon in the freezer. Help yourself..."

Curiously Scyathica asked,

"Thought you might have some Knubb bacon."

"Heavens, no," responded her uncle with a twinkle in his eye. "Never touch the stuff."

Scyathica found herself some eggs and bread and made herself an omelette with toast and tea and tried to relax.

At Auntie Bea's Steven was also trying to relax. His day had seemed rather stressful. First there was the difficulty of starting the scooter in Canal Street. Then the traffic had really scared him. After that he had a nightmare parking in the concrete car park behind the court. He had been shouted at first by a security man and then by a judge. He was thankful it was one of the District Judges, District Judge Ercol who he had annoyed rather than His Honour Judge Oliver Grasby KC. That was until Derek Devene said he would by way of training be shadowing one of the Julies, Julie Jacobs in District Judge Ercol's court. She explained they would be using a courtroom not a District Judge's Chambers and would be assisted by an usher. The ushers were respectively Nichola, Nicky, Nikki, Nila, Nick, Nicholas, Jenni, Kenny and Khaled. Today Nicky would be the usher, but Steven's head was spinning with all the new people for him to get to know. In the basement of the Royal Courts in London he did not see many people in his old filing job. He also rarely saw any judges unless he was asked to take papers to a particular judge or a particular court. That had become rare since the covid period.

Julie explained the intercom system and how the video link to the prison would work. It seemed District Judge Ercol was dealing with a care case and Julie explained the mother May Lou O'Hanrahan would be appearing by video link from prison. The father Johnny, who was also in prison, was neither being produced in court nor appearing by video link today. Everyone was legally represented. There were two social workers who had chosen to attend in person as had the Children's Guardian whose job it was to represent the interests of the children. Steven understood it was an important hearing. Currently the children were living temporarily with May Lou's mother Audrey Shagg, but Waste Borough Council had applied to remove the children and place them with local authority foster parents since the police were now presenting criminal charges against Audrey too for receiving stolen goods. Just to add to the mix the court had received a late application from someone who said he was the father of Patella rather than Johnny. The application bore the name Lascelles Levi and he was represented by local solicitor Mr Blunt.

Steven watched the usher bring everyone into court who was entitled to be there except Lascelles Levi and Mr Blunt. Julie made initial contact with May Lou's prison and District Judge Ercol entered. Everyone stood up. After he indicated for people to sit Waste Borough Council's counsel Ivan Huff stood up and cleared his throat.

"If it pleases you, sir we are concerned with Petunia, Pansie, Prince, Paula, Persephone, Pearl, Parker and Patella."

There was a loud interruption from May Lou on the video link.

"How many times do I have to tell people there ain't no Persephone... She is called 'Percyfone'."

"Please, Mrs O'Hanrahan don't interrupt. Your lawyer will deal with matters on your behalf," said Eric Ercol.

Ivan Huff continued and pointed out that they needed to deal with the preliminary issue of Mr Levi's application. The District Judge asked for the applicant and solicitor

Mr Blunt to be brought in. A neat, grey-haired man in a pinstriped suit was first through the entrance. He was carrying a file and his laptop, so Steven assumed he was the solicitor. An extremely tall black woman with a beautiful coiffure and a face with strikingly high cheek bones followed him.

"Madam, you can't come in... this is a family case," said Julie.

District Judge Ercol added,

"This is a private matter, not open to the public."

"But it is about mi' daughter," said the woman. "I'm Patella's father."

"Father, father..." said Ivan Huff. "Surely not?"

"Are you some tranny thing now?" screeched May Lou over the video link.

The solicitor Mr Blunt interjected, "My client was Lascelles Levi. She is now known as Lavinia Levi."

District Judge Ercol spoke to everyone. "Miss Levi my apologies to you. Ms O'Hanrahan, one more interruption and I will mute you for the rest of the hearing. Now let's get on with things without inappropriate comments and interjections."

So District Judge Ercol went onto hear the application for party status which was adjourned for DNA testing and after one more interruption he had May Lou muted. Which was just as well; when it came to Waste Borough Council's application to remove the children from Mrs Shagg's home, this was opposed by her. Mrs Shagg had been notified but made no application to become a party and was not present. It was left to May Lou's counsel Miss Faye Leafly to make an impassioned speech while her client mouthed obscenities on the video link. Eventually it was the turn of Johnny's solicitor Max Scott.

"Sir, as you know my client is not present, but I have full instructions. As stated earlier he did not oppose DNA testing of Patella and if Miss Levi turned out to be father... him... her ... er 'em being made a party. He also does not oppose the local authority's application to remove his children from Miss Shagg. He has always felt her to be a bad influence on the children... and er... em... his wife." May Lou could be seen on screen getting up from her chair in prison. She clearly heard every word. It appeared the chair was thrown in the direction of the screen which then went blank.

District Judge Ercol cut in, "We seem to have lost the prison. Miss Leafly unless you want us to adjourn for a few minutes so you can try to ring your client there... I suggest we proceed without her."

"No, sir," said Miss Leafly. "I do have full instructions."

And so the hearing continued. District Judge Ercol rose after he had heard submissions. The court was cleared during that adjournment.

Steven asked Julie, "Has he gone to decide? It sounded fairly clear cut."

"He will have decided already," responded Julie. "He will have gone to make notes to give a water-tight judgment of his reasons."

And indeed some 45 minutes later District Judge Eric Ercol gave a succinct reasoned oral judgement. The hearing did not conclude immediately after his judgment. The Children's Guardian's solicitor, a tall, blonde woman Miss Sue Rosemary made application for psychological assessment of the children for reasons she explained clearly and in a measured way, referring the judge to online documentation. Steven hoped he could have helpful lawyers in court like Max Scott and Sue Rosemary. They were well organised and helped keep the case flowing, reducing the work of the clerk and he imagined assisting the judge.

He sat back in Auntie Bea's easy chair and gradually felt less stressed. She fussed around him and presented him with a tray of tea, toast and sausages, beans and chips. He was pleased he had opted to pay for 2 meals a day... even though they seemed rather plain fare. In his bedsit in London, he had often had to resort to take-aways due to the inadequacy of the cooking facilities. It had been quite a lonely life but one he had been determined to carve out. The rest of the Hovells lived in the Home Counties. He was the youngest of 4 children and his parents had never stopped telling him how much more successful his elder siblings were even though their jobs were mundane. Steven was slight, taking after his mother he assumed who was also slight, but his father was a huge bear of a man. Carter Hovell or as his friends called him, 'Champ', had taken a cruel delight in belittling anything Steven achieved. If Steven attained an 'A' for English Champ would make sure he berated him all evening for his lack of sporting prowess and would dismiss the success in English. Steven was nothing like his older sisters, loud and outgoing girls or his elder brother who looked and sounded much like his father. He often wondered if his mother Deedee had had a brief fling with the postman or milkman but dismissed these thoughts each time as Deedee seemed devoted to Champ.

His parents did not seem bothered when he left home. They never came to his bedsit where he had a particularly lonely existence during the covid lockdown period, so he did not give them his new address when he headed for Waste. He would phone his mother briefly monthly out of duty to tell her he was alright. He visited his parents twice a year for a few hours on Christmas Day and Mothers' Day but was not sure if he would continue this. His siblings did not bother with him, and he did not contact them.

Steven hoped that in Waste he could truly belong. Maybe he could find a young lady... Maybe one day have a family... and be nice to his children.

Chapter 4

A FEW WEEKS LATER ON a **Monday morning** Steven scootered his way with some pride to Waste Combined Court. He drew into the car park and managed to avoid either colliding with the prison van or putting his scooter anywhere near a judge's car. Undoubtedly Waste was a more welcoming place than he had expected and for that he was grateful. He liked most of his colleagues. As a boss Derek Devene could be a little vague but the Julies all had their fingers on the pulse. Julie James was particularly helpful. A neat, mature woman, who did not take fools gladly, her steely demeanour which she put on for public consumption hid a heart of gold. Aside from training about what the usher did with the jury or the lowdown on which judge had what grumble she could be both sympathetic and firm at the same time. Steven passed the time of day with Julie and readied himself for a day with His Honour Judge Oliver Grasby KC.

His Honour was not in the best of moods. His daughter Sheron and son-in-law Les Laybourne had been to visit. Sheron was pregnant again and Les said he was between contracts... whatever that meant. Oliver didn't actually know what Les did for a living, but it never lasted long. Sheron and Les were often on the doorstep seeking a hand-out. The last thing they needed was another baby. Annette left such matters to him because at weekends she was usually exhausted by her High Court work and her journeys. At the moment she was in London having set off at 5am while Oliver slept off his claret hang-over. He had felt particularly in need of fine wine and his pipe and cigars after Sheron and Les's visit. He had given into their sob story asking for money for unborn Laybourne. He had also allowed small, unruly Laybournes to clamber all over him and generally to cause chaos. His two children who still lived at home Christopher and Cressida put in a brief appearance but retreated once the small

Laybournes started screaming for sweeties and 'piggybacks'. His head thumped as he readied himself for the morning case.

Steven peered into his Chambers as he straightened his court attire.

"Morning, Shovel... is the paedo in the dock?"

Steven flinched. "Your Honour, my name is Hovell and, yes, the defendant is available."

And so, the week's trial commenced. Prosecuting counsel was the dashing, urbane Percy Vere and defence counsel was the flustered Miss Faye Leafly. The blonde and suave Percy Vere sought permission for his pupil to attend with him, a spotty young man. Oliver only caught his last name Ellison. At lunchtime Percy Vere sought permission to call on Oliver briefly in his Chambers so he could update Oliver on the dates of some dinners at the local Bar Mess. He had Ellison in tow who hovered at the doorway to the Chambers.

"Where are you from?" Oliver barked in his direction.

"I'm from the Black Country, Your Honour," said Ellison in a strong Birmingham accent.

"Well, mind you watch what young Vere does so he can make a decent lawyer out of you. What did you say your first name is?" Oliver questioned.

The reply in a strong Brummy accent sounded like 'crease'.

"Crease?" commented Oliver. "That's an unusual name. How do you spell it?"

Ellison went a rather pink colour and replied, "That's not at all an unusual name... C H R I S."

Steven, who was in the corridor outside tried not to laugh and he could see the smirk on Percy Vere's face as Percy and Chris left.

"Your Honour," said Steven, "Recorder Ahmed and some of the other judges are in the dining room. Would you like me to bring you a coffee there or would you prefer I brought you a coffee here?"

Oliver indicated that he would go to the judges' dining room. The covid days of working remotely had spoiled this once daily interaction. As Steven was organising the coffee and thinking of his own egg sandwich made by Auntie Bea, Oliver took out a sandwich box and a tin of chocolate biscuits and oat cakes made by the local bakery and headed for the dining room. Steven also considered the contrast between Oliver and Recorder Ahmed.

The Recorder was immaculately dressed at all times. His fine, dark, pinstripe suit fitted him perfectly. He also seemed to possess a number of beautiful silk ties. Today he was wearing a County Cricket Club tie pin. His hair was neatly cut and there was never a hair or bristle out of place. His desk in court and Chambers was always neat and tidy. He was known as the most courteous Recorder on the Circuit. Hearings before him were always a sea of calm. He was tipped for Silk and a glittering legal career. He was alleged to have a beautiful wife who was a top eye surgeon and twin sons who at the age of twelve were respectively a chess prodigy and music prodigy. No-one had a bad word to say about him, not even the defendants.

Aziz Ahmed rose as Oliver entered the dining room. Pleasantries were exchanged. Then Oliver pushed his biscuit tin forward.

"Here, help yourself," and looking at Recorder Ahmed, "unless it's still Ramadan or you're on a diet."

Recorder Ahmed murmured that neither applied. Oliver persisted, "It's from a good bakers... but not sure their Halal."

Recorder Ahmed took 2 biscuits.

"Well, you look like you could benefit from a good meal."

Recorder Ahmed said nothing, but Oliver continued, "How's that wife of yours? Eye surgeon, isn't it? I don't expect she has time to cook or perhaps she doesn't like cooking."

The other judges variously drank teas and coffees and seemed to be poking at lunchboxes and packets of sandwiches and appeared in the main to be ignoring this exchange. Oliver persisted in needling Recorder Ahmed.

"I hear your court is so quiet, people wonder if anything happens in it," Oliver continued and kept making comments as lunchtime continued.

"It's as quiet as waiting for the end of a Test match. Cricket is not my thing, but I hear England won the latest Test match. There's a very good fast bowler from Pakistan but he was bowled out. Looks a lot like you. Do you like cricket?"

Recorder Ahmed said inscrutably that he was not that interested in cricket and much preferred tennis.

"Ahh, that's the tennis club pin you're wearing then," said Oliver still needling.

After what was only 30 minutes in the dining room but what seemed an eternity, lunchtime finished. Oliver waddled back to his Chambers where Steven awaited him, but he was followed by Recorder Ahmed.

Steven stepped into the corridor as Aziz Ahmed followed Oliver into the room.

Recorder Ahmed asked, "Why do you try and provoke me every time I come here? Is it because I'm not white Anglo-Saxon?"

"No, of course not. It's because you're so perfect!" responded Oliver with a chuckle. "I like there to be a bit of spark at lunchtime. I figured you could take it... Some of the others are very dull... or look like they would be very easily upset."

Steven listening outside thought about District Judge Stump who always looked on the verge of tears when she was not in court. Her demeanour tended to make him feel less weak and down at heel.

Aziz Ahmed smiled. "Your Honour…"

"For goodness' sake call me Oliver. I've known you off and on for about a year."

"Oliver, then, you are impossible! Don't you have enough in court without winding people up outside of it?"

Oliver chuckled further. "You're a good sport, here... have a cigar."

He rummaged under his desk and brought a huge Cuban cigar out of his secret stash.

"Don't mind if I do. I'll take it for after court," said Aziz Ahmed. He then sped off up the corridor to the Chambers allotted to him. He reflected on the fact that Waste and its court were full of very eccentric people. He supposed it made a change.

Steven also dashed off. He took what he thought would be a short cut through the old front hall of the building, only to slam into an attractive young woman who dropped her handbag and notebook onto the floor. Steven spotted her press badge.

He became very flustered and said, "Oh, I am so sso sorry... are you alright...?"

Scyathica smiled. "I'm fine, really I am."

Steven looked at her badge. "Miss Wentworth, is it? I am Steven Hovell one of the judge's clerks. I am new to the court... well actually the area so I guess I need to look around me more."

"Call me Scyathica," she responded. "I'm pretty new to the area too. New to the local news as a court reporter."

Steven could not help but notice how attractive she was. Trying not to look as nervous as he felt he asked,

"I finish at 4.40 today. If you are free then the Knubb Arms serve tea and cake in the lounge until 5.30... I saw a sign outside... It looks quite respectable. Perhaps as recompense for my clumsiness we might have tea... or coffee there?"

Scyathica really didn't think Steven was her type, but he seemed so inoffensive… and she had not done any socializing since she came to Waste so she said, "Yes."

Meanwhile she nipped back to the office and saw Stacey. Stacey said,

"I've got a cracking good story for you to look into. It seems the Environment

Agency are bringing a prosecution against Waste Waste for polluting Waste Beck with some type of alcohol waste run-off from the plant. Case is in court next week. Some old farmer reckons that when this happened just after Christmas some of his sheep drank from the beck and were falling about drunk. Three died. However, as long as we get our facts straight I was thinking of a headline 'Waste Waste waste water wastes sheep!'"

Scyathica was mildly amused but did not look forward to going to visit the sheep farmer. It was bad enough that her uncle had a pig farm. She was missing London not that she believed she could find young men who could entertain her and admire her, but she supposed here she at least had tea and cake at the Knubb Arms ahead of her with Steven Hovell.

The Knubb Arms was at first glance an old-fashioned establishment. It was a Georgian building which had been a coaching inn and sat on the edge of the same square as the old frontage of Waste Combined Court. There was an archway which led to the rear of the building which had been a stable yard but was now a small car park. The stables now housed some bedroom accommodation and a function room which took 30-40 people depending on the activity. Every first Wednesday of the month an evening could be spent Morris Dancing and listening to traditional folk and sea shanties since this was the monthly venue for the Waste Borough Alliance of Folk and Morris-men.

The main building had 4 storeys. The top floor was occupied by the landlord Glenn Bullerton and his wife and children.

The third floor had staff accommodation and a couple of single bedrooms for guests. The second floor housed the best of the guest rooms.

The first floor housed a small meeting room for up to 18 people, a fine dining restaurant and the main ladies' and gents' toilets. On the ground floor was a small reception area, a modest taproom with a selection of real ales and a television showing a sports' channel constantly and a larger lounge bar which opened up into a spacious lounge area. It was within the lounge bar and lounge area the patrons could enjoy bar snacks and afternoon tea. Glenn Bullerton was astute enough to realise that his income could not just be derived from the old codgers who came into the taproom to have a few pints and watch the football. Thus, he made sure that the establishment's 10 bedrooms had up-to-date facilities and that the dining experience was of a high standard. This made sure the hostelry was a favoured haunt for the lawyers, and visiting judges would tend to room there rather than in the cheaper chain establishment near the railway station. The Knubb Arms had survived the temporary loss of business in the covid days and once again thrived.

Thus, Scyathica Wentworth and Steven Hovell sank nervously into two armchairs by a coffee table to consume an herbal tea for Scyathica, a coffee for Steven and a plate of somewhat delicate looking afternoon tea fancies. Although the conversation was a little stilted at times and both of them remained slightly anxious each of them derived a secret satisfaction that they had managed to achieve a date of sorts. After spending what was actually a pleasant hour or two in the Knubb Arms they went their separate ways but promised to "do it again next week".

Scyathica did not notice the missed call on her mobile phone until she was back at High Cliffe. Sir Hugo was in Westminster, and she did not expect him until the weekend. Charmaine popped in a few times to make sure the house was in order but otherwise she had the place to herself. And so, she sat down with some trepidation and helped herself to a large brandy. She played the voice mail several times.

'Hi, this is Penny Wayney,' the North American drawl sounding like 'Painy Wayney'. It went on, 'I'm having my fourth go at a dissertation for my Sociology Masters. I was in touch with your mom, and she said you had been sent to northern England,' she pronounced it 'Inger-land'. 'Anyway, I wheedled your address out of her what with us being such good friends and all,' that was news to Scyathica who had been doing her best to avoid Penny for the last few years. After about a year's silence she had supposed Penny had returned to the USA.

Penny carried on, 'I decided to do my dissertation on life in a northern Inger-lish town and I thought you'd be thrilled if I came and stayed with you. We could go everywhere together like at uni... it would be such fun and I'm sure you need a good friend being in a strange place and all. Also, I have really good new vegan recipes I want to try out on you... and your uncle too."

Scyathica dreaded to think of what Sir Hugo would think of Penny's vegan recipes, seeing he was the proprietor of a bacon factory! In fact, she dreaded to think of what Sir Hugo would think of Penny at all; and as for the thought of Penny following her around that really was something which made her shudder. While Scyathica was keen on having company and admirers that certainly did not include Penny and she felt with some justification that most people would agree with her. The voicemail went on and on about how much Penny was looking forward to coming and finished, 'So I'll be with you real soon,' but failed to say when.

Chapter 5

PENNY WAYNEY PULLED HER MICROSCOPIC skirt down as far as it would go and pulled her patent leather plastic boots up over her long, slender legs. She straightened her green artificial feather boa scarf which matched her green retro handbag. She hoped she could impress those northern English folks. The daughter of Senator Brad T Morton Wayney, junior and his English ex-actress wife Alanna Wayney nee Winters (aka Aggie Winterbottom in her hometown) she had been brought up in both New York and California. A year in a Swiss finishing school had not softened her rasping drawl. She had met Scyathica at the University of South Kent when she was making her first effort at a Masters' degree in the UK. At first Scyathica had welcomed having a new friend but after a short time the friendship became a strain.

Penny would follow her everywhere and would in that rasping drawl be quick to utter pronouncements and opinions whether anyone asked her or not. If there was a faddy diet she would be on it. If there was an obscure cause she would take it up. From 'Be kind to Slugs' to a campaign to introduce a vegetarian diet to lions, Penny could be sure to pick it up. When Scyathica last saw her, she had started a vegan gluten free, dairy free, sugar free 'Green' diet. Penny had been trying to gain a Master's degree for all the time Scyathica knew her but she seemed to 'stop-start' and then go off on a tangent. When Scyathica gained her Master's and went back to London, Penny initially claimed to be desolate and sat in Scyathica's room weeping for hours.

However, Penny soon found other interests. At one point Penny had joined Green-Peace but her attraction to them had waned as she had no real understanding of their causes. She toyed with Buddhism for a bit. Another time she went off with a mid-

European alleged aristocrat who had extolled the virtues of his organic vineyards near the Danube; their engagement had been announced in society magazines. On whose side the engagement cooled was not clear, but the romance soon fizzled out. Penny apparently spent 3 months in Indonesia studying native tribes although she went en route via Bali where she spent a lot of time on the beach considering the literature on the subject. She spent a long time in therapy and would go on for hours about her therapy and "dealing with" her "emotions" on the phone to Scyathica. Gradually the phone calls petered out.

Now and again Scyathica saw mention of Penny's parents in magazines. She had met them once at a fine London restaurant. They were somewhat larger than life and perhaps accounted for some of Penny's personality traits. As they sat themselves at a standard table, Scyathica recalled her embarrassment as the senator said to the waiter in ringing, loud tones, "We want a bigger table," and had continued to be obnoxious to the serving staff throughout the meal.

While Penny Wayney was sorting out her attire for her visit to Waste, Steven was chatting to his landlady Auntie Bea. She was explaining how over the years she had had a variety of lodgers including for a time their Labour MP Nat Cartey and that Steven's presence was a pleasant change from some of her former lodgers who could be noisy or had other annoying habits. She mentioned in passing she still had a single room at the top of the house which she would not be averse to letting out since she had her eye on acquiring a new flat screen tv, but mused it was a difficult room to let out as it was a bit on the small side. Steven said he would let her know if anyone was looking for a room. He thought it more likely that a staff member or a trainee might look for a room. He could not imagine the likes of Percy Vere wanting to stay in the homely surroundings. He felt very much in awe of some of the barristers, particularly the debonair Mr Vere. Still, he readied himself for work and confidently went to set off on his scooter.

Scyathica spent her day feeling slightly distracted. Stacey Birch commented that she seemed out of sorts, but Scyathica assured her that she was fine and went off to visit the farmer whose sheep had allegedly got drunk on polluted water. Jim Knight was a laconic sort who lived in a tumble-down house with some tumble-down barns up a rough track up which Scyathica had to walk for half a mile as she did not want to risk her uncle's sports car on it. She took some notes and recorded part of the interview with his permission in case it was of interest to say the Bricey show. She had half a suspicion that Jim Knight was as fond of a tipple as his sheep might have been.

Later in the day when she returned to her uncle's home, she heaved a sigh of relief. Penny had sent no further messages and had not arrived. She checked with Charmaine as well, who was sure there had been no visitors. Perhaps Penny had changed her mind. The house was very quiet. When her uncle was away, he left his Springer spaniel, Piper in the care of the pig farm manager. Scyathica quite liked Piper pottering about since she had been brought up with dogs and her mother still had a Scottie dog.

She made herself a prawn salad and served herself with a large glass of Chablis from her uncle's ample fridge full of white wine. She finished her meal off with a bowl of strawberries and felt replete. She dozed in a chair but woke suddenly. She found she was in semi darkness, and she heard a car engine and loud clattering from outside. She turned on the lights and went with some trepidation to the door. It was gone half past ten; surely her uncle had not returned from London? Could there be an intruder? Could it be… she opened the front door slightly on a chain and there was her worst fear.

"Surprise!" shrieked a raucous North American voice. It was Penny Wayney of course, and the car engine had been her taxi which now sped off.

Scyathica froze.

"Well, aren't you going to ask me in?" said Penny. "I'm just thrilled at staying here… it's so old…" With that she just pushed her way inside.

Scyathica initially felt at a loss what to do next. Her uncle was away, and she had no chance to ask if Penny could stay. The house although grand in appearance had some areas in need of renovation. Her uncle had a bedroom with an en suite and she had the guest room which also had a small en suite. There was a room which still housed many possessions belonging to Uncle Hugo's estranged wife. There was a room which Uncle Hugo used as an office and a tiny bedroom reserved for Charmaine in case she ever had to stay late.

There were 3 other bedrooms and a bathroom on the top floor. The bathroom was still functional but needed a complete overhaul. One bedroom was being used as a storage room for the other bedrooms so was piled full of furniture. The other two bedrooms had been stripped bare to deal with damp and be redecorated.

Downstairs there was an entrance hall, a grand dining room, a rather beautiful lounge, a small library room and a downstairs cloakroom. The basement housed the kitchen, the scullery, a wine cellar and a boot-room which doubled up as Uncle Hugo's gunroom. On the back of the house with views of lustrous lawns was a conservatory orangery with several buckets in it to catch the rain. On the east side of the house was a wing which in the past had housed stables with accommodation for the staff upstairs. It had long since been converted into garages and the upstairs which was fit for use had been converted into offices for Sir Hugo's agent. The rest was ringing with damp and full of old equipment from the former stables. On the west side of the house was a wing which had been abandoned some years ago. It was locked up as it was potentially dangerous to enter.

Scyathica could not think of anywhere else to put Penny other than the library. It had a large couch and beautiful views of the grounds, and she was quickly able to move Piper's dog bed which was perched on the couch as well as his dog toys. She shuddered to think what Sir Hugo would think of Penny and indeed she was right to be apprehensive. She said to Penny,

"I had no idea you were coming tonight so things are not ready… but I hope you will be comfortable in here."

Penny replied, "But I sent you a message… and I was sure you couldn't wait for us to catch up." She pouted a little. "But gee, it's gorgeous and so cute… and so old."

Scyathica felt she needed to offer Penny some refreshment so after Penny had put her bags in the library and freshened up, she took Penny to the kitchen.

"Some tea, maybe?" asked Scyathica.

Penny said, "Sure, do you have any cornsilk or rosebud tea?"

Scyathica indicated that there was Darjeeling, Earl Grey or peppermint which she felt was a pretty good selection.

Penny replied, "Darjeeling… I guess, but only if you have either oat or almond milk, otherwise I'll have peppermint."

Scyathica nodded and also put some oat crumbly biscuits made locally on a plate. Suddenly Penny got up from where she had been sitting and started to look in the kitchen cupboards.

"Whaat on earth are you doing…?" said Scyathica.

"I'm looking at your food. I eat a vegan, gluten and dairy free diet… and I believe in animal rights…" replied Penny from a cupboard.

Scyathica gently yanked her away by her green feathery scarf and retorted, "This is my uncle's house, and I don't think he would like you inspecting his food cupboards."

"I am sorry you feel so emotional about this," said Penny irritatingly. "I can see you have some issues to work through..."

Scyathica sighed and pushed the tea and biscuits towards Penny. This was going to be hard work.

Next day Penny stuck to her more like a leech than a limpet. She followed her around the entire day. The only time Scyathica escaped her clutches was when she went in the office to take instructions from Stacey Birch. Even when she went into a cubicle at the court toilets, she could hear Penny's piercing tones.

"Gee, Scyathica, it's so old… It's like your Buck-ing-ham Palaace in London… and some of the men they are so gorgeous, even in their fancy dress things… those wigs and gowns. Isn't that Percy Vere so gorgeous, just like a Greek god…? I really dig him. Even the young man assisting him that Chris… He was so sweet when I asked him the time."

And on and on she went. "And you were talking to some court clerk too… Steven… He seemed cute but not handsome like those barristers. He looked at you with puppy dog eyes… he really likes you!"

Scyathica shuddered. She had managed to speak to Uncle Hugo briefly but was not sure of his view of Penny depositing herself in his house.

As she passed through the main hallway she bumped into Steven. Penny was still adjusting her feather boa in the mirror in the Ladies' and pouting to put on her sparkly lip gloss.

"Are you OK?" said Steven. "You look a little… well out of sorts."

"An old acquaintance has turned up, Penny and she's a bit… ehm… bit… ehm," Scyathica struggled.

Steven replied, "Much?" He went on, "If you mean the girl with the green feathery thing who has been ogling counsel from the public gallery, Recorder Ahmed actually asked her to stop pulling faces and waving at people or she would be ejected…"

"I hadn't realised," said Scyathica. "I had popped back to the office as there was nothing exciting to report about! Look I hope I can still meet you for tea soon. But she follows me everywhere. She has invited herself to stay and goodness only…"

She stopped when Penny appeared.

By the end of the week Scyathica felt emotionally drained. Penny, however, treated her visit with continued excitement except for Scyathica's efforts to feed her. Scyathica was keen on salads and fruits herself but liked fish, eggs and cheese as part of her meal but struggled with providing for her guest. She had for example found an interesting recipe for stuffing bell peppers with mushrooms and kidney beans only for Penny to say, "I don't like mushrooms." Every building was described as "so old" or "quaint" and every passable looking man was described as "cute".

Uncle Hugo returned on Saturday afternoon. There had been an important but exhausting debate in the House of Commons on agricultural subsidies. He had picked up Piper on the way home so when he returned Piper came bounding through the door first. He made straight for the library where Penny was apparently having a nap. There was a cacophony of growls, barks and squeals followed by what sounded like a 'thwack' and a yelp. Penny came rushing out of the library clad in a flimsy rose pink negligee and a pink towling turban followed by Piper who slunk out with his tail between his legs.

"A dog tried to get on my couch," shrieked Penny.

"I rather think you were on his couch," boomed Sir Hugo. "You must be Penny. Did you hit my dog?"

Penny's complexion soon matched her negligee. "I just pushed him off with a magazine."

"Well, I'll thank you not to touch my dog again," responded Sir Hugo.

The day just went from bad to worse. Penny proceeded to sit herself with her long legs stretched out in places in the house which seemed to obstruct Sir Hugo as he went about settling back into his home. Piper whimpered or bared his teeth each time he saw Penny.

When it came to dinner Scyathica prepared a large mixed salad and some new potatoes. For Sir Hugo she prepared some succulent looking pork chops and for herself an omelette. She also roasted some sweet potatoes and butternut squash and hoped there was something there for Penny to eat. Never a pork eater herself she felt her mouth begin to water as Uncle Hugo's chops sizzled and spat. The table was elegantly set. Some Chablis was chilled and there was a bowl of strawberries and a chocolate mousse for dessert. Piper sat quietly in a corner gnawing on a bone.

Sir Hugo and Penny sat at the table chatting. Penny was babbling about her interests in studying 'Northern folk' for her thesis, her interest in veganism and how cute she found the people of Waste. She several times said, "I love your house... it's so old and so quaint." Sir Hugo's mood became blacker and blacker. Scyathica began bringing in the meal. Penny espied the pork chops.

"Oh, my," she said. "You can't eat that. It's pig... those poor little piggies."

"Don't you know what business I'm in?" exploded Sir Hugo. "Pigs. I breed pigs and have a sausage and bacon factory."

"Aaw gee, but what about the environment? I mean a plant-based diet and plant-based agriculture is much better for the environment… and those poor pigs," warbled Penny.

"Let me tell you a thing or two, young lady. My pigs have the highest standard of animal welfare. Their feed is primarily from grain and crops grown by local farmers. My bacon factory is the second biggest employer in the area. If my pigs went not only would hundreds be out of a job, but local farmers would be affected too."

And so a huge quarrel raged. Scyathica sat with her head in her hands. She did not want to be drawn into the merits of the arguments. Penny, in loud ringing tones was throwing in both valid and hopelessly invalid arguments about rain forests, pig crates, sustainable crops and the environment. Uncle Hugo retorted with his arguments about sustainable pig keeping, the high standard of UK animal welfare and the value of British farmers. Eventually, Uncle Hugo had gone a sort of purple colour and he said,

"Young lady. You come to my house without my invitation... and I believe without my niece's either. You strike my dog, and you insult my business. After dinner my niece will ring the Knubb Arms and the taxi service, and you will leave my house tomorrow morning… permanently."

And so, at 10 o'clock the next morning a vehicle from Khan's cars rolled up to whisk Penny off to the Knubb Arms. Scyathica accompanied her outside and she could see Penny's lip quivering.

"Gee, Scyathica, I don't know what I'm gonna do. I had hoped cos you're my friend that I could stay with you and do my dissertation properly this time. Daddy says all my college fund has been used up by me and he won't give me any more money unless I get my Master's and prove I'm being useful. All my credit cards are maxed out. I can't afford to stay at a hotel for more than 2 or 3 nights."

Scyathica felt very slightly sorry for her. She could see Uncle Hugo glowering out of the window and knew she could not change his mind, nor indeed if truth be known did she want to do so. She suspected that Penny had managed to exasperate all her relatives and friends.

"I'll think of something," said Scyathica, but she had no idea what that might be.

Chapter 6

MICKEY GASSON EASED HIS NOT inconsiderable weight as he contemplated how to galvanize the workforce at Waste Waste. The Frenchman who was the public face of the consortium who owned the plant rarely showed himself there so most of the dealings were with middle management. The current plant manager was a local man, Ron Woodhouse. His daughter Charmaine worked for Sir Hugo Wentworth-Knubb in his house. Despite the questionable conditions at parts of the plant the workforce was worried about losing their jobs as there were not many alternative large employers at Waste. He was aware of the prosecution by the Environment Agency because of the issue of the drunk sheep. More recently a few of the men in the waste sorting plant had developed rashes on their arms. Nat Cartey had at one time been Union Convenor at the plant. This dubious honour fell to him as well as being Nat's agent. Mickey indicated to Nat that he intended to throw a meeting about conditions at the plant and would hire a nearby hall. He suggested they contacted Waste FM and asked Nat to speak at the meeting.

Nat nodded in agreement. "You know I might get that solicitor chappy Bernie Blunt to come... there might be some legal action the workers might consider."

Mickey thought that was a good idea. Nat continued, "We ought to lay on a few refreshments and let it be known there will be free food... people tend to turn up for a free meal. Can your Maureen provide anything?"

Mickey said, "I don't know if the union can run to much," and he also secretly hoped his wife Maureen would not poison everyone.

Maureen worked part-time at Waste Waste canteen. Mickey would have described her main interests as 'talking rubbish gossip on Facebook' and buying scratch-cards if he had had the courage to do so. Maureen was a very large woman whose main motivation for her part-time working at the canteen was gossiping and nicking leftover pizzas. Otherwise, she would have spent her days sitting on the settee watching day-time television.

Nat indicated, "I'll chuck in a hundred quid," and Mickey felt that even Maureen might be motivated to do something about the catering.

They mulled over whether Ron Woodhouse or any other spokesman for the plant should be invited to the meeting. On balance they decided he should be. At that point Brittany, Mickey's daughter came in with some steaming cups of coffee.

"I'm off to work in a minute at the caff." She was manageress at a local veggie café, rather incongruously since her uncle was a butcher. "I'm just taking one of these outside before I go. Uncle Lewis has decided to take his motorbike apart."

It was Lewis Gasson's day off from his job as a senior butcher at Knubb Bacon. His Harley- Davidson was his pride and joy. He was nearly a generation younger than his brother Mickey, being something of an 'afterthought' and only a couple of years older than Brittany. He was proud of his physical appearance, with rippling muscles and sleek jet black hair. He kept trim not only with weight training but also fell running, but he still always made time for his beloved motorbike which thus far was the only love of his life. He did not share Mickey's interest in politics and thought Brittany a dim air-head. Good luck to her setting her sights on that sleezy MP fellow, he thought.

Monday was not a day off for Steven. He was clerking for old Oliver again who was still calling him 'Shovel' and was getting rattier and more impatient by the hour. Oliver's mood was not assisted by the fact that it was Miss Faye Leafly in court yet again in a very flustered state. Percy Vere's pupil Chris Ellison had also knocked over a plastic water jug in the middle of the hearing causing a waterfall which resulted in a brief adjournment.

At lunchtime he spotted Scyathica. Penny was facing the other way gazing at Percy Vere who had just emerged from court resplendent in his wig and gown, his gold locks just curling slightly from under the edge of his wig.

"Are we on for tea this afternoon?" whispered Steven. Scyathica nodded in the affirmative.

At the end of the afternoon, she suggested to Penny that Penny might like to try 'Crunchie's Veggie Café' on the other side of town near the station and claimed quite falsely that some local barristers liked to go there. She also told Penny more truthfully that the food was cheaper than the Knubb Arms. Steven stood in the corner of the court lobby pretending to look in his bag while this conversation took place. Fortuitously, Penny took the suggestion and went striding off in her long boots. Scyathica figured if the café was closed, they had about an hour and a half as it would take 45 minutes to walk each way but if it was open they might have a little longer. In any event, Scyathica and Steven sat in the furthest corner of the Knubb Arms' lounge.

Steven said, "What's this café... how did you find out about it?"

Scyathica explained she had had to help out on an article about the small number of vegans in Waste. She also unburdened herself to Steven about the row between Penny and her uncle, Penny's lack of resources and needing a place to stay. Steven recalled his chat with Auntie Bea and mostly in an effort to please Scyathica he indicated stutteringly that Auntie Bea was looking for another lodger.

"She is very wearing," said Scyathica. "Are you sure you'd want her lodging in the same house?"

"Well," he replied anxious to help Scyathica, "I'll be working in the day and I'm sure Auntie Bea will sort her out."

Steven and Scyathica phoned Auntie Bea to explain matters as frankly as they could; they did not hold back on Penny's loud manner or lack of funds or general fussiness over food. Auntie Bea was not bothered. Then they sank back in their armchairs and enjoyed tea and sumptuous cakes. After a while they agreed they should part company for now so that Penny did not get suspicious that she had been sent off on purpose. Scyathica agreed she would wait in the hotel lobby for Penny who she knew had to check-out tomorrow. Steven slunk out just 5 minutes before Penny strode in with a rather red face and a brown paper bag.

"What are you doing here? You sent me miles... they were about to close but I bought some vegan brownies to take away," exclaimed Penny.

Scyathica calmly told her that she might have solved Penny's accommodation problem. She was quite vague about Steven rooming in the same house. Soon she whisked Penny off to 3 Canal Street to meet Auntie Bea. Steven quite wisely kept to his room.

Auntie Bea showed Penny the room which was very small. It housed a single bed, a small wardrobe and one chair. A very small tv sat on a shelf on the wall.

"There's a toilet and basin up the corridor. Bath is next floor down," said Auntie Bea. "But mind you don't take too long in the bath... that's a shared facility."

Penny was about to make some gushing comment but before she said much more

Auntie Bea said, "The cost of the room includes breakfast and a light meal early evening. I hear you're a vegan and a bit picky… so I hope plain porridge, fruit and tea will do for breakfast? For tea I can make you a green salad and a jacket spud, but we'll have to find you something veggie you might like on your spud…"

Then she went into details of cost which she seemed to be very reasonable. Penny agreed to the terms and tried to tell Auntie Bea how quaint and cute the house was but Auntie Bea kept talking across her.

"I have another lodger," she said, "a very quiet gentleman. I expect you to respect his privacy and mine too. You're an American I know so I don't know what you're used to… but just to make it clear no loud music or coming in at all hours. I may let out the odd room, but this is my home."

Scyathica smiled inwardly. For once someone was putting Penny in her place.

Penny confirmed that after she checked out of the Knubb Arms she would take a taxi to 3 Canal Street tomorrow morning. Indeed, that is what she did.

Steven found he was largely able to avoid Penny in the mornings by leaving for work before she came down for breakfast. Auntie Bea did not mind staggering breakfast time. Sometimes he had his evening meal at the same time as Penny in Auntie Bea's dining room. Sometimes he met Scyathica for a bar meal. Their afternoon teas had extended somewhat. He had joined the local Philately club although he didn't have many stamps and he also had found a crossword group at the public library, so he also spent the odd evening out pursuing a hobby and taking a sandwich in his room when he came home. He was also careful to give Auntie Bea warning if he was going to be late.

As the month into another month progressed, he managed to avoid Penny for the greater part of the weekends, as did Scyathica. Sometimes Steven and Scyathica spent time together taking rambles near Waste Water, both claiming to each other that it got them away from Penny and into the open air. On one occasion Steven and Scyathica passed Jim Knight's sheep farm. She suggested they walk a bit up his farm track as it would get them off the road and she had half a thought that she might get a bit more out of old Mr Knight. She was aware the Environment Agency's case was due in court soon. They did not get very far, however, as their path was blocked by two large men.

"Why are you here? What are you doing?" said an accented voice.

"Just strolling," replied Scyathica. "I know the owner… Mr Knight… well a bit… Who are you?"

"We are Pawel and Karol. We both work for Mr Knight. Does he know you are coming? He is very busy right now."

Scyathica admitted he did not expect her and Steven and Scyathica decided to make a hasty retreat, although they commented afterwards that the little incident was rather strange. Scyathica thought she might mention it to Stacey Birch.

On one of the occasions that Scyathica was out with Steven, Penny was sitting in Auntie Bea's living room glumly drinking a camomile tea.

"What's with the long face?" asked Auntie Bea. "I thought you liked that sort of tea?"

"I'm considering my future," responded Penny. "Scyathica is busy doing her own thing. I'm short of money. My research for my dissertation doesn't take up all my time. I guess I need a part-time job."

"I think I know just the man who might be able to help you! I'll ring up my nephew Easy... well Norman actually. There's always jobs going at the council. He'll know what there is."

"Easy? Norman?" questioned Penny.

"My nephew Norman Ryder is Mayor and Leader of the Borough Council... He's called 'Easy' because he is always keen not to offend people. Shall I call him?"

Without waiting for an answer Auntie Bea was speaking to her nephew and soon gave Penny a response.

"Norman says they have several temporary part-time positions for people to conduct a survey for the council on Waste's local environmental needs. It's between 12 and 16 hours a week and you can apply through the council's website... I should give it a go..."

And that's what Penny did. Somehow, she managed to control her gushing manner. Scyathica gave her a reference (missing out the bits about Penny annoying people). She got the job. She found she was required to canvass passers-by in the local shopping centre which suited her outgoing side. She soon learned to navigate the temperamental local bus service. Now and again, she would meet Scyathica for a tea in the veggie café, Crunchies', and find her way back to the town centre by bus.

One day as she was canvassing near the Court House a veritable god drew up on his motorbike.

Said god was Lewis Gasson set to deliver a letter to Bernie Blunt solicitor who had an office near the Combined Court. The delivery was a favour to Mickey. The meeting about the workers' grievances at Waste Waste had been a disorderly affair. The people who attended had scoffed down the food which appeared to have given the energy to make 'boos' and catcalls against Ron Woodhouse. It appeared that there was some disquiet about whether the gloves, helmets and coveralls were adequate. Five men complained of mild rashes and one woman too… but she worked in the canteen. One of a gaggle of women at the meeting muttered under her breath, "Oh, Maureen, I thought it was that curry you made for lunch."

Waste FM had done a short piece the next day on the Bricey Show but the real substance of a plan had been discussed after the meeting between Mickey, Nat Cartey, and half-a-dozen militant members of the union. They had agreed to instruct Bernie Blunt to send a letter to the plant's owners and also to seek a barrister's opinion. Bernie suggested Dr Gordon Flaughtersdough (pronounced 'Flowerdew') as reasonably priced and keen. So, the letter contained funds to seek counsel's opinion from Dr G Flaughtersdough of Counsel of Peasegood Chambers, London. Mickey had liked the look of the good doctor's impressive website. He was not sure that a Doctorate in Applied Sociology of Anthropology was immediately relevant, but it showed the man was well-educated. He had not heard of the University of Morton in Marsh before, but he understood it was near to Oxford. And Dr G Flaughtersdough said he was an expert in criminal law including frauds, assaults and murders, civil law including every type of contract, trust or tort, constitutional law, local government law and divorce and all aspects of family law.

Lewis parked his motorbike and took off his helmet to reveal his dark hair. He looked as if he had been poured into his black motorbike leathers. Penny stood there with her mouth open. All thoughts of Percy Vere or past loves fell away. This was her true love, her god.

Lewis was most amused by the girl staring at him and thought her quite attractive with her long legs and her tall boots. She had some sort of green stringy scarf which had seen better days and was holding a clipboard and asking questions.

Once he had delivered the letter to the solicitor, he decided to saunter over to long legs.

"What's your name, darling?"

Penny stammered, "Pain...eee."

"Pain...eee?"

"Penny as in Penelope. Will you take part in my survey?"

Lewis decided to do so, in order to spend a little time with Penny. He let her ask the dull questions and gave dull answers. He liked her appearance although her American drawl was less attractive to him.

"Fancy a drink, sometime?" asked Lewis.

"I would just love that," said a hot and flustered Penny.

"Don't get too excited. It won't be the Knubb Arms. Probably be the 'Roebuck and Hog' over in East Waste."

And so he took Penny's number and said he would ring her mobile soon. And then he left on his Harley.

Penny Wayney hugged the clipboard to her. Everything was just wonderful. She was gathering her research. She had a place to live. She had a part-time job. Maybe she could also reel in this Greek god too.

Chapter 7

STEVEN HOVELL HAD A PRODUCTIVE meeting with Derek Devene and the two Julies about progress at the court. Unlike his time working in London, he had fitted in very well. Later he went over the lists with Julie James who remarked that his quietness worked very well with old Oliver. They talked about the locality and local issues. Julie's husband Martin had previously been manager of the local prestige car showrooms and repairers and in semi-retirement he still kept his hand in repairing a handful of classic cars. Julie on the other hand, had a second career making celebration cakes. They looked at some of the more challenging matters in the lists.

"There will be a lot of press attention to the Environment Agency prosecution of Waste Waste in a few days' time," said Julie. "I'll need to let security know. Also, this week the O'Hanrahans are back in court. It's their care case… Her Honour dela Notte will have that one as District Judge Ercol is away on a course. She'll also have to take Parsival and Grubbins. She won't like that… Listing have not inflicted that on poor DJ Stump… it needs a firm hand…"

"Parsival and Grubbins? I have not met them."

"You have not met our self-styled Knight of the Round table? He is in dispute with his ex over their 2 kids Lancelot and Guinevere…"

District Judge Stump was indeed not in a fit state to deal with these cases. Her fountain pen had snapped, spraying her with ink and she had dropped her coffee. She looked relieved when Steven took her the message, she would be dealing with all the court's small claims today which was a list of cases about minor road traffic damage. When Steven knocked at the door of Her Honour dela Notte's Chambers to announce he was her clerk, he found her already engrossed in details of her cases on the computer.

"It seems today is just a procedural hearing on O'Hanrahan," said Her Honour. "I believe the lawyers are just seeking listing directions for various contested aspects so most of them will appear by video and apart from the main social worker and the Children's Guardian we will not, by agreement of all the lawyers have any parties. You will I trust have the video link good to go?"

Steven nodded confirmation. "Your Honour we will have attenders on the next case... Bagshaw aka Parsival v Grubbins. They are not represented. I believe a social worker Desmond St Vincent will attend too…"

Her Honour observed, "That looks like a case where we may have more unknowns… It's a new one to me…"

The O'Hanrahan case went without incident. In respect of the next case the usher, Nichola, brought the parties in and Steven announced,

"Gavin Bagshaw versus Naomi Grubbins… in the Family Court sitting at Waste numbered…" He was interrupted,

"Name's not Gavin Bagshaw anymore… it's Sir Parsival…"

Steven looked up. There was a short weaselly looking young man clad in a long medieval robe. The robe was worn over what looked like chainmail but as Steven squinted, he saw it was actually a grey knitted affair. He was unaware that the wearer had had to leave a helmet (wooden) and sword (wooden) with security.

"Mr Parsival have you changed your name by deed?" asked Her Honour dela Notte, haughtily.

"Well… no... but as I believe in the principles of chivalry and laid down by King Arthur that's what I prefer to be called... and it's Sir… not Mr…"

"Mr Bagshaw… Parsival," continued Her Honour, "have you been knighted by our current monarch...? What name is used by the DWP and the Inland Revenue?"

Sir Parsival looked a bit uncertain. "DWP say Bagshaw… but I don't recognise their authority. I am a knight most pure of the Round Table and I only recognise the principles of chivalry and the laws of King Arthur."

"Well, Mr Parsival, this is my court and I enforce the law of the land, so I expect you to behave appropriately. You must not lose sight of the fact that I have jurisdiction over the decision about how much you will see of your children."

Almost inaudibly Miss Grubbins said, "Nutter," under her breath.

Her Honour caught the utterance. "Miss Grubbins… You will not inflame the situation. Any more inappropriate comments from you and you will receive a formal warning about contempt." Miss Grubbins looked chastened.

Mr St Vincent was asked to give Waste Council's interim oral report about his observations of the self-styled knight's interactions with the children and his knowledge of the family. It transpired the family had not been known to social services until a few months ago. There was on file a brief mention of a police call out for a domestic disturbance at the family home about a year ago when neighbours had heard some shouting. Mr Bagshaw had become totally fixated on King Arthur more recently and had lost his job at the local supermarket when he attended work in his knightly regalia which the manager had found unsuitable for shelf-stacking, and he had further frightened customers with his sword (wooden). He was arrested for public order offences and was bailed to appear before the magistrates for breaching the peace.

Thereafter he had been kicked out of the family home by Miss Bagshaw and was living in the shed at the bottom of the garden. He was only being admitted to the downstairs loo or to see the children if either a social worker or Miss Bagshaw's mother was in the house. Mr St Vincent was clear he was capable of keeping the 6 and 8-year-old children safe from physical harm; the issue was whether his fixation was capable of causing any psychological harm and whether the children might be harmed accidentally if their dad started waving his sword (wooden) at anyone. Miss Grubbins had been observed to be a good mother but there was concern about her racist language to social workers. She told the current social worker for example, 'No black cunt who aren't from round 'ere should tell me what to do'. Mr St Vincent commented that his only temporary contract with Waste Council was ending soon so he would not be assessing the family further and he did not know when there would be a new social worker.

Her Honour dela Notte did not look pleased but pressed on with asking the parties more about themselves.

"Do you have any job applications?" she asked Sir Parsival in haughty tones, and he replied he had applied for a job at Waste Waste. "Apart from King Arthur do you have any hobbies?" she pressed. Sir Parsival looked perplexed. "You know, hobbies. For example do you keep pigeons?"

Sir Parsival looked more puzzled, and Steven felt himself cringe inwardly. "Well," came the eventual answer, "I used to watch the footie... follow the Wastrels."

Her Honour dela Notte obtained an agreement that conditional on Sir Parsival reverting to Mr Bagshaw attire and leaving his medieval gear including helmet and sword in the shed he could take his children out for a burger after school once a week unaccompanied as well as see them supervised at the house. She indicated she would find a date for the case in her court in about 3-4 weeks' time. At that hearing she expected a new social worker and a legal representative from the council to present the court with an assessment plan.

The morning soon passed, and Steven was eventually able to take a short lunchbreak. He phoned Scyathica and said,

"What time are we meeting at the Knubb Arms tonight?"

"I'm glad you phoned," said Scyathica. "I have to go and interview 'Easy Ryder' about 6 ish. Waste Borough Council has got together with Eastern Waste Moorlands Council to outsource the control centre for 999 calls. My boss Stacey thinks there's a story in it...That there could be problems having 999 calls answered in Mumbai or wherever. I'd love to meet you, but it couldn't be until later..." She sounded wistful. "Look, you couldn't get out to my uncle's place could you about 8 maybe? I can make omelette. My cooking is not up to much else. And I'm sure my uncle won't mind. He only threw out Penny because she was dreadful."

Steven felt nervous about meeting Sir Hugo and responded, "Why don't I pick up an Indian takeaway? I could get a mixture of things. I found a place near the station which is quite good. Then if I brought it for about 8 you wouldn't even have to make omelettes."

Scyathica sounded enthusiastic and gave him directions to her uncle's house.

Scyathica hoped her uncle would be pleasant to Steven as she was aware Steven was rather shy and quiet. She knew from her weekly phone calls to her mother that Pandora still nurtured a hope that she would return to London and perhaps settle down with some city type. She let it be known that there was still a room for her in the flat in Kensington. Scyathica had not in the past felt like settling down with anyone. She had gone out with her fair share of Jeremys, Julians, and Justins from Chelsea and also City types... most had bored her stiff. As to other newspaper reporters she did not share their desires to do hatchet jobs on people as a way of advancement and they in return found her snooty and remote.

At 6.15 Scyathica arrived at the council offices. No-one was in the main mahogany panelled chamber. A security guard showed her through the chamber to a little cubby hole of a room off the council chamber. Its mahogany walls made it feel even smaller than its actual dimensions. It was only furnished with a polished wooden table and two matching straight-backed wooden chairs. There was a tiny window about 6 foot from ground level with mesh over it. Norman Ryder was already seated there, and he rose to shake Scyathica's hand.

A man of about 60, Norman was so tall he tended to stoop when speaking to anyone shorter. His handshake was limp and his smile benign He had a pair of spectacles hanging from his neck on a chain.

"How can I assist you?" he asked, despite the fact he knew the purpose of the interview.

Scyathica asked if she might make notes and record the interview as well.

"Tell me in your own words why you are outsourcing the 999 control centre?" asked Scyathica.

"Well," said Norman. "We needed to save a bit of money in this authority and the neighbouring one did too. We have a really good IT officer at the council... and he came to us with a scheme from a company who had approached him… said it would save money… Scarlett IT Solutions Inc."

Scyathica felt herself flinch.

Norman continued, "Well he was really enthusiastic, and my council group was keen on saving money."

Scyathica asked, "But what did you think?"

He replied, "Well... everyone else seemed very keen. The council officers recommended it. I am not out to make waves."

She continued, "Has the company you are using got a good track record for this sort of thing?"

The reply was, "I don't really know. I am advised by the council officers."

She persisted, "Do you know of any other areas using this company and scheme?"

Reply, "I don't really know. I am advised by my officers."

Scyathica again, "Does the company have any UK base?"

Reply, "I don't really know. I am advised by my officers."

And so the interview went on with Scyathica gently probing and Norman not knowing. By about 7.15 she had thanked Norman for his time and was on her way home to her uncle's house. She had a horrible feeling the company mentioned was owned by a holding company which was owned by another holding company and so on until a path led to her father. She knew before his disgrace he had been trying to get into IT and call centres. She did hope there would not be any unfortunate repercussions.

Steven loaded the paper carriers containing foil trays into the back of his scooter. He had erred on the generous side as he was not sure what Scyathica would like. The owner had also included a load of poppadoms and complimentary pickles. He followed the route out of town as instructed and as he reached The Mount he went past the gates with the intercom and headed for Knubb Pigs. He navigated his scooter up the track past the barns and in due course drew up in front of the Georgian house. His knock at the door provoked a large amount of barking. He heard voices one of which he recognised as Scyathica. He knew she was there anyway as he had spotted the sports car.

The door opened and Scyathica said, "Uncle Hugo, please can you hold Piper back… I think he smells the takeaway Steven has brought."

"What… yes, yes," said Uncle Hugo looking somewhat red in the face as he pulled Piper back with one hand while trying to shake Steven's hand with his other hand; this was difficult for Steven too as he was carrying bags of takeaway.

"You must be Scyathica's young man?" said Sir Hugo.

"Yes, I think I am. I am Steven Hovell. Please call me Steven."

After a moment's confusion Steven and takeaway came in and the dog calmed down. Steven found himself in Sir Hugo's grand dining room.

"I put a collection of plates, glasses, mats out… Some juice… a couple of cans of cold beer... if you want one… If you think it's okay for you?" said Scyathica to Steven. Uncle Hugo didn't seem to withdraw.

"Indian is it? I love a good Indian takeaway?" said Sir Hugo.

Steven had not expected to be feeding the MP for West Waste too, so he was glad he had erred on the generous side.

"Oh, Uncle," said Scyathica rolling her eyes. "Have you not had anything?"

"Well… Erh," came the noncommittal reply.

"There is plenty here," said Steven helpfully. "I'm sure it will be too much for two."

And so the MP, the young reporter and the court clerk tucked into an Indian takeaway on a Georgian dining room table with Piper the Springer sitting underneath it wagging his tail every time his master accidentally on purpose dropped a little something.

"Oh, I do like poppadoms and a good biryani," said Sir Hugo tucking in.

If Steven had been concerned as to how to break the ice with Scyathica's uncle, he need not have been. The Indian takeaway did the trick. They soon were chatting away on all manner of subjects including what Steven's job entailed and on what House of Commons' Committee Sir Hugo sat. They touched on Sir Hugo's sister Pandora having a preference for London. Steven mentioned he did not really get on with his parents. He indicated he had different interests. That got them onto hobbies and soon transpired that Steven and Sir Hugo shared an interest in philately.

After they had cleared away the debris of the takeaway, Sir Hugo brought out a few of his stamp books to show Steven. Scyathica felt a small pang of jealousy. On the one hand she was very pleased how well the two men got on together, but on the other hand she had invited Steven to the house so she could spend a little time with him. Nonetheless, it was a very convivial evening.

"We must do this again," said Sir Hugo. "That is if Scyathica doesn't mind…? And I'll order in a takeaway… I can see why Scyathica gets on with you…"

Steven and Scyathica both smiled a little. After Steven left Sir Hugo mentioned he'd had a call from her paternal uncle, Lord Coldharbour.

"Says he has sent you texts, or you haven't picked up your calls. Told me he's had some good reports on you from your office so he says he's thinking you might be able to give it another go in London… He's short staffed on one of his evening rags."

Scyathica sighed.

"Oh dear, I really ought to ring him tomorrow. The truth is I'm happier in Waste than I ever was in London."

Sir Hugo smiled. "Yes, I can see that."

Steven was also deciding what to do about messages from family. When he reached 3 Canal Street he noticed he had both texts and voicemails. The texts were from his mother Deedee followed up by 2 voicemails. The first text pointed out he had not been in touch for about 6 weeks. The second text asked him to phone. He listened to the voicemails. In the first voicemail his mother sounded relatively calm but did inform him his father had been taken to hospital. In the second voicemail she sounded very upset so despite the fact it was about 20 to midnight he decided to ring her.

Deedee spent the first few minutes of the call sobbing and berating him for not being in touch. The pangs of guilt subsided somewhat when he learned what had happened. Champ was employed as an Engineering Manager for Network Rail. He was leading a crew modernising some points near Clapham Junction. Deedee said, "Some bloke in the crew called him 'a fucking great bully' so Champ well… he had to do something… He gave the bloke just a little shove to show him who was boss. But this bloke took a swing at him back and Champ tripped over the rails to avoid him… and now he's broken his leg in three places."

Steven felt sure that Champ had been bullying and reflected to himself that he was surprised there had not been any such incident long ago.

"Wish him a speedy recovery," said Steven.

"No, no you don't understand," said Deedee. "Once they've stabilised his leg the hospital will send him home... but he'll be all in plaster. They expect it will be in about 3 days."

"What's that to do with me?" asked Steven.

"Well, I can't look after him alone and the rest of the family are busy working, so I need you to come back home."

Steven breathed in, "I'm busy working too."

Deedee said, "Yeah... well, it's only some northern thing in an office."

"Mother," he said somewhat formally. "I'm a judges' clerk and I'm well settled here. Dad can't stand the sight of me anyway. I am afraid someone else in the family will have to help out. I doubt if I will visit you and Dad again this year... although I do hope he recovers soon. I promise you I will ring more often but that's about..."

He heard silence. It appeared his mother had hung up. He did not ring her back. He resolved to use some online service to send a 'Get well' card and gift in the morning. He did not think his father would appreciate it, but he felt he ought to do so. He was sure one of his large, loud sisters could look after his father and he knew that if he was ever ill or injured not one of his family would come to his aid. The only thing which was a wonder was how his father had also as yet avoided getting the sack from work.

Chapter 8

NEXT MORNING STEVEN FELT VERY guilty about his conversation with Deedee. He knew they had been lousy parents to him, but they were the only parents he would ever have. First, he rang Scyathica. Despite the fact she was feeling nervous about a planned visit to interview Jim Knight again she did her best to be sympathetic.

"Why don't you talk over your situation with your colleagues or your boss? It might help to know if they can spare you for a day or two," she suggested not mentioning her own worries.

Steven went to see Derek Devene and explained,

"My father has had a bad accident at work… broken his leg… My mum sounded worried, but I know we are very busy here."

Derek replied, "I really would prefer not to let you go but you are clearly not going to be at your best if you mope about worrying…"

Steven nodded and Derek went on,

"If you work until 1pm today there is a London train at about 2.30 I know… You could be in London by early evening. I will put you down as on leave this afternoon and tomorrow… but after that unless it's really serious I hope you will back here." He paused. "You are a valuable member of the team so I really can't afford to be without you."

Steven expressed his appreciation and at 1 o'clock zoomed off on his scooter to get an overnight bag and tell Auntie Bea what was happening. He got a cab from Auntie Bea's at just before 2 and booked a b and b on his phone as the cab drew into the station. He just had time to buy a ticket before the London train came into the platform.

At about half past 7 that evening Steven found himself outside the parental home. He knocked hesitantly at the door. He still had a key but felt he should start by knocking at the door. If his mother was at the hospital, he would resort to using it. He had dropped off his overnight bag at the bed and breakfast but had with him a couple of gifts in a carrier he'd picked up at the London train terminus, being a copy of 'Cars Monthly', a box of Ferrero Roche chocolates and a paperback of some celebrity's exploration of Route 66 in the US. No-one answered so he started to fumble for his key. To his surprise he heard his father's voice calling, "Find out somebody who's at the fucking door."

The door was opened by his sister Denise. She was panting as presumably the exertion of going a few steps had made her out of breath. A somewhat large lady, the tight pink shell suit did not suit her. Her blonde hair was pushed back with hair grips.

"'Allo… wa you doing 'ere, bro?" she queried in between mouthfuls of the packet of crisps she held in her hand.

"I've come to see the old man… I thought he might be in hospital, so I guess I also wanted to make sure Mum was okay."

"You best come in… I suppose," said Denise chomping.

Steven headed straight to the living room. His father was lounging in an easy chair with his foot on a footstool. There were some cushions on the stool and the foot was encased in plaster which covered part of his lower leg and ended just short of his knee. His right hand and wrist were strapped up as well. However, in Champ's left hand was a pint glass which Steven suspected was full of lager. Deedee could be heard clattering around in the kitchen which led off the living room and singing to an inane pop tune which was blaring out on the radio.

"Hello. I thought you were at death's door…" said Steven.

"Well hello, Wimp. How nice of you to grace us with your presence," responded Champ who continued, "I've fractured my ankle and got a small crack in my wrist… but what do you care Mr La-di-da…?"

"I've brought you these," said Steven handing over the gifts.

Champ replied, "Beer would have been better," and paused. "So I suppose you have come back with your tail between your toes… thinking if I was laid up you could just waltz back in?"

"No," responded Steven. "Everything is fine… at work… and generally."

"So you say," said Champ. "With your poncy court job… I suppose you're still Billy no mates... no friends… no girl."

"As a matter of fact I have friends... and one of them is a girl... Please stop being nasty, I was genuinely worried, so I have travelled hundreds of miles to get here," said Steven.

Champ smirked. "A friend who is a girl? Eh eh, could it be our Wimp is in love, but the girl is not interested in him...? Not a girlfriend... but a friend who is a girl..."

"I have got a girlfriend," said Steven thunderously but regretting it as he heard his mother drop something in the kitchen before emerging.

"What is she like? What does she do?" said his mother.

"She is very smart and clever," said Steven. "She is a journalist." In for a penny, in for a pound he added. "Her uncle is an MP, and we all ate a meal together at her uncle's house."

He did not mention it was a takeaway he'd brought round.

At that point he faced a barrage of questions, and he was even offered a lager and easy chair. He was persuaded to eat a meal with his parents for the first time in a long time. Although their interest in him derived from a sort of social climbing curiosity Steven no longer felt intimidated by his parents. Even their remarks about Scyathica's name didn't bother him. He had his job, his scooter, the friendship of colleagues and Auntie Bea, his clubs and yes, his girlfriend Scyathica. He somehow felt he belonged in Waste so he could approach his life with a little more confidence.

The evening passed and soon it was getting on for 11.

"I'm glad all is okay here," he said. "I'll be going back tomorrow but I will keep in touch."

"OK, Stevo," said his father. "Keep us posted of your news... Maybe bring your girl for Christmas?"

"That's kind," said Steven not having the heart to say there was no way he wanted to bring Scyathica there for Christmas. "I'll have to see nearer the time."

Steven set off early next morning. He envisaged that by catching the 7am train he might be able to go to work at the court in the afternoon if he was not too tired and then maybe meet Scyathica after work. While he was snoozing on the train Scyathica was setting off for Jim Knight's farm. Although she was expected around 10am she hoped she did not meet the two heavies who had appeared on the farm track. She wondered what help they were giving him with his sheep; somehow, they did not seem farming types. She recollected that they both wore tight black leather jackets and what might be described as designer sunglasses. The clothes did not seem suitable for tending sheep.

She parked her car at the end of the track. She had deliberately worn trainers so as to more easily navigate the bumpy track. There was no sign of the heavies. Down the track she could see the ramshackle buildings. There was strangely a strong smell of alcohol. She was nowhere near the beck which had apparently become polluted. Some sort of steam or smoke was coming out of the side of an outbuilding about 20 metres away. She could just about see Pawel and Karol take what appeared to be a crate of bottles out of the outbuilding and then take a large container into it. She thought whatever they were doing seemed unlikely to be connected with sheep. As she got closer Jim Knight appeared at the gate to his yard. He seemed to be shouting at her and waving at her to go back.

"Stay where you are…" she could just about make out. He started to say something else.

There was a tremendous roaring noise and something akin to a bang mixed with a rumble. Scyathica felt the ground shake and found herself flung to the ground. Just for a second, she could not hear anything. She lifted her head. The gate to the yard was now on the ground as was Jim Knight. She struggled to her feet and brushed bits of stone and dust from her hair. There was a slight wetness on her forehead from a small cut on her brow. She could see Jim Knight struggling to his feet. Most of the outbuilding had gone. One wall still stood and there was a gaping hole out of which smoke and flames were being emitted. The farmhouse appeared to have the glass blown out from the windows and the front door blown off. Guttering was hanging down and many slates were off the roof.

Scyathica stood there winded. She struggled for her phone. As she did so she could see Pawel pushing his way out of a pile of rubble screaming, "Karol, Karol." Even from where she stood shakily she could see he was covered in black dust and had blood running down his face and neck.

Her hands were shaking but she managed to still make her call to emergency services. To her surprise the call was answered as follows by a recorded voice: 'Thank you for calling Waste Emergency call centre. Your call is important to us. Please say 'fire' 'police' or 'ambulance'.

"All three," said Scyathica shakily to hear the response 'I'm sorry your answer could not be understood. Try again'. She was non-plussed and the recorded voice said, 'Please say 'fire' 'police' or 'ambulance'.' She drew in a deep breath and was about to say, "Ambulance," when the recorded voice said, 'Call terminated' and the line went dead.

For a minute Scyathica did not know what to do. Her hands were shaking. Her ears were ringing. While she sought composure she randomly photographed and videoed the scene on her phone but then quickly rang emergency services again. Once again, the recorded voice said, 'Thank you for calling Waste Emergency call centre. Your call is important to us. Please say 'fire' 'police' or 'ambulance'.' This time she quickly said, "Ambulance," on the basis that surely the ambulance people would notify the fire brigade and the police. To her amazement she got another recorded voice. 'Thank you for calling. You are number 79 in the queue for Waste Ambulance. Your call is important to us. Please continue to hold'. Then there was some tinkly music.

She stumbled down the track towards the scene of devastation. Jim Knight was calling to her, "Please get us some help... it's all gone terribly wrong."

Pawel was sitting on a mound of rubble crying, "Karol, Karol." She could still hear tinkly music and the repeated message, 'Your call is important to us'. After a good 5 minutes she was only number 78 in the queue!

Jim Knight was sobbing, "Are you phoning 999...? The other one is buried under the rubble... He was closer to the still... It blew... It blew... I never should have got involved."

Scyathica confirmed she had phoned for help but was really worried about the delay. She said,

"I'm in a queue on the phone... it's taking too long... I'll get my car and drive for help... Do you want to come, Mr Knight?"

He shook his head. "You go, I'll just slow you down."

She stumbled back down the driveway as quickly as she could. By the time the phone connected to the 'hands free' kit in the sports car she was number 74 in the queue. The nearest place she could think of to reach quickly was Knubb Sausages where she believed there was a landline. It took a few minutes to get there. She was only at number 73 in the queue. There was no-one in the office and the door was locked but there was a window slightly ajar. She pushed on the window as hard as she could, and it sprung open. She pushed an empty plastic barrel under the window to give herself a leg-up and scrambled through the window landing on a desk from which papers went flying. Her handbag strap was round her neck with her phone in it which was on speakerphone, and she could hear, 'Your call is important to us. You are number 70 in the queue'.

She looked around the office and spotted a landline phone on a wall. She made a call to Stacey Birch at the newspaper office. The words came tumbling out.

"I don't know what to do… Jim Knight's blown up and I'm number 70 in the queue on 999."

"Woah. Slow down," said Stacey. Scyathica did her best to calm herself and explain what had happened. "Okay… me and some of the others from the office will go round to the police, fire and ambulance people… Sounds like a major emergency. Where are you? Are you okay?"

"I'm at the sausage factory… I had to break in to use the phone. I feel shaky but I think I'm okay," she replied.

Stacey said, "You should go and get checked out at the hospital."

"No. I'll go back to Jim Knight's… But I'll send you some pictures from my phone you might want."

Scyathica hurried back to Jim Knight's and parked her car leaving the track accessible. Within 3 or 4 minutes of her arrival as she was stumbling back down the track she could hear sirens. She flattened herself against a wall as 2 fire engines squeezed down the track closely followed by an ambulance and a police car. She continued down the track to be met by a burly police officer. "Who are you?" he said.

She gabbled out her name, showed her press card and explained what happened. Soon they were joined by 2 further ambulances, another police car and a rescue helicopter.

She leant against a wall. From her bag her phone said, 'You are number 39 in the queue'. She ended the call. Her knees felt wobbly. She saw a press car from the radio station pull up. Her world seemed to wobble.

"Miss, miss, we should get you checked out," said a friendly voice. She found she was sitting on the ground with an ambulance man leaning over her. She nodded and found herself being led into a waiting ambulance.

As she was whisked away in the ambulance, she rang Steven.

"Steven, Steven… Jim Knight's blew up," she said tearfully.

"What?" said Steven. "I can't hear very well I'm on the train back from London."

Somehow, she managed to make herself understood. "I'll be with you soon, Sy…," said Steven. "You get checked out by the medics… It won't be long before I'm back. Do you want me to ring your uncle and the farm so you can concentrate on being checked out?"

Gathering that she did, as soon as the brief worrying call was ended Steven managed to ring Sir Hugo's constituency office and Knubb Sausages. The manager of

Knubb Sausages expressed both relief and concern; relief there had not been a burglar and concern about the situation at Knight's Farm. Steven initially only managed to speak to Sir Hugo's agent and also Charmaine, but as he alighted from the train Sir Hugo returned his call. He sounded full of concern for his niece. The two men agreed to keep in touch.

Sir Hugo managed to contact Scyathica who was between X-ray and consultation at the hospital, and he arranged to have the sports car picked up.

Scyathica had had 2 stitches to the cut on her forehead. "They are just ruling out that I have not had a head injury and then I can leave."

Sir Hugo agreed to fetch her later on all being well.

Steven made his way back to Auntie Bea's in Canal Street.

"How'd it go?" she asked. He briefly told her of his trip to see his parents but then told her of the worrying call from Scyathica.

"Oh my goodness," said Auntie Bea. "I was just listening to Waste FM. They had a bit on breaking news. I never realised Scyathica was there… There's been sirens and helicopters and all sorts for the last hour. Let me make you a cuppa and then you can ring that uncle of hers in a bit to see if she's okay."

Steven sat nervously sipping his tea and decided to ring Derek Devene to explain he was back in Waste, but he did not expect to be in until tomorrow. Derek had also heard the sirens but nonetheless expressed his hope Steven would be in next morning. As he was starting to call Sir Hugo, he heard a key in the lock and the rasping tones of Penny Wayney.

"Hi, it's little old me… anyone at home?"

"I'll speak to her," mouthed Auntie Bea and left Steven to his call. To his relief Sir Hugo replied.

"She's just home… rather shaken up… Seems old Knight let some dodgy fellows try and distil some sort of alcohol…I assume to sell… and the place just blew up!"

Steven asked if he could call round briefly. "I'm sure she'd be reassured to see you," said Sir Hugo.

Auntie Bea turned on the local news. It appeared that police suspected an illegal vodka distilling operation. Karol had been pulled from the rubble seriously injured. There was some footage from immediately after the explosion. It was rather blurry but quite dramatic. The local news broadcaster said, "This is footage taken by local news reporter Scyathica Wentworth who was on the scene just after the accident and received minor injuries herself."

Steven set off on his scooter to see Scyathica. Sir Hugo and Piper were at the door to let him in. He was shown through to the elegant lounge where Scyathica was sitting on a chaise lounge with her feet up. He could see the wound to her forehead and that she was extremely pale.

"I haven't brought you anything," he said.

"It doesn't matter," replied Scyathica, "I am just so pleased to see you."

Steven listened intently to her account of her ordeal, and she then asked him how his father was and how the trip to see his parents went. He was able to say his father was not too badly injured and that he had parted with his parents on reasonable terms.

"When you feel better we should do something really nice... an outing of your choice," said Steven.

Scyathica smiled. "That would be lovely," she said.

Uncle Hugo came into the lounge. "I've been trying to get her to have a brandy, but she says it won't go with some pain killers she got from the hospital."

"I expect Scy's just following medical advice," said Steven, he hoped diplomatically.

Sir Hugo started going on in loud tones about certain elements of the Emergency Services not knowing what they were doing. "They have even outsourced 999... quite disgraceful... I will ask questions in the House."

Steven could see Scyathica looked very tired.

"Scy... I think I'll go now... not cos' I don't want to stay with you but because you need some rest. Don't try to work tomorrow. I'll come here as soon as I leave court and then we can plan something nice for the future."

Sir Hugo showed him to the door and Scyathica drifted off to sleep.

She slept there until about 6am. Sir Hugo had placed rugs over her. She awoke to hear the dawn chorus and went upstairs to her room where she undressed and slipped into bed. She slept further until after 10. She had a long bath being careful not to get her forehead wet and when she came downstairs it was mid-morning.

"Charmaine is here and can get you some coffee and something to eat," said her uncle. "I hope you feel better?"

She indicated that she did and gladly accepted some coffee and some toast. Sir Hugo retired to his study, Charmaine's boyfriend picked her up and Scyathica sat and looked at the newspapers.

All of a sudden there was the sound of a car outside the house. Scyathica looked out of the window and saw a cab from Khan's cars. The taxi sped off and there was a loud knock on the door. Piper started barking. Scyathica went to the door and opened it gingerly. She was sure it was not Steven or Penny. She wondered if her uncle expected anyone. She saw a sun -tanned figure on the doorstep. Her jaw dropped in horror when she saw who it was. A voice said,

"'Allo, my darling daughter... Aren't you going to ask your dear old dad inside?"

Chapter 9

"WHAT ON EARTH ARE YOU doing here?" said Scyathica not opening the front door any further.

Sir Hugo and Piper were quickly behind her, Piper barking loudly and unusually for him snarling. Sir Hugo pulled the door open wider.

"Get your bleeding dog under control," said Davey Scarlett. Davey was a stoutish man of medium height, and slightly balding. He wore a pair of faded jeans better suited to someone 20 years younger and a white shirt slightly open from which some chest hair curled out. He was very tanned. There was a small black holdall at his feet. There was a glint of a Rolex watch at his left wrist.

"He doesn't like you and nor do I," said Sir Hugo. "Go away."

"You can't tell me to go away, I've come to see my daughter," said Davey.

"I can. It's my land. Go away before I call the police... They probably want you for something and if they don't, they should want you..."

Scyathica interjected, "It's okay, Uncle... I'll talk to him outside for a few minutes." She went outside and led her father to a bench in the gardens.

"You look a bit rough," he said.

"Didn't you see the news? There was an explosion. I was caught up in it..."

"Oh, that," Davey responded. "Your name was mentioned when they showed some photos, but I didn't fink you were really there." Scyathica raised her eyebrows.

"Why have you come to Waste, Dad?" She pronounced it Waast in local fashion. "I thought your creditors were after you..."

"Well mostly I keep on the yacht... on the move... but while I was in Blighty I thought I'd check on one of my business ventures and visit my only daughter..."

"What venture is this?" said Scyathica having a horrible suspicion where the visit was going.

"Call centres for emergency services... got the first one set up in Mumbai to service Waste and area. Seeing as I got my crew to bring the yacht up the River Clagg to Waste Water so I could moor in Waste Yacht harbour I'm killing 2 birds with one stone. I thought I would call on Waste Borough Council and also see you... to see if you wanted to get away from this dump and come away with me on the yacht..."

Scyathica sighed. "Dad don't go to Waste Borough Council... or anywhere near Waste... you may get lynched. Your call centre thing is a disaster. Not only was I in a queue of about 80 when Knight's Farm blew up... but in the last few days anyone phoning 999 has had similar problems. They are even talking possible deaths being linked to the emergency service call centre."

She continued, "They'll probably sue... Mind you, as usual you'll be hiding behind God knows how many corporations in the Cayman Islands or whatever... If you lose a bucket of money I don't care except for any ramifications for Mum."

Davey said, "Why do you care for that bitch Pandora...? You were never close... nothing like her."

Scyathica responded, "She may be a bit of an airhead but unlike you she wouldn't hurt a fly."

Davey went on, "Well why not get out of this dump anyway...? There's nuffink but northern oafs here."

Scyathica sighed again. "This is not a dump... Despite nearly getting blown up I feel very at home here... probably more content than I've been for a long time. I don't want to leave... and I'll thank you not to call people who are better people than you 'northern oafs."

Davey got up and without speaking to Scyathica started to phone for a taxi. "Yeah, yeah... you only dropped me off about 30 minutes ago... Yeah same place out of town... Yeah, if you can take me back to the yacht harbour on Waste Water."

He started feeling about in his bag and drew out a bundle of notes.

"There's about 20 grand here," he said. "I thought you might not come with me."

"I don't want your dirty money," said Scyathica.

"Take it, take it... I won't come again. If you don't want it for yourself, give it away..."

Scyathica said, "It's not stolen, is it? Or got from something nasty like drug running?"

"Well," said Davey, "even I would not go that far."

"Okay," Scyathica said, "I might give a bit to Uncle... to help him fix the house... and some to local charities."

"I don't need to know what you're doing with it," said Davey, who started walking away from Scyathica. She followed. He stopped at the wide area of driveway in front of the house and stood there waiting for his taxi.

"Goodbye then," said Scyathica and went inside. She stood in the hallway looking out of the window for about 15 minutes. The taxi came. She saw her father get in and the car disappear down the driveway. Apart from the money in her hand it was as if he had never been.

"What do you have in your hand," said Uncle Hugo appearing. She told him about the money. He said, "Well I'm not sure you should have taken it... but you've got it now."

They sat down and counted it.

The money came to £26,300.

"Uncle..." said Scyathica, "I'd like to give you some for being so kind to me... and maybe give a lot to charity."

Uncle Hugo looked thoughtful.

"Charity tends to begin at home... Here's a thought. The West Wing would be ideal to turn into a self-contained wing. I had a quote about 5 months ago. It can be treated for damp and the floorboards fixed for about £10,000. I could get that work done and sell you the West Wing for say £50,000... £10.000 down and either you get a mortgage for the rest, or pay me off in instalments... You could use the money to help pay for it... do the place up... something like that."

"Uncle," said Scyathica, "you're thinking on the hoof... the West Wing is worth vastly more than £50,000 surely, and I want to give a large amount to charity to help the people who suffered due to my father's outsourced call-centre."

They resolved to do their sums. As long as Scyathica was able to give a sizeable sum to charity she felt her uncle's idea had merit.

Penny on the other hand was not thinking of money. She was thinking of Lewis. She'd been on 2 dates with him at the Roebuck and Hogg but today they were going on a picnic. She dreamed of him putting a large wicker basket on the back of the bike and riding along with her hair flowing in the wind while she clung to her god, naked to the waist.

Reality was different. Lewis was about 20 minutes late and said grumpily there had been a queue at the café where he had waited for some takeaway butties for them. He was of course clad in his leathers. He kept his helmet on just opening the visor to speak. He proffered a helmet to Penny and insisted she put it on. As they rode along Penny was clutching Lewis's motorbike leathers and really felt quite scared.

They stopped at a car park which was on a slight rise and had good views of Waste Water including the yacht harbour. They took their helmets off and sat at a picnic bench just by the car park edge. Lewis took 2 cans of pop from the brown carrier bag which housed the take-away sandwiches. Then he passed her a sandwich.

She bit into it. "What is it?" she said. "It's really, really tasty."

"BLT," said Lewis chomping.

"BLT... whawt's that?" said Penny drawling and chewing.

"Bacon... Lettuce...Tomato..." was the response.

"But I'm a vegan," screeched Penny.

"Take the bacon out," was the practical response.

Penny was not sure what to do. She did not want to go against her principals, but she was enjoying her sandwich, and she did not want to upset her god. She mumbled something about the environment. Lewis smiled wryly.

"Well, it's local meat from local farmers fed on local feed from local produce... not soya from South America..." he commented.

Penny said, "I guess I also feel sorry for the poor little piggies."

Lewis replied, "Poor piggies? Do you know what my job is? I'm a butchery manager with Knubb's Bacon and Sausages... Pigs exist to be bacon."

Penny looked crestfallen but Lewis went on, "A pig is a domesticated hog... it would not be kept if it were not for the fact it tasted good."

"But Lewis... they could be kept on reserves," said Penny intently.

Lewis guffawed. "Pig safari parks, I like it," but more gently, "next time we have a picnic if you really are insistent, I'll get you something veggie."

Penny smiled. Lewis tucked an arm around her. She felt all was alright with her world. She could overlook Lewis being a butcher because he was respectful of her wishes.

As they sat enjoying the view the London train was making its way to Waste. Aboard it today was Dr Gordon Flaughtersdough and his pupil Verity Timpson-Saunders. Dr Flaughtersdough quite enjoyed his forays north to Waste. The Knubb Arms was a good place to stay for a couple of nights. Bernie Blunt seemed a good source of work, so he was happy to oblige. As they had reclined in first class, he had let Verity go over the briefs on her laptop. The main event as far he was concerned was a conference with various employees of Waste Waste leading to an injunction application. They were also acting for a mother called Whitney Knight in a separate case. Dr Flaughtersdough asked Verity to explain what she had read. He thought it would be good experience for her (and save some of his time) albeit he had read the main reports. Gordon Flaughtersdough sat back being careful not to spoil his plum-coloured velvet jacket. He curled the end of his handlebar moustache with his little finger. It was good to not be just doing video hearings, which had been the norm in covid lockdown days. There was nothing like a trial with people in court.

"So," said Verity. "This is a final day's hearing in respect of Cortina and Popsicle Ford, aged 2 and 1 respectively. Their mother is Whitney Knight aged 19 and Garry Lee Ford aged 25. Waste Borough Council seek care and placement orders; that means they want the children adopted, doesn't it? The threshold document has been agreed; that's the basic grounds saying the children have suffered significant harm and are at risk of significant harm..."

"Yes, that's right," said Gordon. "You can just summarise..."

Verity started speaking, her strawberry blonde locks cascading over the shoulders of her impeccable cream trouser suit.

"It says Garry is in prison for armed robbery and he took Cortina and Whitney out for a ride in the car and left them outside a newsagent while he went in with a crossbow. Also, both parents have histories with drug abuse. The police raided a squat known to be used to supply crack cocaine and found Whitney living there with the children - Popsicle was only 2 months old... The children have been with foster parents ever since that date. There have been efforts by Whitney to get her drug habit sorted but it has not gone too well. She puts forward a case for the children to be placed with her mother Dusty Knight who has been living at a farm with her father Jim Knight. But there may be a problem..."

Gordon raised an eyebrow. "The local authority was not able to do a proper assessment of Dusty or speak to Whitney's father Karol Luca... Dusty did not turn up for appointments and they could not get Karol on the phone or get enough information to do any police checks on him. There were some court directions about immigration disclosure, but no-one knows if his name is accurate or what his date of birth is... they think he is from Romania. It is assumed Dusty knew him years ago somehow, but he has come back on the scene recently. The great grandfather didn't allow social workers to visit his farm... But now... well... have you seen the news...?"

Gordon responded, "Don't tell me it was the farm which blew up?"

Verity said, "Yes. Karol is in hospital. Jim Knight the farmer is on bail, and I think Mr Blunt has not been able to contact Dusty Knight. He thinks our client Whitney is still living in a hostel."

"Ah well, I am sure I can put on a show for the client. Who am I against?" said Gordon.

Verity's small rose-bud mouth pouted. She looked perplexed. "Well, the local authority is represented by Ivan Huff; Mr Ford has Max Scott and the children's solicitor is Sue Rosemary... What do you mean... put on a show?"

"It's all theatre," replied Gordon in plummy tones which were the verbal embodiment of the colour of his jacket. "Unless the client can instruct us of something new, all the reports and assessments of her are negative. So she will lose her children. But she will want a good show... She will want to think her barrister gave his all. I am sure I can think up some argument to put forward to make her think I am fighting tooth and nail."

Verity replied, "Aren't you going to annoy the judge if there is nothing of merit to put forward?"

"Possibly. But I don't do all my cases in Waste, do I? Fortunately, we are likely to have a different judge on the other case. I am more worried about that one. Also, Waste Waste might try to make something of the fact it's now likely to wriggle out of the Environment Agency's prosecution."

He sipped on a glass of red wine served by a train steward and looked at the plate of sandwiches in front of him with a dissatisfied look.

"The wine from these little bottles never tastes as good as wine from a proper bottle even if the label purports to say it is claret," he mused. "The sandwiches look and taste like... train sandwiches!"

Verity poked her pre-prepared salad in its plastic container disdainfully with a fork and nodded her agreement. She stretched out her long legs.

"So I understand we are having an initial conference on the injunction case late afternoon when the intention is to see if any draft papers need tweaking. Then there is the day care case... and we go back to London probably after the day case unless a further conference is needed in the injunction case... And then we will be back sometime soon for the injunction application?"

"Yes, that's right," said Gordon with a yawn. They did not speak much for the rest of the journey. Gordon did not believe in social chit-chat with his pupils.

Things went much as he had planned. First, they had the conference with Mickey Gasson, Bernie Blunt and half a dozen vociferous workers from Waste Waste who all complained of "them rashes" and "that gloves were no good what they gave us". Bernie was assisted by a downtrodden looking young girl introduced as "my new trainee Sonja Sidebottom". Her cheap-looking navy blue jacket over black t-shirt and black trousers contrasted markedly with Verity's immaculate cream trouser suit. Sonja said nothing in the conference and when she was not making notes on a laptop spent her time chewing a ball-point pen. The conference took place in a room Bernie had hired at the Knubb Arms due to the numbers likely to attend.

Nat Cartey had dropped off Mickey Gasson for the conference and decided to go for a stroll in the square outside before going to his constituency office. Scyathica had called on Stacey Birch that afternoon having had the morning off to recover. She was on her way to the Knubb Arms to have tea with Steven Hovell. As they both passed the alleyway between Waste Combined Court and Knubb Town Hall they almost collided.

"Nathanial? It is you," said Scyathica. "It's me... your cousin Scyathica."

Nat Cartey froze. He was of course aware his cousin was in Waste, particularly since the news reports of the explosion but had hoped to avoid her.

"I am Nat Cartey... your MP... You are mistaken..." he tried.

"I know it's you, Nathanial... Why are you calling yourself Nat Cartey?" Scyathica continued.

"Shuushh... no-one is supposed to know... Not even Dad knows I'm here." He pulled her into the alleyway.

"Why is it a secret?" said Scyathica.

"Because I'm a Labour MP, for Christ's sake. No-one knows my public-school background or that I'm related to a Tory press baron," hissed Nat.

"That would make a good story," said Scyathica without thinking.

She had never really liked her cousin. He had been a whiny, spoiled little boy who always demanded presents whenever he arrived at family get-togethers. He had teased her and cat-called her "bad-back". He had dropped earwigs and worms down her back when they were 10 or 11 years old. He pulled her mother Pandora's Scottie's tail and when the dog yelped falsely claimed it tried to bite him. He had then turned into a morose, selfish teenager who had struggled at his public school and who had been frequently suspended due to his tendency to extract money from younger, weaker boys. When Scyathica was about 13 she could remember him pushing her over when out of sight of adults in the garden so he could riffle through her handbag and take her pocket money.

Nat shoved her against a wall in the alleyway putting his arm across her neck.

"Don't you say anything about me to anyone." Scyathica could not move but he continued, "I bet people don't know about your father... What would they think of you?"

Scyathica managed to just about breathe out a reply. "I don't think many people know... I really won't say anything, Nat."

Just then Steven came down the alley. He had come out of the rear court entrance to avoid defendants and was heading for the Knubb Arms. He immediately hastened his speed and seeing Scyathica pinned against a wall and fearing the worst gave Nat Cartey his best right hook. Champ would have been proud of him.

"Leave her alone," he shouted.

"Ouch...," cried Nat. "I'll report you to the police." His arm was no longer against Scyathica's neck.

"I don't think so," said Scyathica. "You don't want it getting in the papers do you?"

"What IS going on?" said Steven.

"What is it to you?" said Nat.

"I'm her boyfriend," said Steven. Scyathica did not disagree.

After a few minutes discussion they all agreed they better go and talk about things somewhere more private and agreed to go to Auntie Bea's in Canal Street.

Auntie Bea asked few questions and showed them into her small dining room. She went and fetched a small pack of frozen peas which she offered Nat.

"Sorry, no ice," she said. "Hope this helps." She closed the door and left them to talk.

It was agreed Scyathica would say nothing about Nat's true identity to anyone and he would not publicise the identity of her father. Nat would not press charges and would tell people he tripped over a loose stone. They would all 3 keep their distance from each other and the incident was agreed never to have happened.

"All finished talking?" said Auntie Bea suspiciously just after they had finished talking.

"Yes," said Nat quickly. "I tripped over a stone and eh... eh..."

"Steven," said Steven.

"…Suggested I came here in case I was hurt," continued Nat. "And of course, I told him I used to lodge here. Then he introduced me to his girlfriend."

"Well," said Auntie Bea, "I suppose you didn't have any ice or frozen peas in your own flat, Nat?"

"Well, no," he said absurdly lying. "I really do thank you. It was nice to see you again, Auntie Bea. I don't think I will have time to come back this way for some time… I will be needed in the House of Commons."

He wondered how he would look going with a shiner to the House. He hoped Scyathica would respect their agreement in full and that her uncle on the opposite benches would not suspect a thing.

Chapter 10

IN THE MORNING STEVEN GAVE Scyathica a quick call to make sure she was alright. They had had a long talk the previous night about their respective families. Scyathica reassured Steven she would be working from home for the day, writing up a couple of articles. He drove his scooter into the court car park only to be greeted by His Honour Judge Grasby KC who was leaning against the back of his car smoking his pipe.

"Morning, Shovel," he said with a twinkle in his eye.

"Morning, Your Honour," Steven replied smiling.

"I've loaned you out for most of the day to Her Honour dela Notte. I have a couple of bail applications in half an hour and then a plea and directions so by 10.30 you can go and clerk in her care case. I'll be writing some judgments."

"Thank you for letting me know," said Steven as he headed inside.

Moments later Her Honour dela Notte parked her BMW sports car with its personalised number plate DNOTT 1.

"Good morning, Oliver," she said.

"Well, it is for me," said Oliver. "But I am not sure about you."

"Why?" she replied.

"Rumour has it," said Oliver smiling, "you have that dreadful man Slaughter–duff!"

"Oh, no," said Davina dela Notte. "I suppose you mean I have the good Doctor Gordon on my care case?"

"Yes indeed," said Oliver puffing on his pipe. "I'd like to be a fly on the wall. By the way, our esteemed sporting colleague the Phitt-one has apparently gone on a sabbatical for 3 months to study sports' arbitration."

"Golly," said Davina. "That was kept dark. Who is going to cover for him?"

"Well I hope it's our friend Aziz. He knows what he's doing…"

At that moment a taxi drew to a screech near the car park entrance and who should clamber out carrying a suitcase and a suit bag, but Aziz Ahmed uncharacteristically clad in a pale grey tracksuit.

"Good God," said Oliver. "I was just talking about you and saying I hoped you would join us for a bit. But I didn't expect you to have borrowed clothes from a prison!"

"My dear chap," said Recorder Ahmed. "You did not expect me to ruin my suit getting here… By the way, I have brought you something, Oliver."

He put his bag down and searched for something inside it. He took out a small box with a clear cellophane front. At first glance it looked like a pipe made from very dark wood. Oliver held it up after it was placed in his hands. Davina started to smile wryly. In gold writing the box bore the message 'Finest dark chocolate'. Oliver started to laugh. He was sure he was going to continue to get on with Recorder Ahmed.

Oliver finished smoking his tobacco pipe for now and capped it.

They all went inside.

Steven had got Her Honour's court set up. There was a video link with the father's prison, and he had done a quick test run. He had checked with the usher that everyone had arrived as expected. He had liaised with the usher to make sure Her Honour had received a coffee, that there was water in the court, the judge's notebook, any paper documents were there and as far as he could be aware all electronic and recording equipment was working. Nichola, the usher, brought in the parties and the lawyers and lastly Her Honour who was dressed in a black pinstripe trouser suit and had her hair tightly tied back in a bun. Steven announced the case.

"Waste Borough Council versus Knight… The Family Court sitting in Waste Combined Court before Her Honour dela Notte."

Ivan Huff rose to his feet. A striking middle-aged man with a slight accent which was perhaps that of the Newcastle-on-Tyne area. He was made striking by the fact his dark hair had a streak of white down the middle which made him look like a badger.

He began to address the court.

"If it pleases Your Honour, I represent Waste Borough Council. My Learned Friend Dr Gordon Flaughtersdough represents the mother Whitney Knight, my Learned Friend Mr Percy Vere instructed by Max Scott represents the father Mr Ford and the children's solicitor Miss Sue Rosemary is also here to represent the children,

Cortina and Popsicle through their Children's Guardian Mr Tim Weary. The mother is present, and the father will attend by video link. As well as the Guardian also in court is the social worker Mrs Mary Yeo and her manager Mr Richard Nay. Dr Flaughtersdough asks that his pupil Miss Timpson –Saunders can remain to assist him and likewise Mr Vere asks that his pupil Mr Ellison be present…"

Before Mr Huff could finish Dr Flaughtersdough rose to his feet. Today he was clad in a black corduroy jacket which seemed a little on the long side. The problem might have been that the good doctor was a little on the short side. He had a crisp white shirt and a huge black velvet bow tie. He curled the edge of his handle-bar moustache and started to speak in ringing tones.

"Your Honour, I must insist on an immediate adjournment... under articles 6 and 8 of the Convention on Human Rights my client can neither have a fair trial today nor can her right to family life have been respected..."

Her Honour dela Notte leaned forward. "Dr Flaughtersdough, Mr Huff has not even finished opening the case..."

"It's alright, Your Honour... let him make his application. The local authority can then oppose it. We are ready to proceed today."

The judge sought the positions of the father and the Children's Guardian. Mr Vere said,

"My client had no notice of this application, but my instructions are to support the local authority's case for adoption. My client cannot care for the children, and he does not believe the mother, or her family can either. He has bravely come to the conclusion the best future for his daughters is adoption."

Mr Weary whispered something to his solicitor Miss Rosemary who rose to her feet.

"If it pleases Your Honour the Children's Guardian supports the local authority's case for adoption. The drug –testing of the mother and the expert psychological reports on her are all sadly negative to her abilities to safely parent the children at this time and she has accepted their contents. The Guardian is deeply saddened for the mother but very concerned about the effect of a delay on the children so would oppose an adjournment. Indeed, the social worker has told her this morning a suitable family has been located by the adoption team for these little girls."

"Very well I will hear the application to adjourn now," said Her Honour in an impassive tone.

Gordon continued in ringing tones, "Your Honour, my client was to have advanced a case for her mother Dusty Knight to care for the girls... who she deeply loves... at Knight's Farm... but that ship has sailed, nay, blown apart... literally due to the unfortunate circumstances at the said farm. But fear not, there may be another solution for these poor dear babes.

"My client's grandfather has a sister Mrs Audrey Shagg. I understand she was recently looking after children for another family member but that no longer is the case. There must be an assessment of her urgently to see if she can care for the beloved babes..."

Mr Huff rose to his feet and interrupted. "Your Honour, I seek permission to interject..."

"Yes, Mr Huff, what is it?" said Her Honour dela Notte.

Gordon went a sort of deep purple. "Your Honour, I do protest at the untimely interruption."

Her Honour retorted, "Well, you did interrupt Mr Huff's opening... so I will allow him to make a point."

Mr Huff said, "Your Honour, Waste Borough Council already has information on Mrs Shagg... but I don't think I can divulge it without her having the opportunity to object... Further, I am not aware whether Mrs Shagg wants to be assessed. Her name was not put forward in any of the previous hearings."

"Dr Flaughtersdough," said Her Honour, "has she said she wishes to be assessed?"

"Well, no... my client does not have her number so she couldn't ask her," he replied.

Mr Huff then responded,

"Your Honour, I believe the social workers do have her number... If I could suggest the matter be stood down for half an hour to see if at least there can be some initial contact with her? I make it clear the local authority oppose an adjournment but understand the mother's situation."

Her Honour agreed to the short break with some frustration. During the brief adjournment Steven had a quick coffee but all too soon the court re-convened.

Gordon rose to his feet. "Your Honour, my client has decided not to pursue this avenue... Mrs Shagg has made it clear to one and all she does not wish to be involved."

What he didn't describe was what had really happened. In an interview room Mary Yeo had managed to get through to Audrey Shagg and was met with a mixture of suspicion and incredulity. She had obtained permission to pass on Whitney's up-to-date number to her. Once Mary Yeo had finished the call Whitney immediately received a call from Audrey. She was sat in an interview room with her legal representatives. Audrey Shagg was so loud her voice seemed to reverberate off the walls.

"You're not getting me involved with your bleeding brats as well… I had enough with the other children, and I am looking after your great granddad just now. After all, 'ee was nearly blown up, you selfish little cow..."

The long and the short of it was that there was no adjournment to a later date. The case had to proceed.

The evidence was overwhelmingly unfavourable to poor Whitney who, as, unfavourable comment followed more unfavourable information visibly seemed to shrink into her seat. She looked younger than her 19 years, a thin wisp of a girl. Her face was grey, and her lip was quivering. It seemed all Gordon's verbose and pointless questions and speeches were making things worse.

His final speech by way of closing argument referred to the Magna Carta,

Habeas Corpus and the Freedom of Information Act, none of which really had much to do with the law on care proceedings and adoption. The speech was peppered with reference to the "darling babes" and the "sweet innocents". Just after this Whitney said,

"I feel sick," and bolted out of the court.

Steven felt very sorry for her. All Gordon's verbosity had done was prolong her agony. Although hardly the most experienced court clerk his instincts told him that there might have been better and less painful ways an advocate might have presented what little case she had.

"I will reserve my judgment until 9.30 tomorrow morning," said Her Honour dela Notte with an inscrutable expression. "I think this has been a long enough day."

Gordon actually looked pleased. The thought of another night at the Knubb Arms was appealing as fortunately he was not due in another court in the morning.

When tomorrow came and Her Honour dela Notte gave judgment Whitney did not attend. She clearly knew what to expect.

After she had given judgment Derek Devene gave Steven the unenviable task of taking an urgent civil injunction application to His Honour Judge Grasby KC. He explained to Steven that although it was good news that Recorder Ahmed was with the court for a further period the Recorder could not undertake this civil matter.

Oliver was just finishing preparing a judgment he was due to deliver at noon.

"Shovel," he said, "stop hovering at the door."

Steven cleared his throat and entered the Chambers placing a file in front of the scowling Circuit Judge.

"Your Honour, Mr Devene says you have retained a civil ticket to deal with urgent matters which need a Circuit Judge... District Judge Ercol has looked at the file and says it needs to be listed before a Circuit Judge as soon as possible."

His Honour sighed and then after he had read the first couple of pages guffawed.

"Well, well... an injunction application against Waste Waste... that should be interesting. Leave it with me and I will give some initial directions."

And sure enough it found its way into the court list for the next week; but in between was the weekend.

Steven arranged to call on Scyathica on Saturday. Since he had still to pass his test and she did not want to ride on the back of his scooter she drove them some 20 miles away to a stately home up on the fells, Screwhampstead Hall, which Steven had seen advertised as an attractive place to visit. He bought her a cream tea and they explored the formal gardens. She talked vaguely of her uncle and his proposal to sell her the West Wing.

Steven talked vaguely of wanting to buy somewhere in due course. He mentioned more specifically he was resuming learning to drive a car and that subject to passing the test he wished to buy a car. They agreed Steven would bring a takeaway round on Sunday afternoon and Sunday needed to be a lazy day.

Penny on the other hand spent an active weekend with Lewis. She crept out of Auntie Bea's just before dawn. Lewis picked her up with his motorbike.

He whizzed her off to the other side of Waste Water, crossing the suspension bridge over the River Clagg. There was a swimming place there well away from the Waste plant or the yacht harbour, which was deserted at that hour.

"Come on, darlin' let's jump in... it'll be bracing," said Lewis stripping off.

Penny Wayney undressed to reveal a very tiny white bikini.

"Do you need that?" he said, undoing her top.

She shrieked at the cold as they jumped into the water and splashed each other. Afterwards they lay on some towels for a while listening to the dawn chorus.

"Breakfast now," said Lewis and first produced a thermos of hot coffee from the container at the back of his motorbike. Then he produced a tiny camping stove and a tiny pan. From one pocket of his leathers, he produced a hunk of bread and from another a pack of Knubb's bacon and from yet another some foil containing 2 odd looking sausages.

"Brittany... that's my niece... said they were veggie," he said. "They are pre-cooked."

Penny wrinkled her nose but thanked him nonetheless. The bacon sizzled appetisingly. Penny dutifully bit into a veggie sausage. She didn't say anything, but it tasted disgusting.

After they had breakfasted Lewis took them on a long bike ride to the coast where they walked along the sand dunes for about 6 miles and wandered into a small seaside town where they ate candyfloss and ice-cream.

On Sunday Lewis wanted to take her fell-walking but Penny said her feet still hurt after Saturday. They hit on a compromise. They agreed on a short walk near the yacht harbour which would finish at the Harbour View Pub. They took a taxi so they could both drink alcohol and they whiled away the afternoon and early evening drinking cider. Lewis had the house special to eat the 'Mammoth Sausage Surprise Burger' which he wolfed down and Penny picked at the vegetarian pasta bake. Some of Lewis's colleagues from the factory were present having lunch too. The 'Mammoth Sausage Surprise Burger' with ample amounts of cider was a hit and laughter could be heard echoing out across the yacht harbour.

Penny felt most content... apart from the vegetarian bake which she had not enjoyed. She let Lewis and his friends do most of the talking. She fell asleep in the taxi back to town. When she stirred she found she was tucked in on a sofa in Lewis's flat. She vaguely remembered him helping her inside. It was about 7am... she could hear Lewis snoring. She needed to be at the council offices at about 9.30am collating some of her material. Fortunately, she was not too far from Canal Street. She wrote a quick note and tip-toed out making sure the door only shut with a click. She put her key in the lock at Auntie Bea's at about quarter to 8 only to find Auntie Bea standing in front of her.

"If you are going to stop out you might at least tell me... I was a bit worried you'd come off that lad's motorbike."

Penny nodded and quickly went to get washed and changed for work.

Steven left for work well before Penny. He knew today would be busy. The Environment Agency's prosecution of Waste Waste was in court today. Scyathica was likely to be in the press benches. He knew His Honour Judge Grasby KC was not likely to be in a good mood.

"Morning, Shovel," he said in the car park puffing on his pipe. "Are we prepared for the onslaught?"

Steven said, "It's only 8.30am… Your Honour, I've only just arrived."

"Well, you better get inside… and get ready, then," said His Honour Judge Grasby KC in acid tones.

Steven waited to sigh until he was inside the court building. This did not sound like a fun Monday. He liaised with the usher. He made sure the court was ready. He checked who was representing whom. Percy Vere was representing Waste Waste, but Faye Leafly was representing the Environment Agency and Ivan Huff represented Waste Borough Council. His heart sank. He had an impending feeling of doom.

About this time Lewis was waking up with a pounding head. He looked at his clock. Fortunately, he was on an afternoon shift at Knubb Bacon. He called for Penny but realised she had gone. He had a shower and set off for the factory calling briefly at Mickey and Maureen's to cadge some late breakfast if anyone was at home. As it happened Mickey, Maureen and Brittany were all there. Brittany looked both flushed and flustered and Mickey and Maureen looked rather stern.

Pointing at Brittany Mickey said,

"She's up the duff… that MPs got her in the pudding club."

Maureen said, "It'll be lovely to have a baby in the family, but I do hope he'll look after Brittany and the bairn."

"Does he know?" said Lewis to Brittany.

"Yeah. Told him yesterday. He's gone to London today."

"What did he say?" asked Lewis.

"Not a lot," said Brittany. "I think he's been feeling off colour since he fell over and got that black eye. Said he'd sort things with me when he's back again… I trust him."

"Fell?" said Mickey. "Looks more like someone took a swing at him. I'd be happier if he'd told our Brittany something more helpful… I mean he's not married as far we know, and I've always got on well with him. MPs have relationships and children too… It just seemed a little off that he's been so vague."

Lewis nodded in agreement. He had never been quite sure what Nat Cartey was hiding but always felt there was something.

Nat himself was contemplating his deceptions as he arrived at Westminster. He felt he should marry Brittany. It would embed him further in the community. The concern he had was whether he could use his acquired birth certificate or his real one plus the change of name deed. On the one hand he didn't want to store up some sort of issue with the Registrar which potentially could be a criminal offence but on the other hand if he used his real identity his party, not to mention the electors, would be furious. It was enough of a risk that he had not declared his Trust Fund money to the register of members' interests. Then there was the financial side. His MP's salary and the Trust Money kept him in a comfortable lifestyle with his flat in Waste and a bedsit in another MP's large London flat. He'd need somewhere bigger for Brittany, the child and himself... whether they married or not. He also thought about his father. Maybe if he came clean on what he had been doing the old man would be pleased to support his grandchild. He needed to formulate a plan.

Chapter 11

STEVEN HAD COURT 1 WELL prepared for the Environment Agency's prosecution of Waste Waste for polluting the beck. He had previously noted Waste Borough Council were also on the indictment. He knew they were responsible for monitoring local water courses but did not understand the 'ins and outs' of the criminal case. He had plied His Honour Judge Grasby KC with strong coffee and even found a chocolate biscuit for him. He was not sure it put His Honour in a better mood but at least his mood was no worse.

A handful of press representatives were on hand to report on the case, including Scyathica and Stacey Birch. An outside broadcast car was stationed outside the courthouse since the issue was worthy of report on the local television news.

Everyone was soon assembled in Court number 1 except His Honour Judge Oliver Grasby KC. Miss Faye Leafly was accompanied by a couple of civil servants from the Environment Agency. Ivan Huff was on his own. Percy Vere was accompanied by his pupil Chris Ellison. There was a solicitor's clerk Steven did not know from Waste Waste's solicitors who were out of town plus the plant manager Ron Woodhouse sat there with a slightly worried expression.

There was an expectant hush before His Honour Judge Grasby KC came in and as he entered and went to sit down Faye Leafly dropped all her papers on the floor. Steven attempted to announce the case, but Miss Leafly had dived under the desk in front of her. Even Steven was nonplussed by her actions.

"Lost something, have we?" barked His Honour. "And we haven't even started."

Miss Leafly emerged from under the desk with a pink face, looking extremely dishevelled. "I give profuse apologies, Your Honour, but I've lost my dongle."

"Your dongle?" said His Honour questioningly.

"For my laptop," came the response. "I can't get it to work otherwise."

"Can anyone help her?" His Honour said in a weary tone.

Chris Ellison dived under the desk and a minute later in broad Brummy tones said, "Here it is I think."

"Now can we get on?" said His Honour.

Percy Vere rose to his feet. A golden curl peeked out from under his wig on his forehead above his aquiline nose.

"Your Honour, I have an application on behalf of the first defendant which is supported by my Learned Friend for the second defendant. I have also notified my Learned Friend for the prosecution of this application... It is for the indictment to be dismissed on the basis there is no case to answer."

"Miss Leafly, were you aware...? Is this opposed?" His Honour asked.

Faye Leafly looked even more flustered. "Yes, Your Honour, I have had notice. I thought I would leave the matter to Your Honour."

His Honour looked annoyed about her response. "Carry on, Mr Vere," he said with a slight sigh.

"Your Honour," said Percy Vere, "you will recall this prosecution arises from an allegation that Waste Beck was polluted by outflow from Waste Waste Waste Processing plant. Waste Borough Council has the legal responsibility for monitoring and managing the beck. The allegation was that polluting alcoholic substances had got into the beck and killed a number of a local farmer's sheep. Your Honour not to put too finer point on it, in the light of recent events the Prosecution's case has been blown out of the water... literally."

There was uproar in court.

"Be quiet, everyone, unless you want to face contempt charges," growled His Honour at the press and public's laughter.

"Continue, Mr Vere... but without show-boating, please."

Percy Vere carried on,

"Your Honour may be aware that the local farmer was a Mr James Knight and that there was an explosion fairly recently at his farm. Your Honour, there has been a joint investigation by the Police, HMRC, the Health and Safety Executive and Trading Standards. I understand it has been a complex investigation and that the Crown Prosecution Service are shortly to proceed with a criminal case against several individuals who have no connection whatsoever with my client. The allegation, as I understand it will relate to an illegal vodka still which will be alleged to have been situated in a building just next to the beck... a building which is no longer there. Your Honour, the first defendant alleges the only evidence the prosecution ever had was that some sheep died. In short, they have no case to answer."

He sat down and Mr Huff leaped to his feet and said,

"Your Honour, the second defendant has always taken its statutory responsibilities seriously and is aware that strict liability might normally apply. However, if there is no evidence the beck was ever polluted the second defendant would concur there is no case to answer."

He sat down and His Honour looked at Miss Leafly with a piercing stare.

"Well?" he said, "Surely you must have something to say?"

"Your Honour," she replied meekly, "could I just ask for the matter to be stood down for five minutes? It would really be so helpful."

Grumpily, Oliver Grasby granted the five-minute adjournment. Miss Leafly went into a consultation room with the civil servants. When the case resumed Miss Leafly offered no evidence and requested the indictment be dismissed. Percy Vere smiled smugly. Ron Woodhouse looked relieved. Miss Leafly and the civil servants seemed to melt away.

Everyone filed out of court. Scyathica and her colleagues from the press cohort made for the Knubb Arms. As she walked from the court to the pub, she noticed men with ladders and a cherry-picker seemed to have started erecting bunting in the square. To her surprise sitting in the bar with an orange juice she spotted Penny Wayney. She had a pile of leaflets in front of her and looked a bit glum.

"Hello, you look a bit out of sorts," said Scyathica.

"I guess I am a little sad," said Penny. "The survey for the council has finished. They have kept me on for a few more weeks to deliver leaflets to do with some pageant thing... and a bit of admin to do with it. But then I am out of a job..."

"Will you have any trouble with your visa?" asked Scyathica.

"No, that's okay because I got a way to go on my Master's degree."

"Can I look at a leaflet?" asked Scyathica. Penny handed one over.

Scyathica looked at it. It was advertising festivities in a few weeks' time to celebrate the tri-centenary of Waste worthy Sir Charles Whitewhisker's birth. Neither Penny nor Scyathica knew anything about him and Scyathica looked on the Webopaedia page on her phone. Stacey Birch was also in the pub of course and heard them talking. She came over,

"That won't tell you everything," she said. "Read it out and I'll fill in the gaps."

Scyathica began with his birth and death date and went on,

"Sir Charles Hengist Whitewhisker was a philanthropist and Abolitionist. He was born near Waste and after spending time in the West Indies he returned to Waste and lived at Whitewhisker Hall. He became the town's MP until his death. He married a freed slave from his plantation, Solange who was known as a great beauty and for her generosity.

"He had three daughters and no sons. His eldest daughter Madeira inherited Whitewhisker Hall but the family died out eventually and the Hall fell into some disrepair. It was eventually taken over by Waste Borough Council and most of it was demolished. The site is now utilised as Waste General Hospital. One wing remains which has been incorporated and houses the hospital's imaging suite and private patients' rooms..."

Stacey interjected, "The council could have saved it... but didn't want to spend the money. They also sold off what had been a walled vegetable garden and stable block and that is where the Magistrates' Court stands."

Scyathica continued,

"During his time in the West Indies Sir Charles decided to free his slaves who worked on the family plantation on St Pernicious Island. He took up the issue of Abolition subsequently in Parliament prior to Sir William Wilberforce's involvement but at that time without much success." Stacey interrupted.

"What the official account does not tell you is that St Pernicious Island was only 10 miles long and 5 miles wide, so the slaves had nowhere to go... they all stayed working on the Plantation anyway. Later on when back in Waste, Sir Charles took over a cotton mill. He offered some of the slaves a chance to leave the island and work in the cotton mill... the poor sods swopped one lot of servitude for another... I think he intended good things, but it didn't work out quite right."

Scyathica continued,

"Sir Charles was keen on alleviating poverty. He also introduced a bill into the House of Commons called the 'Cake Bill' which would have made it mandatory for every Borough to make sure all poor children under the age of 10 had cake each Sunday. The Bill failed. However, Sir Charles continued his anti-slavery campaigning and his philanthropy. He set up the Pernicious Foundation which was a philanthropic foundation whose original aim was to supply bibles and cake to those still working on the plantations."

"What happened to it?" asked Penny.

Stacey replied, "I remember when I was a child it used to sponsor one or two children a year to attend Waste Grammar School for a year and live with host families. Poor mites I can recall one or two... isolated for a whole year from their families, often the only black children in a class... and then sent back home just when they had got a tiny bit used to things. These days I think it funds libraries in schools in the developing world..."

Scyathica continued reading,

"Sir Charles had a strong belief in law and order and felt it was inappropriate for the assizes to be held in the Knubb Arms as it was at that time. He therefore funded the building of a fine courthouse on Knubb town square. The building was designed by Thomas Eve.

"Sir Charles also funded the first sewerage system in Waste. He complained that the odours from the town square put him off his cake which he enjoyed eating at the Knubb Arms.

"There used to be a saying amongst the people of Waste 'There can be no justice without cake'.

"It is not clear what sort of cake was preferred by him, but he did name his daughters after cakes. They were respectively called Madeira, Torte and Eclaire. A portrait of Sir Charles attributed to Gainsborough, holding a plate of cakes flanked by his wife and daughters can be seen in Waste Town Hall Council Chamber."

At that point she stopped reading. "The rest is just footnotes. I'd never heard of this man before today..."

"Not a lot of people outside Waste have," said Stacey. "But he is very much part of our history and culture here. Having a festival to celebrate his birth will give people a chance to enjoy themselves. We'll probably run some competitions in the local paper and on the radio, for example bake the best Waste cake."

"Is there a particular Waste cake?" asked Penny.

"Now you have opened a can of worms," said Stacey. "There are three competing theories. One theory is that Waste cake was a bit like a Cornish pasty filled with a mixture of sausage meat and rum-soaked raisins from the West Indies... a recipe brought back by Sir Charles from St Pernicious. The second theory is that Waste cake is actually a boiled apple or pear dumpling. The third type of cake which claims to be Waste cake is a bit like a Bakewell tart except it has a pool of jam in the middle of it to signify Waste Water... If we run a competition, we won't specify a right or a wrong cake. We don't want fistfights over cakes as happened many years ago!"

"Do tell," said Scyathica.

"Not long after the Second World War," said Stacey, "the town had a competition supposedly to raise morale to decide on which cake was Waste cake. Several local bakers competed... a chef from London even came. Because there was rationing it was difficult to source ingredients. Unbeknownst to anyone most of the London chef's cake was made of cardboard. He won on appearance but when they tried to slice into it and found it was papier mâché all hell broke loose. He was nearly lynched and fled back to London... Great care will be needed!

"Mind you, that being said there was no issue when they did that TV baking competition here a couple of years ago... the inhabitants of Waste went cake mad, so the newspaper ran a kids' cake baking championship and all the children had a whale of a time."

Penny commented, "Gee... what a cool story and I've never heard of anyone before who named their children after cakes. If Waste is having a festival to celebrate him, it sounds a great idea."

Meanwhile, Nat had also heard of the festival. It gave him an idea for a plan. He would need to be careful. But hopefully he could marry Brittany and work things to his advantage. He telephoned his father. He supposed he should not have been surprised if his father knew exactly what he had been doing for the last few years.

"I control newspapers and radio stations," said Lord Coldharbour. "And even though I have not seen you for years do you really think I am not going to recognise your picture when backbench MPs are discussed? More power to you for re-inventing yourself, Nat... I can keep your secret if that's what you want... but why are you in touch?"

Nat told him about Brittany, her pregnancy and trying to work out a wedding plan. His father agreed to go along with the plan.

When Brittany heard about most of the plan she was delighted. Immediate contact was made with the Registrar. There were a few bits he left out when explaining his plan to Brittany and her family. Soon invitations were dropping on the doormats of Gasson family wedding guests and the great and the good and the significant of Waste. He felt it was a masterstroke on his part to combine his wedding party with the festival on the Harbour Green that day in celebration of Sir Charles.

The main wedding party would be in the Harbour Arms and the festival could carry on just outside. If Lord Coldharbour were to attend it would be assumed he had come to attend the festival. He had already arranged to book most of the Harbour Arms for the wedding. He had also paid for the Harbour Arms to have a marquee so all their regulars could drink outside on the green.

When Sir Hugo received his invitation, he guffawed and supposed he better attend. When Scyathica received an invitation to her plus one she was suspicious of it as a peace offering but supposed that she would no doubt attend with Steven. Easy Ryder received an invitation as did the judges and court manager at the court. Auntie Bea received an invitation. Lewis and Penny obviously received invitations. All the great and good and not so good of Waste were invited to the wedding of Waste East's MP to one of their own on the date three hundred years after Sir Charles Whitewhisker was born... and there would be cake, wedding cake.

C h a p t e r   1 2

SONJA SIDEBOTTOM HAD COME INTO Bernie Blunt's office at 6am. She wanted to get the paper-work right for Mr Blunt's important injunction case. She did not like Mr Blunt, and Dr Flaughtersdough really terrified her, but she wanted desperately to become a solicitor and prove to her parents she was a success. She had done reasonably well at Waste Grammar School but with parents who had a medical background and an uncle who was Mayor and Council Leader she sometimes felt a bit overwhelmed.

Mr Bertram Sidebottom was the most important Consultant General Surgeon at Waste General Hospital; at least he thought so. His wife, Sonja's mother Marjorie had been a hospital Sister, but these days devoted herself to fundraising in support of the hospital and riding her horse 'April's dawn' at three-day events. Marjorie was Easy Ryder's much younger sister. This made Auntie Bea, Sonja's great-aunt. Sonja did not see Auntie Bea that often but was very fond of her. At school she found Maths to be difficult but excelled at English and History. She also felt faint at the sight of blood. Medicine was not something she felt was for her. Her parents tended to treat her as a disappointment since she did not train for a medical career but did a law degree at a Red Brick University and managed a creditable 2nd Class Honours. Auntie Bea on the other hand was never judgmental.

And so she felt if she could make sure her drafting skills were of a high standard at least, she might succeed in her training contract with Bernie Blunt. Bernie would no doubt charge the client at top rate for the work she had done and pretend it was his. She had already proved her worth in drafting a particularly complex lease for the landlord of the local taxi company. She did have an uncomfortable feeling about the injunction application. Dr Flaughtersdough seemed very optimistic but to her the case seemed very thin.

The good doctor had enjoyed another night at the Knubb Arms. Although the weather was somewhat warm, he had ploughed into his steak and kidney pie with relish and polished off a bottle Rioja. He had then guzzled sticky toffee pudding and ice-cream and finished his meal with Stilton and a glass of port. Verity had picked at her crab salad but was told to enjoy it and her glass of Pinot Grigio "because after all the union can pay for this". At breakfast he still had room for fried eggs and Knubb bacon. Verity picked at a grapefruit.

As they entered the court building Verity stifled a giggle as Dr Flaughtersdough belched and then farted saying in plummy tones, "Squeaky shoes, don't you know." They found Bernie Blunt and Sonja Sidebottom in the largest of the interview rooms. Six of the claimants were in attendance and the rest were reachable by telephone. It was a bit of a squeeze. There was Mickey and Maureen Gasson, a colleague of Maureen, Doreen Spenders, and three men off the waste sorting line, George Tassel, Bill Frond and Fred Hemme. After a few minutes' discussion Sonja was sent to make contact with the court usher, so she was aware the claimants were present and who represented them. This was a task she was happy to do as the room had developed a strangely unpleasant odour.

Percy Vere, Chris Ellison and Ron Woodhouse sat quietly in another interview room having reported in to the usher well on time.

His Honour Judge Oliver Grasby KC smoked two cigars in the car park that morning. He knew his wife Annette would not approve. He felt he needed fortifying against that awful man Dr Gordon Flaughtersdough. Steven Hovell brought him a strong coffee and two chocolate biscuits to his Chambers.

"How are you this morning, Shovel?" he asked with a twinkle in his eye. "Ready for the fray? We have that dreadful man Slaughter-doo this morning..."

Steven had learned to ignore the mispronunciation of his own name, but he said,

"I believe the claimant's counsel's name is pronounced Flowerdew."

"Pity he can't spell it like that, eh, Shovel?"

Steven withdrew. Oliver then studied the invitation on his desk. That MP seemed to have incorporated the forthcoming festival into his wedding, a clever ruse no doubt to get the great and the good to attend. He was not aware that the father of the bride was one of the claimants before him. 'Gasson' was not an unusual name in the area, and he was thinking more about the suitability of persuading Annette to attend. It would be nice to attend something jointly. He assumed Davina dela Notte was invited; would anyone see her seldom seen husband Jerome, he wondered.

Oliver carefully read the claim and the supporting statements. The claim was made by 19 employees of Waste Waste. They sought exemplary damages and an injunction from their employer. Today's hearing was for an interim injunction. The claimants sought head to toe protective gear for 17 of the 19 claimants plus the company to build new showers within 21 days. The crux of the complaint was that there was noxious material passing through the sorting room where employees sorted paper, tin and plastic for recycling, and this had caused the claimants skin ailments. It was pleaded in a very wordy way that the current gear in the sorting room of heavy long gloves, plastic boots, aprons and helmets was inadequate.

The medical evidence appeared to be short GP letters from six of the claimants' GPs indicating that each of them had suffered an allergy rash. Two had had rashes to the arms. None appeared to have been referred to hospital. It was unclear how the two female claimants were involved. Granted they said they had had rashes, but they worked in the canteen.

Pre-action correspondence was exhibited. Waste Waste denied the claim or that its gear was inadequate. An extraordinary assertion was raised. It was suggested that Maureen Gasson had brought something into the canteen of her own, which had not been authorised by the company which she had either used to flavour the food or offered as a drink. And this had caused the rashes. It was mentioned Maureen had received a written warning not to bring 'extras' into the canteen. The documents for the defence were succinctly put together. He noted Percy Vere had drafted some of them. The morning would either be trying or entertaining; maybe a little of each.

The usher, Nichola, went to fetch everyone to get them into court. There was a brief hiatus as Dr Flaughtersdough had disappeared. He emerged from the Gents' toilets after some minutes,

"Bit of a dicky tummy," he said. "Must be the weather."

Chris Ellison pulled a face at Verity Timpson-Saunders behind Percy Vere who smirked back at him. Eventually everyone piled into court and awaited the entrance of His Honour Judge Oliver Grasby KC. The case was announced. Oliver took his time in getting himself comfortable. He shifted in his chair. He arranged his pens. In the silence of the courtroom a stomach could be heard gurgling.

Eventually, Oliver looked forward and said, "Yes, Doctor Laughing-dough, this is your client's application."

Gordon said, "It's pronounced Flowerdew, Your Honour."

"What is?" said Oliver. Steven Hovell could see the glint in his eye.

"My name," Gordon responded.

"What about your name, Dr Slaughters-doo? You referred to someone called Flowerdew," carried on Oliver wickedly.

"Your Honour, my name is spelled F-L-A-U-G-H-T-E-R-S-D-O-U-GH but pronounced Flowerdew," said Gordon.

"I see," said Oliver impassively. "Please do carry on."

Dr Flaughtersdough then started to make a long, flowery impassioned speech. After a few minutes Oliver interrupted him.

"This is all very well but you have some issues. First of all the medical evidence is inadequate. And indeed, linked to that you have issues of causation."

Gordon responded, "Once I had finished with the interim injunction application, Your Honour, if it pleases you, I was going to seek a direction to instruct Mr Yorick Platinum, Consultant Dermatologist from Harley Street..."

Percy Vere jumped to his feet. "If it pleases Your Honour, I was when we got further, going to suggest a joint instruction of a local consultant dermatologist Mr Hedley Etch."

Oliver said, "Let's go back to the interim injunction. There seem some anomalies here. Why have we canteen ladies? How did they get affected by the sorting shed issues if any... What is the initial evidence as to how the rash was caused? What of the defence assertion that Maureen Gasson gave people something which caused the rash...?"

"Your Honour," responded Gordon, "I understand my clients Mrs Gasson and Miss Spenders would say if asked... that they obtained the rashes from bringing coffees and teas to the men in the sorting room or off their gloves when they came to the canteen..."

Ron Woodhouse whispered something to Percy Vere who leaped to his feet.

"Your Honour, taking hot drinks from the canteen to the sorting room is against company policy and instructions as is wearing the work gloves to go to the canteen."

Oliver sighed. "Dr Flaughtersdough, I really do not think the interim injunction is going anywhere... I am minded to adjourn the case to a District Judge for costs estimating and directions."

"With Your Honour's indulgence, I could perhaps call some evidence... perhaps from Mrs Gasson?" Bernie Blunt was attempting to poke Gordon in the ribs and was furiously shaking his head. Percy Vere looked quite pleased, and Verity Timpson-Saunders buried her face in her hands.

"Yes, do have Mrs Gasson called," said Oliver in an unusually oily way.

Maureen Gasson came forward. There was a bit of a look of a rabbit in the headlights about her. She was duly sworn in and then she was asked to give her full name and address by Gordon and to confirm her statement was true. Gordon then asked,

"Mrs Gasson do you maintain noxious material from the sorting room caused your rash?"

The reply was, "Yes of course... and it hurt real bad."

He continued,

"Do you serve teas and coffees to the sorting room operatives in the sorting room?"

The reply was, "Not really. They know where the canteen is."

He then asked, "Did you cause the rashes?"

The reply was, "I don't think it was me."

Gordon sat down looking pleased with himself.

"Cross-examination?" said Oliver.

Percy Vere rose and said, "'Not really' is not a definite 'no' is it?"

Maureen shrugged and Percy Vere continued, "Isn't it the case that you occasionally DO take hot drinks to the sorting room?"

Maureen went slightly pink and said, "A very few times."

Percy continued, "So maybe there are a few other things you haven't told us?"

Maureen looked embarrassed. "What about the bottle you brought in on Doreen's birthday?" said Percy while Mickey looked increasingly thunderous.

"Well, it was a birthday," said Maureen. "What harm is a little drink going to do?"

Percy persisted, "Wasn't the bottle you brought in bought from a man who the managers had to ask to leave the work's car park after he was seen selling suspected illegal booze from the back of his van? And wasn't that bottle of the type later seized by the police when they raided Knight's Farm after the explosion?"

Mickey hissed furiously from the back of the court, "You didn't?"

Maureen looked as if she wished a deep hole could swallow her up. "I swear it was just the one bottle. I just wanted to treat people to a birthday drink. It's not true if they say I put it in the cooking... I didn't..." She started to cry.

At this point Oliver intervened.

"I think in the interests of fairness and justice we should leave it there."

Percy Vere did not seek to continue his cross-examination, nor did Gordon ask to re-examine poor Maureen.

His Honour continued, "Dr Flaughtersdough, I trust you will not continue the application for an interim injunction today? The case needs a two-hour case management and costs management hearing at a minimum... I am minded to transfer this case to the Circuit trial centre... Any objections?"

Gordon did not seek to go on with the interim injunction and both counsels indicated agreement to the transfer. Verity looked at Percy Vere and Chris Ellison who both looked a bit smug and wished she could swap places with Chris Ellison. She realised that if she was to have a decent legal career, she might need to have a pupillage elsewhere. Sonja looked at Bernie Blunt. He looked impassive. She did not want to be blamed for the courtroom disaster.

Oliver said,

"Dr Flute-enough, Mr Vere, this brings this morning's case to an end. Good day."

He rose to his feet. Everyone stood while he made for the door.

Steven then announced, "Court now stands adjourned."

Once Nichola and himself had ensured the court was cleared, Steven went to check on His Honour's requirements.

"I believe I have a bail application at 2pm, Shovel," he said. "I trust the CPS and the defence will be punctual?"

Steven said, "We can but hope, Your Honour... especially as most parties are on video. Can I assist with anything else until this afternoon?"

"No," said Oliver. "I suggest you get your lunch while the going is good."

So, Steven left His Honour to thoughts of the afternoon's work and to thoughts of Claret.

Mickey and Maureen Gasson left the court glowering at each other and did not speak to each other on their journey home. Bernie Blunt was philosophical in discussions with Sonja Sidebottom. It might have been that the recently received wedding invitation had brightened his mood.

"That's clients for you...you just can't trust them! Could have been worse though. The whole case could have been thrown out. At least His Honour had a decent bundle. I've seen old Oliver in much fouler moods. But I am not sure Flaughtersdough is the right counsel for this sort of work."

Mickey was less philosophical when he got home with Maureen, he was still angry,

"You stupid cow," he said. "We could lose the whole case. We are lucky the judge did not dismiss the case straight away."

Maureen looked sheepish. Mickey's mood was black for the rest of the day until Nat turned up to discuss wedding plans with Brittany. There really were only a few weeks to the wedding. Nat had booked the Registrar, the pub, the marquees and catering. Brittany needed to get a dress and there was the issue of a wedding cake, flowers and seating.

"Don't you have any family?" asked Brittany when seating was discussed.

Nat replied, "They all died years ago." His deal with his father was that he would be a last-minute attendee purportedly attending the festival. His mother had left when he was a baby. He did not know what had become of her.

Maureen said, "Me and the girls in the canteen could make the cake?"

Mickey pulled a face. "Don't be daft. You'd poison everyone."

Maureen looked very deflated. Nat tried to calm things.

"I've had a bit of a look... and I think there is a lady at the local court who bakes cakes on the side. We should see if she can help. I'm sure Maureen will have enough to do... supervising flower arrangements and suchlike."

Soon they were joined by Lewis and Penny. They all sat drinking beers in the back garden, except Brittany who sipped some fizzy pop.

"How are you feeling, Brittany?" said Penny. "I expect you're real excited... wedding and baby... Wow!"

Brittany responded, "It is all happening so quickly. I have been feeling a bit under the weather. I am not sure I can manage all my hours at the café. I'll have to go on maternity leave eventually anyway..."

"Gee," said Penny. "My contract is up in a couple of weeks. Working at a veggie café would be just my thing, if you think they'd have me... I mean just temporarily?"

Brittany said, "Yeah, I think you'd fit right in. I'll tell the boss."

Brittany did not think Penny would "fit right in" but a quick taking on of Penny would reduce some of the pressure on herself. She found Penny's whining voice irritating and her comments often quite stupid.

Penny on the other hand felt delighted. She had a chance of another part-time job when her contract ended. She was sitting in the bosom of her boyfriend's family. She felt she was mending bridges with Scyathica too. She had no idea what had really happened between Nat and Scyathica and Steven and Nat. She thought about a new outfit for the wedding.

Scyathica was contemplating the wedding with Uncle Hugo as they sat in his garden.

"I suppose I will have to go," he said. "He is the town's other MP... but I won't have a wife on my arm as she is still with that fitness instructor."

"I don't think it's compulsory to have a plus-one..." said Scyathica. "I think it will be informal. Besides, Steven and I will both be going."

That placated Uncle Hugo. "Well," he said, "make sure you wear something nice; I will treat you to an outfit. You're much prettier than the other girls who will attend. You have really come out of your shell since you became settled here and you look much better for it. I like your young man too. When I first met him, I didn't rate him at all, but somehow, he seems to have turned into a confident, reliable man... a good egg I think."

"As do I, Uncle," said Scyathica. "As do I."

Chapter 13

THERE WAS GROWING EXCITEMENT IN Waste as the main festival in respect of Sir Charles Whitewhisker approached. Already there had been some preliminary events including an opening firework display and a folk concert. In the town square there had been displays of Morris Dancing and then overnight two huge sculptures had appeared for temporary display. One sculpture was an eight-foot-tall tin can cleverly fashioned out of old tin cans and the other was an immense sausage, about twenty foot tall, made of plastic sausage wrappers. Both were intended to symbolise the main industries of Waste, waste disposal and sausages and bacon. The tin can did look a little like a giant bin and the sausage looked rather phallic. The locals wryly called them "the dustbin and the willy".

Steven had settled down to a routine for work. He had somehow managed to fit in a rapid course of driving lessons as well as seeing Scyathica. He was spending a little less time on crosswords and stamps but was in contact with his parents more frequently. They had progressed to video calls and although he felt he would never be on the same wavelength as Champ and Deedee he was content that contact was more cordial. They were talking vaguely of visiting Waste one day, but Steven was relieved this would not be a reality for quite a while as Champ was on a long course of physiotherapy before he could return to full mobility.

One morning during this period Scyathica received a phone call from Uncle Hugo who was in London.

"Your mother is threatening to visit you," he said.

"Oh, Lord," said Scyathica.

"She says you have not been home since you came to Waste and you don't ring her enough," continued Uncle Hugo. "I don't want her in the house with that Scottie dog. Piper doesn't like him. I don't think she really enjoys coming to the house anyway. She'll complain about everything... It's a few years since she came here."

"Oh, dear," said Scyathica, "I suppose I better go and visit her. I have not been back to London since I came here. I agree she is much better in Kensington. I don't suppose she has been here very often since she was sent off to boarding school as a child. Presumably that's why she never brought me to Waste... I'll try to go this coming weekend."

Scyathica rang Steven next. He was sad but understanding about the shape of the forthcoming weekend. He even offered to accompany Scyathica to London, but she declined the offer and told him he might use the extra time, if he wanted, on his intensive driving lessons. Then she rang her mother. Pandora feigned surprise that Scyathica might think of visiting.

At the end of the weekend Pandora felt relieved her London trip was over. She didn't like London anymore.

While she was fond of her mother, she felt she had very little in common with her. Pandora was very much a "lady who lunched". She enjoyed a little fundraising and rarely left London. Scyathica often cringed at some of her mother's actions and ideas. Her mother had for example called her Scottie 'Kitty' and had later acquired a Persian kitten who she named 'Woo woo'. Hopefully, Pandora was placated for the time being.

Bunting and marquees were soon erected on Harbour Green for the main festival and wedding. Ladies went to Waste's one high class dress shop or indeed out of town. Some outfits were ordered online. Nat had talked to Brittany about taking her to London to buy an outfit, but she was not keen. In the end they had found a local dressmaker. Their honeymoon was to be local as well, at a luxury spa hotel in the next county. Waste's florist had an uphill task in keeping the flowers fresh in the hot early autumn weather. It was something of an Indian summer.

The night before the wedding Nat had a few quiet drinks with Mickey and Lewis Gasson and his agent. He did not feel that as an MP he could go and get plastered nor did he want to draw adverse media attention to himself. The hen night was relatively quiet as well. While Nat had drinks at the Knubb Arms, Brittany had colleagues from the café, her mum's friend Doreen Spenders, two former school friends Liz and Les, and Penny Wayney round to her mother's house for nibbles and cakes.

Down by the yacht harbour men were doing the finishing touches to the 'Waste

Bake a Cake Competition Tent' and the night ended with a firework display over the harbour arranged by Waste Borough Council.

When the sun rose next morning, it shimmered and gleamed over Waste Water. The lake looked still and glassy and a slight mist hovered over the surface giving the lake an air of mystery. The town seemed to hum; there was an air of expectancy.

While wedding guests and participants were seeing to their finishing touches the Waste Bake a Cake Competition started, hosted by Bricey who was giving a running commentary on his radio show. The last six participants of some previous heats were having to bake 'live' in the marquees. It was rather a warm day for baking but there was no shortage of enthusiasm and a small crowd stood outside the tent.

It was not long before the wedding guests assembled at the Harbour View Pub. Nat and Brittany had decided to have the ceremony in the gardens going down to the yacht basin. The food and the drink was going to be available buffet style inside. The pub's large, lounge sliding doors had been opened fully and trestle tables arranged in and outside. The two 'top' tables were just inside to gain some shade and the rest of the tables spilled out into the pub garden. There was a gazebo to one side where a string quartet was tuning up. Nat had insisted the quartet played "tasteful" music during the ceremony and wedding breakfast. They would later be replaced by disco equipment and Bricey would then be the DJ for a disco. Festivities were expected to end at midnight with yet another firework display.

The bride was dressed in a cream satin wedding dress with purple floral tiara also dotted with a few little yellow flowers. She had a little posy with similar flowers tied by a ribbon to one of her wrists. Maureen Gasson was kitted out in a hideous purple concoction with an enormous purple hat which looked like a spare sail off one of the nearby yachts. Liz and Les who were apparently "maids of honour" also sported hideous low-cut purple dresses and purple hats. Nat wore a well cut dark grey suit. Mickey on the other hand looked as if he would burst out of his suit. Lewis looked very uncomfortable in a modern style pale grey suit. Penny looked to have acquired a nineteen seventies' peasant style smock dress which looked rather incongruous. It floated down over a pair of long white plastic shiny patent leather boots which must have been very uncomfortable. She had what appeared to be real daisies woven in her hair, so they were wilting rapidly.

His Honour Judge Oliver Grasby KC sat with his wife Annette in an area which seemed to have been set aside for dignitaries. He wore a morning suit even though that was not specified on the invitation. He puffed on a cigar and squeezed his wife's hand. He was glad she had come with him. Next to them sat Recorder Ahmed and his wife Amina, a youngish woman of great poise and elegance. Not far away sat Her Honour Davina dela Notte. She was accompanied by a young boy who Oliver understood was Flavio, her son. He looked very hot in what must have been formal school uniform from his boarding school. Her husband was nowhere to be seen. As senior District Judge, Eric Ercol and his wife had been invited and he sat nearby as well with his wife. His children were outside enjoying festivities on Harbour Green. Michael Phitt and Cecily Stump did not appear to be amongst the judicial contingent.

Amongst the dignitaries sat Derek Devene and his husband Julian, Mayor Norman Ryder and his wife, Mr and Mrs Sidebottom and Bernie Blunt who had surprisingly brought Sonja as his 'plus one'. Not far away sat Auntie Bea, Stacey Birch (presumably representing the newspaper) and Melvyn Brice from the radio station who was DJ later, Julie James who had made the wedding cake and her husband Martin. Steven and Scyathica sat with Uncle Hugo and Percy Vere who had presumably been asked as a representative of the local Bar. Dr Gordon Flaughtersdough was not there but Percy had Verity Timpson-Saunders on his arm.

Various friends, relations and hangers-on sat on rows of chairs and benches and there was a sort of makeshift aisle between the seats strewn with rose petals.

The string quartet started to play and there was a hush. The Registrar stood at the front with Nat Cartey under what appeared to be a home-made flower arch. It was slightly lop-sided, and the flowers were wilting. One side was propped up by a Knubb Sausages' crate with the lettering very visible. Mickey began to walk Brittany up the makeshift aisle followed by the two maids of honour.

At that moment a chauffeur driven Bentley drew up outside the Harbour View Pub. A suave older man alighted and came into the gardens. He stood discreetly at the back. Few people noticed him. The Registrar started the ceremony which was simple and short.

After the ceremony something occurred which quite plainly Nat had not expected. As people were milling around offering the bride and groom congratulations Lord Coldharbour walked forward.

"Good heavens," said Stacey, "it's the big boss from London. I had heard a rumour he might look in on the festival, but I didn't expect him here."

Scyathica moved a little further forward. She did not know what to expect. He nodded to her very slightly. Then he stepped up to Nat and Brittany.

"May I offer many congratulations," he said.

"Thank you," said Nat with pleading uncertainty in his eyes.

"I own the local press here," he said facing Brittany. "I also knew Nat's father. I understand you are due a happy event. I hope you might permit me to be the child's godfather... to preserve family ties so to speak."

Brittany smiled and said, "How lovely."

Nat looked relieved and said, "Thank you. Yes of course."

Lord Coldharbour said, "I hope it is okay if I stay for the reception?"

Nat nodded agreement. He had expected his father would watch the ceremony from the back and take part in some of the civic festivities but not this. But of course, he should have figured out how clever his father was.

Liz and Les started calling over to Brittany.

"Throw your flowers, throw your flowers."

Brittany smiled and pulled the posy from her wrist. Penny clutched Lewis's arm and looked hopeful. Scyathica and Steven had sat down again. Steven had his arm around her shoulder. Penny leaned forward expectantly. Brittany sent the posy spinning through the air. It seemed almost to hover. Then it fell and landed straight in Scyathica's lap. She smiled and said graciously,

"Thank you. I'm not sure this was meant for me."

Brittany responded, "Take it. I didn't aim for anyone." Steven tied the posy to Scyathica's arm and Penny looked crestfallen.

The string quartet started to play softly in the background and champagne corks could be heard popping. The party continued from the afternoon into the evening. The wedding cake was cut and distributed. There was a brief interlude when the quartet packed up and Bricey set up his disco.

Outside on the Harbour Green many of the other inhabitants of Waste drank beer in the beer marquee or admired and ate cakes in the cake tent. The Waste United Football Club had a stand all of their own and their supporters sat about planning for the next season. Knubb Sausages had a stand where it was barbecuing sausages and there was even a hog roast of a Knubb pig. Waste Waste had a small stand with leaflets about its work. There were small glasses of wine for anyone who called in there, but most of the time Ron Woodhouse sat there glumly with his daughter Charmaine.

As the evening wore on the bride and groom slipped away. Penny had been munching something which looked suspiciously like a piece of pork pie when she looked at Lewis and said,

"Gee... I wish I'd caught the flowers."

Lewis gently kissed the top of her head still decorated with dead flowers.

"That's just tradition, Penny," he said. "You wouldn't want us to have a traditional relationship, would you?"

"I guess not," came the answer. They spent the evening entwined in each other's arms throughout the discotheque. He said nothing about the pie.

Sir Hugo, Oliver and Annette Grasby, Percy and Verity whiled away the evening quaffing champagne and then port and brandy and swopping humorous anecdotes. Aziz and Amina Ahmed chatted amiably to Oliver and his wife Annette as well. As the evening continued Oliver and Annette and Aziz and Amina swapped humorous stories and discussed children with increasing enthusiasm. Aziz explained how Waste was growing on him and Amina talked of seeking a better environment for her talented children. Annette agreed that Waste was a better environment than London where she spent a great deal of her time. The two couples agreed they should socialise with each other in the future.

Davina left a little early with Flavio to take him to the cake stall. All the guests enjoyed the ambience of that warm early autumn evening. Even Lord Coldharbour could be seen raising a number of toasts before he too left a little after Davina and Flavio. Soon enough the mists of late autumn and the chill of winter would be on everyone.

When the disco started Scyathica and Steven didn't dance. He led her by the hand down to the lake shore. They followed a path away from the garden and the yacht harbour until they reached a bench with a view of the open water. After a while the moon was reflected on the glassy expanse which seemed to shimmer slightly. The noise from the disco seemed distant and there was the occasional sound of a water bird. They sat there for a very long-time side by side with their fingers touching saying nothing at all. Eventually Steven said,

"I am hopeful of passing my driving test very soon so I can get a car and move out of town. You know your uncle talked about selling you the West Wing. Do you think we should talk seriously about it and make some future plans?"

Epilogue

The writer galvanised his thoughts and wrote his final comments of the day.

'Waste Water seemed to blink as if it knew there was more to come. The town of Waste was far from finished with the people who lived there or visited it frequently. And so those people continue with their ambitions, their failures, and their achievements. When you next hear someone say, "Don't let that go to waste" or "it's such a shame he" or it could be "she" "just let things go to waste", hesitate for a moment. Think carefully. Going to Waste could be the making of some people.'

Then he added a note.

AUTHOR'S NOTE

If you have any doubts as to whether this is a work of fiction and think you are described here, then the author suggests you have a problem. The characters are very real to the author but should not seem real to anyone else.

R e t u r n   T o   W a s t e

S p r i n g

THE AUTHOR OPENED THE WINDOW and breathed in the spring air. This would be a good day to draw on his life experience, the people he knew and had met and a place he had come to know.

'One crisp spring day in early March, Steven Hovell climbed to the top of the wing of the old house he was renovating with his girlfriend Scyathica Wentworth. He had recently discovered that there was a door leading from the attic to a small flat area of the roof and from this area he was able to have a panoramic view of Scyathica's uncle's property, the lake of Waste and the town which bore the name of the lake.

Steven shivered a bit. He hoped Scyathica was still tucked up in bed in her uncle's house. The caravan he was currently living in could be seen just below the house to the rear. Scyathica's uncle Sir Hugo Wentworth-Knubb MP for West Waste owned the house, High Cliffe, and he and Scyathica had made a rather complicated contract with Sir Hugo to renovate the West Wing and in return it would become their property. As yet the West Wing needed more attention before he could move into it.

The slight odour of pigs filled Steven's nostrils from Sir Hugo's nearby pig farm. He could not see the Knubb Bacon and Sausage Factory which was the other side of Waste which was the eventual destination of the pigs. He could just make out the chimneys of Waste Waste on the other side of Waste, the town's waste processing plant. He could see the rooves of the Town Hall and the courthouse where he worked. Steven was a court clerk to the judges.

He could not make out the roof of the newspaper and radio station where Scyathica was based as a court reporter. He thought he could just see the top of the Knubb Arms, the best hostelry in town. There was a mass of rooves of older houses too. One of them was the house of his former landlady Auntie Bea. He was not sure from this distance which was her house. Scyathica's friend from America Penny Wayney lived there and his old room had recently become occupied by a young Brummy barrister Chris Ellison. Another older house would be that of District Judge Ercol and his family. Steven had sometimes been clerk to District Judge Ercol.

Nearer at hand Steven could see the golf course and Links Road. His Honour Judge Oliver Grasby KC for whom he clerked lived somewhere in the vicinity. Steven could also see the executive developments off Links Road. He understood the town's other MP Nat Cartey (who unbeknownst to East Waste's residents was actually Scyathica's cousin and a media baron's son) had recently bought a house at the far end of Links Close. He had been to Nat's wedding to Brittany Gasson and knew they now had a baby.

He could not see all the houses on Links Close as it was heavily tree-lined. He was also aware that a recently appointed judge, His Honour Judge Aziz Ahmed had moved into a house at the beginning of Links Close with his wife Amina and their children.

Steven shivered again. It was a pretty good view. The railway station, the hospital and the football stadium to the south of town were out of sight. He could not see Knight's Farm which was beyond the waste plant. It had caused consternation when this old sheep farm blew up due to an illegal vodka still. He could see the Harbour View pub by the yacht harbour and its just completed upmarket hotel wing. He also could not see the outlying villages such as Gitthwaite. But the lake glistened in the cold spring air and looked slightly mysterious under a small bank of slow-moving mist. It seemed to wink at him as if to tell him something was going to happen here at the town of Waste. But in Steven's limited experience there was usually something to surprise him in Waste.'

The writer smiled as he continued.

Chapter 1

STEVEN HOVELL CALLED INTO THE house at High Cliffe and shouted to Scyathica who he could not immediately see.

"Do you want a lift to work or are you driving yourself?"

He was very proud of his little old Japanese car he had acquired after recently passing his driving test. A disembodied voice replied,

"No, it's okay, you go on. I have to take Piper for a little walk."

Piper was Scyathica's uncle's Springer Spaniel who had been staying with the pig farm manager when Sir Hugo was in the House of Commons but nowadays Scyathica and Steven kept an eye on him when Sir Hugo was in Westminster.

Steven set off for the court. He believed he was clerking for old Oliver today. His Honour Judge Oliver Grasby KC had become less grumpy since Recorder Aziz Ahmed had been appointed Circuit Judge and had come to sit permanently in Waste. The two men shared a taste for good cigars and cricket. After His Honour Judge Michael Phitt who used to sit in Waste Combined Court had finished his sabbatical studying sports' arbitration, he obtained a transfer to a court where he could sit hearing technical civil cases and those related to sport. Steven understood His Honour Judge Ahmed and his wife had rented Judge Phitt's house. He believed Her Honour dela Notte would be sitting at the court today. Steven found her rather haughty and abrasive, but the lawyers seemed to find her decisions sound. He also expected both District Judges to be there, District Judge Cecily Stump and District Judge Eric Ercol; so there would be a full house.

Steven had seen Her Honour dela Notte's teenage son Flavio at a couple of functions. The boy spent most of his time at boarding school and the rest of Her

Honour dela Notte's family seemed invisible. As a contrast to Her Honour dela Notte's highly confident and sometimes superior manner, District Judge Cecily Stump always seemed very nervous and easily upset.

District Judge Ercol was a robust character who lived in the centre of town. Steven felt he knew where he stood with Judge Ercol.

Steven parked his car in the court car park taking care not to get in the way of the judges' cars. He headed for the court office only to be cornered by the court manager Derek Devene. Derek was usually calm and calming to everyone else but today he looked unusually flustered.

"Steven, Steven, Steven…" he begun.

"Whatever is the matter?" said Steven Hovell.

"Julie Jacobs is going," came the reply. Julie Jacobs was the Senior Judge's Clerk and Steven's Line Manager.

"Going where?" asked Steven.

"And Julie Johnson is going too…" Derek went on.

Julie Johnson was a Team Leader and Derek's Deputy.

"They've been nabbed."

"Who has nabbed them? When… where?" Steven began to ask.

Derek showed Steven into his office. Derek cleared his throat.

"I knew the manager of the Magistrates' Court was retiring but Julie Johnson did not tell me she was going for her job. What really irks me is the Circuit Central Court have nabbed Julie Jacobs as chief clerk there. She will have to commute… but I hear she has family that direction. No-one said anything. They are both going relatively soon… The girls in the office are more interested in throwing leaving parties than what it will mean to the court here…"

Steven said, "Well I'm very happy working here and I am not going anywhere."

Derek smiled weakly.

"I had hoped to see my time out here before I retired without too much disruption. I thought Julie Johnson would succeed me. I know Julie James does not want promotion. Look, Julie Jacob's job has actually been on temporary promotion for years so I doubt they will allow me 2 permanent senior members of staff. If I were to amalgamate the roles so the person who applied definitely had the seniority would you apply? I might then ask for 2 additional junior members of staff one to fill your old job… if you apply…"

"I'm not sure what to say," answered Steven, "I've only been here just under a year, and I found my application for the job here hard enough. There was a time when I might have said I was not interested but I think I am... and the extra money would be useful for the building project. Am I up to it?"

Derek replied, "You might have competition, but I would see what I could do to help you with your application... but don't say anything."

Steven nodded. He could not help wondering if it would stop his parents continuing to denigrate his efforts. His father 'Champ' had managed to wriggle out of disciplinary action at his own work in the southeast on Network Rail, after he had punched someone. Deedee his mother tended to follow his father. Both Scyathica and himself felt their parents were 'unsatisfactory' but in different ways. Steven was grateful his parents remained in the London area. Although he had mended some bridges as far as they were concerned, he felt far more confident away from them and his overbearing sisters.

There was something of a spring in Steven's step as he took himself down the corridor and upstairs to the Judges' Chambers. He narrowly avoided bumping into District Judge Ercol.

"I'm sorry, sir," said Steven.

"That's alright," said Judge Ercol, "I was miles away. I just got given my Court of Protection ticket."

"Well, done, sir," said Steven slightly nonplussed.

"Come and see me next week," said District Judge Ercol. "Some of the lists need re-organising."

Steven nodded.

Eric was pleased to be allowed to hear this additional type of cases. He felt it was a feather in his cap. His wife Tina, who was a local solicitor, had encouraged him to apply. Yet he had misgivings. The training seemed to indicate that he would be spending half the time on such cases hearing challenges from old people who did not want to stay in care homes. The other half would be hearing issues about how money for such people would be looked after. Very little of his workload in the Court of Protection would be likely to be about anything else. Personally, he thought if an old dear or old bloke did not want to be put in a home, they shouldn't be.

While Steven was setting up the morning court Scyathica was arriving at the newspaper office to report to her boss Stacey Birch. She paused to pass the time of day with Waste FM's best known DJ Melvyn Brice. Everyone in Waste listened to the Bricey show.

"Morning, Stacey," said Scyathica. "Anything exciting I should know about?"

"Well," said Stacey who was ever well informed and well organised, "there is a rumour that the main man… the French boss is going to visit his football club and his stake in Waste Waste this year. Maybe Davey Scarlett might appear too!"

Scyathica shivered and hoped Stacey had not noticed. David Scarlett had disappeared off to the Caribbean after various financial scandals involving companies with which he was involved. His investors tended to lose their shirts while he tended to get richer. He was in fact her father but so far she had managed to keep it dark. Last time she saw him in September she had accepted a wad of cash from him, somewhat against her better judgment. She had sent some money to a charitable trust supporting people her father had defrauded. The balance was being used by Steven and herself to renovate the West Wing of High Cliffe. Davey's brother Lord Coldharbour was a media baron and had managed to keep some of Davey's misdeeds out of the press. Lord Coldharbour owned the Waste Telegraph and Waste FM and had 'banished' her from his London press operation in effect for not being ruthless enough. And she was so pleased, as it turned out, that she had gone to Waste.

Lord Coldharbour of Southend and his son harboured further secrets. Her Uncle Sir Hugo was on the maternal side and was not party to these secrets, nor was her mother Pandora who lived in Kensington.

"Scyathica…," said Stacey. "You seem miles away."

"Oh sorry," she responded.

Stacey went on, "Isn't Xavier Didier Le Perte a splendid name? And he looks like a dish too. Anyway, I was kind of hoping we could do a piece on him when he came to Waste. I thought that he might respond to you better than asking him to just do an interview with Bricey. You have a softer touch with people... they respond warmly to you."

"Hopefully not so warmly that they blow up," said Scyathica with a laugh.

Last year she had been sent to interview an old, sheep farmer Jim Knight. He had complained the local Waste Processing plant Waste Waste was poisoning his sheep. In the event it was his own illegal vodka still. When Scyathica arrived to interview him, the farm blew up. She narrowly avoided injury, but the incident helped her standing with the local media as she had filmed a bit of the immediate aftermath on her mobile phone.

Stacey continued, "I think said Xavier wants to check on his investments. I believe he may plan to build a new stand at Waste Wanderers Football Club and there is a rumour he wants to expand the Waste plant to include a plant manufacturing recycled paper. I believe it is to be called Waste Paper. Now that the Environment Agency prosecution is a thing of the past and the injunction case has gone too, he may see investment opportunities. The rumour is he is after Jim Knight's farm as the land adjoins the site of the Waste Waste factory."

The Environment Agency prosecution was as a result of the allegations about the sheep. The civil injunction proceedings had been spearheaded by union convenor Mickey Gasson and backed by Waste East's MP Nick Cartey. The proceedings had fizzled out after it had come to light that Mickey's wife Maureen had laced some of the cooking in the canteen where she worked with illegal vodka. This probably made people ill rather than their work at the plant. Mickey and Maureen's daughter Brittany was of course married to Nick.

Scyathica of course agreed to interview Xavier if and when he arrived. Today, however, was a slow day for local news. The Leader of the Council Norman Ryder aka 'Easy' Ryder had not said anything interesting. Mind you he rarely did. There were no exciting newsworthy court hearings. So at the end of the afternoon, she took herself to visit her American friend at Crunchies' Veggie Café.

Penny Wayney was just preparing to close up. The manager had left her to do this. She had been working here since Brittany had gone on maternity leave last year. She had arrived in Waste uninvited. The term 'friend' might be used loosely as Scyathica often found Penny's accent and manner irritating. Not for nothing did she sometimes refer to Penny as 'Painee' when talking to Steven. Penny had trouble sticking to things and would tend to gush. She had been 'finishing' her dissertation for her master's degree for years. It surprised Scyathica that Penny had remained in Waste and had also remained in a relationship with Lewis Gasson, Mickey's brother who was head butcher at Knubb Sausage and Bacon and a Harley-Davidson enthusiast.

"Hello," said Scyathica. "How's it going?"

Penny grimaced. "Well, it's a job... I guess. I would prefer to do something that had meaning... like a campaign or something."

Scyathica responded, "Any particular campaign...?"

Penny replied, "Well, gee... I don't know. I guess there are so many issues."

Scyathica smiled. "Well it's a nice café. And they must trust you as they have left you in charge." She continued, "How is Lewis?"

"Well, I guess," said Penny. "I think we may go out somewhere at the weekend. I do sometimes feel I take second place to his motorbike."

"Surely not," said Scyathica. She then made an invitation she hoped she would not regret for Lewis and Penny to call on Steven and herself at the weekend and see how the building work was doing.

As she drove away from the café a car pulled out in front of her coming from Waste East. She had to jam on the brakes but further up the road the said car and her own vehicle ended up side by side at the lights. She instantly recognised Nat Cartey MP, aka Nathanial Coldharbour son of Lord Coldharbour of Southend. The media baron kept his public schoolboy son's true identity secret. It would not have gone down well with the voters or the Labour Party. Scyathica and Steven had promised not to reveal Nat's real identity in return for keeping the details of her father out of the local press. Recently, Scyathica felt she no longer cared whether people knew Davey Scarlett was her father. She and Steven were making lives for themselves, and she was not responsible for her father's misdeeds. It would be easy enough for the press to dig up the connection anyway. But she had no reason to go back on her word to her cousin and felt if the connection came out it might somehow affect her maternal uncle Sir Hugo Wentworth-Knubb. It was not her uncle's fault his sister Pandora, her mother, was married to Davey Scarlett.

Sir Hugo was an old school paternalist Tory MP. He had sacrificed his own wealth to make sure jobs continued at the sausage and bacon factory when it hit a rough patch. He enjoyed his 'countryside pursuits' such as the occasional pheasant shoot. He believed that an Englishman should promote fair play. She was very fond of Uncle Hugo.

Nathanial sped off to his new home. Despite being MP for Waste East he had hastily purchased a house on Links Close before Brittany's baby arrived. He had used an out-of-town lawyer who he had paid extra to speed the transaction along. He had brushed aside any queries about boundaries or the high trees at the end of the garden. He was pleased there would be a big garden for his child to be able to play in. It was quite a while since he had lived in the humble lodgings run by Auntie Bea in Canal Street, near the railway sidings in East Waste. In his own way he missed her.

Not all Nat's neighbours were that enthusiastic about him. His long back garden bordered the garden of Mr Bertrand Sidebottom and his wife Marjorie who had the oldest house on The Ridings another part of the executive development in that area. They liked the area because it was close to where Marjorie stabled her horse 'April's Dawn' and Bertrand felt it was not too close to the hospital where he worked as a general surgeon, so he could separate work from leisure. They were particularly proud of their giant willow trees at the end of the garden. They had built a large pond where Bertrand kept ornamental koi carp. Bertrand was probably prouder of his fish than his daughter Sonja who had recently qualified as a solicitor.

As Nat sped home Sonja was having a quick after-work drink with young Brummy barrister Chris Ellison at the Knubb Arms on the town square next to the court. She still worked for local solicitor Bernie Blunt with whom she had trained. Chris had joined the Chambers of Percy Vere, the debonair barrister who had trained him. He did, however, have competition from Verity Timpson-Saunders who was also a new tenant and 'new' barrister. She appeared to have a very sharp intellect and Chris reckoned she would make mincemeat of Faye Leafly the other female barrister who frequented Waste Court. They both considered the local legal scene and wondered if Waste's courts would ever be visited by Verity's ex pupil master Dr Gordon Flaughtersdough. Chris did speculate there might be more cases available as Percy Vere was taking a strong interest in politics these days, writing articles for a Labour Party journal.

If truth be told the person with the biggest foothold in politics of recent arrivals in Waste was Amina Ahmed. Amina had taken a post as eye consultant at Waste General Hospital, but it was a fifty percent job share with the previous eye consultant who was wanting to reduce his hours as he was thinking of retirement in the near future. Aziz had thought his wife would spend even more time with their super talented twins Helal and Ali who were now attending Waste Grammar School. He was surprised when Amina quickly became a local Labour Party activist. He was even more surprised when she told him early that evening, she was going to run for the local council.

"There is a by-election in the Central Waste Ward. The local councillor on the Borough Council has had to step down due to ill-health. Somebody has to shake that complacent lot up and I am just the woman to do it!"

Amina told her husband.

"But what about the twins…? How are you going to have time?" he responded.

Amina continued, "They are 13 nearly 14… they will be joining plenty of clubs and societies at that age. They are not babies. Besides, as you have finished at the Bar you are mostly home in the evening… you should spend more time with them. Oh… and before you start I shall be careful not to create any conflicts of interest with your job… Mr High Up Criminal Circuit Judge…"

Aziz Ahmed knew when he was beaten. Maybe he would contact Oliver later and they would smoke cigars and talk about cricket.

His Honour Judge Oliver Grasby KC was as it happened not having a good evening either. He had come home to his house on Links Road not far from the executive developments. It was a rambling Edwardian house he shared with his wife Annette, a High Court Judge, when she was not away sitting in London. These days she was spending more time at home sitting in the High Court at the local Circuit Centre Court which was a 90-minute commute by road or 2 hours by train. He was smoking his pipe in the potting shed and adjoining greenhouse and examining his tomato plants and more particularly his concealed cigar collection when he heard Annette calling.

"Oliver... where are you?"

"Here, dear," he said quickly emerging. "Just having a very quick pipe smoke in the garden to avoid fumes in the house."

"I have some news," said Annette. "The Stiffles have invited themselves for a weekend in the near future."

"Oh no," said Oliver. "Couldn't you have refused them?"

"It would have been rude," said Annette. Oliver grimaced.

He had never understood why they had remained friends with Nick and Lena Stiffle. Nick was a retired barrister who had once specialised in corporate law. Annette and Oliver had met him early in their careers. Lena, his wife, was a retired music teacher. Since retiring Nick had become heavily involved in the UK Society of British Cheesemongers and was essentially obsessed with cheese. Lena was a keen amateur singer who would try to entertain others with what Oliver called behind her back "a ghastly warble". They had no children which Oliver regarded as a blessing for future generations.

Annette said, "Well at least we get a few weeks' peace as they are not coming immediately."

"Thank God," said Oliver and went back to the potting shed.

Chapter   2

DISTRICT JUDGE ERIC ERCOL SAT in his Chambers looking at the computer screen. He was looking at details of his Court of Protection cases. He should have been proud to start work on cases which had the serious point of looking after the best interests of people who lacked mental capacity but somehow, he could not muster much enthusiasm. The first electronic file bore the name Mrs Axe. Her first name was apparently Betty, but someone had made a typo in the statements, and she was referred to on several occasions as 'Mrs Battle Axe'. She lived in a sheltered bungalow at Pither's Court just near Canal Street, Waste. Waste Borough Council wanted an order for her to be placed in a home which was something she opposed.

The complaint was she kept wandering the streets. There were worries for her safety. Fortunately, there was no canal at Canal Street and there never had been. He supposed she might get on the railway line, but it was well fenced in. Neighbours were concerned she often wandered in her underwear. It seemed unfair to Eric that youngsters could wear next to nothing, but he supposed a half-naked eighty-two-year-old might shock some people. The council was worried that Mrs Axe was not eating properly either.

Mrs Axe was legally represented, and her lawyer argued that she had her faculties, so she could do what she liked within reason.

The other electronic file was about money. A youngster with severe brain damage had a fund from his damages which was there to provide for his needs. His dad was making a court application to arrange a holiday costing thousands of pounds so the lad could trek with alpacas. He argued it was a once in a life-time experience. Eric was dubious.

He sighed. His thoughts turned to his own mother. He thought smugly how he had kept her in her own bungalow; no old folks' home for her. Maude Ercol had previously lived some 60 miles away with her farmer husband, Ernest, Eric's deceased father. After Ernest died it became clear within months that Maude could not run the farm. She made it absolutely clear she did not want to have a 'granny flat' at Eric's house.

"I must have my own front door," she said. "I was talking to Mrs Tomkins and her son defrauded her because she did not have her own place."

Eric had felt somewhat aggrieved. His eldest son Mostyn who in those days still lived at home studying GCSEs at the grammar school had come to the rescue. He had trawled the internet and found the village of Gitthwaite just a few miles away from Waste. There was a bungalow with a large garden for sale. So when the farm was sold Maude moved to number 3 Wattery Lane, Gitthwaite. With her came an elderly Jack Russell dog 'Rats', a large black and white cat 'Tibbles' and half a dozen hens and a cockerel. That was nearly 8 years ago. Sadly, Rats and Tibbles had died a few years ago. Before she died Tibbles had produced a litter of kittens. All had been given away except one. He was called Claudius.

Claudius was a huge black cat with a tiny white tip to his tail. Not a sign of any other colour or lightness could be found on him apart from that white tip. The rest of him was jet black and shiny. His bright yellow eyes had a very slight green tinge. He was very imposing. He was a prodigious hunter, but he left Maude's hens alone. Although the hens had been replaced over the years, she still had the same cockerel known as 'the Emperor'.

Gitthwaite was a tiny village of 40 houses, a Norman Church, a small village hall which sat 30 people maximum with a playground in its grounds and post box. The locals pronounced the title of the village "Gifwaite" but the inhabitants of Waste referred to the village as "Git-thwaite" and its residents as "Gits". As the years had proceeded Eric found that many residents deserved this title.

The name 'Wattery' did not denote a particularly wet place but was the name of a local family. Wattery Hall had once been a 'lordly' pile near Gitthwaite. Eventually the Wattery family had financial difficulties and it fell into disrepair. The locals then pillaged as much as they could from the property. Many a cottage in Gitthwaite was built or extended with materials from Wattery Hall. The door to Maude's rear garden was reputed to once have been the door to the Great Hall at Wattery Hall. As it turned out the inhabitants of Gitthwaite continued to have a reputation for being grasping. If there was grant money to be had, their Parish Council was first in the queue. Outsiders were welcome if they brought something the 'Gits' valued to the village but were soon abandoned if they only need help from others.

At first Maude managed on her own and was welcomed by the 'Gits'. She did flower arranging for the church and made coffee for the mothers' union in the village hall. Her hens were welcomed as she was generous with boxes of eggs. There were a few complaints about the Emperor, but the initial reception was good. However, about four years ago Eric found his mother was becoming confused and a little forgetful. One day after visiting a grocery store on the outskirts of Waste she became disorientated and could not remember her address. She stopped her car outside Waste station in the taxi rank and it was fortunate that the proprietor of Khan's cars, Baz Khan was alert enough to realize something was wrong. With the help of one of his daughters who ran the taxi office they were able to help Maude get home and notify Eric Ercol.

It took a further 6 months for Eric to persuade Maude to hang up her car keys. By then Eric and his wife brought groceries to Maude and Eric managed to find a care company prepared to provide his mother with carers. Polarity Care began by calling on Maude once a day but more recently that had been increased to four times a day. Maude still took pleasure from her bungalow, her garden and her cat but she often forgot to eat unless food was put in front of her. These days the carers slung a handful of corn to Emperor and the hens and collected a handful of eggs when they could. She was tending to get too deaf to hear his early morning crowing.

Maude found it too much to continue making coffee for the mothers' union or even to do flower arranging as she gradually began to find daily tasks difficult. The response of the 'Gits' was to abandon Maude. They stopped visiting her. They did not offer any assistance to her whether to assist attending church services or church functions. No offers to fetch shopping materialized. No villagers popped in to say, "Hello, are you alright?" Occasionally notes were put through her door saying 'Shut up your bloody cockerel' or similar.

Maude had very little mobility but from somewhere she had acquired a traditional broom or besom and could be seen on a daily basis sweeping in front of her bungalow. Eric was proud he had managed to keep her at home and just dismissed as eccentric her querulous question,

"Eric, do you think I have turned into a witch and that is why people don't visit me anymore?"

He also dismissed the fact Maude sometimes referred to herself as 'Mordred the witch' and referred to Claudius as 'Claw-Deus' and said that Emperor was her familiar.

"My cat is a lovely witch's cat you know. He is a god that is why he is called Claw-Deus because Deus means God," she said.

The carers did not think Claudius was a god. They hated his little gifts. He could be sure to wait for a carer who hated mice to catch a mouse and leave a dead or better still, live mouse on the doorstep. One young girl had climbed on a chair screaming as the cat chased his prey round and round before dispatching it. Sometimes Claudius would pick the carers who disliked cats the most and would lie in wait around corners before sticking out a paw and giving them a quick swipe.

The carers also had to contend with the 'Gits' of Gitthwaite. Wattery Lane was very narrow, and the village hall had a surprisingly large car park. Initially they had parked in the car-park. They had then had letters pasted to their cars 'Parking for Gitthwaite residents only'. They then started to park on Wattery Lane. Often the 'Gits' would call the local police who incredible as it would seem, would actually come out. The complaints were vague, for example 'selfish parking' or 'Wheels on the pavement'.

Even Eric was concerned when the villagers had called the police when a District Nurse had called on his mother. Maude had recently needed the help of the District Nurses for various ailments of the elderly. It appeared the District Nurse had the temerity to park outside Maude's house with two wheels on the pavement. Eric was not sure why the police turned out for such seemingly trivial matters. He suspected one of the 'Gits' was related to a local police officer but had absolutely no evidence to support this. It was important to Eric that Maude's equilibrium in her own home was not upset by such intrusions.

Eric decided he would call on his mother as soon as possible but then went back to reading his Court of Protection cases. However, he was soon interrupted by a knock on the door of his Chambers. It was Steven Hovell.

"Come in," said Eric with a sigh. "How can I be of assistance?"

"Sir," started Steven. "The Legal Advisor... eh m... Magistrates' Clerk... has been on the telephone. There is a case listed before the lay justices at the Magistrates' Court which she feels should be transferred here as the care case was, I think largely before yourself. She asked if you could take it and give it a listing fairly soon."

"What is the case?" asked Eric.

Steven replied, "You may recall the O'Hanrahan children? The mother May Lou was in prison. I believe you made full care orders. You may recall the child Patella O'Hanrahan? Well his father had transitioned to a woman, Lavinia Levi. Miss Levi applies to have the care order discharged and to be Special Guardian for Patella. She also applies to change the child's name to Pauline."

Eric smiled. "Well she ought to get somewhere just on the grounds of choosing a better name! Of course, I will take the case."

On the way back to the court office Steven popped his head round the door of Oliver Grasby's Chambers. Oliver was peering out of the window but somehow knew Steven was there.

"What do you want, Shovell?"

"Just to check, if you needed anything, Your Honour," Steven replied.

Suddenly, Oliver smiled.

"Can you do me a favour?" he said to Steven. "It's not strictly speaking work, but can you find out the name and type of the smelliest British cheese there is?"

Steven was taken aback. "Why, Your Honour?"

"I want to wind some people up," said Oliver.

Steven chuckled at the response and said he would do his best. He knew better than to ask for details.

After work that evening Oliver Grasby arranged to go for a walk with Aziz Ahmed. They met on the corner of Links Close. Oliver brought a few of his best cigars with him and proffered one of them to Aziz. They both stood on the corner in a sheltered position lighting their cigars before heading across the road to the golf course to take the public footpath across the links. They both had winter jackets since it was a cold evening and there was a little sleet. Aziz was wearing a woollen ski hat and Oliver was wearing a very impressive Russian hat he had picked up on holiday in St Petersburg a good many years ago.

They puffed away at their cigars and at first discussed cricket. Aziz then turned to Amina's political ambitions. After he had had some time to vent his feelings Oliver then told Aziz how Annette had chosen to inflict the Stiffles on him. He did mention he had a plan. A wicked smile came across his face.

Aziz said, "I know that look. You are going to do some dreadful wind-up... aren't you?"

"Yupp," said Oliver looking pleased with himself. They turned around now and headed for their homes.

About this time, Penny was waiting in the pub for Lewis. He was a bit late.

"Hi, Pens," he said when he arrived. This was a new nickname for her. She didn't like it.

"Sorry, I am late. I was just checking on the bike."

Penny grimaced. "Can't you get a car? Even Scyathica's Steven has a car?"

Lewis looked cross. "That bike means everything to me," he said.

Penny now looked cross as well. "Everything?" she pouted. "Don't I mean anything? I only meant a car as well as your bike... so we could do more together."

Lewis put his arm around Penny. "I am sorry, Pens. I can see what you are saying. Sometimes I think it might be useful, but I need to see what I can afford."

They carried on chatting and discussed going out for a meal on Saturday. Lewis walked Penny back to Auntie Bea's. She needed to be up early to open the café so declined Lewis's invitation to come back to his flat. She did accept a cup of tea from Auntie Bea who was more than a landlady but a support to her various tenants.

"What's up, lass?" said Auntie Bea. "I thought you were happy and settled?"

Penny replied,

"I think my job is boring. I am tired of competing with Lewis's bloody motorbike... and I don't think I will ever finish my Master's."

"As to the last," said Auntie Bea, "who cares if you don't! As for the motorbike... well, that is men for you. You will have to find a way to get him to sit up and take notice. As for your job, well, it is paying your bills so instead of flitting from one thing to another and another which I believe you have done in the past, use the time to find out what you really want to do."

Penny felt better. Auntie Bea was so sensible.

Steven had found her helpful too when he lodged with her. Now he spent his nights stuck out in the caravan. Scyathica's uncle was rather old fashioned, so he understood why he was not sleeping in the house. Scyathica and himself had been having a good look at the West Wing that evening. It had had to be virtually gutted to treat all the different rots it suffered. They were pleased and relieved all the treatments were finished. It now had sound floorboards and a sound roof. The wiring had been done. It had no working bathrooms, toilets, kitchen or central heating but at least it was now sound.

"I think we should be able to do some basic decorating ourselves," said Steven.

"Yes," agreed Scyathica, "but we will still need kitchen and bathroom fitters and so much more."

Steven agreed but knew they would need to be very economic with the balance of the money Scyathica had left and his own meagre savings. They retired to her uncle's kitchen to make hot drinks. Suddenly, the landline began ringing.

"That can only be Uncle Hugo, hardly anyone else uses it."

Scyathica answered the phone and Steven could tell she was speaking to her uncle. She looked concerned. Her brow was wrinkled, and it was obvious that all was not well. After she came off the phone she spoke to Steven.

"Uncle went to see mother after she phoned him crying. I thought her finances were safe from Dad but that may not be the case. Her income comes from a family trust. The trust is quite modest; there is just enough to pay mother something to live on. Uncle has never had a penny from it as he knew it was Mother's only source of income. Dad does not pay a bean and my mother has no training for anything. I thought the flat in Kensington was safe… in Mother's name."

She gulped and went on.

"Uncle says there used to be a leasehold but some years ago Dad persuaded Mum to buy the freehold. Because it was a long lease, and she was in occupation the freehold was relatively cheap for a place in Kensington. Apparently, some Act of Parliament which helps leaseholders assisted. Obviously, Mum did not have the capital, so an acquaintance of Dad's put up the money. He also lent extra money which Dad said he needed for the business. It seems the money was secured on the property and the loan is now due to be paid in full. Uncle says as it is classed as a business loan, not a commercial mortgage it has to be paid off all at once… and Dad has disappeared without paying anything…"

"How much is it?"

She mentioned an eye-watering figure.

Steven uttered an expletive. This was unusual for him. Then he said,

"What will that mean for your mother?"

Scyathica replied, "I think there is a real possibility my mother will lose her home."

Chapter   3

XAVIER DIDIER LE PERTE RECLINED on a wicker chair in the orangery of his house just outside Paris. He flicked ash from his cigarette on the floor. That cheeky little bitch of a maid could clean it up later. He took a sip of brandy and thought about his next move. He would miss this house and its elegant rooms and wine cellars so convenient for Paris and so great for having parties. It would all be there when he got back. He pushed back his lank grey hair and stretched his long legs which were encased in tight jeans a little further. With his equally tight leather jacket he felt no-one would imagine that he was 58 years of age. He thought of going to the Caribbean like his erstwhile business partner Davey Scarlett, but he did not really want to go near him and although the Caribbean was a huge area they both tended to frequent the more sophisticated watering holes. He did not care for heat either. He had been intending to go to Waste in mid-summer when the weather might be better but there was no reason why he should not bring forward his trip.

He had an excuse. He had let it be known he was thinking of building a new stand at the football stadium. If truth be told he was more interested in working out what to ask for it. There were several parties interested in buying Waste's football club. He did, however, want to consider the feasibility of paper making in Waste, using recycled paper from the waste plant. The project of Wastepaper had been in mind for some time.

Hopefully the authorities would not think to look for him in some northern English backwater of a town. He could lie low there for a while as surely the Gendarmerie would not listen to the warblings of a bit-part film actress. He would get his publicity people to make sure there were rumours all over social media that

Monique spent most of her time high on drugs and that she kept company with the Paris underworld. He took a few more sips of his brandy. He had no trouble attracting women. He felt sure he could find someone with whom to have a dalliance in this funny little English northern town. He was only sorry the choice would not be more cosmopolitan. He had really fancied finding some American bimbo; now that would be fun.

He called his assistant to him and asked him to obtain the best but most discreet accommodation in Waste and to arrange for his private jet to be ready to depart to the nearest regional airport to Waste. He also would need transport when he arrived. Pierre came back to him within the hour. The jet was fuelled and ready to go. He had booked the whole of the new rooms at the Harbour View inn indefinitely. He had hired a sporty Alfa Romeo for Xavier and a non-descript car for himself.

Pierre Bruele knew part of the issue with Monique, but he had an unfortunate feeling he did not know the half of it. Still perhaps visiting this godforsaken English place would enable Xavier to lie low. Pierre was a complete contrast to his boss. A non-descript neat man in his forties he often asked himself why he continued to work for Xavier. It was not an easy one to answer. One day he wanted to open a little business of his own. He was saving up and would leave when the time was right. He hoped he would be less of a crook than his boss.

Little did he realise, but news travels fast in Waste. The landlord of the Harbour View was so proud of his booking he bragged of it not only to his staff but to all his customers. Everyone in Waste soon knew Xavier was coming.

Sir Hugo came home for the weekend in quite the most upset state Scyathica had ever encountered.

"It's so cruel to your mother," he said. "She has taken legal advice and there is no defence. She has had a letter before action. If she surrenders the house to the lenders, they will sell it to cover the loan and she will get the balance back. It won't be very much. If she does not surrender the house, they will take her to court and win."

Steven interjected, "Scyathica and I have a little money meant for the renovations, would paying that buy any time to say track down Davey?"

Sir Hugo shook his head. He indicated that generous though the thought was he knew Pandora would not take the money and he also knew it would not be enough to help the situation. Steven cleared his throat.

"Scyathica and I have been talking. The other option would be for Pandora to come here. Scyathica would move into the caravan with me, and your sister could then have her room. After all, if we get on with things there will also soon be a habitable West Wing. I understand Pandora lived here as a child…"

Sir Hugo said, "It seems the only option, but I am sure she will hate it. What about that dog Kitty and cat… Wuwu is it?"

Scyathica interjected, "I should ring Mother and sell this plan to her on the basis she can advise Steven and I on colour-schemes for the West Wing and also be on hand to keep an eye on your business. I am sure that if Kitty is gradually re-introduced to Piper, they can become playmates. If need be, Steven and I can have the cat in the caravan."

Sir Hugo had some misgivings about Kitty and Wu-wu… and not just their names!

Scyathica and Pandora had a long video call. During parts of it Pandora was tearful. For parts of it Steven and Sir Hugo joined the call. Steven even agreed to ask his own mother Deedee to go over and help Pandora with her packing as Pandora was too embarrassed to ask her London friends. Deedee would no doubt be honoured to be asked. Steven had striven to improve his relationship with his parents, although thus far he had managed to avoid them visiting Waste. And thus, Sir Hugo, Steven and Scyathica planned for an orderly departure from London for Pandora.

It seemed there was less order that weekend at the village of Gitthwaite. Eric and Tina Ercol went to visit Maude. They drove a few miles from Waste, taking the road past the entrance to Knight's Farm. Gitthwaite was actually technically in the next county, Eastern Waste Moorland. However, the nearest large town was undoubtedly Waste some twelve miles from Gitthwaite, whereas Moorland the county town of the neighbouring county was some thirty-five miles away from the village.

Eric and Tina had to stop their car briefly to open Maude's gates only to be accosted by an angry neighbour.

"Who are you?" he shouted. "You can't stop there."

"As you can see," Eric responded, "I am just gaining access… to visit my mother."

"Well tell her to shut that ruddy cockerel up," yelled the neighbour who clearly would have recognised Eric and Tina from their many previous visits.

They parked on the driveway outside the bungalow. The bungalow was a nineteen seventies construction made of mellow stone. It was really rather larger than was needed for an eighty-seven-year-old lady, but Maude had taken to it. It had two bathrooms and three bedrooms and ample grounds in which Emperor and his ladies had a small house and run. Claudius had a cat-flap in the backdoor so he could come and go as he pleased. The carers had a key safe just in the front porch, so they too were freely able to come and go.

Eric and Tina beat a retreat inside.

"Mum, where are you?" Eric called.

Maude emerged from the toilet clutching her besom. "I was hiding in here from the witchfinder. I don't want to be taken away," she said tremulously, looking rather frail.

"Mum," said Eric. "There is no witchfinder, and you are not a witch, although your cockerel does upset people."

"Emperor? Upset people? He doesn't make a sound... It's so quiet here. Isn't it, Claw-Deus?"

She bent down to stroke her cat. Eric wanted to discuss having the cockerel re-homed but lost his nerve.

"Tina and I have brought you some lovely cake, shall we all sit down and have some?"

"Who?" responded Maude.

"Tina... my wife who is just here."

Maude answered obliquely, "Yes, we should have some cake. We all get on well together."

Tina made some tea and put the cake on a plate.

Maude asked, "Have you met my cat? He is a god you know. He is called Claw-Deus. Have you met the Emperor?"

They both replied they knew her cat and the cockerel. Eric tried,

"I think the Emperor might want to live with a lot more hens, maybe at a chicken farm."

"I don't think so," said Maude. "He is happy here." She seemed very clear on the subject, so Eric decided not to persist. Then she said,

"Do you know my cat? He is a lovely cat. He is called Claw-Deus. He is a god you know."

Eric and Tina did not argue with her. They were pleased when Maude appeared to be enjoying her tea and cake. After tea Tina checked Maude's food cupboards and fridge while Eric looked in the Polarity carer's book. Maude seemed to be enjoying her cottage. There had been a few occasions when the District Nurse had been summonsed and the odd occasion when she had refused to change her clothes. The feature of concern was the fixation that the villagers were out to get her because she was a witch.

As Eric and Tina got into their car Eric commented,

"She seems well and happy, but I am not happy about this witch fixation. I wish I could have got her to agree for me to remove the cockerel too."

Tina agreed. "I am worried your mother's mental state is deteriorating and the neighbours do nothing to help. The carers find her rather difficult as well. She keeps turning down their help and unfortunately many of them don't like her cat. I am sure the neighbours just like to spy on everyone without giving a hand."

"Yes," said Eric. "I think they are peering at us through the net curtains now," which of course they were.

Oliver Grasby's weekend had thus far been altogether more satisfactory. His daughter Sheron and her husband Les Laybourne had made a brief visit to tell him that Les had been offered a "very good job" and they were moving away! "Hooray," thought Oliver; less handouts to Les the layabout. He supposed they would dump the grandkids on him anyway when he took leave in the summer holidays so he would still see them but not so often.

Davina dela Notte had called in briefly with the unfortunate Flavio. She had decided to move from her country 'estate' to a flat in town so the unfortunately named Flavio could leave boarding school and go to Waste Grammar School. Oliver thought this was a good move for the boy who always looked miserable and did not seem to be enjoying boarding school. He mused to himself that she might have to think of changing Flavio's name to something like 'Frank' if the lad was ever not to be teased. He was now out walking with his friend Aziz Ahmed. Both men were smoking large cigars out of sight of their wives. He brought Aziz up to date with his cheese plan for when the dreaded Stiffles came to visit.

"Got Shovell at the court office to do some research. There is a very smelly cheese called 'Stinking Bishop'."

Oliver said what he had in mind. Aziz laughed. Then Oliver asked,

"Haven't you got Ramadan soon...? Won't you have to stop smoking? I really enjoy our walks."

"It's OK, old thing," said Aziz. "I should still be able to smoke once it's dusk... we might have to walk a little later sometimes."

Oliver asked Aziz how he found Michael Phitt's house.

"It's a bit bland with its white neo-Georgian cardboard look pillars but it is convenient."

"Do you think he wants to sell it to you?" persisted Oliver.

"Probably," said Aziz, "and I might even buy it."

Oliver chuckled. "You could always jazz the house up. Paint the pillars in garish stripes! That would shake the neighbours up."

"Oh, so I can stir up some stereo-typical racist comments?" quipped Aziz in return. Both men laughed.

All was going well on their walk until they heard shouting. They had chosen to walk around the estate tonight rather than on the public footpath by the golf links. They were just rounding Links Close when they saw a furious looking Bertrand Sidebottom hammering on Nat Cartey's front door. Nat had his door open slightly and was looking out.

Bertrand had gone a purple colour and was shouting, "Tree murderer, vandal."

Nick was responding, "Stop bloody exaggerating and shouting on my doorstep."

Aziz and Oliver hung back in the shadows.

"This does not sound good," said Aziz.

"I think we should skidaddle out of here, we don't want to be witnesses," said Oliver.

"Agreed," said Aziz. "They could end up in front of one of us."

"Let's go to my potting shed, my dear chap. We can finish our cigars there relatively undisturbed," responded Oliver.

Fortunately, Bertrand Sidebottom and Nick Cartey were so engrossed in their quarrel they never noticed Oliver Grasby or Aziz Ahmed. Recently Nat had been concerned about some brown patches on his lawn near the end of the garden. He employed a jobbing gardener who ventured an opinion, "It's them willows drawing the moisture out of the lawn." Nat decided the trees could do with an initial trim. It was a bit more than Taz the gardener could handle so he looked online and made contact with 'Shady Trees. The people for trees and hedges.'

'Mr Shady' had come and after a lot of sucking of teeth said he would need to erect a scaffold around the trees at the end of the garden (obviously at considerable expense to Nat) and then give the trees an initial trim and survey them. The scaffold had gone up in Nat and Brittany's Garden and a few branches which had hung over their lawn had been removed. 'Mr Shady' had commented, "You know two or three of them trees are smack on the boundary, mate so you will need to be careful before you go much further." Nat was not going to take much notice. He did not like the nasty patches on his lawn and the offending branches seemed to be his side.

Bertrand Sidebottom had of course noticed the scaffolding going up. No-one had discussed matters with him. He liked the oriental look of the willows which grew near his carp pool. He carefully shaped the branches his side each year. The last thing he wanted was for the willows to be hacked about or worse still cut down.

He had sent Nat Cartey a carefully worded, if not stiff and starchy little note which Nat had of course ignored. That morning Nat had noticed a branch which was not cleanly chopped through by 'Mr Shady' and was dangling in a somewhat hazardous fashion. He had taken a small saw and climbed up the scaffold himself. He had quickly lopped off the offending branch and carelessly tossed it to one side. It had come to rest in the Sidebottom's Garden on the neat path just feet from the carp pool.

Bertrand Sidebottom had been staring out of his French windows at his garden which was something he did frequently in his leisure moments and saw the whole thing. If he had been worried before, he was now furious. He had not been able to go round to Nat's house that morning because he was due to work at the hospital. During the day every time he had a break, he could not help but think about the trees. By the time he got home he was seething with anger against Nat Cartey.

"They are not just your trees; they are on the boundary. You can't just vandalise them," he was now shouting.

Nick responded, "They have only had a little trim my side. I will only cut them my side."

"We'll see about that," huffed and puffed Bertrand.

"I will not be shouted at in my home," retorted Nick before closing the door.

He scratched his head. The man would surely get over it. It was such a storm in a teacup. He would carry on and get the trees trimmed but would make sure any work was carried out on his side. Bertrand stomped off home. He would take advice. His daughter was of course a solicitor. She might be useful for once. He would see if Sonja would write a solicitor's letter.

As it happened Sonja was not as sympathetic as he might have wished. "I can get a solicitor's letter done for you," she said, "but you may wish to consider some sort of arbitration or mediation with your neighbour. Getting into court cases about boundaries is not a good idea."

Instead of heeding what she said Bertrand huffed and puffed and called for backup from Sonja's mother. "We can pay that man Blunt you work for... if that's what worries you?"

Sonja sighed. "Look, Mum and Dad, I know you are good for the money. I just don't want you bogged down in a court case about some trees."

Bertrand Sidebottom was not listening. And he certainly was not going to listen to his daughter.

C h a p t e r   4

PENNY HAD DRESSED IN HER long boots and her shortest skirt to go and meet Lewis. She had hoped to distract him from his motorbike. She had taken a bus to the Harbour View pub where they were meeting for a meal. She stood outside fiddling with her artificial feather boa wishing she had a coat. She thought she might have been a little early.

Xavier had slipped into the country the previous day. He was standing on the balcony of the Harbour View's newly completed accommodation wing looking at the mist roll over the lake as dusk set in. He began lighting a cigarette and turned out of the breeze in order to do so. As he turned, he happened to glance downwards and see Penny. She was illuminated by a lamp at the pub entrance and looked extremely striking, and a little younger than her actual years.

Having stubbed out the newly lit cigarette, Xavier went quickly downstairs since he was immediately attracted by what he saw. He pretended to stumble as he passed Penny so that he could slightly bump into her.

"Mademoiselle, a thousand pardons for my clumsiness," he said. This trite line tended to work for him.

"Oh, gee, no harm done," said Penny. Xavier's pulse raced just a little. An American girl: it could not be better. "You sound French," she said.

"And you sound American," said Xavier. "Mademoiselle, we are both foreigners in this country. Let me buy you a drink as an apology."

"Well, I don't know," said Penny, "I was waiting for my boyfriend."

"Who evidently isn't here," responded Xavier.

"Well I guess, one little drink would be nice," said Penny who almost immediately found herself led to a private terrace on the other side of the pub which was attached to the new accommodation wing.

Xavier rang a bell on the wall and Pierre Bruele appeared. Xavier spoke quickly to him in French asking him to see if the pub could manage a decent champagne, but if not at the very least a good bottle of white wine. He also asked Pierre to make sure that if the young lady's boyfriend arrived, he did not find her.

"Gee," said Penny, "my boyfriend might be looking for me. He is called Lewis, and he rides a Harley. Can you tell him I am here?"

Pierre smiled and found the information helpful so he could identify who to make sure was kept out of the way.

Surprisingly the landlord was able to serve a decent champagne.

"It's going up my nose," said Penny giggling.

Xavier said, "Well, enchanting nymph with bubbles up your nose, what is your name?"

"Penny," came the reply sounding inevitably like 'Painy', "Penny Wayney."

"Do tell me a little about yourself."

Penny gave him a brief potted history of how she was trying to finish her dissertation for her master's degree but was working in a vegetarian café.

"What are you doing in Waste?" she said giggling some more. "Business," said Xavier, "but I prefer not to talk about it."

"Hush, hush," said Penny still giggling.

"Why don't I buy you dinner? It doesn't look like this boyfriend is coming."

In actual fact Lewis had made a special effort that evening. He was dressed smartly, not in motorbike leathers. He had borrowed his brother's car so he could surprise Penny by driving her home after dinner, rather than expecting her to perch on the back of his motorbike. He had bought a small box of specialist expensive vegetarian chocolates as a gift for her. He was perturbed that Penny was nowhere to be seen. Pierre had given the bar staff twenty pounds to keep quiet so when Lewis asked if anyone had seen a tall, slim American girl all he got was shoulder shrugging.

Lewis tried ringing her mobile phone. It went straight to voicemail. Crestfallen he turned and left.

Penny was giggling so much she had not heard her phone. She agreed Xavier could buy her dinner.

"Although I am a vegetarian," she added.

"Pity," thought Xavier. He would have to charm her with his good looks and guile and plenty of alcohol. She seemed quite pliable to him and frankly easy entertainment.

Penny enjoyed her evening being flattered and plied with champagne by the French man. At the end of the evening, he gave her a fairly chaste kiss on each cheek initially.

"My man Pierre will drive you home," he said. "But I will see you again? Perhaps the day after tomorrow, for dinner again? Tell Pierre where to collect you."

Penny blushed and nodded. Xavier then kissed her hand. "Ma cherie, I can hardly wait to see you again and to become more intimately acquainted."

Pierre drove her home to Canal Street hardly saying a word. As she got out of the car he said quietly, "Are you sure about this with Xavier?" Penny brushed his remark aside and flounced inside to be met by Auntie Bea.

"I've had Lewis your bloke round here looking for you."

"Well, he's not my 'bloke' anymore," said Penny. "He stood me up."

"He kind of said it was the other way round," said Auntie Bea.

"Well, you don't know. I was there. Actually, as a result of him leaving me in the lurch I have met someone else."

"Best tell poor Lewis then," said Auntie Bea.

Next morning Penny tried to speak to Lewis on the phone, but he had just started his shift and there was a cacophony of noise. They could not hear each other well, let alone understand each other.

"I think I have just been dropped by my girlfriend," said Lewis to a work colleague. "I don't know what is going on."

He tried not to think about it, but Penny had got right under his skin.

Oliver on the other hand was not letting the issue of the Stiffles get under his skin. He had his strategy. The one thing he hoped was it would not upset Annette. Annette had taken the day off tomorrow to make something of a long weekend out of it. God knows why!

He had let Aziz know he might not be able to go walking with him and left court punctually. Both Oliver and Annette were at home when the Stiffles arrived in their MG sports car. Annette had taken some care over the dinner and had laid the dining room table with appropriate crystal and silverware.

Annette brought into the dining room a homemade consommé which had taken her hours to cook.

"Lena probably won't have any," said Nick Stiffle before Lena had a chance to speak. "It's her nerves again you know."

Nick was a thinnish man with silver hair and bundles of nervous energy. Lena was a short, slight woman who when her husband was being loud looked just like a dormouse.

"Well, I'll try a bit," she said rather quietly. "It's just that I've been a bit upset by my music society."

They all started their consommé and Nick started discussing whether the pubs and restaurants of Waste served any decent cheese. He indicated plenty was to be had in his hometown.

"There's a restaurant near us which serves fourteen varieties of British cheese on its cheeseboard," he said.

Oliver said quietly, "Well I have arranged a little cheese surprise during your visit."

Nick looked momentarily intrigued but went back to talking about cheeseboards.

Annette served the main course of roast chicken.

"Not hungry are you, Lena," boomed Nick.

"Well, I'll have a bit. I like chicken," said Lena.

"What has happened at the music society then? "queried Annette.

She was aware that Lena had retired a few years ago when her nerves had got the better of her when she was teaching at a small school. These days she understood Lena was the leading light of the amateur operatic society. She put on amateur operatic productions and excerpts from grand operas. In their younger days Oliver and Annette had attended a concert given by Lena when she was still teaching. Annette had wondered if Lena's quavery slightly off-key soprano was affected by nerves.

"They cut my aria," said Lena and started sobbing slightly over her ice-cream dessert. "The other singers said my voice was not right for it and if they didn't have it cut, they would vote me out of office, and I could not be President of the Society anymore."

"There, there," said Oliver although he did not mean it at all. He thought Lena's voice was absolutely terrible and he did not know how her music society had put up with it for so long.

Cheese and port were offered. Annette had sourced some fine vintage cheddar and some stilton. Lena stopped sniffing and sobbing.

"Not bad for cheese amateurs," said Nick putting his nose so perilously near the cheeseboard that Oliver was not sure he wanted any cheese anymore.

Oliver took the Stiffles to the lounge and offered teas and coffees while Annette started clearing up. He switched the television on by way of background. There was an updated version of Macbeth on screen.

"I am not watching this... far too violent," said Nick loudly when less than 5 minutes of action had been shown.

Oliver turned the television off.

"I think," said Lena, and she named a particularly dreary soap which pretended to be a costume drama, "is on tomorrow."

Oliver said nothing. Then Lena added, "But I think I'll go to bed now it's getting on for quarter to nine and I can't manage staying up late."

While Annette was clearing up Oliver was therefore left with Nick who told him of the thoughts of the committee of the UK Association of British Cheesemongers on pasteurised milk and the making of a number of cheeses. Nick also told Oliver about a cheese tour he intended to do in the autumn. If Oliver and Annette had not been going to bed themselves Nick Stiffles would still have been discussing cheese. As Oliver and Annette settled down, Annette remarked,

"I'd forgotten how wearing the Stiffles could be."

"I did warn you," said Oliver.

"You have been remarkably well behaved," said Annette. "I'm sure you're up to something."

Oliver pretended to be asleep.

Next day they tried taking the Stiffles for a scenic drive but felt almost worn down by diatribes about cheese. Oliver offered Nick cigars, but this was rebuffed on the grounds it would upset his palate for cheese. Lena on the other hand was rather quiet and it was hard to draw her into conversation. At lunchtime they ventured to take the Stiffles to a bistro pub for lunch some 15 or so miles away at the end of their scenic route in the village of Farthwaite. Oliver was well behaved enough not to refer to the pub as the 'Fart-weight' Arms which is what he usually called it.

The pub specialised in French bistro style cooking which it did rather well. Oliver enjoyed a speciality of the pub, pigeon cooked in sherry with peas. Of course, Nick complained about the cheeseboard as the cheeses were mainly French, Oliver on the other hand was concerned to hear the landlord was thinking about retirement as he rather enjoyed this little place.

After they arrived home the evening seemed to drag on. At one point there was a knock at the front door.

"I'll get it," said Oliver and quickly went outside to take delivery of an extremely well-sealed package from a uniformed delivery man who had come in a little van labelled 'Nationwide Gourmet 24 hours'.

"It is vacuum sealed," said the delivery man. "Keep it cool and don't open it until you want it."

Oliver thanked him and paid for the delivery.

Afterwards, Oliver quickly put extra wrapping around the parcel and hid it in the cool of the potting shed.

Next morning the Stiffles expressed a wish to get on their way straight after breakfast.

"Meeting of cheese committee tonight and Lena is rehearsing," said Nick.

Oliver said just before the Stiffles drove away,

"Hang on one moment," I have a little gift for you.

He dashed to the potting shed and came back with the parcel which had been delivered just the previous evening...

"Remember," he said, "don't open it until you get home; best looked at in that cosy little kitchen of yours."

Both Stiffles expressed thanks not only for the gift but for a 'lovely' weekend. Nick checked the hood of the MG was in place. It was after all, only April. They drove off.

Oliver cleared his throat. "Just going to see if Aziz is free for a walk. Will be nice to chatter to him after that pillock Nick."

"OK," said Annette. "I need to pack up for London. I will be spending a couple of weeks there again as you know."

Oliver strolled along Links Road to the corner of Links Close and went up to the door of the neo-Georgian property which was first in the road. He rang the doorbell. Initially one of the boys answered. A few minutes later Aziz and Amina appeared.

"Come in, come in," said Aziz in jovial mood. "We were just talking about Amina's famous victory. She won the council by-election you know. Meet Councillor Amina Ahmed!"

Oliver congratulated her. He genuinely believed she had done very well to be both an ophthalmic consultant and a borough councillor at such a young age.

"I bet you'll give 'Easy' Ryder a run for his money," he said.

Although Aziz had not previously been in favour of Amina being on the council he was now glowing with pride.

"Once you've finished Ramadan and Annette is finished with her latest stint in London you will let us take you both out," said Oliver affably.

"Thank you," said Aziz. "By the way, has Nick had your gift, yet?"

"Yes," said Oliver. "But he hasn't opened it yet as far as I know." He looked smug. Amina looked puzzled and said she ought to look at some council minutes.

Oliver continued to chat to Aziz for a while and then took himself home where he went in the potting shed and cleaned out his pipe. Once he had cleaned it, he sat himself in the battered old armchair he kept in there and began a quiet smoke. The shed afforded some shelter from the elements, and he still had his warm outdoor jacket on, so he dozed and smoked for a while. Then he heard Annette's voice ringing in his ears.

"Oliver, Oliver. I know you are there. How could you?"

Oliver emerged and smiled. "I take it Nick found my gift?"

"I have had Nick and Lena on the phone furious," said Annette. "It seems they were halfway home and had a little break in their journey. Nick could not resist opening your parcel. The contents smelled so rank they had to continue their journey with the roof down… and it rained. Lena says she is worried she will get laryngitis and she will not be able to sing with her operatic society…"

"A blessing surely?" muttered Oliver.

"Nick says the seats in the car have got a little wet as there was an April shower. They say they will never visit us again. What on earth did you give Nick?"

"Stinking Bishop," replied Oliver.

"I beg your pardon," said Annette.

"Stinking Bishop cheese. It is reputed to be Britain's smelliest cheese. It is a speciality. It surely can't be a bad thing if they don't come again," said Oliver enjoying the outcome of his prank. "Nick being Nick probably kept the cheese anyway to try and review when they got home," he added.

Annette scowled at him. "Oliver, you are incorrigible. But you will have to rein-in your jokes and wind-ups. You do not want to jeopardise your judicial career or indeed your judicial pension. Promise me you will not do anything as wicked as this again. I do not want to spend my time in London worrying about your behaviour."

Oliver smiled. "I don't think they would have a leg to stand on complaining to anyone. Stinking Bishop is a very rare cheese and Nick is a self-appointed cheese expert and I just made a gift of unusual cheese to him. It is no bad thing if we don't see them again. They are a miserable pair with whom we have nothing in common."

Annette raised an eyebrow. She was not sure she could trust her husband not to engage in further jokes.

"However, I promise not to be so naughty!" said Oliver still smiling.

"I hope I can trust you," responded Annette, really doubting him.

"I one hundred percent confirm I will take no action which will jeopardise my judicial career or my judicial pension,"

said Oliver looking serious to reassure her.

"Now," he said with a twinkle in his eye once again, "it's getting near tea-time. What shall we have for tea, cook? Cheese on toast?"

Chapter 5

DISTRICT JUDGE ERCOL HAD NOT been long at his desk on Monday when his phone rang.

"Sir," said a disembodied voice from the office, "it's your mother's carers on the phone. They say they got your court number from your wife. Can I put them through?"

"Yes," said Eric somewhat surprised.

"This is Trudy from Polarity Carers. We have had a lot of trouble with your mother today. Aside from that cat leaping out at everyone, today the carer we sent in found herself prodded by your mother with her sweeping brush. Your mother has sat herself in her armchair and refuses to get out of it. She has been there since 7am and says if she gets out of it the witchfinder will get her."

Eric expressed dismay and said he would call on his mother as soon as his list finished. Fortunately, his morning case settled, and District Judge Stump had a very light list, so he was able to persuade her to take his afternoon cases. He rang Tina his wife and she cancelled her appointments. By 3 o'clock they both arrived at Gitthwaite. There was a carer in the kitchen.

"She won't get out of her chair whatever I say," said the carer. "She's in her lounge."

"Hello, Mum," said Eric as he went into the sitting room.

"Hello, dear," said Maude. "Have you met my cat? He's a very nice cat. He's a god you know."

"Yes, Mum, Tina and I have met Claudius many times," said Eric. "I was just wondering if you might come to the kitchen and have some tea with us there or take a little walk to see Emperor and his hens."

"Oh no," said Maude. "If I move the witchfinder will get me."

"Mum, you are not a witch," said Eric.

"Yes I am. I am Mordred and my cat is Claw-deus… Have you met him? He is very nice. He is a god you know," was the answer he got.

"Mum, you are not a witch."

"Yes, I am. You are just wanting the witchfinder to get me."

"No, I'm only trying to help you."

And so, the conversation continued in similar vein.

Eric eventually turned to Tina. "This is doing more harm than good. I think we should pop home and call the doctor."

They left the carer in charge. As they drove the few minutes home Tina said, "I'm sorry to say your mother needs a mental health assessment, maybe even sectioning."

By the time they got home Eric was agreeing with her. He therefore quickly rang the surgery.

The receptionist said, "Oh, it's far too late... if she is an emergency take her to A and E."

"You don't understand," said Eric. "She won't move out of her chair. She needs a doctor to visit her. She needs a mental health assessment."

"Best I can do is for Dr Siddartha to ring you at the end of his list," said the receptionist.

Eric had no option but to agree.

At about half past six he received the call. He explained the problem.

"A most perplexing and worrying issue," said Dr Siddartha. "You need her to have a mental health assessment. A nearest relative can request one…"

"Yes, that's what I want."

"I will give you a number," which he did. "They should help you."

As soon as he finished the call to Dr Siddartha, Eric rang the number.

"Waste Social Services, Duty Officer," said the person who answered.

Eric explained the issue.

"Your mother's address?"

"No, that's not us, that is East Waste Moorlands, I can give you the number?"

He took down the number and rang it as soon as he finished the call.

"North Clagg Council," was the answer.

Eric terminated the call and cursed and rang back Waste Social Services. He was given a further number. It was now nearly 9 o'clock.

He got through to the Duty Officer at East Waste Moorlands.

"It sounds like your mother needs a mental health assessment," said the voice exasperatingly. "Surely if her doctor is in Waste he can organise it?"

Eric expressed his concern. "Look," said the voice, "I will pass your enquiry to the day-time team as it sounds as if your mum needs an elderly person's assessment."

Eric came off the phone. It was after 9 o'clock. He said to Tina,

"Nothing doing tonight. I think we should start again tomorrow but we will quickly call round to see if Mum's okay," he said wistfully. "Maybe she will have got out of the chair."

They drove around to Maude's bungalow and crept in. She was still in the armchair, fast asleep with the cat settled on her lap.

Next morning Eric checked with the early carer if Maude was still in the chair and as he expected Maude was refusing to move.

"You get off to court," said Tina. "Get yourself sorted and see if you can make a get-away while I phone the doctors,"

Eric arrived at court to find he had Lavinia Levi's application to have Patella live with him. He was relieved Steven Hovell was clerking for him, so everything was well in hand. He could see Lavinia Levi was represented by Bernie Blunt. The council was represented by Ivan Huff and the child was represented by Miss Sue Rosemary. There was a Children's Guardian appointed, Mr Tim Weary and the mother May Lou O'Hanrahan was unrepresented and was appearing by video link from prison. Eric explained to Steven that he had some personal difficulties, so he wanted to leave after this case. Steven immediately liaised with the office to try to get lists re-arranged.

The case was ready to start. The parties were in court and the video link established.

Ivan Huff rose to his feet.

"If it pleases you, sir the advocates have agreed I should outline where the case has reached."

He was interrupted by May Lou. "I ain't agreed nuffink."

Eric said, "Miss Hanrahan, I think all Mr Huff is going to do is outline where things have got to in the case."

Ivan Huff explained that as a result of previous court orders made by the lay magistrates the local authority was well advanced with preparing a report as to whether a special guardianship report would be appropriate. The magistrates had re-appointed Mr Weary and Miss Rosemary who had represented Patella in the care case. Miss Rosemary had application before the court for a psychologist's report on any psychological challenges to the placement.

May Lou began shouting, "It's freaky that's what it is."

Eric said, "If you interrupt one more time my clerk will mute you."

Ivan Huff outlined some more of the case. He explained that since the final care order Patella had thrived in a foster placement and had spent increasing amounts of time with her father which was now once a week including one overnight stay. Since Miss Levi had transitioned it was understood she had ceased all offending behaviour, but the council were awaiting written confirmation.

"He's a freak…" yelled May Lou again.

Steven pressed the mute button, and she could still be seen mouthing profanities.

Ivan Huff continued,

"All three advocates can see this is an unusual case. If Patella is subject to a Special Guardianship order to Miss Levi she would be in a very different position to her siblings and generally in a unique position. Her mother has only 6 more months in prison and is not represented. We would ask you, sir, to list the next hearing before a Circuit Judge."

Bernie Blunt rose. "My client concurs. While she would like Patella to come and live with her as soon as possible and a change of name from Patella to Pauline to be affected she would like this done in an orderly fashion. My client now lives an exemplary life and is training to be a therapist to assist alcoholics and drug abusers."

Sue Rosemary added, "Sir, I agree with a Circuit Judge listing. Apart from Mother's clear opposition to the orders, some of the siblings are in family placement and the issue of interaction with the family and contact will be needed."

Eric Ercol cleared his throat.

"I will ask my clerk Mr Hovell to find this case a listing in a few weeks' time before Her Honour dela Notte, once the reports are available."

Mr Huff rose to his feet. "It is the local authority's position that the current level of contact between Patella and her parents and also her siblings should be maintained in the meantime, sir. I know this is supported by Miss Levi and the Guardian, but I believe the mother opposes this."

District Judge Ercol looked at the video link screen.

"Miss O'Hanrahan, my clerk will shortly unmute you so you can give me your views but if you start shouting insults, I will ask him to mute you again. In the next few weeks I would recommend that you seek legal representation. I am going to ask the child solicitor to send you a list of solicitors who do legal aid cases not only in this town but where the prison is. Unfortunately, legal aid for such a case will not be automatic but you are in a difficult situation so you may well qualify for legal aid."

Sue Rosemary confirmed she would send the list and Steven pressed the button to unmute Miss O'Hanrahan.

"I demand more contact," came the voice from the prison. "Once a fortnight for 90 minutes is not enough. I'm her mother and when I get out, I want all my babies with me. And another thing, I want that freak's time stopped… those bloody social workers have no idea. And you Mr Stuffy Judge… she ain't your daughter… and if you keep this up when I get out, I'm going to get you."

District Judge Ercol had just waved his hand in a halt motion when Steven pressed the mute button.

"In the paramount best interest of the child," he said, "I am not going to change current arrangements. However, if the mother behaves in anything like this way during contact, I expect an urgent application by the local authority to suspend or stop her contact. While many judges might consider having a contempt hearing for your misbehaviour, I see little point at the moment as you are already in prison, Miss O'Hanrahan. However, I would strongly urge you to take legal advice. The video link will now be cut, and this court stands adjourned."

The link was cut, and everyone filed out of court.

"Thank you, Steven," said Eric. "I have to dash now. I have a lot of issues with my elderly mother."

As Eric started walking down the backstairs he rang Tina.

"What's happening?"

Tina replied, "It was a locum, Dr Dornier, not Dr Siddartha and she only agreed to send an Emergency Practice nurse to rule out physical ill-health. I said I would go round to your mother's place if you could not be there."

"I'm on my way," said Eric, "but I think dementia has set in… and she needs a mental health professional, probably to section her and give her a short stay in a mental health hospital to get her sorted out."

He started the journey to Gitthwaite again. On his arrival he was met by a Polarity carer.

"She is still in the chair and won't get out," said the carer. "It is getting on for 36 hours now. I am worried she will have horrible sores."

Eric agreed with the concerns. "Hello," said Maude, "have you met my cat? His name is Claw-deus. He is a god you know."

"Yes, Mum," said Eric, "I have met your cat."

There was a knock at the front door. "Hello, I'm Dick Smith the emergency practitioner. Where should I see your mum? Bedroom? Bathroom? Living room?"

Eric looked thunderous. "Since the problem is she won't get out of her armchair... you will have to see her in her armchair in the living room."

He showed Dick to where Maude was. "Mum, people are worried about you, so this nice man is going to see if there is anything wrong."

Maude beamed. "I think we have met before. Have you met my cat? He's a god you know."

Claudius was sitting next to her hissing. He tried to swipe Dick with his paw. "Don't do that to the nice man," said Maude.

There was another knock at the door. A slight, very young-looking woman with a doctor's bag stood on the doorstep.

"I'm Dr Dornier. Dr Siddartha told me to come."

Eric showed her to the lounge and made the introductions. "Please also take a blood sample," said the doctor to Dick.

The examination was soon over. Maude was still beaming. Dr Dornier said to her,

"Mrs Ercol, do you think you could with a little help, stand up and come away from your chair? Your blood pressure and oxygen levels are all good, but it would be nice to see you away from the chair."

"Oh no," said Maude, "Claw-deus says not to... He's a god you know. I'm a witch."

Dr Dornier and Dick began talking across Maude. Eric showed them to the hallway but there was a knock at the front door. An angry man stood there.

"Who's parked on the pavement? I can't get my son's tricycle past. If they don't move soon, I'm calling the police."

"I think it's me," said Dr Dornier. "I'm a doctor. I've been visiting a patient, but I'll be gone in 5 minutes."

"Oh," said Mr Angry. "As long as it's only 5 minutes," and flounced off.

"Well," said Dick, "your mother seems physically okay so if you want her taken to hospital you may have to wait until she has an infected sore and ring 999."

"That can't be right," said Eric. "She surely needs to be sectioned under the Mental Health Act? She can't be left sitting in an armchair thinking she's a witch."

"I'll speak to Dr Siddartha as soon as possible," agreed Dr Dornier before Dick and herself departed.

Eric checked with the carer who had stayed in the background that she would call in on his mother around 9.30 if he had made no other progress. Feeling rather despondent he headed for home.

As he was driving along his mobile rang so he pulled into a layby. It was Dr Dornier.

"Dr Siddartha says you can ring and ask for a nearest relative Mental Health assessment. We will get the number for you."

On his arrival the landline was ringing as he entered his home.

"This is Dr Siddartha's receptionist," said the voice. "I have a number for you to ring about your mother."

Eric took down the details. As soon as he could he tried the number. "This is Waste Borough Council, press 1 for rating service, press 2 for refuse collection, press 3 for street lighting and parks and press 4 for children's services."

Eric groaned and put the phone down. He rang the surgery. After being in a queue for 10 minutes he eventually got through and explained he had been passed the wrong number.

"Well Doctor gave it to me," said the receptionist and hung up.

Feeling very frustrated he phoned the number for East Waste Moorlands he had tried last night.

"Ah," said the Duty Officer, "I think my colleague was trying to ring you a little earlier. Hang on a moment."

Eric did. "Hello. This is Andy Addefull. Please do update me."

Eric explained the latest. "Look, your mum needs a mental health assessment organised by an Adult Mental Health Practitioner," said Andy. "The GP could have formally requested it from us if Waste Council say Maude is not under their jurisdiction. The irony is that if your mother needs to be sectioned, she will be taken to Tall Pines in Waste because her GP practice is in Waste. I will try ringing the GP and if nothing is on track by early morning, I will ask for the assessment myself."

"Thank you so much," said a relieved Eric.

Steven on the other hand was rather less relieved by the news he got when he got back to High Cliffe.

"I have had Uncle on the phone plus my mother and your mother."

Steven thought that an unlikely but slightly worrying combination.

"My mother will have packed up by Friday with the help of Deedee but there is no way Uncle can get all she wants to bring in his car plus the dog and the cat."

"I thought Pandora was hiring removers and what she can't get into the house she is storing in that empty office in the East Wing?" said Steven.

"This is stuff she immediately wants apparently," said Scyathica raising her eyebrows, "and there is a plan for it… but you won't like it."

Steven said, "Out with it then!"

"Deedee and Champ will load the excess luggage in their campervan and will follow Uncle's car up here on Friday! They are then hoping to stay until Sunday to help my mother unload, to meet me and have a little visit with their son," said Scyathica.

Steven was initially speechless. Then he laughed.

"Well, in the past my parents have never done anything to help me. So, your mother's problems are indirectly getting them to help me… by helping you, help your mum. So, it's a first!"

Both Scyathica and Steven contemplated how they were going to cope with an influx of parents. Scyathica was already in the throes of moving into the caravan. They decided to finish the move that evening. There was then the matter not only of settling in Pandora but entertaining everyone for the weekend. They decided they would cook something filling and wholesome for Friday dinner. Scyathica hit upon an old recipe issued by Knubb Sausages. It was a version of the German Meatloaf known as 'Falscher Hase'. They also decided to book a table at the Harbour View for Saturday night.

Later that night they peered out of a side-window of the caravan looking at the moon.

"It's not too bad in here," said Scyathica. "Even a little romantic!"

"Well," said Steven laughing, "I am not sure how romantic your winter pyjamas and two dressing gowns are or my heavy old tracksuit, but let's have a nightcap of something strong and warming!"

They both were surprisingly good humoured in the circumstances.

The Sidebottom household was not a good-humoured household that night. Sonja had arranged for the solicitor's letter to be sent to Nat and Brittany Cartey. Bertrand had been furious to come home to an envelope addressed to him which contained nothing but the solicitor's letter which was torn to shreds. He had not been able to see the trees in the gloom but had gone outside with a torch. He knew the willows were just beginning to bloom, but he could not see well. He went to his carp pool. He noticed one of his carp looked as if it was swimming at a slight angle.

He came stomping indoors,

"I hope they haven't been poisoning Tinkerbell!"

he said referring to his koi carp.

"Oh dear," said Marjorie.

Sonja retreated to her room and shut the door.

Chapter 6

STEVEN WOKE EARLY AND FELT very nervous. It was the day of his interview with the bigwigs from the Circuit Office. In the past he had never been ambitious, but he now felt keen on this promotion, and of making something of himself at Waste Combined Court. Scyathica stirred. She gave him a hug.

"You will do well. I know it," she said.

Steven tried to put on a brave face and got himself ready for work.

Eric was getting ready for work at this time when he received a phone call.

"Hello, this is Henry Mcnally. I am an Approved Adult Mental Health Practitioner. Will it be alright if I come with two doctors including a consultant psychiatrist to your mother's home at 4 o'clock? Andy has told me the story. The doctors will do a mental health assessment."

Eric agreed that was just what was needed and he and probably his wife as well would be there. When he arrived at the court, he managed to swap around some cases with District Judge Stump so he could leave at 3.30. It meant foregoing a lunch-hour, but it was worth it.

Eric and his wife Tina made sure to pull their cars well into Maude's driveway and left the gate open so at least one of the doctors could park on the driveway if not both. At just a few minutes after 4 o'clock Henry Mcnally and the two doctors arrived. Henry introduced himself to Eric and Tina at the front door and introduced Mr Enstile, consultant psychiatrist and Dr Stroller, general practitioner psychiatrist. Some discussion followed about Maude's medical history and the lack of any diagnosis of dementia.

"Is Maude still in her chair?" said Henry.

"I spoke to the carers this morning," said Tina. "They believe she got out of the chair late at night and fetched some biscuits as they found some crumbs but at 7am she was back in it refusing to move."

Eric brought Henry and the doctors into the bungalow. The tea-time carer was just making Maude a cup of tea, so Eric explained to her what was happening. He then brought everyone into the living room where Maude was sitting.

"Mum," said Eric, "these nice gentlemen are here to help you and find out why you can't get of your chair."

Maude beamed. "Hello, have you met my cat? He's a very nice cat. He's a god you know."

"Alright," said Dr Stroller, "I am just going to ask you a few questions. So let us start with what your name is."

"Mordred," said Maude.

"And your last name?" asked the doctor.

"It's a secret," was the reply. "I don't want the witchfinder to know. I'm a witch you know. Have you met my cat? He's a very nice cat."

"What's your address?" persisted the doctor.

"It's a secret," was the reply.

"Alright," said Dr Stroller, "who's this gentleman here?" pointing to Eric.

"That's my son," said Maude.

"And his name?"

"My cat can tell you. He's a very nice cat," came the response.

The doctor pointed to Eric's wife Tina. "Who is this lady?"

"My cat knows. Have you met my cat? He's a very nice cat?" was Maude's reply.

"What year is it?" said the doctor.

"That's a hard one," said Maude.

"Well, what about the date of your birthday?"

"My cat will know it. He's a god you know," was the inevitable response.

"Alright," that's quite enough questions.

The doctors asked if there was somewhere they could sit and talk, and Eric showed them to a small dining room. Dr Stroller said as Eric showed them through, "Well, I think that was nil points, but we need to just discuss things." It was not long before they called for Henry and then for Eric and Tina.

"Your mother needs sectioning under the Mental Health Act," Mr Enstile said.

"Dr Stroller and I will leave shortly but Henry here will do the paperwork and look for a hospital bed."

Henry sat at the dining room table trying to speak to the admissions officer at Tall Pines. It took him some time to get through and discussions followed.

"I'm sorry," he said. "There is no bed tonight. I really don't think it would be good for your mother to be sent away a long distance since they should have a bed tomorrow. I will come back at midday tomorrow. I think she can be left just the one more night. Can someone be here tomorrow?"

Tina said she would take the day off.

While Eric and Tina were arranging to leave, over at Auntie Bea's house Penny was dreamily getting ready for her next date with Xavier. She had a small bag packed as Xavier had asked her to spend the weekend with him. She applied some eye liner but was interrupted by her phone. The call was something of a surprise.

She had not heard from her parents for some time, but she recognised the number. Senator Brad T Morton Wayney junior and his wife Alannah rarely if ever travelled to England. Penny had never discovered her English mother's hometown. Alannah aka Aggie Winterbottom had never told her. In her youth her mother was often seen in minor American soaps and made for tv movies. These days she graced the side of her wealthy, loud and powerful husband.

"Hi, Penny, your mom and I have decided to come to little old England. I have been thinking of buying one of your English soccer clubs and your mom wants to find the house where she was born… well, so all roads have led to Waste," said the senator.

"Was Mom born in Waste?" said Penny incredulously.

"Yupp," said the senator and before she could say anymore, "so I've booked your mom and I the best room at this quaint inn called the Knubb Arms."

He ended the call without saying anymore, not even when Alannah and himself were due to arrive or the identity of the football club.

Penny tried calling back but only got a busy signal. She sent texts and emails to her parents but gained no immediate response, so she finished getting ready.

"I hope you know what you're doing, girl," said Auntie Bea as she came downstairs. "I don't trust that French fellow one little bit. No-one has seen him and then he suddenly shows up… It all sounds a bit off to me."

"Auntie Bea, I love it that you are concerned but Xavier is sooo wonderful," said Penny. Then she added, "Hey and I have extra news, my folks may be visiting Waste soon."

"Well," said Auntie Bea, "maybe they can talk some sense into you."

At that moment Pierre Bruele drew up in Canal Street and honked his car's horn. Penny climbed in the car and was whisked away to be wined and dined by Xavier. Her swain had done his best to get the chef at the Harbour View to find vegetarian specialities. There was candle-light and soft music. Xavier turned on his Gallic charm and it was not difficult for him to lure Penny into his spider's web of seduction.

That evening Steven had a quiet dinner with Scyathica and contemplated his progress with his interview.

"As far as I can tell, it went well," he said. "I think double mothers tomorrow might be more of a strain!"

Things were not so quiet at the Sidebottom residence. Nat had insisted that Mr Shady Trees cut more branches off the willows. Marjorie had been at home and had called out to the gardener as he cut a few branches,

"Cooeee, please stop... my husband won't like it."

Mr Shady's man had paused and called Nat Cartey who was in his constituency office. He drove home at speed and came stomping down the garden path.

"Look," said the gardener, "those trees are on your boundary. I am not prepared to get caught in some dispute. I'll come back another time... give you time to talk to your neighbour."

Nat scowled and he picked up a handful of small branches and twigs and threw them over the boundary. One very small branch landed in the carp pond with a slight slosh. He went back to his office.

Bertrand Sidebottom returned home at the end of the day and Marjorie told him what had happened.

"I persuaded him to stop but he threw a few twigs," she said.

Bertrand stood by his carp pool. Tinkerbell was floating upside down.

"He has murdered Tinkerbell," he shouted. "That man is an evil menace."

Sonja just about managed to calm her parents down by agreeing to speak to the senior partner Bernie Blunt in the morning to arrange an appointment.

The very next morning Sonja approached Bernie with some trepidation.

"So," he said, "your parents want to sue the sitting Labour MP who just so happens to be a supporter of the union who is a client of this firm. You managed to slip a solicitor's letter through, but I really cannot involve the firm any further. It would be a conflict of interest. I think your parents have two choices. They either can go to another firm, and I can give you some names. Alternatively, if they act in person as long as nothing goes through the office, I can't stop you helping them. I can give you a list of barristers too who not only take direct access cases but also are regular visitors to Waste."

Sonja felt she knew what her parents would do, and her heart sank at the prospect. She also noticed that at the top of the list was the name of Dr Gordon Flaughtersdough (pronounced 'Flowerdew'). He was a barrister she had met before, plummy, and self-opinionated with a tendency to flatulence. It would be just her luck if they ended up with him.

As Sonja was gloomily contemplating her parents' future litigation, Tina Ercol arrived at Maude's bungalow. Just as she drew up, she saw the angry neighbour on the warpath towards Henry who was just parking up, so she quickly opened the gate and beckoned him inside.

"The bed is available, so now I have to summons an ambulance," he said. "I hope the ambulance technicians can coach her from her chair as it would seem over the top to have to get police assistance."

They waited just over an hour.

"That's pretty good going," said Henry. "Sometimes I have waited all day."

The ambulance pulled in as far it could up Maude's driveway and the ambulance technicians got out. Tina and Henry discussed the situation with them.

"I think I should get the cat out of the room," said Tina. "I will say to Maude that if she lets you lift her onto the stretcher you will help her fly away from the witchfinder."

Tina shut Claudius in the dining room. He didn't try to scratch her as he was surprised by being picked up. He miaowed a little and scratched the door.

Tina introduced the ambulance technicians to Maude.

"They are going to put you on a special bed which will help you fly away from the witchfinder."

Maude beamed and let herself to Tina's amazement be lifted out of the armchair. She was whisked out of the house to the ambulance.

"Shall I meet the ambulance at Tall Pines?" said Tina. "I have her bag of clothes."

Henry responded that the clothes should go with Maude in the ambulance and in Maude's case it was better to let the dust settle before family visited at Tall Pines. The driver of the ambulance then seemed, however, to be having some difficulty starting the ambulance. He turned the engine over a couple of times but if anything, the engine noise was getting fainter each time. He then rolled the ambulance off the driveway. It was now situated clean across the country lane. There was just a slight clicking noise. He got out.

"It's broken down. I'm sorry. I've just radioed for another ambulance. Should be here under 30 minutes."

"And the ambulance?" smiled Tina thinking of the awkward residents of Gitthwaite.

"I think they may need to send a forklift to lift it from its position and a tow-truck. An all day job. But don't you worry about getting out of the drive. There is just enough room. I can see people out."

Henry took up the offer and went off to see another client. Tina first went to check on the chickens. She gave them food and water. They would have to make do with someone calling each day until they could be rehomed. Eric and Tina could not keep them in the town. Tina decided she should probably take Claudius with her. She opened the door of the dining room, and he shot out between her legs and headed to the open front door.

"Claudius, Claudius," called Tina but the cat was nowhere to be seen.

Angry neighbour had appeared to berate people for blocking the road. Indeed, a number of vehicles had already had to turn around. He was crestfallen that there was nothing he could do since the blockage was a broken-down ambulance, so he shouted at Tina,

"And if I see that bloody evil looking cat I'll make sure I catch him."

Tina was glad Maude was deaf and was safely sitting inside the ambulance. She hoped Claudius would keep away from the residents of Gitthwaite and resolved to look for him when she next visited and with the help of the ambulance driver extricated her car and left. As it happened, Claudius was never seen again in the village. Eric put signs on the lampposts in the village saying 'Missing pure black cat with white tip to tail. Answers to the name of Claudius'. The signs were soon ripped down and Claudius seemed to have disappeared. There was said Eric, first a poetic justice that the lane was blocked for the evening and second, sense on the part of the cat that he appeared to have left the village. With Maude safely in Tall Pines it was for now a great relief to Eric.

That Friday evening Steven returned to High Cliffe with some good news, namely that he had received a telephone call to tell him that subject to a mass of red tape the promotion would be his. Scyathica and Steven had a very quick celebratory toast before readying themselves for the onslaught. Sure enough, come early evening there was a loud tooting and Uncle Hugo's car drew up at High Cliffe followed by a campervan.

Scyathica held an excited Piper on a lead and Pandora tried to restrain Kitty. The two dogs sniffed and bounced and managed to get Scyathica and her mother tied up in dog leads. With some trepidation Scyathica let both dogs off their leads to bound round the garden. It was plain that actually they were going to be firm friends and playmates.

Champ and Deedee parked the campervan close to the caravan as requested. Although Scyathica and Steven did not relish having the campervan next to them for the night, this was the most appropriate place to put it. Deedee and Champ then stood staring up at the house. Deedee was wearing a bright pink shell suit with sparkles on it. Champ was attired in jeans which looked far too tight and a black t-shirt which bore the motif 'Old rockers never die'.

"Ooh," said Deedee. "Isn't it huge."

Champ was uncharacteristically affable to Steven and slapped him on the back. Embarrassingly he said in ringing tones, "Fallen on your feet, eh, boy?" Steven hoped that Scyathica and her uncle had not heard this.

Everyone including Uncle Hugo then did their best to help Pandora with all her luggage. Her cat 'Wuwu' was still in its carrying case. Scyathica suggested that initially the cat had a limited range and he just be placed in the kitchen.

"William and I are really good friends," said Deedee making an enormous fuss of the tabby Persian cross.

"William?" asked Steven.

"I call him William," said his mother. "I don't see him as a Wuwu...it's... well... too foreign."

Pandora just smiled amiably. She just seemed relieved to be surrounded by people helping her.

Scyathica was delighted everyone was getting on so well. While Pandora unpacked with the help of Deedee, Uncle Hugo took the two dogs for a walk and Steven gave Champ a tour of the West Wing. William as he was now called settled himself in front of the Aga and purred contentedly.

"As you can see," said Steven showing Champ around, "it's smaller than the central part of the house although it is the same height. The rot has been treated. The rewiring done. Many rooms have been plastered. The plumbing is in place. I think we will probably leave the cellars for storage.

"On the ground floor there is space for a huge kitchen diner with a big utility room next to it and a shower room and toilet. We can have a big lounge and there is a little room which could be a study. On the next floor we hope we can have three bedrooms and a bathroom. Then in the attic I would like there to be at least another bedroom with the potential for another one and a boxroom."

"Wow!" said Champ, clearly impressed. "I should try to give your master bedroom an ensuite."

"It's a question of money," said Steven. "Scyathica and I have done a deal with Sir Hugo which meant concentrating on getting it sound. Basically, the wing is ours, but we spent a lot of money on things like the roof. I think we can only do so much at a time."

"I'm surprised that Sir Hugo is letting you spend all your money," said Champ sounding more like his former self.

Steven explained that appearances could be deceptive and that Sir Hugo's generosity to others had left him short of money. He explained how Sir Hugo had prioritised the workers' job at the pig farm and the Knubb Sausage and Bacon factory which he owned over his own comfort. Surprisingly Champ did not argue. Steven supposed Champ knew something of Pandora's predicament. They were then interrupted; Scyathica was now calling people to dinner.

She had laid the table in Sir Hugo's formal dining room using his best silver cutlery and crystal glasses. Sir Hugo, ever affable, asked her about wine. Scyathica produced a Chablis she had chilling for her first course. She had kept it simple and had assembled a prawn cocktail using supermarket prawns and supermarket sauce. She had done her best to use salad and lemon to make it look pretty.

"What's for mains?" said Sir Hugo. "And is there a pud?"

"I've used an old Knubb pig recipe for the main course. It is a version of the old German 'Falscher Hase', false hare meatloaf. The Knubb pig recipe book version is called 'Yummy sausage bunny'. I've done loads of roast potatoes, Uncle, as well, just the way you like them. Pudding is a crumble. There is either cream or ice-cream with it."

"Or both!" said Sir Hugo with a twinkle in his eye.

Sir Hugo offered everyone some claret and with some trepidation Scyathica served everyone piping hot meatloaf, roast potatoes, vegetables and gravy. There were a few minutes silence while everyone tried their meatloaf and roasties. The silence was suddenly broken by Deedee,

"Some ketchup would go lovely with this," she said.

Chapter 7

ON SUNDAY MORNING STEVEN AND Scyathica waved off Steven's parents in their motorhome. Saturday had been spent assisting Pandora to get sorted out followed by an early evening meal at the Harbour View. It had been a surprisingly affable affair. Champ and Deedee expressed a wish to visit again. They had been really surprised by the pleasant scenery. The pub went down well with them as well. Sir Hugo had opted for bar meals rather than the more formal restaurant. Champ indicated he could take a little time off in the summer and he would help Steven and Scyathica with decorating.

"The missus can chat to Pandora, and we can go for some pub meals," he said.

Steven was not sure if it was the effect of Waste or whether his parents had mellowed or whether he had matured or whether it was a combination of the three, but he was getting on with his parents better than he had ever hoped.

Waste's two members of Parliament also left for London on Sunday, Sir Hugo to a room in another Tory MP's flat and Nat to a tiny bedsit in Lambeth. Scyathica was left with the realisation it was just herself and Steven to deal with Pandora's adjustment. Kitty thankfully had made a strong doggy friendship with Piper and William was enjoying his time snoozing in the kitchen. Piper was not interested in chasing the fluffy tabby, so William now had the run of the house. Pandora for the first time looked glum.

"I will miss my London friends," she said. "Even though many of them were very shallow and abandoned me when they knew I had troubles."

Scyathica said, "It's many years since you have been in Waste. Why don't you start exploring it afresh on Monday? We can always give you a lift into town."

Pandora nodded but still looked gloomy.

Sonja Sidebottom had been hoping Nat Cartey would return to London. If he was in London it would hopefully give her some breathing space to calm her father down. She doubted that Brittany Cartey, Nat's wife, would do much to the trees in her husband's absence. She knew Brittany slightly. She had been a few classes below her at school, being younger than Sonja but they had both briefly been in the school choir. The driving force for her brief stay in the choir was her parents; however, she did not stay there long as she had no singing voice. Now, her parents were insisting they took legal action against Nat Cartey "to stop him hacking the trees and to avenge Tinkerbell's death". Sonja knew she would be drawing up statements and court applications in her free time. It was not something she relished.

Penny rose late at the Harbour View; she felt elated by Xavier's talk that sometime in the future they should marry, and he would get her a huge diamond ring. Xavier had already been up for hours. Pierre Bruele had been to see him with some interesting information. One of the Americans interested in buying the football club was said to be heading for Waste. He mentioned the name of the US senator. It was so familiar. Pierre, however, told him there were others who were not so welcome on the way to confront Xavier. Xavier had therefore spent the day interrupting both his French and English lawyers' Sundays. There were exchanges of emails and numbers of phone calls. By the afternoon Pierre was in possession of a Power of Attorney which would let him complete the sale of the football club at a price Xavier had set out if Xavier had had to leave. He also had details of a numbered account where he could send the money once it had been paid to his company. Xavier's plane was ready at the regional airport some miles west of the town of Moorlands if a quick exit was needed. However, for the time being Xavier was enjoying his stay at the Harbour View.

He was, however, put out when he found Penny sitting on the terrace with her bag packed, drinking a coffee. She said,

"Gee, Xavier, darling, can Pierre take me back to Canal Street? I gotta go to work to tomorrow and I got this situation where my folks might show up."

"Cherie," said Xavier, "I thought you were leaving your place behind and going to go travelling with me?"

"Aww, no, gee travelling sounds lovely. I thought we were just seeing each other for the weekend, and we would not be travelling straight after… I hardly see my mom and dad and they are due at Waste. My dad's a US senator so he's so busy…"

Alarm bells rang for Xavier.

"Is he Senator Brad T Morton Wayney junior?" he asked.

"Yeah, why?" said Penny in all innocence.

"Because, you little bitch, as well you know he wants to buy the football club from me."

Penny looked perplexed. "Xavier, I don't know what you mean. Dad hardly speaks to me. Don't be nasty."

"Nasty? Nasty? You are just a spy." Xavier was getting increasingly annoyed.

"'Course I'm not," Penny said in her worst drawl.

"Liar," said Xavier. "Spy."

"You're just being horrible and nasty." Penny started to cry, and because she was upset added a jibe, "I should have stuck with Lewis. He is younger and much better looking than you."

That made Xavier lose it. He slapped her hard across the mouth catching her lip with his signet ring. Penny, as a reaction, picked up her coffee cup and attempted to throw the dregs at him. That only made matters worse. He struck her again with the back of his hand across the face so that she fell off her chair.

Penny screamed, "Help, help… stop, stop."

No-one heard as there was a hubbub of Sunday dinners at the next-door pub. Xavier began yelling at her in French. She tried to get off the ground, but Xavier had her hair. She could feel she was being pulled along the concrete by her hair and she was being kicked every time she resisted. She put a huge effort into turning sharply and biting Xavier in the thigh. Her teeth did not go through the denim of his jeans, but he was just sufficiently surprised to loosen his grip on Penny. She took that opportunity to break free and run. She did not stop for her overnight bag. She did not stop at the Harbour View pub. She just ran and kept running. She ran past Harbour Green. She ran onto Links Road. She ran past the golf links. By the time she got to the executive developments she had slowed to a trot. Every time a car passed, she flinched and hoped Xavier was not looking for her. She felt in her jacket pockets. Her keys and her wallet were there. She was pleased she had not put them in her bag. Her phone was probably there in her pockets too, but she did not want to stop; not until she felt safe.

As she left Links Road and started walking along The Mount, she had a vague idea where she was. She took a footpath into the grounds of High Cliffe. While she knew Scyathica's uncle did not like her some instinct told her that Scyathica would not turn her away.

She approached the house and knocked on the brass doorknocker on the big front door. There was a chorus of dogs barking. Penny half collapsed on the doorstep as the front door opened. Scyathica, Pandora and Steven looked down on her as she sat in a crumpled heap on the doorstep.

"Let's get her inside and find out what's happened to her."

"Pandora?" said Penny recognising Scyathica's mother.

"I live here too, now," said Pandora as they got Penny onto a chair.

She had a split lip, a black eye, there were grazes on her arms and matching rips in her jacket and scrapes and tears to her tall boots which seemed to have largely protected her legs. Penny complained her ribs hurt (where she had been kicked).

"Surely, Lewis didn't do this?" said Scyathica.

"No," said Penny, "I broke up with him," and she told her story.

"I think this should be reported to the police and perhaps we should take Penny to hospital," said Steven.

Pandora and Scyathica both agreed but Pandora said,

"I think we should let Penny just have a little time to compose herself. Also, I know it seems harsh, but Penny, dear, I think I should take some photos of your wounds and your clothes. I'll find you a clean top and jacket from my things, but you should keep your things to show the police. And Steven, dear, make her a cup of strong, sweet tea…"

Steven did as he was told.

Penny sat sipping her tea. She shivered a bit.

"I don't want my parents to see me like this. I know they are coming soon." Scyathica and Pandora tried to reassure her.

"Look," said Pandora. "Scyathica will drive us to the hospital. I'll come in with you if they will let me. Steven can mind the fort. Perhaps, Scyathica, as you know Penny's parents you could email them... something vague… when might they be in town as you might be able to meet up...?"

Scyathica had never known her mother so assertive. Dealing with Penny's problems had certainly distracted her from her own woes.

Penny and Pandora spent several hours at the hospital. Fortunately, apart from one slight crack to a rib there were no other serious injuries. The hospital also photographed Penny's face and bruised torso. Scyathica waited at the newspaper office where she sent the vague email as planned. She caught up with a little work and then collected Penny and Pandora who she took to the police station. The police took an initial report and arranged for Penny to return to give a statement next day. They handed Penny some leaflets on Domestic Violence support agencies.

It was quite late when Scyathica collected them. "Please don't take me to Auntie Bea. He might find me there," said Penny.

"I won't," said Scyathica. "I'll take you back to High Cliffe but one of us should ring her."

Although it was very late Steven telephoned Auntie Bea to explain what had happened.

"I knew no good would come of it," said Auntie Bea. "Her room is waiting for her again when she wants it."

Steven and Scyathica went to work on Monday and Pandora took it upon herself to support Penny. They spent the day between the police station and a domestic violence support group 'Waste women against Violence' (known as 'Wav 'for short). Apart from a brief call at Crunchies' café for refreshment and for Penny to explain she needed a few days off they had no respite. By late afternoon not only did the police have a full statement ("we will look into it further in the next few days") but she had also filled in all the paperwork to apply for an injunction against Xavier. She was advised that although the relationship was relatively short the 'Wav' worker thought she could get a Family Law Act order as there had been apparent talk of engagement to marry and hopefully Penny could therefore get an order to stop Xavier going to Canal Street. She agreed to meet the 'Wav' worker at court at 9.30am next day. Pandora said she would come with her. They took a taxi back to High Cliffe.

Steven and Scyathica were relieved by Pandora's involvement. Steven knew to keep clear of Penny's application at work next day. Scyathica did not think she could break her friend's confidences about what Xavier had said and done, but she saw nothing wrong in telling her boss at the newspaper, Stacey Birch that Xavier was in town. As far as she was aware the press did not know the owner of the football club and part owner of Waste Waste was visiting Waste. Stacey thanked her for the tip and very soon the online version of the local paper had an article titled 'French football boss in town'. This headline was picked up quite far afield by those monitoring the press and web for news of Xavier.

Penny attended the hearing at Waste Combined Court. Pandora sat in the waiting area while Penny had her papers processed and then went before District Judge Cecily Stump with the Wav worker.

District Judge Stump read the papers and looked at Penny's injured face.

"You were not with Mr Le Perte very long, Miss Wayney. I can see you have injuries, but I don't know if you were with Mr Le Perte long enough for the Family Law Act to apply…"

"Madam, may I speak?" asked the Wav worker. The District Judge nodded. "Madam, they did agree to marry so surely that counts?"

"Very well," said the District Judge. "I will grant an order for him not to assault you or harass you or contact you except care of Wav and he will not be allowed to enter any part of Canal Street. I will ask the court bailiff to serve Mr Le Perte. There will have to be a further hearing. The date and time will be on the order. It will be in about a week to ten days' time. I will ask the court to see if a Circuit Judge can take the case because of the potential the case might generate publicity, even though this is a private hearing."

"Will I have to be in court with him?" said Penny. "I really would be very nervous."

"In the circumstances you may enter via the rear entrance to the court and be present via video link from the vulnerable witness room in another part of the building," said the District Judge.

The hearing was soon at an end. Penny and Pandora waited for the paperwork. Penny said she would rather spend one more night at High Cliffe while she waited for the bailiff to give the papers to Xavier, even if Piper the dog tried to share the couch where was sleeping. She phoned Auntie Bea while they waited.

"You've done the right thing, girlie," said Auntie Bea. "Although I think you were unwise to drop poor Lewis, maybe you need to be a bit more independent. In fact, I've got the perfect thing for you when you get back. Steven didn't need the scooter anymore, so I've got it back from him. Get yourself licensed and insured and have a long hard think about your life…"

Penny agreed that Auntie Bea spoke wise words. She collected her order and found a taxi with Pandora. As they rode along, they listened to a report which focused on Knight's Farm, the farm to the east of Waste which had been badly damaged by an explosion last year due to an illegal vodka distillery being present. It appeared residents were concerned about its apparent abandonment and plans for re-development. Bricey from Waste FM was interviewing newly elected Councillor Amina Ahmed.

"Councillor Ahmed, won't a redevelopment of the farm to Waste Waste Waste paper plant bring jobs?" asked Bricey.

"There would be a great cost to the environment with yet another factory to the east of Waste," said Amina.

"You are a new councillor. Isn't it true the council officers are in favour of the planning application and the other councillors are unlikely to vote against it?" said Bricey.

"I think the council has been half asleep. There is no environmental impact study. The farm is in an area not designated for industry," replied Amina.

"But" continued Bricey, "is it not the case that the owner Mr Knight has had to abandon the farm and go into a home since he is too frail to live in a near ruined property?"

"That may be so," said Amina. "But I understand local people favour something more in keeping with its agricultural history. Indeed, I hear Mr Knight left about a dozen sheep behind and local farmers from Farthwaite have been coming over weekly to check on their welfare."

"Aaaw," said Penny listening. "Poor sheep. I don't know why someone doesn't buy the place and turn it into an animal rescue centre."

Pandora said, "That's a lovely idea, but from the sound of it, it might be expensive."

They speculated as to why it was that farmers from Farthwaite and not the nearer village of Gitthwaite or the hamlet of Halfthwaite visited Knight's Farm.

Eric and Tina Ercol were also thinking about Gitthwaite and Halfthwaite. First, there was the matter of looking after Maude's bungalow. They agreed to take turns visiting it and feeding Emperor and the hens. Eric had received a telephone call from the psychiatrist Mr Enstile first thing that morning. It appeared Maude had settled well at the unit at Tall Pines. There would in due course be a 'best interests' meeting which he would be invited to attend. The meeting would discuss Maude's future, so he recommended Eric started to consider the possibility of a care home. Eric recalled there was a highly recommended home at Halfthwaite, Ivy Bank, so he indicated to Tina that they should research Ivy Bank and other homes in the area.

Tina recalled there was no love lost between the residents of Gitthwaite and the hamlet of Halfthwaite because the residents of Gitthwaite nastily called Halfthwaite 'half-wit' due to the dementia patients in the care home.

Eric said,

"One day that nasty lot will be old too."

Chapter 8

SONJA SPENT MOST OF HER free time drawing up the papers for her parents' case. Her father came home each evening and would gaze at his koi carps, Wendy, Peter, Hookie and Never-never to check they were all well. Then he would spend a good thirty minutes examining the hedge and trees on the boundary, which in the light early May evening had a pleasant green sheen. After several days of this Sonja was pleased to be asked to join up-and-coming barristers Chris Ellison and Verity Timpson-Saunders for a drink after work. Steven Hovell and Scyathica had also dropped into the Knubb Arms. It was somewhere which they both enjoyed visiting as a break from their everyday cares. They enjoyed sinking into the old-fashioned armchairs for tea and cakes. On this occasion, Sonja who knew them slightly, beckoned them over.

They were enjoying socialising and discussing local issues.

"I'm pretty new here but even I can tell no-one wants a paper plant on the old farm," said Chris in his Brummy accent. Scyathica said she had heard that local 'Green' campaigners were intending to have a demonstration.

"Who is that?" said Chris suddenly.

A very graceful woman with extremely large dark sunglasses and white leather luggage was leaning against the reception desk in the adjacent hall pinging the bell saying, "'Allo, 'allo ...anyone there?" in what sounded like a French accent.

The landlord Glenn dashed across from the bar and said, "Can I help?"

"I am sorry, I do not 'ave a reservation but I wondered if you might have a room."

"For how long?" said Glenn.

"I am not sure... but I think at least three nights. Can you help?" said the woman.

"I have a room which I'll have to get made up as it has only just been vacated but it is available. I'll have to take some details and a credit card," said Glenn.

"My name is Monique St Pernice," said the woman.

"That's a very unusual name," said Glenn.

"My ancestors came from St Pernicious Island in the West Indies," replied Monique.

"Oh," said Glenn. "This town had a kind of lord of the manor in the eighteenth century, Sir Charles Whitewhisker who freed his slaves on St Pernicious Island. He married a girl from the island too, Solange."

"Yes, it is that island," said Monique. "I think I am descended from some sort of cousin of Solange, Desiree. She left the island and went to France... but zis Sir Charles was not a very good abolitionist because it was such a small island, most people 'ad nowhere to go."

"Are you visiting to check out local history, then?" said Glenn.

"Non," said Monique, "I am trying to track down my 'usband... He is wanted by the police. 'is name is Xavier Didier Le Perte...'e as business interests 'ere. Do you know him?"

Scyathica had heard part of this conversation. She shot out of her seat towards Monique.

"Excuse me," she said, "I am a local reporter. Did you say you were married to Xavier Didier Le Perte?"

"Can I see your press card?" said Monique suspiciously.

"Can I have proof you are his wife?" answered Scyathica.

"Why don't the two of you sit and talk in the lounge bar while I sort out Miss St Pernice's room," said Glenn.

Monique and Scyathica found a quiet table in a corner. Steven looked on as they passed him. Scyathica showed Monique her press card. Monique showed her a French National identity card which named Monique as 'Madame Monique Le Perte'.

"What do the police want him for?" asked Scyathica. "I thought he was a wealthy business man?"

"They want him for two things. One for buying stolen artwork and second, for what he did to me," said Monique.

"What did he do?" asked Scyathica.

Monique took off her sun-glasses and revealed a long scar that ran just above her left eye, causing the eye-lid to droop slightly, and continued just under her eye, and marred her otherwise flawless smooth, black skin.

"I was lucky not to lose my sight in this eye. Xavier was angry with me because I wanted to continue my modelling career and 'ave a little money of my own. 'e said 'e earned more than enough from his businesses and took a glass to me," said Monique. "I ran away and went to the Gendarmerie. It took some time but 'zen the examining magistrate said 'e should be charged. Zen it turned out zat two of the masterpieces in his chateau were paintings originally looted by the Nazis in the war... and sold on by crooks over ze years to people who don't care. There is an international arrest warrant out for him. The police 'ad not located him but I was looking on the internet and saw something which said he was 'ere."

Scyathica said, "I'm amazed they have not caught up with him." She then explained about Penny's troubles.

"I suppose the local police have been given the run-around by him after the bailiff served him with the injunction. Each time they have tried to interview him, there has been an excuse. I am surprised they do not know about the international arrest warrant. Xavier may still be in Waste. After he was served with the injunction papers, he let it be known to the court he wanted to defend it and is due to appear in court tomorrow... if he turns up. He has been staying at the Harbour View pub."

Monique said, "I want him caught. He should pay for what 'e did to me... and did to your friend. I will liaise with the police in London and also go to the local police station here. Please give me your number so I can tell you what is happening."

"My boyfriend is clerk to the court," said Scyathica. "If you don't mind I will tell him what is happening... and Penny. Steven, my boyfriend can alert the court security guards we may have an issue."

Monique agreed with this and Scyathica returned to Steven's side.

"We need to go, Steven," said Scyathica. "I have information which affects Penny and possibly the court tomorrow. We can't talk here. Let's make haste."

First, they called in to Penny who had returned to Auntie Bea's house in Canal Street, where she was recuperating before returning to work. It was unclear what shocked Penny more; the level of violence he perpetrated on Monique or that he was married.

"I can't be the clerk tomorrow, because I know you," said Steven. "But I will go in at seven in the morning to brief the security guards and other staff. Her Honour dela Notte will be hearing the case so I will send a message to her in the morning too."

Penny was also reassured by Scyathica that Pandora would come to the building with her tomorrow, even though the Wav worker should also be there.

When Scyathica and Steven arrived at High Cliffe it was quite late, but Pandora was still up. They told her all the developments. She smiled and said,

"Well I won't be idle. I had a phone call from Hugo. He is having a new prize boar delivered to the pig farm from a farm near Moorlands. The animal has a long name, but I am told they call him Barry. Hugo asked me to go down to the pig farm in the afternoon and take a picture so I could send it to him. Not really my sort of thing at all but of course, I agreed."

Everyone went to bed.

Xavier did not go to bed. He had decided to pack up and make an early departure to the regional airport. He had already instructed his lawyers to have counsel at court to oppose the application on the grounds of jurisdiction. His vanity was such he could not bear to have such an injunction against him even though by the time of the hearing he would be nowhere to be seen. His London lawyers had found an experienced barrister Dr Gordon Flaughtersdough (apparently pronounced 'Flowerdew') who was willing and able to travel from London to Waste. Pierre Bruele would keep him informed and would also stay at Waste to complete the sale of the football club if that could be done quickly. He needed the money. He would need to lie low for quite a while. Thus, very early in the morning he slipped quietly away from the Harbour View pub.

In the early hours of the morning, MPP Farms (Moorlands Pedigree Pigs) started the job of attempting to load Barry, the prize-winning large, white pedigree boar into the animal container. Barry was due to be delivered at Knubb Pigs that morning, but it was going to be a difficult job loading him. A fairly young animal, Barry's main interests were servicing the female porkers and food. He could charm the farmhands if he was in a good mood, and they would scratch him between the ears as they passed. But if Barry did not want to do something it was entirely another story.

That morning he was inside a steel barn in a pen made of concrete breeze blocks with a metal gate. The animal trailer had been backed right up to the gate and had its ramp down. A farmhand had scattered some pig nuts leaving a trail up the ramp into the trailer. Barry was initially asleep in a comfortable heap of straw. The manager and three farmhands peered in at him and opened the gate.

"Cummon, pig, cummon, pig... cummon, Barry," said the manager.

Barry opened one eye. He grunted a little.

"Cummon, pig, cummon, Barry," he said again. Barry stood up but faced the wall away from the opening.

"It's no good," said the manager, "we'll have to go in… Get some pig boards."

The four men got in with pig boards. Barry turned and faced them, and his grunts turned to snarls.

"I'm not staying," said one lad and immediately leaped out. Further help was summonsed as Barry was one very angry pig. Eventually, there were eight men in Barry's enclosure. Four used hurdles to narrow the area where Barry could move. One man had a bucket of food, three men had pig boards and one man had a long yard broom which he pushed at Barry's behind. Barry grunted and snarled and frothed at the mouth. This was not what he had in mind. Eventually, he capitulated and aimed for the trailer where the bucket of food was waiting for him.

"Right," said the manager. "Hopefully we should miss the commuter traffic on the Moorlands' bypass and get him over to Knubb Pigs quite early still. I'll drive. I want two of you with me to help with unloading."

Things, however, did not go according to plan.

When Steven and Scyathica got up that morning they switched the radio on in the caravan. Waste FM gave traffic reports every thirty minutes. Most of the time there was nothing serious to report for the Waste area. The usual accident blackspots tended to be round Moorlands and its bypass. The traffic reporter, whom Scyathica had met a couple of times announced,

"Waste traffic is fairly free flowing although there is some minor congestion near the station car park due to some re-surfacing work. Slightly further afield drivers are advised to avoid the Moorlands bypass which is closed at present due to a serious accident at the Stumpbottom roundabout at about 6 o'clock this morning. Police are trying to clear the roundabout after an accident between a tractor and trailer carrying fertiliser, a small animal transporter and a car. Apparently, there are several tons of manure blocking the roundabout. One person had to be taken to hospital. The area should be avoided for at least the rest of the day."

Scyathica yawned. "I'm glad we are not going that way. Mind you, Uncle's new boar Barry was coming from Moorlands."

When they went in the house they met Pandora in a state of consternation.

"The pig farm manager has told me Barry the boar has been in an accident."

Steven said, "You mean the accident at Moorlands?"

"Yes," said Pandora. "I don't think the animal is injured but they are having terrible trouble trying to get him re-loaded and the police have threatened to get a marksman out and shoot him if there is any danger to the public. I won't phone Hugo for now in the hopes they can load the boar up again."

"There's always something," said Scyathica.

Penny would have agreed with her if asked. As she got ready to go to court, she received a phone call from her father.

"It's Dad, here. We have landed in Enger-land," he said. "We are gonna rest up in an airport hotel. Then we will travel to you tomorrow. We will be staying at a little old inn called the Knubb Arms. But we will come and visit you and see where you are living."

"It's okay," said Penny, "I can visit you."

"No, we want to see where you are living… see how you are doing."

Penny said she looked forward to seeing them and wondered what Auntie Bea would make of them. She mentioned nothing whatsoever about Xavier's attack on her. She was nervous enough about going to court without wanting her dad's business dealings mixed up in her personal life. She did tell them how she was learning to ride a scooter and was doing a quick course so she could legally ride the scooter. The call ended affably enough. Before Scyathica and Pandora picked her up she spoke to Auntie Bea.

"If I didn't have enough to worry me I'm sorry to say my parents will roll up here tomorrow."

"Don't worry," said Auntie Bea, "I'll make sure I get the kettle on. Did you say your mum came from these parts?"

"Yes, in those days she was called Aggie Higginbottom," said Penny.

Auntie Bea started to laugh. "Aggie Higginbottom? Aggie Higginbottom? …Goodness gracious if that is who I think it is her family lived just round the corner in Pither's Street. She got expelled from school if I remember rightly. She truanted a lot to chase the local lads and was made to stand up in front of the whole school in assembly with a cardboard banner saying, 'I am a slut'. As revenge she went out the next day and caught some frogs from the beck. She sneaked them into school and left them somehow in a shoebox in the headmaster's private toilet. He had the fright of his life when he opened the box and the frogs jumped out!"

Penny and Auntie Bea discussed details of her mother's age and when she left Waste. They both agreed this was one and the same person.

Somehow, Penny felt more respect for her mother and wished her mother had talked to her more about her time in Waste. As she was thinking about this Pandora and Scyathica arrived to take her to court. The journey was only about five minutes duration by car. Scyathica stopped at the rear entrance to the court where Penny's Wav worker stood waiting. Scyathica and Pandora drove off to park the car nearby while the security guard showed Penny and her Wav worker to the vulnerable witness room. Penny knew Scyathica and Pandora would not be allowed to come into court, but they had agreed to sit in the waiting area. Scyathica had said nothing to her newspaper employers about the case but had told her manager Stacey Birch she was going to be at court today where she "might or might not" have news of Xavier Didier Le Perte.

Nicky, the usher came to see Penny.

"Is he here?" asked Penny nervously.

"No," said the usher. "There is a barrister Dr Flaughtersdough who is representing him and two police officers who are looking for him, who I've put into a side room. There is a man called Pierre Bruele who says he is his business manager. I've told him he can't come into court and mentioned him to the police."

"I think he has run away," said Penny.

Chapter 9

DR GORDON FLAUGHTERSDOUGH LOVED HIS visits to Waste. They usually involved him staying overnight at the Knubb Arms where he would gorge himself on steak and kidney pie and sticky toffee pudding. He seemed oblivious to the fact that he was not well-liked either by other members of the legal profession who practiced in Waste or the judges. He was wearing a deep purple corduroy jacket which would have better suited a bandleader of the nineteen-fifties and a large black velvet bow-tie. His large floppy moustache had been carefully combed.

The usher Nicky approached him. "Her Honour dela Notte wants to know if your client is coming."

Dr Flaughtersdough replied in ringing tones, "He is not coming. He had other important business. I believe his business manager Mr Bruele is here to assist the court."

He waved his hand towards the waiting area, where Pierre Bruele was sitting.

"This is a family matter so unless he can shed some light on Mr Le Perte's whereabouts he cannot assist the court much," said Nicky.

"Monsieur Bruele," called Gordon in a loud plummy stage whisper. "Where is my client?"

Pierre Bruele sidled over. "I believe, he should have taken off from the airport, although I know I have some missed calls on my phone," he said. "Just a minute."

He phoned and there was a rapid conversation in French.

"That was the pilot. My boss never arrived at the airport," he said.

"One moment," said the usher and went to see Her Honour dela Notte.

"Your Honour," she said, "you know the injunction between the American lady and the football club owner, you've got first, well it's all a bit of a tangle. Miss Wayney and a Wav worker are in the vulnerable witness room. Counsel, Dr Flaughtersdough is here but Mr le Perte is not. His business manager, a Mr Bruele is here. He says Mr Le Perte headed to Moorlands Regional Airport early, but he also says Mr Le Perte never arrived. There are two police officers in the building too and they say they have a warrant to arrest Mr Le Perte."

The usher's internal mobile phone rang. "Sorry, Your Honour, it may be security." She quickly answered it. "It seems more police officers have arrived and Mr Le Perte's ex-wife."

The usually composed Davina dela Notte put her head in her hands. Then she said,

"I suggest you relay the information about Mr Le Perte's whereabouts to the police. You should also update Miss Wayney. I will have my coffee. By the time I have done that I will get my clerk to convene the court. Please let Dr Flaughtersdough know I may require him to call Mr Bruele and I will allow one of the police officers to sit in court while we deal with the issue of his client's whereabouts."

The court convened. Derek Devene the court manager acted as clerk today. He made sure the video link was established to the vulnerable witness room. Dr Flaughtersdough and a police officer were in court. The usher brought in Her Honour dela Notte.

"Court rise," said Derek.

"I have an application," said Dr Flaughtersdough before being invited to speak. "I am instructed that the application should be struck out because Monsieur Le Perte is not an 'associated person'… and for want of jurisdiction… he is a French National and he is not in the country."

"Oh," said Her Honour dela Notte. "But he may well still be here. You should have waited until I invited you to address the court and heeded my message that I might want to hear from Mr Bruele."

"I protest, Your Honour," said Dr Flaughtersdough, looking like a rooster puffing up his chest. "It is an outrage for my client's character to be sullied when the court does not have jurisdiction."

"Usher, please call Mr Bruele," said Her Honour, having none of it.

Pierre Bruele was called and sworn in to give evidence. He explained he was employed as an all-round assistant for Mr Le Perte and gave his address as "usually Paris but currently staying at the Harbour View, Waste".

"Monsieur Bruele, the applicant, Miss Wayney is not represented, and it appears Dr Flaughtersdough represents your employer. The court bailiff signed a certificate that he served your employer at the Harbour View Inn. Has Monsieur Le Perte been staying there?"

"Until recently, Your Honour, during his visit to Waste, but he has left."

"Where was he going?" said the judge.

"I believe he set off early morning for Moorlands Regional Airport," answered Pierre Bruele, "but the pilot of his private jet said he never arrived."

"Did he know the police wanted to arrest him?" asked the judge.

At that moment there was a slight commotion at the back of the court as one of the other police officers tried to come into the courtroom.

"Your Honour, I am sorry for the interruption, but I have vital information about the whereabouts of Mr Le Perte," said the plain clothes officer.

The judge granted a short adjournment to clarify matters. At the resumed hearing some thirty minutes later, it reconvened without Pierre Bruele or the police officers.

"Dr Flaughtersdough is it correct that your client is currently under guard at the United Moorland Hospital pursuant to an international arrest warrant and when he is sufficiently recovered from the injuries he sustained in an accident this morning he will be appearing at Westminster Magistrates' Court since France wishes to extradite him for serious assault and fraud charges?" asked Her Honour dela Notte.

"Your Honour, I fear this is true," said Dr Flaughtersdough, looking deflated. "Can I have an adjournment?"

"Miss Wayney," said the judge. "If Mr Le Perte is extradited you may have no need for an injunction. I propose to time limit your injunction to 3 months. Your application is adjourned generally. You may request it be restored on 48 hours' notice at any time before the order expires in case Mr Le Perte returns after all. Mr Le Perte may also ask the proceedings to be restored on 48 hours' notice... but why he should I don't know. If no-one asks the proceedings to be restored within the life of the order, the proceedings will then be automatically dismissed with no order as to costs. Hope that suits everyone. The court stands adjourned."

The Wav worker nodded enthusiastically to Penny who was a bit overwhelmed. Dr Flaughtersdough's mouth just opened and closed silently like a fish.

To say that Xavier had been unlucky would be one version of what had happened. The Stumpbottom roundabout was a notorious accident blackspot. Nonetheless, lorries and tractors needed to pass through it to bypass the town of Moorlands. Early that morning Xavier in his sporty vehicle, Barry in his animal trailer and a large tractor with a trailer full of manure converged on the roundabout. Xavier, who saw no need to wear a seat belt, should have given way to the tractor and trailer coming from his right but failed to do so. Barry's animal transporter was already established on the roundabout. The tractor driver braked sharply to try to avoid the collision causing the trailer to jack-knife and topple over covering the road with heaps of manure. The animal transporter managed to avoid a collision but came to a halt. Xavier's vehicle skidded into the tractor causing Xavier to catapult out of the car. The manure broke his impact. His injury would have been confined to a fractured wrist if it hadn't been for what he did next.

It took some fifteen or twenty minutes for Xavier to extricate himself from the stinking heaps of manure by which time two police cars had appeared on the scene. At the sight of the police arriving Xavier urgently looked for somewhere to hide and espied the pig trailer. He opened the door at the back of the trailer to let himself inside. Barry had first of all not been happy to be loaded in the trailer but had now been woken from his snooze by an uncomfortable jolt. He was a very angry pig and took the opportunity to sink his teeth firmly into Xavier's leg in protest. He then pushed his way out.

Xavier was actually lucky the police were on the scene to administer first aid and stem the flow of blood. They saved his life, but his leg would never be the same again.

As it happened Barry nearly lost his life too. Moorlands Police were all for getting in a marksman. He stood on top of the heap of manure grunting and growling. The men from MPP pigs were terrified he would move away from the scene. One lad had the idea to try and quell Barry's no doubt building thirst. He ran about one hundred metres to a nearby pub, the Moorlands Windmill Inn and returned a short time later with a half-full barrel of beer. He opened the bung and let the brown hoppy liquid run out into the adjacent gully. Barry lapped it up and then did what any self-respecting pig would do; settled himself down for a snooze on top of a heap of manure.

The MPP men took the opportunity and after some pushing, coaxing and shoving and help from half a dozen police officers Barry wobbled his way back into his trailer where he promptly went to sleep.

The marksmen were disappointed, but the police were insistent they took advice as to whether Barry would have to be put down in the circumstances. Eventually they agreed it was Xavier's fault he had got bitten; besides, Barry had done the police a favour in making sure he didn't get away. Better late than never a hung-over pig was delivered to Knubb Pigs.

Dr Flaughtersdough went off to the Knubb Arms to find something for lunch. The plain clothes police had an interesting discussion with Pierre Bruele who reassured them he would be at the Harbour View for some time to come. After he had finished his conversation, he too went into the pub for a drink. He went to the bar rather than the lounge area to avoid the good doctor who was tucking into a large steak pie. As he swirled the brandy in his glass, he looked up to see Monique standing beside him.

"Merde," he said.

Monique laughed. She had by now heard what had happened to Xavier. They indicated to each other that during their remaining stay in Waste they would be civil to each other. Monique said she was only staying on a short time longer to discover a little of the history of Waste and its connection with her ancestors.

Penny, Scyathica, Pandora and the Wav worker had been sitting in an interview room in the courthouse digesting the outcome of the hearing. Penny was glad the hearing was all behind her before her parents arrived. She did not know what impact the incidents would have on her father's purchase of the football stadium. She hoped knowledge of her brief and unfortunate entanglement with Xavier would not come to her father's attention. If it did she would have to deal with it. Penny thanked the Wav worker. Pandora added,

"Could I please have a card. If it is possible, I would like to train as a volunteer to assist people…"

Scyathica was pleasantly surprised by her mother's interest. Pandora continued, "I have a driving licence but I need to do a refresher course and get a little car so I can get to your offices and the court or other venues independently. It may be a few weeks before I am in touch. I have been very impressed with your work."

The Wav worker seemed genuinely pleased as well and handed a card to Pandora before she left.

Scyathica said, "Is it okay if I call you a taxi, Mum? I have somewhere to go for a story for the paper. Auntie Bea's is on the way so I can drop off Penny. I am going back to Knight's Farm. There is supposed to be some sort of demo there against redevelopment to Waste Paper."

Penny said, "Do you mind if I come?"

Pandora said, "I'm in no rush. I'll come too. I doubt there will be some huge demonstration."

How right she was.

Scyathica drove to Knight's Farm and parked her car where she had parked it on the day of the explosion. As they walked up the track, she thought how lucky she was not to be badly injured the day it blew up when she went to interview Jim Knight. It had given her a 'scoop' for the news media, but it also left her feeling a little nervous today. It started to rain; the early May weather was unexpectedly dismal. As they proceeded up the track they passed a rather forlorn 'For sale' board from a local estate agents, which was leaning at an angle into the dry stone wall. There was initially no sign of any demonstrators. It was only as they approached the entrance to the farmyard that they saw four rather forlorn figures with a banner on a stick saying, 'say no to the paper factory'.

"Who are you?" said one of them.

"I'm press," said Scyathica and indicating to Pandora and Penny, "and they have just come out of curiosity."

"Are you the only local press coming?" said the spokesperson.

"Well, I can't speak for other news outlets," said Scyathica taking a quick photo on her phone of the four figures and their banner, "but from Waste FM and the related paper, it's just me."

"Right then," said the spokesperson, "we are off then. No point in staying. We will try for a demo outside the Town Hall next time," and with that the bedraggled bunch set off down the track away from the farm.

"Gee," said Penny. "Not much of a demo." Then she looked about her. "I'm having a look at the farm." The gate had a padlock on it but before anyone could stop her, she shinned over the gate.

"Penny," said Scyathica, "haven't you had enough trouble?"

"I'll just have a little look; I won't go in anywhere," said Penny and with that she had a quick look around.

A low, stone outbuilding which must have once been a small barn was just a heap of rubble. The neighbouring outbuilding had a gaping hole in the roof. Half a dozen sheep had come to a small gateway and were peering through the aperture. The windows in the house were boarded up. To the rear of the house was what should have been a small cottage garden, but it was now quite overgrown. A bird of prey wheeled above the farm looking for mice making a "peewit" sound, and there were a few bleats from the sheep. The only other thing to be heard was the splashing of the nearby beck.

Penny came back. "What a peaceful place," she said. "It's not as badly damaged as I expected. It would make a great place for an animal rescue centre. I don't think it should be a factory. I think when I can ride my scooter in a few days I might take another look. Maybe some animal charity might be persuaded to buy it."

"Oh, Penny," sighed Scyathica.

After Scyathica had dropped off Penny at Canal Street, she called in quickly at the newspaper office to tell Stacey Birch she would send in what there was of her story complete with picture of damp demonstrators later that afternoon. Pandora stayed in the car and phoned Knubb Pigs. She was able to establish that Barry the boar had only recently arrived and was being examined by a vet. She asked Scyathica on her return to drop her off at the pig farm. She would come up to the house later, on foot. Scyathica continued to be pleased and surprised by the changes in her mother. Here was a "lady who lunched" now not only contemplating becoming a domestic abuse support worker, but taking a definite interest in matters agricultural.

Pandora tried not to give her life in London too much thought. Here were people who had helped her but also people she could help. She did not think the years of being idle while supported by Davey Scarlett were valuable years anymore, save it had resulted in a daughter of whom she felt proud.

She was greeted by the pig farm manager who proffered an overall and some shoe covers before she entered the particular barn where Barry was situated. He had been placed in a separate enclosure in a corner which had a strong breeze block wall and metal gate. Barry was standing in the corner eating from a food trough, his male equipment clear to see.

"He's a big boy," said the manager, "so I hope he'll do the job he was brought in to do. The vet could not find anything wrong with him. As he's a new animal to the farm we'll let him be on his own for a couple of weeks… and then there is a door at the back of the enclosure … we'll hopefully be able to open that, and he can join a paddock of outdoor gilts…"

"Gilts?" asked Pandora.

"Females who have not yet farrowed a litter," replied the manager, "from which I hope we will get a lot of litters if Barry proves his worth."

With the agreement of the manager Pandora took some pictures of Barry to send to Hugo. Then she walked up to the house. That evening after Pandora had dinner and a bottle of wine with Scyathica and Steven she phoned Hugo.

"You would not believe the adventure your new boar has had in arriving at the farm," she said. She recounted the story to Sir Hugo.

"Good heavens," he said. "The media was banging on about a pig and a road accident near Moorlands and the pig helping to secure a man wanted by the police. I never dreamed it was Barry the boar, or how close he came to being shot. It seems to me I am now the owner of a famous pig."

Chapter 10

HER HONOUR DAVINA DELA NOTTE met District Judge Eric Ercol in the car park, and they talked as they entered the building of the courthouse.

"How is your mother, Eric?" she asked.

"Actually, there is a 'best interests' meeting this afternoon. The hospital wants to discharge her soon. Tina and I have sadly concluded she cannot go home. We have found a suitable home, Ivy Bank, not far from her bungalow, actually. They are used to dealing with old people with Mum's issues. Thankfully she has stopped talking about being a witch. I don't think she can even remember her bungalow or her cat now," he replied.

"Changing the subject," said Her Honour dela Notte, "I have a case today which started with you. Do you recall Patella O'Hanrahan?"

"Yes of course," said Eric.

"I hear that dreadful man Gordon Flaughtersdough has been in Waste again," said Davina dela Notte. "I just hope he does not turn up on this case. As you know it is quite complex."

She need not have worried. Steven Hovell was her clerk. Ivan Huff as usual represented the council, Bernie Blunt the applicant and Sue Rosemary the child. May Lou O'Hanrahan had been released from prison under an early release scheme and was represented today by Chris Ellison. When the matter came before the court, she seemed a lot quieter than she had been in prison. The report from the council and the Children's Guardian were hugely favourable to Lavinia Levi. It was felt that she could cope with the challenges of parenting Patella (or 'Pauline' as she was to be called) as a woman despite starting as the child's father. There was a little less certainty as to how she would cope with May Lou. There was a surprise, however, in store.

As the hearing begun Chris Ellison rose to his feet.

"If it pleases, Your Honour," he said in his strong Brummy accent. "There are some developments of which my Learned Friends and the court need to be aware since they were expecting a contested trial today."

"Please continue," said Her Honour.

"My client was released from prison only a week ago. She is staying in supported accommodation. We have had time to have the benefit of a long conference. My client has come to the conclusion she cannot have her daughter where she is… and that she has a great deal of work to rebuild her own life ahead of her. We have had a long talk about the reports and how the court will view them. My client also now realises that…eh hm... Patella … is more likely to be used as a name for a bone than a child…"

Steven Hovell bit his lip to stop himself from laughing. Her Honour dela Notte remained poker-faced.

Chris Ellison continued.

"My client also realises that as well as her daughter being called Pauline in the future, Miss Levi would be able to give her the home she needs. Your Honour, I know there have been some questions raised about the management of contact. My client would like the local authority to start with supervised contact at their children's centre, but she suggests things might be able to quickly move on to some sort of community-based contact. She appreciates Miss Levi will need to have confidence in her."

May Lou O'Hanrahan sat quietly peering into her lap. Lavinia Levi smiled nervously.

"I think you may wish me to stand the case down, while you have a discussion," said Her Honour dela Notte.

And indeed, the case was stood down and after about forty-five minutes the parties returned with their counsel. An adjournment had been agreed. Steven Hovell confirmed he could find the case a suitable date in the correct timeframe. In the meantime it appeared that all was satisfactory for Pauline, as she was now to be called, to start living with Miss Levi albeit with the care order still in place. Davina dela Notte was very pleased that Chris Ellison seemed to be the exact opposite of Dr Gordon Flaughtersdough. It would serve him and his clients well.

Bernie Blunt was pleased at the early finish to this case. He was not so pleased when Sonja Sidebottom came into his office and asked for a day off at a time when he knew he would be short staffed.

Sonja had helped her parents issue their application against Nat Cartey. Things had remained quiet when he had been in Westminster, but he then came back for a few days. Although no further work had been done, the scaffolding still stood erected around the trees. On one occasion when Nat Cartey seemed all too aware that Bertram Sidebottom was in the garden, he had gone to the end of the garden with a pair of secateurs and stood provocatively next to a gap in the hedge closing and opening them. During the time he was home Sonja's father would peer frequently through the trees into Nat Cartey's garden. He was constantly checking his koi carp. He had taken Tinkerbell to the local vet for a post-mortem, but the local vet had laughed and said that he was not a fishmonger! The proprietor of the Waste aquatic centre said that most likely Tinkerbell had had a parasite, and the pond might need some filtration. Much to Marjorie Sidebottom's disapproval Tinkerbell had then been placed in the freezer she had in the garage for fruit and extra bread.

"Really," she said. "Much as I support the case against that awful man Cartey, I don't want us to accidentally eat Tinkerbell."

Sonja was relieved that the court had given the case a listing slot in June.

When Sonja told Bernie he would need some time off to support her parents at the court, he expressed his displeasure.

"I don't want anything to do with it and I would rather you didn't... but if you must... you must."

He then gave her a list of eighteen witnesses to interview in a road traffic case resulting from a pallet lorry overturning on the Stumpbottom roundabout near Moorlands.

Things, however, went a little better for Eric and Tina Ercol. All the professionals agreed that Maude should go and live in Ivy Bank and by the end of the week she had arrived there.

"What a lovely hotel," she told the staff.

Eric was pleased Maude had forgotten Claudius because he had never found a trace of him. He hoped he could rehome the Emperor, and the hens soon and he put a little note on the court noticeboard and an ad in the local paper. Penny read the ad and thought wistfully of Knight's Farm.

Her parents had arrived the day after her court hearing. They had settled into the Knubb Arms and had then taken a taxi to 3 Canal Street.

Auntie Bea had astutely put out the best crockery for tea or coffee in the front room and a tin of fancy biscuits.

"What a lovely quaint little place you have," said Senator Brad perching gingerly on the largest armchair.

"Thank you," said Auntie Bea. "Would you like tea or coffee?"

"I don't like your English coffee," said the senator, "so I'll have a cup of your English tea."

Penny took her mother to see her room.

"It's not very big, but I have everything I need," she said before they returned downstairs.

"Now tell us all about your stay in Waste," said Penny's father. Penny told them about her time in Waste leaving out her adventures with Xavier. Fortunately, the physical evidence of his assault had all but faded away.

"And now?" said her father.

"Well, I've nearly finished the formalities so I can ride the motor scooter on the road. I have been practicing at the back of the allotments. I am going to keep on with the job at the café and look into doing something with animals. I have always rushed into things in the past but this time I will try not to do it. I will also give myself six months to complete my Master's and if I do not do it... so be it."

"What sort of thing with animals?"

"Some sort of animal rescue work. There does not seem to be an animal rescue centre here. There is a tumble-down farm which would for example make an ideal place. I don't have the resources but maybe one of the local animal charities might be able to do something. It has a house and land and is by a stream. But anyway, that's the general idea," said Penny.

"And boyfriends?" said her mother.

"There was someone, Lewis, but I broke up with him," said Penny. "I wish I hadn't."

Auntie Bea had been listening and decided the subject needed changing.

"Now then," she said to Alannah. "You're Mrs Wayney now, but as I live and breathe, I believe you are Aggie Higginbottom whose folks used to live round the corner, who used to play with my nephew Norman Ryder. You are the girl that got expelled from school for leaving frogs in the headmaster's cloakroom."

The senator looked stunned. "I've never heard about this before. I knew you came from round here."

Alannah said, "Yes, that's me, 'frog girl'. That's partly why I left Waste. The name of 'frog girl' was used by everyone and I had enough of it."

"Gee, Mum, I wish you said," said Penny. "You always seemed so perfect compared to me."

Alannah spoke a little about her time in Waste and explained that she had been expelled from school and that the nickname she had received locally had made her feel hugely embarrassed and hurt. She had left Waste in order to make a fresh start. However, she added,

"Somehow, I think inwardly I missed the old place and I'm glad to visit now."

Penny and Alannah both smiled, and Penny felt more confident in herself than she had for years.

The senator smiled. "You know what?" he said. "I'm proud of both my girls," and put an arm around each of them.

Auntie Bea looked smugly satisfied.

She then asked Penny's parents about their immediate plans. The senator replied,

"I have a meeting tomorrow with Monsooor Le Perte's business manager, a guy called Brew or Broole at the soccer stadium. Le Perte is not around apparently but this guy has Power of Attorney so if I like what I see I'll buy the club. Other than that, I hope to sight-see a little and spend time with my daughter."

Neither Penny nor Auntie Bea blinked when Xavier was mentioned.

Alannah added, "We might also take some of your friends out for dinner while we are here. Your father was also thinking of getting a little place if he was buying the football club and if he felt you were putting down roots here. To be honest I was not so keen. My parents are dead, and I have mixed memories of Waste."

"Well," said the senator, "maybe I should look at the tumble-down farm you mentioned, Penny, if I buy the stadium. If it is worth renovating it might be a nice quaint little place, we could vacation in… in little ol' Waste without bad memories for your mum."

Auntie Bea accepted an invitation to be taken out to tea with Penny by Alannah while the senator visited the football stadium next day. They went to some tea-rooms by Waste Water not far from the Harbour View pub and sat eating scones and Victoria sandwich as boats went in and out of the yacht basin. The senator found his visit to the stadium enjoyable and fruitful. The players put on a demonstration of their skills, and he was given drinks and snacks in the Directors' box. He was pleased to see the fabric of the stadium looked fairly solid and well looked after to the naked eye. Pierre Bruele had documents ready prepared and the price was as previously discussed so the senator was happy to close the deal. He then took a taxi to the tea-rooms and spent a little time admiring the view with Penny, Alannah and Auntie Bea. He downed a cool glass of lemonade and tried a piece of cake.

"It's real pretty here," he said. "Think I'll see if I can look at that farm soon."

Pierre Bruele headed to the Knubb Arms. He was aware that although the senator was staying at the Knubb Arms he was joining his family near the Harbour View, and he particularly wanted to avoid Penny. He did not want to cause awkward questions. He was standing at the bar enjoying his brandy when a voice said,

"I take it you've sold my 'usband's stadium?"

"Hello, Monique," he replied. "Yes, I have."

"So, he gets money, yet again," she said.

"Not exactly," said Pierre. "He thinks I am sending the money on from the company account to a numbered account, but I had to agree with the police not to do anything like that, otherwise they spoke of arresting me as well."

Monique smiled. "My divorce lawyer in Paris will be pleased to know that. But what will you do now?"

Pierre smiled back. "I think I will stick around. Maybe buy a bar or something and get a visa to remain…"

"With what money?" said Monique. "Let me guess; you took agent's commission!"

"It was all above board in the documents," said Pierre. "But what about you?"

Monique replied, "I will finish my little holiday in Waste and hope my lawyers can get my divorce settlement money. Then I hope I can go to the island of St Pernice; perhaps buy a little place out there."

She slid off her bar stool. "Au revoir, Pierre."

Pierre downed his brandy and headed back to the Harbour View pub. Next morning, he contemplated his next moves. There was something about the area which had got to him. Even if Xavier wriggled his way out of things and it was hard to see that he would do so, he was done with being a dogsbody for a crook. It was time to move on and have an honest business of his own.

The senator was also contemplating his moves. Alannah and himself sat in the lounge of the Knubb Arms going through brochures collected from the local estate agents in the town square.

That afternoon Eric and Tina were able to visit Maude for the first time at about 4 o'clock at Ivy Bank.

As they were shown into her bedroom initially there was no flicker of recognition from Maude. She was sitting in a high-backed armchair at first peering out of the window at a hedge but then she turned her head. She looked at them for several minutes and said,

"You look just like my son and his wife."

"That's who we are," responded Eric as he brought some pictures and ornaments from out of a bag to personalize the room.

"Shall I call for them to bring you tea?" said Maude as if she was the lady of the manor.

"It's alright, Mum," said Eric, "we just had tea," which wasn't true. They showed her the pictures for the walls and gave her a book with photos of kittens playing with balls of wool.

She asked no questions about Claudius or her past life and seemed well and happy. The visit was a success.

As they drove away Eric breathed a sigh of relief that his mother had settled in so well. He turned on the radio. It was the tail end of the headlines.

"And in local news," said the newsreader, "the issue of Knight's Farm came before Waste Borough Council today. Councillor Amina Ahmed gave an impassioned speech against the outline planning application made by Waste Waste to redevelop Knight's Farm as a paper plant. The full council voted to reject the application. Mr Woodhouse, manager, at Waste Waste said there was now doubt whether the company would buy Knight's Farm. The Knight family were not available for comment. And now the weather…"

"I wonder," said Tina, "who on earth would want that place. Unlike Maude's bungalow, it's a bit of a wreck. Still, I suppose we have the job of sorting out what we do with Maude's place for the future."

She was obviously not aware that the senator had spent the day booking a hire car and appointments to view properties and that Knight's Farm was top of the list.

Chapter 11

SENATOR WAYNEY AND HIS WIFE enjoyed touring the area. There was slight irritation on his part, when, what was supposed to be his vacation was interrupted by Waste FM seeking an interview about the acquisition of the football club and he also found he was invited to attend a fans' forum at the stadium. He need not have worried. Waste FM decided the slightly softer tone of Scyathica was needed for the interview than a full onslaught by Bricey. The interview was broadcast on Melvyn Brice's show and the senator's involvement was by and large well-received particularly when he revealed his wife came from Waste and his daughter lived in Waste. At the fans' forum, held at the stadium bar, he was offered sausage sandwiches and pork pie and plenty of beer. Perhaps, his one concern was that the fans seemed keen for him to build a new stand and to spend money on players. Otherwise, he was pleased with his involvement.

Knight's Farm was of considerable interest to him. The farmhouse, although run-down had four bedrooms. There was about twenty acres of land which included an area of waterfront. The agent was encouraging and told him the local council was very supportive of ecotourism. Whereas an attempt to build a paper plant had failed, the agent felt the council might be more amenable to say a planning application for some yurts or log-cabins for eco-tourism purposes. An idea was growing in the senator's mind that he could end up with a vacation home, fulfil Penny's ambitions and set her up running a little business for him. It appears the Knight family were now prepared to accept a very low price for the property so he hoped he could persuade his wife and daughter to support his ideas.

He arranged to take Penny out to dinner with Alannah and invited Scyathica and

Steven to join them. He thought he might sound out Penny in the presence of her friends. He hoped it was not too underhand. He had booked a table at the Harbour View pub in its restaurant. Initially he was irritated as they were placed on a corner table which he felt was a little cramped.

"Say," he said, "I want a bigger table."

They were duly moved but the restaurant was having a bad day, so service was very slow. Nonetheless, the senator managed to throw off his dissatisfaction with English establishments and have a discussion about Knight's Farm. Any bad memories of Harbour View for Penny were cast to one side by thoughts of Knight's Farm.

"I was just giving thought to whether the little old farmhouse might be modernised inside. Penny, how would you feel about say living there, but your mom and I using it on visits?"

Penny gave a cautious, "Yes… but what about an animal rescue centre?"

The senator said to Scyathica and Steven, "Do you think there is any need for an animal shelter in these parts?"

Scyathica said, "Well, I think the nearest rescue centre is at Moorlands and it takes mainly cats and dogs. What sort of animals were you thinking about, Penny?"

Penny replied, "I guess mainly farm animals which no-one wanted like those abandoned sheep, chickens which had stopped laying… that kind of thing. Maybe even some cats and some small dogs. I was a bit nervous around Piper because he was so energetic."

Scyathica said, "I know there is an ad at the moment for someone trying to rehome a cockerel and half a dozen hens."

Steven said, "That's one of our judges. They were his old mum's hens. She had to go into a home. I think an animal sanctuary is a good idea."

"Well, if you are to have an animal sanctuary, it would have to be paid for," said the senator. "So there is a catch, Penny, as long as there would be a market for what I have in mind. What I was thinking is that you might run a little eco-tourism business, looking after some cabins or yurts which we might get erected with views of the lake. People would not be completely 'off-grid' since I am sure they would want water and such like…"

Penny said, "That's a great idea. Do you think customers would come, Scyathica?"

"Correctly marketed, I do," she replied.

Penny said, "Do you think I am up to running it?"

All the other persons at the table unanimously said, "Yes."

"That's settled, then," said the senator. "I'll buy Knight's Farm and pay for renovations and infrastructure for the shelter and eco-tourism. The rest, Penny, will be up to you."

Scyathica and Steven remarked to each other as they drove home that they were glad that it sounded like Penny would be entering a better phase in her life. They also commented that the West Wing was progressing well enough that hopefully they would not have to winter together in the caravan. The kitchen was finished and there was a useable bathroom. If Champ was as good as his word and helped with the decorating in his summer holiday in August, the West Wing would be finished quite soon. They could conclude the formalities with Uncle Hugo and then they would have the job of furnishing it. Steven's slightly higher salary would help with expenses a little. Scyathica did not see a means to increase her salary. Her paternal uncle, Lord Coldharbour of Southend, who was in reality her boss had tried to lure her back to London, but she was settled now with Steven at Waste.

Neither Steven nor His Honour Judge Oliver Grasby KC were looking forward to their next day in court. It was a hot fine summer day in the first week in July. The case of Bertrand and Marjorie Sidebottom v Nathanial and Brittany Cartey looked horrible on paper and Oliver felt it would be even more horrible in court. His nerves felt a bit frayed as it was. Since the weekend with the Stiffles, Annette had exacted revenge on him by making him cut down his cigar smoking. When she was home from London she would appear in the potting shed and forestall his efforts to have a quiet smoke. His walks with Aziz Ahmed had continued. It was during those walks that he had the main opportunity to smoke his pipe or a cigar. Oliver had not slept well. That evening he had received by email an opening submission by Dr Gordon Flaughtersdough, who it appeared had been instructed by the Sidebottoms under the Bar direct access scheme. The urbane Percy Vere was representing the Carteys. He supposed he should not have been surprised by that, since he understood Percy Vere now had political ambitions in the Labour Party and of course Nat Cartey was Waste East's Labour MP.

Oliver did not like neighbour disputes. Give him a good criminal trial for affray or robbery any day! There were long pleadings, submissions, and statements. There were references to dead koi carp and dead patches in lawns. There were references to old case law about the right to trim overhanging trees, there were references to the Party

Wall Act and there were references to old trespass and nuisance cases. The long and the short of it was that there were four trees and some hedging growing right on a boundary. The owners of the neighbouring properties, should, in Oliver's opinion have gone to arbitration led by a Chartered Surveyor but both of them had now dug in their heels. Bertrand Sidebottom was obsessed with his koi carp and Nick Cartey now felt he had his reputation to protect.

Steven was aware of the difficult characters involved and the possibility the case might attract publicity. He also was training a brand-new court clerk who was shadowing him. Lindy Pinney had taken early retirement from teaching due to stress; her husband had been a police officer in London and was retired from the police. They had moved to Waste to start a new life. She had now joined the court service and he thought there was considerable irony in this. She was extremely quiet, but he of course recalled how quiet he had been when he arrived.

Steven got the usual, "Morning, Shovel," from Oliver Grasby and responded politely.

Speaking to Lindy he explained, "It's his little joke. I used to correct him but now I ignore it. He seems fierce and gruff, but he has a tremendous sense of humour. From time to time, he will pick somebody to wind up. If he says anything to you which seems jokey, best to just smile! He is a very fair judge when it comes to it."

Lindy nodded, looking unsure. He continued, "When we are in court just watch and listen, particularly to what I do. The case involves an action between a local surgeon and his wife and a local MP and his wife. There were no TV people around outside and only a couple of reporters so thankfully the national press doesn't seem to have caught up with it. We have one barrister, Mr Vere, who really is rather good and another barrister Dr Flaughtersdough, who, shall we say is a character."

With the assistance of Nicky, the usher they got everyone assembled in court.

Dr Gordon Flaughtersdough was attired in pinstripe trousers but his jacket in no way matched his trousers. At least it was black, but it was black corduroy and colourless and had two pockets with zips on each breast. He sported a small pink bowtie with green spots and a pink shirt. He had no gown or stiff collar. Percy Vere was correctly attired with wig, gown and tabs over a pinstripe suit. He was looking at his opponent with an almost imperceptible smirk on his face.

His Honour Judge Grasby KC did not look pleased.

"Dr Flaughtersdough, I may not be able to hear you," he said.

Dr Flaughtersdough boomed in response in his thick plummy voice, "Your

Honour, is that because you have an affliction with your hearing today? I thought there might be a problem with my attire."

Oliver sighed audibly. "There is nothing wrong with my hearing. Dr Flaughtersdough you should know my comment was a question about your attire, phrased in a traditional way. I could have been blunt and asked you not only where your correct court dress was… but why you have arrived looking like a cross between a waiter and a bandleader."

"I fear half my clothes were lost on the train, Your Honour," said Gordon. "I came up early this morning and when I reached court, I noticed I was only holding one bag, not two… but I do have all my papers!"

"Couldn't you have tried to borrow something?" said His Honour.

"I did try," was the reply, "but all other counsel said they needed their robes."

Sonja Sidebottom who was sat at the back of the court, looked at the floor wincing. Her parents had said they wanted older experienced counsel and of course not all counsel on the direct representation scheme were free to come to Waste. The more she argued not to have Dr Flaughtersdough, the more her parents wanted to have him.

"Well," said Oliver, "I want to get on with the case, we have only three hours as this is listed for an interim injunction and directions not a full trial. I will allow your improper dress this once but see it does not happen again."

Both counsel gave opening submissions. There were no surprises for Oliver save for some histrionics from the good doctor who had a big tear rolling down his face, when referring to "the tragic death of Tinkerbell". Oliver had a determined effort to persuade the parties to go to arbitration, but they were having none of it.

When Dr Flaughtersdough called the Sidebottoms to give evidence, without making much effort Percy Vere managed to demolish anything worthwhile in their evidence. Bertrand Sidebottom had to admit he had not an iota of evidence that Tinkerbell had been killed by the Carteys or that her death was connected to the trimming of the trees. Nat Cartey, on the other hand, thus far performed well in the witness box. Scyathica was sat in the back as court reporter when Nat was giving his evidence, going on about his good reputation as the town's MP. She wondered what everyone would have thought in court if they knew his true identity. However, she had made a pact with him not to disclose he was really the son of media Baron Lord Coldharbour in order that he would not mention her father, disgraced financier and businessman Davey Scarlett. These days she was not so bothered that people knew who her father was for her own sake but did not want to embarrass either her mother or her Uncle Hugo. She just hoped that Xavier Didier Le Perte's involvement and her father's involvement in the investment company which had a large stake in Waste Waste did not do harm to the town. As for Nat Cartey aka Nathanial Coldharbour, she doubted his wife Brittany knew his real origins and did not think he could keep things dark forever.

The case had plodded for what seemed an interminable time due to frequent issues with Dr Flaughtersdough; it took up the whole morning and went into the afternoon. He was a few minutes late back at lunchtime. He seemed to need extra toilet breaks.

"Look," said Oliver, "we have only just started Mr Cartey's evidence. I have a criminal plea and directions I need to hear this afternoon. Realistically I don't think we are going to finish in the thirty minutes I can afford to give you. This case will have to go part heard."

No-one seemed very pleased about this since there would now be difficult questions of co-ordinating everyone's availability. It could be many weeks before the case resumed.

Steven whispered to Oliver, "Your Honour, you do have a week in August. That car-ringing trial has just gone out of the list."

"Right," said Oliver, mentioning the dates, "I can set aside a full day... that is, unless everyone else is on holiday?"

"I never go on holiday," said Dr Flaughtersdough in plummy tones. "But I'll check with my clients." The Sidebottoms nodded agreement.

Percy Vere replied, "I can put back my departure to Tuscany for a few days. My client says he was only planning a 'staycation' in the UK this year."

"The date is settled then," said Oliver. "I'll rise," which he did. Everyone shuffled out of the court except Steven and Lindy Pinney.

Scyathica said, "See you later," in a stage whisper as she left.

"My girlfriend," said Steven to Lindy; but as he said it he realised she ought to be more than that.

Oliver went back to his Chambers and rummaged for his pipe and some tobacco. He would do his plea and directions and then get outside for a smoke. Steven went to see him with Lindy trailing in his wake.

"Your Honour, can we resume quickly before the prison van takes him away again?" said Steven.

"That would not do at all," said Oliver. "I can't leave Mr Dennis Shagg unsentenced, well Shagg by name, Shagg by nature."

As they headed back to court, Lindy asked, "What did he mean?"

Steven replied, "While Mr Shagg was on bail for stealing some shagpile carpets out of the back of a truck, he was arrested with a ring selling shag tobacco which had been imported illegally. Unfortunately, he was bailed again. He then allegedly got high and was spotted by a goods' train driver on the way to Waste Waste doing something unfortunate to one of Knight's sheep. They say they don't know who was more surprised... the train driver or the sheep."

Lindy went red and then started laughing. "Well the work isn't dull, is it?"

When Steven arrived at High Cliffe that evening he found Scyathica in the kitchen of the main house.

"Uncle Hugo has popped back for a couple of days," she said, "so I'm just making dinner for all four of us. Mum said she is doing well on her driver refresher course and is picking up a second-hand car she has decided to buy, tomorrow."

"Well," said Steven, "I did want to have a word about something without Pandora and Hugo. Can we go for a walk after dinner?"

"Yes," said Scyathica. "It won't be long. It's a quick salmon thing. Can you get a nice, chilled chardonnay out of the fridge?"

It was not long before she was taking new potatoes and a crisp green salad through to the dining room. She then brought out a dish from the oven, filled with salmon fillets and a mixture of cream cheese, chives and cherry tomatoes.

"Just the thing for a summer evening," said Pandora.

After dinner, Steven took Scyathica by the hand. "Let's walk," he said, and they did for about twenty minutes.

They sat down on a fallen tree at the edge of a coppice of trees.

"Today," said Steven, "I said to the trainee clerk Lindy that you were my girlfriend. I don't want to do that anymore."

Scyathica looked crestfallen and horrified. "We can't possibly be breaking up," she said in a panicked voice.

"No, no," said Steven, "I've put it all wrong. I want to refer to you as something much better, more permanent than a girlfriend. It ought to be wife."

"Are you trying to propose to me?" said Scyathica laughing now.

"I suppose I am," said Steven. "But I'm doing a dreadful job of it, aren't I?"

"Yes, you are," said Scyathica laughing again. "Well, you're not exactly on one knee and where's the ring?"

This time Steven looked crestfallen. "Well, I thought I might take you to choose something at the jewellers or the antique centre on Saturday. I can go on one knee if you want?"

He tried to get on one knee but came into contact with sharp stones on the ground and started swearing.

"Get up, you twit," said Scyathica. "Of course I'll marry you. I thought we would get round to it at some point anyway."

"Shall we tell your mother and your uncle when we get back?" said Steven pulling Scyathica close to him as he sat down on the log again. "Should I phone my folks?"

"Naw," said Scyathica. "Let's keep it to ourselves just for a few days so we can figure out whether we are having a long engagement, a short engagement, a big wedding or a little wedding..."

"I hadn't thought of any of that detail," said Steven. "I just thought you should be my wife."

Chapter 12

STEVEN AND SCYATHICA LOOKED A little sheepish for a few days. They opted to visit the local antique centre and Scyathica chose a diamond and amethyst Edwardian ring which she did not wear until Sunday morning.

On Sunday morning they sat at the breakfast table with Pandora and Hugo. Hugo was in a good mood as he had been out for a drink with Melvyn Brice from the radio station. Melvyn was seriously interested in taking an active part in Waste Conservatives and Hugo thought he had progressed in persuading Bricey to have a political career rather than spend his life as a DJ. Pandora was saying,

"Well, I have my car now and I am well into my training with Waste Women against Violence so soon I can be a Wav worker. They are letting me mentor a young woman who has recently come out of prison already. My car will also be useful when Penny goes out to Knight's Farm. She has just started riding that scooter. Have you thought of lending her the caravan as I think it will be some time before she is able to stay in the farmhouse and you two will soon be living in the West Wing?"

From behind his Sunday paper Uncle Hugo said, "What do you think, Steven? You bought it off my pig manager. I'm sure for a tenner for fuel I can get him to tow it to Knight's Farm when you have finished with it."

"Sure," said Steven. "We will let you know when. But we have something else to tell you."

Pandora said, "What?" and Hugo turned over the next page of his paper and reached for his toast in a rather convoluted way.

"We've got in engaged," said Steven.

"Pass the marmalade," said Hugo.

"We've got engaged," said Scyathica.

Pandora said, "I thought you would," and this time Hugo seemed to be listening.

"But you haven't got a ring," he said to Scyathica.

"Yes, I have," she replied, showing off her ring.

"Jolly good. Where's the marmalade?" said Sir Hugo.

Steven and Scyathica explained their wedding plans, once they had managed to get the attention of Pandora and Sir Hugo. They had opted for a small wedding just before Christmas. Guests would include Sir Hugo, Pandora, Penny, Auntie Bea, Penny's parents if they were visiting for Christmas and Steven's parents. There were a couple of people from the court Steven felt he might invite, perhaps Julie James the Usher Manager and her husband Martin and the court manager Derek Devene and his husband Julian, and Scyathica wanted to invite her manager, Stacey Birch. They would not be inviting Scyathica's father or her other Uncle Lord Coldharbour. Steven did not want to ask all his sisters but was not sure how he would deal with this issue. They would marry at the Registry Office at Waste Town Hall and as long as the Knubb Arms were agreeable, have a wedding breakfast limited to about twenty people in a function room there. They did not plan to go away immediately on honeymoon, choosing instead to go away in the spring. They might go to Italy or Scotland. That was yet to be worked out.

"Are you sure you want such a small wedding?" queried Pandora.

"Absolutely," confirmed Scyathica. The thought of hats, flower arrangements and large seating plans had no appeal for her.

"Well, let's have some champers tonight!" said Sir Hugo beaming.

Her Honour dela Notte had recently moved to a flat near the middle of Waste. It was actually the top half of a Georgian House, around the corner from Eric and Tina Ercol. She had originally hoped to move her son Flavio sooner rather than later from his boarding school to Waste Grammar School, but in the end, it had transpired the grammar school could only accept him in September. He was at least home from boarding school for the summer holidays, getting used to his new accommodation. He had acquired a bicycle and although she constantly worried about the traffic, it was pleasing to hear his enjoyment about exploring the neighbourhood. She hoped her husband Jerome would join them soon, but she seemed to see him less and less. She was pleased this Monday morning she did not have to rush. She had a pleasant walk before she arrived at court on foot clutching a take-away coffee.

As she settled in her Chambers there was a knock on the door from Steven Hovell who these days was manager of the judges' clerks and the court's manager's deputy. She found him a capable and reassuring presence. He began speaking to her,

"Your Honour, I am afraid Mr Devene is not in today. You may not be aware his husband has a few health problems, and he feels he needs to support him. I have to deputise for him today. His Honour Judge Ahmed has the start of a difficult jury trial, so I propose to clerk for him. His Honour Judge Grasby KC is writing a judgment today. We are very short staffed, and the District Judges are having to make do without clerks, so Lindy Pinney will be clerking for you today. She has been shadowing me and you will have Nikki as your usher," he said.

"I am sure it will be alright," said Her Honour dela Notte. "The case is about the O'Hanrahan child, now called Pauline and it all sounds very promising."

Indeed, when everyone was assembled in court, they were all smiles. Ivan Huff, Bernie Blunt, Sue Rosemary and Chris Ellison were once again the advocates in court.

"Your Honour," said Chris Ellison, "may my client have her Wav worker with her?"

Her Honour dela Notte nodded agreement and Pandora was shown into court and seated beside May Lou.

The reports were favourable. Miss Levi was taking good care of Pauline. Thus far, May Lou O'Hanrahan had not got into further trouble. Drug tests were negative, and she had behaved in a positive way in contact. The local authority, supported by the Children's Guardian, were content for there to be a Special Guardianship order to Lavinia Levi with defined contact to May Lou of a full day every other Saturday, plus tea once a week. Once May Lou had suitable accommodation, it was recommended that if all continued as well as it was now going, the full day could be swapped for a full weekend. Bernie Blunt said that his client agreed.

Her Honour cleared her throat and said, "Mr Ellison, do you mind if I speak to your client direct at this stage?"

"Not at all," he replied in his Brummy accent.

"Miss O'Hanrahan, on a recent occasion when you were in prison you could not contain your emotions. How do I know you can keep up the positive change?"

May Lou stood up. "I'm getting a lot of help now. I've seen how Lavinia has done good things an' all. It's doing my daughter good. I've got a new Wav worker too. She's a lovely posh lady. She really listens to me an' all. She doesn't treat me as if

I'm stupid. She has made me realise it don't matter where you come from, it's 'ow you end up which really counts."

"I could not agree more," said Her Honour, and she agreed to make the orders.

Court stood adjourned and everyone left the courtroom in a good humour. Bernie Blunt and Sue Rosemary went to the solicitors' room and became engrossed in a matter relating to legal aid. Ivan Huff and Chris Ellison went on their way. Pandora attempted to go on her way but bowled into a man just outside the courthouse. She had not noticed him or indeed Sonja Sidebottom who was standing in the shadows on the steps waiting for Bernie Blunt so she could hand him some papers to take home with him at his request. Her head was too full of the work she had started as a Wav worker to notice people around her.

Pandora looked at the man with whom she had collided. He had dropped some of his own leaflets advertising a Labour Party meeting addressed 'by local Labour MP Nat Cartey' and showing a photograph of him.

"Nathanial," she said to Nat Cartey. "It is! Nathanial Coldharbour."

Nat scrambled to collect his leaflets going, "Schhh."

"Nathanial," she persisted. "It's your Auntie Pandora!" She spotted a leaflet and said innocently, "Why are you Nat Cartey MP on these leaflets?"

"SHHH, be quiet," said Nat. "They don't know."

"They don't know what?" said Pandora innocently. "I heard on the radio the MP for Waste East was Nat Cartey. Hugo must have bumped into you in Westminster. Mind you, unlike me he never knew you as a child, Nathanial. When I used to take Scyathica over for tea, what a whiney little boy you were."

"Please be quiet, Auntie Pandora. I'll take you for a cuppa at the Knubb Arms and explain it all to you."

Nat realised his aunt would have had no interest in who an obscure backbench MP might be when she lived in Kensington, let alone politics in general. In the Knubb Arms he tried to dress up the agreement he had with Scyathica as gently as he could.

"As you appreciate, Auntie there are things we would all rather not have discussed," he said persuasively. She seemed to agree not to talk about his real identity.

As for what happened outside, Sonja heard the whole thing. She had shrunk back into the shadows. She stood there aghast. She would have to think about what to do. She was aware Pandora was Scyathica's mother. If she heard things correctly Nat

Cartey was not who he said he was. She assumed he had not seen her. She did not wait any longer for Bernie Blunt. He would just have to pick up his own papers from the office. She went home immediately.

Her father was not yet home. She tried talking to her mother.

"Maybe you heard wrong," was Marjorie's immediate reaction, "or you could ring that nice Mr Flaughtersdough for advice... Mind you, your father is not so keen on him anymore."

It seemed her father was working late undertaking a clinic with private patients so with a racing pulse, she decided to contact Scyathica. She had Steven's number from contact at the court. She rang him and he answered straight away. He passed the phone to Scyathica.

"I was on the steps outside the court..." started Sonja.

"I think I know what this is about. Did you overhear a conversation involving my mother?" was the reply.

"Yes, with Nat Cartey," said Sonja.

Scyathica replied, "My mother has come home and told me of a conversation. She thought she was not overheard but you apparently heard her."

"Can I meet with you?" said Sonja.

Scyathica agreed to meet her the next day. She had a quiet chat with Steven while they painted some woodwork in the West Wing.

"I don't think you can keep a lid on things forever," said Steven. "I think you better warn your uncle."

Scyathica was less than happy about the situation but that evening they sat down Uncle Hugo and Pandora together. Scyathica explained about the agreement with Nat Cartey aka Nathanial Coldharbour not to disclose his true identity in return for him not disclosing to the people of Waste who her father was.

"The rotter, the bounder," said Uncle Hugo.

"It's a long time since I heard names like that!" said Steven.

"Look," continued Sir Hugo, "as long as my sister and my niece are okay, I could not care less if the world knows I have a remote connection to Davey Scarlett. However, I don't know how the Labour Party are going to feel about a former public schoolboy and media baron's son masquerading as something he is not. You will have to tell the truth to this Sonja. And you are sure Nathanial didn't know she was there? What happens next is up to her."

So Scyathica explained exactly who Nat Cartey was to Sonja Sidebottom. They met at the Knubb Arms. They sat in the most remote corner of the Knubb Arms' lounge with a pot of tea.

"Gosh," said Sonja. "Gosh... some MPs... Gosh. With your uncle everyone knows he's the posh old bloke with the pigs and sausages... but this Nat Cartey he's something else."

Scyathica just nodded. She could have said more in defence of her Uncle Hugo but felt she needed to concentrate on the disclosures.

"I can't stop you using the information," she said before she left, "but please be careful how you go about it. I don't want my mother, or my uncle harmed. I suppose conceivably, also, I could get the sack as Lord Coldharbour owns the newspaper and radio station."

Later, Sonja explained who Nat Cartey really was to her parents.

"I think this can be put to him in cross-examination to discredit him. Mum and Dad, I think then we should try and extract an undertaking from him not to do any more work on the trees until both sides have been to binding arbitration about the future of the trees and the boundary... because your case was not going very well..."

Bertrand Sidebottom had himself started to have misgivings about Dr Flaughtersdough but nonetheless he decided to have a call to him to seek his views about the revelations.

"Oh, noo, noo, noo, no," said Gordon slurring his words slightly, "I can't put that to an MP. That would impugn his honour."

"Honour? Honour? What he has done sounds very dishonourable," said Bertrand. "We were losing in court. Although I am sure he killed Tinkerbell, I don't think I can prove it in court, and we must get something out of it."

"My dear old thing," started Dr Flaughtersdough who sounded as if he had had a bit to drink, "we must behave like gentlemen."

"You're sacked," said Bertrand and ended the call.

Marjorie looked stunned.

"Who will do our case now in court?" she queried. "I did like that Dr Flaughtersdough... so old-fashioned and amusing."

"I want Sonja to do the case," said Bertrand. "I should have listened to her before. That chap Gordon Flaughtersdough is an idiot... and as for his Doctorate; don't get me started! Sonja has provided hugely valuable material against the enemy, and he just wasn't interested."

Sonja explained that she could only assist as a 'McKenzie Friend' since Bernie

Blunt had not allowed his firm to take the case. She would need the judge's permission to undertake any type of advocacy.

"And I don't like your boss either," said Bertrand, who was clearly in a combative mood, although of late Sonja had felt less than happy with her treatment by Bernie.

As a trainee she had expected to spend some time doing menial tasks but since she had become a qualified solicitor Bernie had taken to giving her vast amounts of legal work, as well as piling her up with photocopying and expecting her to make the tea. She certainly did not feel valued, and it might be she would need to find another job.

That same evening Penny was discussing the beginning of works on Knight's Farm to her parents on the phone and the plan to borrow Steven's caravan. She sat down with Auntie Bea after the call.

"I guess you'll be one lodger down," said Penny. "I don't want to make it difficult for you."

"It's alright," said Auntie Bea, "I already have someone interested but I hope you won't be cross who it is. Apparently, that Pierre Bruele who used to work for that horrid man has decided to stay on in Waste. The Harbour View is too expensive for him, and a friend of a friend says he might be interested if I have a room available."

"Doesn't matter to me," said Penny. "As long as you're happy."

"It will be a bit different having a Frenchie," said Auntie Bea. "But he'll soon learn our ways."

Pierre Bruele had come to the realisation he would use up all his commission on accommodation if he continued living at the Harbour View pub, now Xavier was in custody. Recently he had had to start paying for his hire car himself. He wanted to make sure he had enough capital to buy the sort of place he wanted. He thought some sort of bar or inn with lots of character would fit the bill. He so much wanted to escape his old life.

He had been sent some particulars which really interested him. There was a nearby village called Farthwaite where the landlord was looking to retire from a pub which had a little bistro. It had limited living accommodation but if he bought it, he would not need more than a bedroom and a bathroom. The landlord and his wife lived in a cottage in the village so the particulars said the landlord would be prepared to work part-time for a few months to show a newcomer the ropes. His wife cooked in the kitchen, and she was apparently prepared to be employed in the future in the kitchen on a part-time basis. He hoped he could purchase the Farthwaite Arms or something similar.

In High Cliffe that same evening, when Scyathica had returned home she decided to send a brief communication to Lord Coldharbour of Southend. She hoped it might be some small protection to herself and her immediate family, particularly from Nat's potential anger. It would be a matter for Lord Coldharbour if he let Nat know but she did not want to contact Nat herself. She sent Lord Coldharbour an email to his personal email address,

'Dear Uncle

A third party overheard a conversation with Nathanial; between my mother and himself. The third party may well disclose what she heard. I stress I was not there, and it appears mother met Nathanial by accident. She had no idea he was in Waste. She tends not to keep up with current affairs. If you feel you need to do so, no doubt you will contact me.

Regards S.'

The response was an automatic 'out of office' reply. Scyathica did not hold a personal phone number for him, and she did not want to leave a message about this with his office.

Chapter 13

BERNIE BLUNT WAS NOT PLEASED when Sonja did not stay waiting on the steps for him. When they were both next in the office, he expressed his concerns. Sonja made him even more angry when she said,

"I had to leave because I obtained a vital piece of information in my parents' case. Also, I will be taking a day off in August to assist them as the hearing was adjourned."

"You can't," said Bernie.

"My parents need me," said Sonja. "I have had very little leave since I qualified. In August things are usually quiet, surely? Please, I really have to do this."

"You have two choices," said Bernie, "be involved in this ridiculous case of your parents, or work for me."

"I'll get my handbag and go," said Sonja, deciding she had had enough of Bernie. With that she was out of the door.

The West Wing only needed final decorating and furnishing. Champ and Deedee were arriving in a few days' time. After Champ had helped with the decorating, providing they could get a bed delivered in time, Steven and Scyathica were moving into their new home. They had rummaged through items stored in the East Wing and attics which Uncle Hugo and Pandora offered and knew they would have a dining room table and chairs, a nineteenth century writing desk, one large Persian rug and a mahogany wardrobe. Steven had spotted a second-hand green velvet three-piece suite in a charity shop for £320 so he had put a £50 deposit on it. It was in impeccable condition. Those items would have to do for now. Pandora said she could get more items out of storage in due course.

Steven was concerned about how he would deal with the thorny issue of his sisters' possible attendance at the wedding. Scyathica was worried about the fall-out from Sonja's discovery. She had heard nothing from Nat or Lord Coldharbour. She did not particularly want to be in court when the Sidebottoms' interim injunction application returned to court. She made an excuse to Stacey Birch the day before the hearing that she was coming down with a migraine. Steven was due to be court clerk so he would keep her informed. Nat had no idea that Steven was now engaged to Scyathica. On the day of the hearing there was indeed more press interest than on the last occasion. A couple of reporters from the National Press and Stacey Birch sat in the back of the court. A news crew from the TV station based at Moorlands were outside the court.

The Carteys, the Sidebottoms, Percy Vere, Sonja and a clerk from the solicitors instructing Percy waited expectantly in court for His Honour Judge Oliver Grasby KC to come into court.

A dark grey limousine with darkened windows drew up briefly the other side of the town square. A dapper suited figure got out. The man slipped quietly into the back of the court without being noticed. If Nathanial Coldharbour had turned around he would have been surprised to see his father sitting there.

His Honour Judge Grasby KC had been made aware that Dr Gordon Flaughtersdough would not be present and that the Sidebottoms were now litigants in person assisted by their daughter. He had mixed feelings about this. On the one had that ghastly man would not be here but on the other hand it was always difficult when people were unrepresented and did not know procedure. He hoped their young solicitor daughter could help them, but in the past she had seemed such a non-entity when she had been in his court.

Steven announced the case and then said,

"Your Honour, Mr and Mrs Sidebottom are in person today, but their daughter Miss Sidebottom is their McKenzie Friend. I understand she seeks permission to act as their advocate."

"Stand up," said Oliver to Sonja. "I understand you work for a local firm, but you are here in a personal capacity?"

"Yes, Your Honour."

"Well, I prefer if your parents have some sort of help, so you better come to the front bench then, and join Mr Vere."

Percy Vere smiled, no doubt with the expectation of making mincemeat of Sonja and her parents. Sonja had a neat folder of documents in front of her. They included Nathanial Coldharbour's birth certificate and a certified copy of his change of name deed.

"I am going to ask you again," said His Honour Judge Grasby KC, "is there a prospect of the parties going to binding arbitration?"

Sonja said, "My parents, I mean clients, would be prepared to go to arbitration if Mr and Mrs Cartey undertake not to touch the trees pending the result of the arbitration."

Percy Vere smiled. "Your Honour, my client is prepared to continue with his evidence and then I have instructions to seek summary dismissal of the proceedings with indemnity costs. With Your Honour's leave, may I call my client back to the stand? I don't have much else to put to him."

Nat Cartey was recalled to the witness box and reminded that he was on oath.

"Mr Cartey," said Mr Vere. "Did you do anything which could have caused the death of Mr Sidebottom's koi carp?"

"Absolutely not," said Nat.

"Did you cut or instruct anyone else to cut tree branches which were not on your property?"

"Absolutely not," was the reply.

"Did you cause any branches or twigs to be thrown into your neighbours' property or act in anyway which was a nuisance or annoyance?"

"Absolutely not," said Nat. "I am a man of honour."

Percy smiled again "That concludes the examination in chief."

Sonja got to her feet just as Nat started to leave the witness box.

"Stay there, Mr Cartey," said Oliver, "Miss Sidebottom may have some questions for you."

"Mr Cartey," said Sonja nervously. "You have sworn to tell the truth and you understand the consequences of perjury, don't you?"

"Yes," said Nat.

"You have also said you are a man of honour?" said Sonja.

"Yes," replied Nat who suddenly had a sinking feeling.

Percy Vere and His Honour Judge Grasby KC wondered where this was going.

"Nat Cartey is not your real name is it?" asked Sonja.

"Well, eh, eh…" said Nat.

"Were you not born Nathanial Justin Coldharbour?" asked Sonja.

Nat went beetroot and then green.

"If it pleases Your Honour, I have a birth certificate here," said Sonja brandishing it.

Percy Vere rose to his feet. "Your Honour, I must object I have not seen it, I know nothing of this."

"A birth certificate is a document of public record," said Oliver. "I will for now let this line of questioning continue."

Sonja repeated her question. Nat looked very uncomfortable and said quietly, "I did execute a change of name deed."

"I have a copy," she said. "But does anyone amongst your political party or your colleagues know your true background? Rather than being a man of honour have you not concealed your origins? Have you not concealed that you are not a mere former factory worker, but you are the public school educated son of Lord Coldharbour of Southend?"

There were gasps in court from Brittany and from the press.

"A man can call himself what he wants," said Nat.

Percy Vere rose again. "Your Honour, please can I beg for a short adjournment?"

"Only if Miss Sidebottom has concluded her cross-examination," said Oliver Grasby.

"Yes, Your Honour, I think I have dealt with Mr Cartey or Coldharbour sufficiently."

His Honour Judge Grasby KC was ever a man to see the funny side but keeping the straightest face he could he said,

"There will be an adjournment of approximately half an hour. Ladies and gentlemen of the press, may I remind you we are in the middle of the case. Please do not bother the parties or start sending reports through to your offices."

Percy Vere strode out looking most displeased and took Nat into the nearest interview room. Brittany was whispering a question repeatedly to her husband, "Are you really a lord's son?" He still had not noticed his father. Lord Coldharbour mingled with the press. Stacey Birch recognised him and greeted him politely. He reciprocated.

"Is that your son, really?" she asked quietly.

He nodded and said quietly, "He's been rather foolish."

The hearing reconvened. Percy Vere stood up.

"Your Honour," he said, "Mr and Mrs Cartey have decided to accept Mr and Mrs

Sidebottom's kind offer to settle the matter. The parties have agreed they will go to binding arbitration conducted by a Chartered Surveyor to determine the exact boundary and the future of the trees. Mr and Mrs Cartey will undertake to do no further work to the trees, nor will they instruct anyone else, save as may be determined by the arbitration. There will be no order as to costs."

Oliver said, "Please send me a draft order by 4pm tomorrow. I will take your clients' undertakings now."

Nat and Brittany stood up and gave their promises to the court. Oliver warned them they could be sent to prison for contempt if they broke their promises. Then without further ado, he said,

"Court stands adjourned," and went off to his Chambers.

Five minutes later Steven found him chuckling there.

"That turned out to be fun!" he said. "Don't you just love our jobs! It's all just the biggest theatre."

Steven agreed that he enjoyed his job very much. He did wonder whether there would be any fall-out from today.

He need not have worried. After the hearing had finished and Nat was talking in the foyer to Percy Vere, Lord Coldharbour tugged at Nat's sleeve. The press were still hanging around.

"Dad," said Nat, going a funny colour again. "I did not know you were here..."

"We must speak," said Lord Coldharbour and pulled Nat away from Percy and Brittany to the nearest interview room. Stacey Birch said afterwards she would have loved to have been a fly on the wall. People close to the room thought they heard words like "blithering idiot".

Later that evening Scyathica received an email from Lord Coldharbour.

'Thank you for letting me know. Things were bound to come out sooner or later. You have nothing to worry about.'

It was a big relief. Quite late in the evening Scyathica, Steven, Pandora and Hugo sat quietly in the garden sipping some cool white wine. Piper, Kitty and even William lay at their feet. There was an air of quiet contentment. Uncle Hugo broke the silence.

"Things not going too badly, are they?"

They all laughed.

In the morning the tabloids ran stories about Nat Cartey. There were also local news reports.

Penny heard the news as she was getting ready to go over to Knight's Farm. Soon it was to be re-named 'Penny's animal haven'. As she rode over on the scooter, she wondered what Lewis Gasson would make of the deception. He was always so straightforward himself. She felt sure he would greatly approve of her riding a scooter. She felt such a fool to have lost him. Maybe one day she would win him back. For the moment she concentrated on her plans. She would live in the caravan until the house was habitable. She would work part-time at the café until her businesses were up and running. Amazingly she had finally finished her dissertation. She would submit it once she had read it over one last time.

However, when she got to the farm, she went to check on her first acquisitions for her animal shelter. Soon she would stay on site in the caravan so that she could care for further animals.

Fortunately, obtaining and erecting a chicken ark and run were relatively simple compared to the renovations the house needed. Eric and Tina Ercol were much relieved to find a home for Emperor the cockerel and his hens. They would soon finish clearing Maude's bungalow and would then consider putting it on the market. Maude was well settled at the care home.

The week ended for Oliver Grasby on a satisfactory note as well. Annette was home and in a good mood with him. She had clearly forgiven him for the episode with the Stiffles.

He arranged to go for a quick walk and smoke with Aziz Ahmed. They walked across the golf links and stood admiring the lake. Waste Water twinkled a little with the dying embers of the sun. There were a few noises from wildlife. A duck quacked and an owl hooted.

"Summer's nearly over," mused Oliver puffing on his pipe and watching as a little mist settled on Waste Water.

"It's just flown by..." responded Aziz lighting a cigar. "So much seems to have happened I hardly noticed summer at all."

"I suppose, it's better to be busy," said Oliver. "I feel very lucky, you know, with my life."

"You know," said Aziz as they turned and headed for home, "so do I."

E p i l o g u e

ON A CRISP LATE SEPTEMBER Saturday morning, after she had downed a steaming cup of hot coffee, Penny pulled on a sweater in the caravan. First, she went to give the newly arrived abandoned kittens some kitten milk and kitten food. At the moment, they were confined to a crate because they were so small. Later in the day she would let them play on an old rug in the middle of the living area in the caravan. After she had fed them, she went outside and scattered some hen food for Emperor and his girls, in their ark. Her next port of call was a dilapidated shed. She let out her recently acquired pair of elderly geese, Onion and his partner Pickle. She had been warned to shut them up at night to protect them from marauding foxes. Finally, she heaved a small bale of hay over a dry-stone wall for the half dozen old sheep who had been left behind for her to tend. She went back into the caravan and fetched herself another coffee. It would be quiet today because the builders were not working over the weekend. She went outside again and pulled herself up onto an old wooden crate. She sat observing the view. She wished so much that Lewis would come up the drive on his Harley-Davidson. Otherwise, it was a pleasing scene.

Through the farmyard gateway she suddenly saw a small, dark object moving up the driveway. It was obviously an animal. A large black cat climbed through a gap in the gate, mewling plaintively. As he approached her Penny could see that although he was quite a large cat, he was somewhat thin. He was entirely black except for a white tip to his tale. He came up to her and rubbed himself against her legs.

Penny slid off the crate and began to stroke him. The reaction was a loud purring noise. He had no collar and gave all the appearance of living wild for some time.

"Are you hungry?" said Penny scratching his chin. "I only have kitten food for now... but if you stay we can find you something better."

The purring increased. She fetched him a generous portion of kitten food and hoped the kittens would forgive him. He wolfed it down. Then he rubbed himself against her again.

"My, that is loud," said Penny. "Do you want to stay?" More purring followed.

"If you stay, we should think of a name. How about, Panther?" The cat did not react. "Tiddles…? Naw, too silly." The cat blinked as if to agree. "Balthasar, maybe?" The cat did not react. "What about Claude?" The black cat hissed, as if to show disapproval. "Okay, okay." Penny momentarily thought of Lewis and his motorbike. "What about Harley?"

Harley as he was now to be called purred loudly in approval and lay on his back to have his tummy tickled.

"Well, Harley," said Penny, "I reckon we're gonna be friends and bring each other luck."

If Harley could have spoken, he would have stated his complete agreement.

The writer stopped at this point; he thought that it really was going rather well.

A l w a y s   W a s t e

M a y

THE WRITER WAS KEEN TO finish his manuscript; soon it would be summer, and he was keen to get out and about.

'It was one of those bright May mornings when the English countryside looks its best. The vivid sheen of green on the trees and the early blossom made it look as if the town of Waste and its surrounding countryside was decorated, ready for something to happen. The birds were particularly active, and their song rang out on the soft May air.

Steven Hovell and his wife Scyathica Wentworth-Hovell sat drinking their morning tea on the roof of the West Wing of High Cliffe House. Scyathica's uncle, Sir Hugo Wentworth-Knubb owned the family pile High Cliffe House where he lived with his sister Pandora, Scyathica's mother and he had been Waste West's Member of Parliament for many years. Scyathica and Steven had brought the West Wing back to habitable condition and now owned it through a ninety-nine-year lease. Every morning, if the weather permitted, they liked to sit on the roof area for a few minutes and reflect on events. From their vantage point they could see Waste Water, the huge lake to the north of Waste, and many parts of the town of Waste. They could see the tops of the chimneys at the town's Waste processing plant Waste Waste from whence a wisp of smoke emanated. Nearby but out of sight, was the Knubb bacon and sausage factory which was owned by Sir Hugo. Sir Hugo's pig farm was not far from High Cliffe House. Waste golf links was also nearby. Waste Water itself glinted in the sunlight. The golf links which bordered Waste Water looked like green velvet.

Opposite the golf course was Links Road where there were some executive developments. Scyathica's cousin Nat had previous lived in one of the developments but had had a spectacular fall from grace from his position as Waste East's Member of Parliament. He had sold his house to a local Circuit Judge. The area around Links Road seemed popular with judges, hospital consultants and the like. Steven had knowledge of the judges due to his position as Senior Judge's Clerk and Team Leader at Waste Combined Court. He could see the roof of the court and something of the town square from where they both sat. Scyathica worked for the local paper and radio station just off the town square. He could not make out the house of his former landlady Auntie Bea in Canal Street either. It was with her he had lodged when he first arrived as a rather shy young man from London.

Neither of the couple came from Waste but it was here their lives had developed and here that they had found each other and made a home.

Steven said, "I hear Penny has a couple of lambs from the sheep over at Knight's Farm." He should have called it 'Penny's Animal Haven and Eco Camping Centre'. However, it was easier to say 'Knight's Farm', its old name. Their friend Penny Wayney had taken on a dilapidated farm with financial help from her American senator father. Scyathica could well remember the explosion at the farm from an illegal vodka still as she had been going up its track at the time to interview its former owner for the paper. Penny had followed her to Waste, when Scyathica's media baron uncle Lord Coldharbour had effectively banished Scyathica to Waste. Penny had initially been something of an irritation. Somehow, after some bad experiences Penny had belatedly grown up and Scyathica now warmed to her.

Scyathica said, "She has no experience with sheep and the local farmers were not interested in taking the old sheep when Knight left so it is something of a miracle!"

Steven replied, "I like this time of year. So full of new life."

"Yes, it is," said Scyathica with a smile on her face. "We have the beginnings of new life too. You will be a father by Christmas."

"Ahh," said Steven smiling, "I hoped that might be the case."

He put a protective arm around her and then they held hands and sat listening to the bird song. Waste Water glistened and gleamed and seemed to be winking at them.

They reflected on the changes which had happened in the last few months and their hopes for the future.'

The writer paused.

Chapter 1

STEVEN AND SCYATHICA'S WEDDING HAD taken place the previous December. They had married at Waste Registry Office and had a wedding breakfast at the Knubb Arms on Waste town square. They had tried to keep their nuptials intimate, but they still had a number of guests. Obviously, Scyathica's Uncle Hugo and her mother Pandora were significant guests. Penny and Auntie Bea were there. Steven invited his colleague from the court, Usher Manager Julie James together with her husband Martin. Julie was a sensible down to earth person sharing the same practical good sense as Auntie Bea. He also invited his boss, the court manager Derek Devene and his husband Julian and the most senior judge at the court, His Honour Judge Oliver Grasby KC, and his wife Annette, who was a High Court Judge. Derek Devene declined due to his husband's increasing health problems, but Steven was pleasantly surprised when Oliver Grasby accepted the invitation. His Honour Judge Oliver Grasby KC loved his pipes and cigars and had a tremendous intellect and a wicked sense of humour.

Scyathica did not invite her cousin Nat. He had been so unpleasant to her before his fall from grace that she saw no reason to do so. He was not in the good books of the Labour Party or his father. His career as an MP had been built on a lie, that he had been a simple factory worker Nat Cartey and not a former public schoolboy and son of media tycoon Lord Coldharbour. As a courtesy she invited her paternal uncle Lord Coldharbour. He declined her invitation politely but sent a bouquet and he also sent Steven and herself a thousand pounds of tokens for the department store which was never "knowingly undersold". As for her father, she had no address for him. Davey Scarlett had gone off to the Caribbean to avoid his dodgy business dealings being scrutinised. She sent him a text telling him of her news but received no reply.

On the day before the wedding a courier arrived with a small parcel. When she opened it she found a small card saying, 'Good luck my darling Scyathica'. It was unsigned. With it was a small presentation box containing half a dozen full size Krugerrands. The courier had melted away and there was no return address on the parcel. She knew instantly it was from her father. She shared her mixed feelings with Steven over the gift; on the one hand she was concerned as to how her father made his money but on the other hand, she was touched he recognised her nuptials. Steven said that she should keep the gift. One day they might want to put the money aside for their children. Also, Davey had let down Pandora very badly. His financial shenanigans had lost her, her London home. Scyathica would have the means to help her mother if she needed a little luxury.

Scyathica was pleased that her boss Stacey Birch from the local paper and her colleague Melvyn Brice who had a radio show came to the wedding.

Steven's parents Deedee and 'Champ' were thrilled to come to the wedding and came up to the house in their camper van. Steven had been worried about his sisters descending on Waste en masse. His oldest sister Sharon was married to a man called Don who did something in scrap metal, and they had three children under ten, Stan, Maynard-Roy and Tilly-Lilly, who Steven had thought were completely feral last time he saw them two years or so ago. At first Sharon did not respond. Then he got a grumpy text 'Why can't you get married in London?'. Then he got a follow up text indicating that they might come. However, when he asked if could book any accommodation for them there was silence. Two days before the wedding he received a message that they were not coming since Maynard-Roy and Tilly-Lilly had chicken pox.

His sister Denise came up with Deedee and Champ in the campervan. She was a year older than him. His younger sister Jade came with her son T.C. aged three and her partner Jazzy Joy. Steven had managed to book them a room at the Harbour View pub which he hoped they would like since there was a children's playground on the green opposite it.

Denise seemed to warm to Piper, Sir Hugo's Springer Spaniel, Pandora's pets, Kitty the Scottie dog and William the cat who were all resident at High Cliffe House.

"I do love dogs," she said. "I can't really have one in m' flat."

She seemed to "ooh" and "aah" with pleasure at the local scenery and pubs. For the big day she squeezed into a very tight, purple, satin dress which really was too small for her bulk. She topped off her appearance with an enormous red silk flower.

She looked very garish compared with the bride's understated tailored cream trouser suit. However, Steven was pleased she had made the effort. He wore a smart dark grey lounge suit and a dark tie with the Waste Borough coat of arms on it.

Jade and Jazzy Joy were dressed entirely in black. They had matching hairstyles. Both of them had their hair dyed purple, their nails painted purple and their eyes shaded purple. T.C. was clad in a Batman costume. At the wedding breakfast at the Knubb Arms introductions were being made between the various guests and Jade pushed the bewildered little T.C. forward to Scyathica.

"'Spect one day you might have one of your own," she said. "This is T.C. 'e's an 'alf-caste."

Scyathica would have ignored the entirely inappropriate reference to the little boy in order for there to be peace at the wedding, but Penny butted into the conversation.

"You can't say that" Penny said, completely horrified.

"Why not?" said Jade.

"That's racist," said Penny. "If he is of mixed race you don't say things like that… let alone introduce him like that."

"You stuck up cow,". said Jade. "You can't talk to me like that."

"Look," butted in Steven, "the day belongs to Scyathica and I… so everyone calm down. The grown-ups should have some champagne and T.C. some ice-cream." Jade still looked annoyed and started muttering something under her breath at Penny.

His Honour Judge Grasby KC had overheard the incident. With a smile on his face which hid his shared view that the comment was completely offensive, he said,

"I love the Batman outfit. My morning suit makes me look like the penguin! My wife has put on a nice pretty dress, so I think Batman needs to rescue her from the naughty penguin. Shall we go and play?"

The little boy smiled, and everyone laughed nervously. Steven felt very grateful to the Circuit Judge who gently teased him on a daily basis by calling him 'Shovel' at work. The tension evaporated and the assembled guests enjoyed the food and drink of the wedding breakfast. As the afternoon progressed the bride and groom slipped away. Despite the winter weather they had elected to have a brief honeymoon in a holiday cottage a few miles away up on the moors to the north of Waste Water. As they drove away a few snowflakes came down as if to tease them.

"I don't care if we get snowed in," said Scyathica. Steven had smiled.

Now in May the wedding was a recent memory and they had plenty to plan for in the future. Steven, Scyathica and those in their circle proceeded with their tasks that

May day. Penny had much to do at the animal sanctuary. Pandora went off to do a day's volunteering at Waste Women against Violence. The head butcher at Knubb Sausage and Bacon Lewis Gasson was organising the day's shift and was trying not to be distracted by thoughts of how he might re-unite with his former girlfriend Penny.

Not everyone in Waste was brimming with optimism about the future. The owners of Waste Waste were a shady consortium. One of the investors was Davey Scarlett. Another investor was Xavier Didier Le Perte. Seeing he was currently awaiting trial in France for corruption, receiving stolen goods, fraud and a serious assault on his now ex-wife he had nothing meaningful to contribute to the future of Waste Waste. Penny had been lucky to escape from his violent clutches, having dropped her boyfriend Lewis Gasson for a fling with Xavier.

There were rumours that the Waste plant might be placed into administration. Mickey Gasson (Lewis's older brother), the union convenor had tried to have talks over the winter but there was no-one at the company with any real authority in Waste. Gone were the days when Waste East's MP could help him.

His daughter Brittany was married to Nat Cartey the disgraced Labour MP. He had been booted out of the Labour Party and had resigned his seat. A date for a by-election was awaited. Nat and Brittany had moved out of their house on the executive development both for financial reasons and to avoid embarrassment. They had sold their home to a local judge and bought a bungalow in the village of Gitthwaite a few miles away, ironically from another judge. It was reasonably priced since it had been the home of the judge's elderly mother Maude, who now lived in a home, and now needed updating. Nat was just starting out in a new career as a radio presenter. Scyathica tried to avoid him at the local media offices. Mickey found him something of a disappointment, but Brittany was very excited by his career move. The bungalow was not as grand as the house on the executive development, but she consoled herself she would have a free range with decorating even though she would have to do quite a lot herself.

There were in fact to be two by-elections. Sir Hugo had indicated to Pandora and Scyathica that he was now feeling his age and running his pig and meat business was probably enough for him. So, there would be a by-election as well for the seat of Waste West. No date had been set and it was expected that both elections would occur at the same time. Sir Hugo had cultivated a friendship with radio presenter and DJ, Melvyn Brice. 'Bricey' had been dropping heavy hints on his show that he would be leaving to do something political shortly, so Scyathica felt he must have something to do with the campaign for the new Tory candidate, whoever that might be. It was not clear who would run against him but then it was actually of more interest as to who might run as the Labour candidate for Waste East.

The Labour Party had adopted as their candidate the suave and debonair barrister Percy Vere who until recently could be seen addressing judges at Waste Combined Court. He was handsome and successful. He made no secret of being a grammar schoolboy who had shone at Oxford University. As yet unmarried he had recently rented a flat in Waste East and also would soon no longer grace the corridors of Waste Combined Court. Union men like Mickey Gasson initially did not know what to make of him.

His Honour Judge Oliver Grasby KC was sorry that one of the most competent barristers in the area would not be appearing anymore in his court. As a judge he did not get involved in politics. He was glad to see 'Shovel' happily married. His friend and colleague His Honour Judge Aziz Ahmed had moved house over the winter but still lived in walking distance from his house on Links Road. This meant he could still enjoy evening walks with his friend and colleague. The two judges would smoke cigars and put the world to rights. Sometimes he would smoke his pipe. Not that his wife Annette was that happy about his smoking. These days most of her court sittings as High Court Judge were in the Circuit Centre, just an hour's commute away, rather than in London. This meant she spent more time at home. She had nagged him to get a hobby. He had thought that being a wine connoisseur, collecting pipes and fine cigars was enough, but not according to Annette.

Despite the amount of time, he spent working and entertaining his children and grandchildren she had convinced herself he needed what she termed a "serious hobby". When he had protested that she did not apparently have one he was met with a rebuff, "As a High Court Judge I spend more time away from home than you." And so, Oliver had given his interests some serious thought, and he kept coming back to wine or cigars. As a young man he had spent several years living in South Africa. He had worked on a vineyard and had been peripherally involved in the Anti-Apartheid movement. He still had distant relations living in South Africa. He decided he would write a history of viticulture in South Africa. That at least would give him a reason to drink some of South Africa's better vintages. He pacified Annette by from time to time demonstrating he had written another few hundred words on his laptop.

Aziz Ahmed and his wife had bought the house previously occupied by Nat and Brittany Cartey. They had previously rented a house on the corner of Links Close, which had a brash neo Georgian style. Aziz was never overly fond of it and when its owner offered to sell it to him, he declined. However, when Nat Cartey asked a reasonable price to get a quick sale and to take into account there had been a neighbour dispute at his home, Aziz and his wife Amina jumped at the opportunity. The house had a big garden and a leafy outlook. As soon as they moved in, Aziz and Amina had an affable meeting with the Sidebottoms with whom there had been a dispute. It helped that both Bertrand Sidebottom and Amina were both hospital consultants at Waste General Hospital. There did not seem any reason for there to be a dispute. The Ahmed's teenage sons Helal and Ali were more interested in chess and computer gaming than kicking a ball over the hedge. Sometimes their friend Flavio would come round on his bicycle, and they would all scowl intently at the chess board. Bertrand Sidebottom felt reassured that pieces of hedge would not find their way into his precious carp pond as had occurred in Nat Cartey's day.

Flavio went to Waste Grammar School with Helal and Ali. He lived with his mother Her Honour Judge Davina dela Notte in the centre of Waste. He had been deeply unhappy at boarding school but here in Waste he was flourishing. He announced to his mother one day that all his friends now called him Frank and could she do so as well. As soon as he was old enough, he said that he would sign a change of name deed and change his name to 'Frank Nott'. Since this announcement they had only seen Davina's husband and Frank's father Jerome, once, briefly. All he had said on the subject was, "I haven't got time for this." Davina did not know if he had even listened to what had been said.

Davina dela Notte's flat was round the corner from the home of District Judge Eric Ercol and his wife Tina. Eric was pleased he had sold his mother's bungalow to Nat Cartey. It relieved him of a considerable burden.

While Steven and Scyathica reflected on their situation early in the morning, so did Steven's former landlady Auntie Bea later that day. Her house in Canal Street had proved a haven for many a new inhabitant of Waste. Nat Cartey had lived there when he first arrived in Waste as had Steven. Penny Wayney had lived there until she had moved to Knight's Farm. Chris Ellison the young Brummy barrister who was furthering his career in Waste had recently moved into a flat but had spent some time in Canal Street. A more recent resident was Frenchman Pierre Bruele. He had previously been assistant to crooked businessman Xavier Didier Le Perte. He had managed to somehow not get arrested himself and to come away with sufficient funds to buy a small pub. He was just about to move into the Farthwaite Arms in the village of Farthwaite. The village was amongst a cluster of small villages to the east of Waste. There was Gitthwaite where Nat Cartey now lived, Harthwaite where District Judge Ercol's mother now lived in a care home and Farthwaite where the pub was situated.

Auntie Bea's newest tenant was Bertrand Sidebottom's daughter Sonja. She had recently qualified as a solicitor and had walked out on her old boss Bernie Blunt. She had felt much put-upon and under appreciated by him. She now worked for Tina Ercol (Eric Ercol's wife) who was a partner in a firm of solicitors called Botch, Brath and Ercol shortened on their notepaper to 'BBE'. The name was certainly unfortunate. Mr Botch had long since retired and was reputed to be aged ninety-three and living in Ivy Bank Care Home where Maude Ercol, Eric's mother now lived. Mr Brath was in his mid-seventies and although a little deaf worked three days a week. Aside from Tina Ercol there were now four other partners. Many about the town called the firm 'Bodge, brass and all cold', but the partners had decided to keep the name of the firm as it was to some degree out of respect for old Mr Botch. However, Sonja was pleased to have made a fresh start and to have flown the parental nest. There was a warmth and security at the old house in Canal Street.

Auntie Bea was chatting to her nephew Norman Ryder over a cup of tea. Norman was the Leader of the Council and Mayor of Waste. He was not a man to wish to upset people.

Auntie Bea said, "When Pierre goes, I am going to be one tenant down again. So many changes in the last year or two. I thought he would not fit in, but he's been a proper gentleman."

"Indeed," said Norman, sighing about his own situation. "Since that Amina Ahmed came on the council, I have never had a moment's peace." He was talking about Aziz Ahmed's wife who as well as being a part-time Ophthalmological Consultant was also a very active Labour councillor. "She keeps going on about the Waste plant and what can we do to save it! Well, I don't really know…"

Auntie Bea smiled. "I'm sure something or somebody will turn up. They always do."

Chapter 2

WASTE HAD A LONG TRADITION of playing competitive football. The original football ground had been close to Canal Street and a nineteen-seventies housing development stood on its site. The current home of the Waste Wanderers lay on the southern approaches to the town, some way south of the railway station but in walking distance of it. The nineteen-seventies stadium was surrounded by light industrial sites, car showrooms, out of town supermarkets and a few scrubby fields where discontented ponies grazed. Waste Wanderers was revered by many in the town who saw nothing peculiar in cheering on the 'Wasters' and being labelled the 'Wastrels'. Until the second half of last year those involved with the football club worried for its future. However, Penny Wayney's father, an American senator had long nurtured an ambition to own an English football club. The purchase was all the more special for him since Waste was his wife Alannah's hometown. He therefore had not wasted any time in investing his money in the club. It had a whole new management team and new players were purchased.

The two most important acquisitions for the club were Achille Plinth and Paulino Spitti.

Achille Plinth made much on social media of his unique ancestry. One of his grandparents came from St Pernice, the Caribbean Island with close connections to Waste and she had married a man from Waste. His other grandparents comprised a Greek grandfather and a Canadian Quebecoise grandmother who was partly of First Nation's descent. He had played in the Premier League but now in his forties it appeared that he was prepared to slum it in the lower leagues and be a player-manager. He was reputed to have a huge collection of sports cars including several

Aston Martins and Maserati, although in recent times there was a rumour, he had to thin down his collection for financial reasons. He already had a country estate near Farthwaite in East Waste Moorland, so he had a base within easy reach of Waste. His jet-black hair was beginning to be flecked with grey and his hawk-like face and colouring made him look more First Nations than anything else. An extremely imposing figure of a man it was believed players feared him rather than revered him. He was a popular figure for the sporting press to interview. He said little but in a seemingly profound way. In one of his most famous interviews, he was asked if, perhaps, he received too much attention. His reply was,

"This Plinth should not be put on a pedestal," which only added to his mystique.

It was perhaps, useful in some ways to any team that if you got Plinth, he insisted on bringing his own Assistant Coach an efficient Dutchman Ruud Van Dijk and his own physio Bengt Halverson. Football commentators were apt to say, "If you get Plinth you have to have the whole statue."

Many people in the footballing world worshipped the ground that Paulino Spitti walked upon. A diminutive Italian 'Spitti' had played in the highest leagues in Europe including the English Premier League. Now in his thirties his fortunes were waning. Football aficionados could remember the "Spitti spat" as it was called, being the incident in the World Cup when he was a young man. Having done the most breath-taking header and thereby scoring a goal, the opposing goalkeeper just could not believe it and started shouting accusations that Spitti had a metal plate in his head, giving him an advantage. Spitti was enraged and spat at the goalkeeper.

It was true Spitti had been involved in a terrible motorcycle accident in Rome when he was sixteen, but x-rays proved he did not have a metal plate in his head. The footballing authorities did give him a 3-month ban for spitting. The incident was in the news for weeks. A pop song was even written about it. When he gave demonstrations of dribbling the ball to his adoring the fans, he referred to his style as 'spitter spatting' which only increased his notoriety. However, these days Spitti did not spit; except of course to clean his teeth.

He was still a flamboyant character. He had a mouth full of gold teeth. He wore gold rings, gold bracelets and gold chains when not playing. He had a reputation for womanising and partying. However, he was not perhaps the player he had been in his youth.

The fans of the Waste Wanderers were thrilled to have Plinth and Spitti. The former owner of the house on the edge of Links Close which had recently been occupied by His Honour Judge Aziz Ahmed was only too delighted to sell it to Spitti. It was a quick sale at a high price. Aziz had never been keen on its neo-Georgian style with neo-Georgian pillars. He had thought it rather brash and was pleased to have moved to the house he bought from Nat Cartey around the corner. The house he left was the largest on the executive development. It had 5 bedrooms and 3 bathrooms. Its former owner had been keen on sports so there was a gym in the quite substantial summerhouse with an outdoor jacuzzi next to it. The house had a conservatory, a double garage, and a carport. It was on a corner plot at the beginning of Links Close, so it had the largest frontage. The sweeping lawn going round the corner made a pleasing introduction to the mostly open plan front gardens of Links Close; or it did until Spitti made some changes.

Spitti quickly moved in with his Spanish girlfriend Lini Montserrat. Without any question of planning permission or if he was breaking any covenants the house had some radical changes. The white pillars were soon decorated in Pompeian red and gold with Roman ladies in interesting poses. The fascia around the previously white front porch was decorated in gold. A flagpole appeared from nowhere one day. It was topped off with a red flag which bore writing in gold saying 'Casa Spitti'. Then one day out of the blue, before the neighbours could draw breath a gang of workmen appeared. They soon erected some enormous black railings around the plot, each railing being topped with a spear of gold. Then some large red and gold gateposts appeared at the entrance to the drive. Each gatepost was topped by a half-naked neo-classical statue of a woman painted in gold. Between the gateposts the final touch was some enormous black electric gates with an intercom.

At first the neighbours were thrilled to have a celebrity neighbour. They soon became irritated by his noisy parties. When his 'improvements' had been carried out most of the neighbours became disenchanted. Councillor Amina Ahmed soon found her inbox full of complaining emails. One or two people turned up on the doorstep to moan. It was not just the garish appearance of the property and the lack of the sweeping open plan lawn which upset people, but also the noise of electric gates. They seemed to have a life of their own and would often clang open and bang closed randomly in the small hours. People did try to tell Spitti of the fault and in fairness to him he did ask Lini to, "'ave dem ruddy gates feexed."

Lini's main languages were Catalan and Italian, so she found it difficult battling with 'Scarlett International Electric Gates'. They rarely answered the phone and were slow to reply by email. They would repeatedly ask the same questions – 'Are the gates still under our warranty?' 'Has anyone been abusing our gates?'. She complained to Spitti, and he said dismissively, "They was fast enough to take my money, so you tell 'em they 'as to feex it... I am after all, busy with football."

The addition of Plinth and Spitti meant that after the senator acquired Waste Wanderers things got off to an excellent start. The team won most of its games. By the early spring when the neighbours were complaining about the gates it seemed that nothing could go wrong. One murky evening about ten weeks prior to when Scyathica and Steven had shared their information on the roof, Achille Plinth decided to call on Spitti. As he approached the Spitti house in his soft topped Maserati the gates appeared to be open, so he started to drive into the driveway. With a tremendous clank the gates slammed shut, slamming into the car with force. Before he could do anything, they flew open and slammed shut against his car and this happened again and again and again. Each time the force was greater. There was a huge noise from the banging gates and Achille Plinth was yelling and shouting as well. Eventually the gates gave a shudder after falling shut but failed to open. Achille Plinth and an extremely damaged Maserati were firmly trapped in the driveway entrance. The soft top of the car had partially collapsed. The sides and doors were bent inwards. It had seemed like an eternity, but it had all taken a few seconds.

All the emergency services were summonsed. Firemen with cutting gear cut through the remains of the car and the gates to free Plinth. A bored policeman held local onlookers back. Paramedics and an ambulance stood by. Spitti and Lini Montserrat hovered around their elaborate front porch. Eventually a groaning Achille Plinth was cut out of the wreck of his car. It was a write-off. Plinth was whisked away to hospital and the car disappeared on a low-loader. The firemen packed up and left. As the police officer made to leave as well Spitti could be heard shouting, "What about my gates?" since his front garden was now adorned with a mangled heap of metal which had been his gates.

Achille Plinth had fared better than his car but nonetheless had suffered a very severe whiplash injury. It was unclear if he would play again, and it would be at least three months before he could resume coaching duties. Ruud Van Dijk stepped up to the coaching duties in the meantime. He did a competent job. Spitti was somewhat off his game, so he sat on the bench for several games. Van Dijk had acquired some promising young players recently, so the team continued to do well. Relations between Plinth and Spitti deteriorated because by the end of April, Achille Plinth had instructed solicitors who had sent Spitti a letter before action setting out his claim.

Things did not look good for Spitti. Since he had failed to get planning permission or the necessary consents for the gates his insurers indicated a reluctance to provide any indemnity. He instructed London solicitors to pursue the suppliers of the gates. It turned out that Scarlett International Electric Gates was owned by a holding company registered in the Cayman Islands. Its UK premises seemed to now be occupied by persons who said they were from an unrelated company 'DS Gates and Doors Ltd'. They also belonged to a holding company in the Cayman Islands. Spitti's solicitors suggested they instruct enquiry agents to find out more about the companies. Spitti gulped over the additional costs and agreed.

The remains of the gates had for some time sat as an unsightly mess in the front garden. Then they were placed in the garages. On his solicitor's advice Spitti did not dispose of them but had them moved to a storage unit to free up space in the garages. There was discussion of a need for an engineering report focusing on the door-opening programme and electrics. Spitti's solicitor advised they should try and instruct an expert jointly with Plinth's lawyers. Spitti voiced the opinion,

"I know them bloody gates is crap... make it worse we 'ave a report to prove it."

After having a big gap for weeks where the gates once stood Spitti also gave into pressure and returned the front garden to its open plan format. The decorations to the pillars and porch remained.

Ruud Van Dijk had rented a flat in the centre of town and he would cycle round frequently either trying to calm Spitti down or cheer Spitti up. Either way was an uphill struggle, but the efficient Dutchman was uncomplaining. His time in the UK had taught him that Brits were a load of grumblers and he felt he was above this; even when younger fans sniggered and joked about his name.

Achille Plinth was of course deeply unhappy. It was unclear whether it was his injury or ruined car which upset him the most. Even though he was not in hospital and went out of his country estate to regular private physiotherapy he had not deigned to visit his colleagues at the stadium. He would from time-to-time fire off an email to someone. In due course his lawyers issued proceedings against Paulino Spitti and Scarlett International Electric Gates Ltd.

Senator Wayney was kept informed of developments and toyed with visiting Waste but things at the football club did seem to be under control, for now at least. He was due to visit soon anyway to check how Penny was doing.

As it happened Penny was making good progress with Penny's Animal Haven and Eco Camping Centre even though the locals referred to it as 'Jim Knight's old place'.

Thanks to her father's funding the house had been renovated, the barns and out-buildings repaired, and some yurts installed with eco-friendly facilities down by the lake. Her animals numbered about nine sheep (including three lambs), Onion and Pickle the geese who had produced some goslings, Emperor the cockerel and his hens, some young cats Eeny, Meany, Miny and Mo who came in as kittens, some new acquisitions and Harley the black cat with the white tipped tail who thought he was in charge. The most recent acquisitions included a one eyed pygmy goat called Marmalade, a duck with one wing, Andy and Pandy the lop-eared rabbits and two small dogs.

Penny had previously been nervous about dogs, but her heart warmed to the scraggy, yappy unwanted canines Ronald and Roderick. They had some Pomeranian in them and the local dogs' home over at Moorlands had already tried to re-home them twice. Their yapping had produced neighbour complaints, so they had persuaded Penny to foster them. Harley treated them with contempt. If they attempted to chase him, he would turn and give the dog in question a sharp cuff around the face. Harley sometimes stole their dog food and was first to nestle on Penny's lap.

The eco campsite was just getting off the ground and Penny now found she was busy with either the animals or the campsite most of the day. She had invested in new computer equipment to do the books and regularly keep in contact with her father. Their web chats which of course involved her mother as well, these days were warm and lively. She also had an open afternoon every other Sunday for local people to visit the animals and buy little souvenirs and teas and coffees. She had had some mugs and mouse mats created by a company and they featured pictures of her creatures. She still thought of her former romance with Lewis Gasson and what a mistake she had made ending the relationship. There had been no-one romantically since.

One 'open' Sunday afternoon Mickey Gasson and his wife Maureen rolled up with their grandchild Tiffany, daughter of their daughter Brittany and her husband Nat Cartey. Mickey and Maureen had clearly been given the job of entertaining Tiffany, a lively toddler, that day. Hanging slightly back was Mickey's younger brother Lewis. There were a handful of other people looking at the animals. Mickey and Maureen were attempting to interest their granddaughter in the various animals.

"Look at the lovely Ba-lambs, Tiff," said Maureen to the toddler who was attempting to run around in a circle until she eventually tumbled over and started crying. Lewis stepped forward with a little children's chocolate bar to distract her.

"Look at the baby geese," Maureen persisted to Tiffany. The child was far more interested in the chocolate.

"Lewis, can you get us some teas and see if she has any squash for our Tiff?" called out Mickey to Lewis indicating towards Penny.

Lewis stepped forward looking nervous and spoke to Penny. "Hello, can we have three teas, all with a bit of milk and two with a couple of sugars, please? Do you have any squash for the kid, too?"

"Sure," replied Penny, also looking nervous. "I can get the teas. I also have a sugar free apple squash or sugar free orange for the kids... Which do you want?"

"Orange, please, my great niece has a plastic, kid's beaker... could you put it in that?" he replied taking it from his pocket.

Penny returned with a tray bearing the drinks a few minutes later and Lewis placed a donation to funds in a box in return. He took the drinks over to Mickey and Maureen who were sitting on a bench with Tiffany. He returned with the tray a minute later and spoke.

"Are you keeping well... the animals look like they agree with you?"

Penny smiled. "It took a bit of getting used to and I'm really busy but, yes, I'm well and I love it here. How are you? You're not on your bike?"

"I'm okay," replied Lewis. "I left the Harley at home today."

At that moment Harley the cat came wandering over.

"I think he thought you were saying his name," said Penny. "His name is Harley."

Lewis bent down and stroked him. There was an immediate loud purr.

"I do like cats," he said. "I had one as a kid. Harley is a great name... he purrs like my Harley Davidson."

Harley purred even more.

"Yeah," said Penny. "He seemed to like the name when I chose it."

Lewis cleared his throat. "Sometimes we get off-cuts of meat at the factory. Can I bring you some one day for the dogs and cats? I know you are a veggie yourself."

"Sure," said Penny. "The dogs and cats have meat or fish so that would be great."

She smiled at Lewis but did not want to appear too eager for him to come back even though her heart was racing, and she was very keen for him to call again.

Lewis smiled back in a warm way. If truth be told there had been no woman in his life since his time with Penny and his instinct was to try to slowly rekindle their relationship.

"I best go back to the family, now," he said. "But I'll drop by when I have some off-cuts."

Chapter 3

STEVEN WENT TO WORK AT the court these days with confidence and self-assurance.

"Morning, Shovel," said His Honour Judge Oliver Grasby KC as he puffed at his pipe in the car park. His Honour Judge Aziz Ahmed passed through in a hurry at that moment and winked. District Judges Eric Ercol and Cecily Stump were not far behind. Her Honour Davina dela Notte was already in the building. Steven was now used to the judges and their eccentricities. He was also used to what he felt was the rhythm of the court. Regular attenders on the criminal and family side tended to include members of the O'Hanrahan, Knight and Shagg families.

Regular barristers at the court included Percy Vere, Chris Ellison, Verity Timpson-Saunders, and Miss Faye Leafly. Of course, there were others. The court had not been visited by Dr Gordon Flaughtersdough for some time. The latter was not that popular with the judiciary who regarded him as incompetent and pompous. Waste Borough Council had their own in-house legal team, and they were usually represented by Ivan Huff. Local solicitors included Bernie Blunt and Sue Rosemary. Steven understood that Sonja Sidebottom had now gone to work for a firm in which District Judge Ercol's wife, Tina, was a partner. He would need to make arrangements to make sure Sonja, like other members of that firm did not appear before District Judge Ercol.

Sonja had spent a period doing locum work in the Circuit town before getting the permanent job with Botch, Brath and Ercol. The environment was still new to her. She made her way that morning to a pleasant red-brick Georgian house just off the square. The brass plate said 'Botch, Brath, Ercol & Co Solicitors and Commissioners for Oaths'. As one entered the building one went into a reception and waiting area.

Just behind this area the rest of the ground floor was given over to two interview rooms and a general office. There was also a staircase down to the cellars which were used for file storage. The first floor housed the oak panelled boardroom, Mr Brath's office and the accounts department. The second floor housed the offices of the other partners and a couple of their support staff. On the third floor there were some small offices for junior lawyers and the rest of the support staff. There was no lift, so any disabled clients were generally seen downstairs.

Mr Botch had of course long since retired and was not listed as a partner on the notepaper. Mr Brath was still listed as senior partner although it was quite clear most major decisions were left to the other partners. The next in seniority was Tina Ercol and the other partners were respectively Dan Walpole, Freddy Glasstone, Gemma Palmerstone, and Sally Pitt. Tina Ercol specialised in financial remedy work within divorce and managed the family law team. Dan Walpole was a criminal law specialist and due to his pushy manner at the Magistrates' Court he was nicknamed 'the warpath'. He had slicked back greasy looking black hair and when Sonja had met him briefly she had found him rather intimidating. Freddy Glasstone managed the personal injury and debt departments. Sally Pitt managed the Wills and conveyancing departments. Tommy Mills, a legal executive undertook most of the firm's domestic conveyancing work. Tim Bailey, an assistant solicitor dealt with commercial conveyancing. Erica Gibson a legal executive dealt with wills and probate. Jyoti Patel, a newly qualified solicitor dealt with housing and assisted with personal injury work. A retired police officer, Alan Ritter, acted as outside clerk and police station representative. Sonja had been drafted in to act in children disputes. There seemed to be a pecking order amongst people at the firm and Sonja felt she was at the bottom of the pile, below all the other legal staff including the slightly goofy looking trainee Dudley Dipshaw and below the receptionists Erin and Di, below the whole accounting department, and below the partners' secretaries. She was not sure she was below the two general admin staff who assisted the lawyers who were not partners but at times she wondered if she had swopped being a dogsbody at Bernie Blunt's firm for being a dogsbody at this firm.

As Sonja climbed the stairs that morning, she found herself waylaid by Tina Ercol.

"Can you come and give me a hand with something?" she said.

"Yes, of course," said Sonja and made her way to Tina's office.

Tina explained, "I am trying to finish the financial remedy case for Sir Hugo Wentworth-Knubb. His wife Muriel left him about three years ago, but he has taken his time to sort out his divorce and financial settlement. It's a bit embarrassing… my secretary has arranged a conference with counsel for Sir Hugo for tomorrow, but I am already in court. It's with Alison Oval KC and her junior Dora Smith. Alison is delightful. Could you go tomorrow?"

"Where?" said Sonja looking worried. The answer came that it was in Chambers near the Circuit Centre as the case was being dealt with there, rather than in Waste. The journey did not worry her as she used to commute to that town. She was, however, daunted by the thought of attending a meeting with Sir Hugo and a top silk on a subject which was outside her usual work.

"I don't have much experience of financial cases," added Sonja.

"Look," said Tina. "To work at this firm you must be adaptable, you must be what we call a 'Botch' person, to fit in here."

Sonja nodded looking like a rabbit caught in the headlights. She expressed her agreement, however, and said she would spend part of today preparing. Indeed, she pored over the information all afternoon and in her own time in the evening. Auntie Bea came up to her room and interrupted her to come and have something to eat.

She had recently moved into Penny's old room at Auntie Bea's after feeling that her parents were constantly disappointed with her. Auntie was family of course, being her great-aunt so her mother was not too worried by her moving to Auntie Bea's house. Although she had assisted her parents settle their neighbour dispute with their former neighbour Nat Cartey, her father would still say things which got under her skin. Bertrand Sidebottom would sniff and say, "If I had had a son, he would have become a consultant like me." His wife Marjorie, who had been a nurse, never stepped in to defend Sonja.

Auntie Bea sat Sonja down at her small dining room table and said, "Get that down you, girl," as she placed a plate of cold sliced sausages, potato salad and green salad in front of Sonja.

"That taste's good," said Sonja. "Your potato salad is different to shop potato salad."

"It's got chives and spring onions from the allotments," was the reply.

"Don't you think you should try to take a little time off?" continued Auntie Bea.

"I wish I could," said Sonja. "Mum and Dad were very disappointed when I walked out on my old boss, Bernie Blunt. I want to make something of myself. I want to show I am not a disappointment. That being a solicitor not a doctor is okay."

"Well you should not let those thoughts rule your life. When your mother was a youngster, she was a big scatterbrain, but she got where she wanted to be. Everyone has to climb the greasy pole of life in their own way," said Auntie sagely. "For example, there was that Brummy lad Chris Ellison who stayed here a short while. Do you know him?"

"Yes, he is a barrister. I do know him," replied Sonja.

"Well," said Auntie, "he's just bought a tiny one-bed flat. When he first came here, I think people laughed at his accent. But I reckon everyone thinks well of him. So don't you let Bodge, Brass and All Cold discourage you… I can remember Mr Brath when he was a young man. These days he probably has false teeth but years ago he had buck teeth and a slight stammer. We called him 'Bunny Breath' then. He lost the stammer as I recall and became quite grasping."

Sonja laughed. Auntie continued, "I should go round to your parents if I were you and tell them your bosses are giving you a lot of responsibility. You'll be alright, girlie."

Sonja said, "Yes, I'll probably see Mum and Dad for Sunday lunch."

"You should catch up with your friends too," said Auntie.

"Yes, I will," said Sonja. "But first I have to go to this meeting tomorrow."

Sonja took the train next day while Sir Hugo Wentworth-Knubb allowed his sister Pandora to accompany him and to drive him to the conference. The Chambers of Alison Oval KC were in a large Victorian building next to a small garden in the legal part of the provincial city where the Circuit Office was situated. The Chambers was called 1 Herbacious Court Chambers and Alison Oval KC was head of Chambers. Her junior, Dora Smith was a junior member of the same Chambers. The old-fashioned atmosphere of the Chambers belied the amount of technology present. Certainly, the atmosphere suited Sir Hugo. Introductions were made and everyone became seated in a conference room with an outlook onto the gardens.

Alison Oval KC started talking. "The next stage in the proceedings is what is called a Financial Dispute Resolution hearing. The judge will try to see if he can get people to settle. I understand your ex is anxious to re-marry so now is as good a time as any to have a go."

Sir Hugo nodded. "I am finishing being a Member of Parliament so I would like to get this out of the way. I don't have a great deal of money. I mortgaged some of my land to keep the factory going. The house has covenants on it meaning it can't be sold out of the family. I was able to lease the West Wing to Scyathica and Steven because Scyathica's my niece and they took on restoring it."

"Can I ask you about this jewellery and silver which is referred to in the papers?" asked Alison.

Sir Hugo looked bashful. "When Muriel left as well as the jewellery, I gave her which was worth about £30,000, she took some family heirlooms out of the safe which I had hoped to pass on to my niece, Pandora's daughter, in due course. There were a couple of fine gold pocket watches, a small bracelet with rubies in it and an antique cameo brooch amongst other things. She also took a silver tea service and silver candlesticks out of a cabinet."

Pandora looked horrified and said quietly, "It's a good thing Scyathica was not expecting these things from you. I hope it helps you to argue Muriel should not have any more."

Alison Oval KC said, "Muriel makes some weak argument that as your wife she thought they were hers. She does not exactly deny they are family heirlooms nor that the items she took without your knowledge or agreement were worth another £25,000 or so. It does not make her look good."

Sir Hugo looked even more sheepish. "She drained the joint account as well. She took about £8000 out and left it overdrawn to the tune of about £3000. I could not afford to do repairs to the West Wing, so it was a good thing Scyathica and Steven took it on. But I suppose I will have to settle with her for something more."

Sir Hugo mentioned a modest sum of money he had put to one side. Alison Oval KC smiled.

"Well, it might be enough if she is anxious to conclude matters and remarry. Taking family heirlooms will not look good. It may be useful to have some statements about the history of the items and how they were intended to be passed on within the family. Also, a statement about the arrangement regarding the West Wing. I understand it was a shortish marriage anyway, four years, and she did not bring any resources into it."

"That's right," said Sir Hugo. "My first wife died in childbirth and our infant son with her, when I was a young man serving in the Army in Brunei. She was a local girl. I don't think I realised how delicate she was…" Sir Hugo looked very sad.

Pandora patted his arm. Alison Oval KC continued to be upbeat.

"Who is representing Muriel Wentworth-Knubb?" she asked.

Dora Smith responded,

"She has just instructed Dr Gordon Flaughtersdough under the Bar direct access scheme." Dora Smith pronounced the name as it was spelled.

"It's pronounced Flowerdew," piped up Sonja.

"Do you know him?" asked Sir Hugo and Alison together.

"Yes," replied Sonja. "My old boss used him. My parents had him on a boundary dispute, but they sacked him."

"I've never been against him…"

Sonja responded to Alison, "It's just my personal opinion as a rather junior solicitor but I did not think he knew what he was doing, and he also seemed rather pompous."

Dora Smith added, "That corresponds with the gossip about him. He has a reputation for thoroughly irritating judges, and I understand he plans to retire soon."

"Well," said Alison, "I will have to persuade him and the judge that what you offer is a handsome settlement."

Sir Hugo and Pandora offered Sonja a lift back to Waste which she gratefully accepted. When she arrived at Auntie Bea's house, she felt much more confident. Auntie Bea was in the process of assisting Pierre Bruele to pack up. Pierre had managed to finish improvements at the Farthwaite Arms, so he was able to move there. He now had a habitable bed-sitting room upstairs in the pub with a kitchenette and en suite shower room. He had converted two other attic rooms to compact double bedrooms with en suite shower rooms which he intended to let out for bed and breakfast. The pub kitchen had been greatly improved and the toilets repainted. He had kept the pub going after a fashion while he did the works. Most of the locals eyed him suspiciously but they were pleased to retain their 'local'. He had managed to keep on the wife of the previous owner as a part-time cook and he had taken on a young girl who was training at catering college to assist in the kitchen in the evenings. He employed a local barmaid and cleaner. Everything else he would have to do himself.

"Well," said Auntie Bea, "I wish you luck. We'll make a proper Englishman of you yet!"

Pierre rather put pay to this idea by kissing her Gallic fashion on both cheeks.

"Well, I never!" said Auntie Bea going a shade of beetroot.

Pierre smiled. "I hope you will visit my place soon," he said, and looking at Sonja, "and you too… I hope people from Waste will come out to my pub and enjoy some good French cooking."

As it happened it was not long before His Honour Judge Oliver Grasby KC came out to the Farthwaite Arms. It had always been a firm favourite with him. He wanted to treat Aziz and Amina to a nice meal so he hoped there would be something there to suit them. He took the precaution of checking the brand-new website of the pub bistro and was very impressed. It had all the old favourites plus some welcome new dishes which included some which he thought the Ahmeds might eat without being concerned they were not Halal. The sample menu read as follows:

'Starters

Traditional selection

Chicken parfait with onion marmalade and soda bread

Country chicken and vegetable broth

Warm smoked trout with a rocket salad

Vegetarian selection

Avocado and mango salad

Heritage tomato and beetroot salad (with or without Auvergne goat's cheese)

Mains

Traditional and Bistro… All served with new potatoes, French fries or mash and fresh veg of the day)

Pie of the day (for example, steak and ale, or chicken and bacon)

Steak of the day (for example, sirloin steak with bearnaise sauce)

Pigeon and peas

Beer battered cod or haddock

Poulet au Normandie

Vegetarian (served with salad or salad garnish)

Salmon or wild grilled mushroom burger in homemade bun with fresh salad

Asparagus risotto (with or without parmesan cheese)

Vegetable and bean ratatouille (suitable for vegans)

Desserts

Fresh fruit in season e.g. strawberries or raspberries with choice of cream, yoghurt, or ice cream

Crepes flambee in brandy

Pear or peach upside-down cake with cream or vanilla ice cream (in season)

Choice of homemade ice-creams and sorbets

Pear poached in white wine (in season)

Alcohol free tiramisu

Cheeseboard

Coffee, tea, petit fours'

Oliver sought and obtained Annette's agreement to invite the Ahmeds out to dinner to the Farthwaite Arms. Aziz Ahmed and Oliver Grasby continued a practice they had started when Aziz lived in his previous home which was to meet each evening and do a long walk together when they would smoke cigars and put the world to rights. As they walked near the golf links and admired the scene Oliver raised the issue of having dinner together.

"I have checked the menu. There are quite a few fish and veggie options," he said. "Is it okay for you to go to a pub? At this time of year, we can sit outside anyway."

Aziz smiled. "I am sure it would be very nice to get Amina away from her council work. She has become very engrossed in the fate of Waste Waste. Although we do not drink alcohol, I will pretend I don't see you having your wine."

Oliver booked a table for a date they had discussed, and the two couples sat outside on a balmy early June evening. Oliver was delighted that his old watering hole had only had minor changes such as a lick of paint to the toilets. The food was better than ever. The pub still had its fair share of old codgers. On the next table Oliver could hear three old boys rambling on,

"Is you entering the veg competition later this summer?" said one.

"Naw, reckon since I retired as game-keeper I been so busy don't reckon mi veg'll be up to much this year," one of his companions replied.

The third one said, "Well I 'ope them bleeding caterpillars don't 'ave all my caulis. I 'ad oped I'd sell a bit of mi veg to the Frenchie 'ere at the pub. 'S not doing a bad job I suppose."

The first one said, "I knows more people is coming for the food but at least 'e's kept some decent ales and a quiz night like we always 'ad. One thing he ain't got is decent pork scratchings… you can't beat pork scratchings made the old way."

Oliver smiled.

Amina interrupted Oliver listening to the old codgers to tell him of the concerns over Waste Waste. It appeared the men behind the consortium who owned the Waste plant had unconnected troubles. As far as she could tell the Waste business was quite successful. Despite some controversies about it, the town wanted the plant to keep going. It was a major employer and contributed financially to the economy of the town. Waste Borough Council had had no success actually speaking to the plant's owners who hid behind offshore corporations, but the onsite manager Ron Woodhouse had at least put the council in touch with the company's lawyers in London who promised to tell the council if the plant was to go into administration.

The council was powerless to do anything except lobby. There was a power vacuum too with Nat Cartey having to resign and Sir Hugo Wentworth-Knubb being in the course of retiring.

Mickey Gasson, the union convenor at the plant had also been put in touch with the plant's lawyers by Ron Woodhouse but he could get little information out of them. He talked gloomily to Maureen in his kitchen,

"Faceless cowards, they are. It's the workers who will suffer... the whole town actually."

"You could have a demo," said Maureen.

"And seeing as one investor is in prison, and one investor has run away... who will see it?" said Mickey angrily. "No-one cares about Waste unless they come here."

"Well," said Maureen, "we shall just have to hope someone does come to Waste who can make a difference."

Mickey shook his head.

Chapter 4

SCYATHICA WAS FEELING RATHER QUEASY in the mornings to the extent she preferred to sit in the garden rather than on the roof before she went to work. Steven took her some tea and a ginger biscuit.

"That's a funny thing to have for breakfast," he said.

"Ginger helps with morning sickness I believe and anyway that's what I feel like," said Scyathica.

"Shall I drive you to work today?" said Steven.

"Yes, please. I'm not going anywhere other than the office today. I have a meeting with Stacey Birch about maternity leave and suchlike," replied Scyathica.

"Stacey seems a good boss," said Steven, "so I'm sure things can get properly sorted. Besides, I'm sure Lord Coldharbour will be fair to you... he seems to have been fine recently."

"Yes, he is not my favourite uncle. Uncle Hugo is, but recently he has been fair. I don't know whether it's something to do with having a son who is a disgraced MP... who has now installed as a radio DJ."

Lord Coldharbour of Southend of course owned the radio station and local paper within his media empire. Scyathica had originally been banished by him to Waste for not being hard-nosed enough when she was a reporter in London. Nat Cartey aka Nathanial Justin Coldharbour was his son. Davey Scarlett, Scyathica's dodgy dealing father was Lord Coldharbour's half-brother. Scyathica did not know where he was, other than probably on his yacht in the Caribbean. Steven nodded in agreement. Having dropped Scyathica at work he continued to Waste Combined Court. Since Steven became Chief Judge's Clerk and Team Leader and Derek Devene had frequent absences due to the ill health of his husband, Steven found there were days when he was acting as a 'de facto' court manager.

His Honour Judge Aziz Ahmed and family had settled into Nat Cartey's house very well. They did not do anything to annoy their neighbours and both Aziz and Amina felt more at home in a less ostentatious house. Aziz smiled when he passed his former home. It looked an awful mess now with its garish pillars and tussocks of grass poking up where the railings used to stand. Aziz had his sons in the car as he was in the course of taking them to Waste Grammar School. Both had their noses in books.

"Can we have Frank over for a sleepover so we can do a chess marathon?" said Helal suddenly.

"Frank?" said Aziz. "Who's he? I thought your best mate was Flavio?"

Ali piped up, "He's called Frank these days."

"If your mum is okay with the date," no problem, said Aziz. He concentrated on the road and soon was able to drop the boys off at school before making the journey to court. He was there in a few minutes. Her Honour Judge Davina dela Notte arrived just a few seconds after him.

"Good morning," said Aziz. They had some small talk about the weather and then he said, "My boys want to have your lad over to play chess… a sleepover... or if they play all night... a 'chessover'! They refer to your boy as Frank… is that right?"

Davina smiled wryly. "Yes, he wants to be known as Frank Nott... and of course he can stay at your house. Your boys are such serious lads."

They both carried onto their Chambers. Aziz was not relishing the day as it was the start of a jury trial involving a particularly nasty sexual abuse allegation. A visiting fairground worker was alleged to have brutally sodemised a twelve-year-old boy who was helping out on his candy floss stall last year for pocket money when the travelling fair visited town in the autumn. He was denying everything even though there was very compelling evidence which meant the lad, now thirteen, would have to give evidence. As a father of teenage boys, the case struck a chord with Aziz.

Down the corridor Steven knocked at the door of the Chambers of Her Honour dela Notte.

"Come in," she said smiling.

Steven replied,

"Good morning, Your Honour, I wanted to apologise for no-one telling you that you had this case in your list. It appears the Legal Advisor at the Magistrates' Court conferred with Mr Devene and since you had previously had some of the parties some months ago it has ended up with you. I think I can recall some of the names from when I was fairly new here… In the circumstances I will be your clerk today."

"Don't worry!" said Her Honour, "I read the casefile online at home last night. It seems Gavin Bagshaw or as he prefers to be known Sir Parcival… has been a busy lad. He is now living with Lila Grimmly who likes to be called Lila du Lac and they have a baby Blanchefleur, and she is expecting another child. The thing is it appears that Sir Parcival, probably because he in reality has money troubles, has decided that they should live without modern amenities. Their home has no electricity or gas. There is no television, computer or telephone. Not all such a bad thing! However, the house is lit by candles and heated by open fires. They are attempting to cook over an open fire in the back garden. They refuse to take their child for standard vaccinations or register her with a GP. Recently our friend Sir Parcival brought a dozen hens and three geese to the back garden of the terraced house. They are not enclosed, and he is threatening to get a pig…"

"Oh dear," said Steven. "I hope he comes without his sword. I have notified security."

"But that's not all," said Her Honour. "His older children Lancelot and Guinevere have been staying for extended periods, but there is little supervision, so they appear to be virtually feral. Their mother Naomi Grubbins also has another child, Arnie. The dad is a local body-builder Lou Stafficoco. There is a question as to whether he is on steroids. Social workers say he can be a bit aggressive when they ask any questions."

"Ahh," said Steven. "I have some of the names of the representatives. I'll be back in five minutes with the rest," which he was.

"Your Honour, apologies if you have some of this information. Representing the local authority is Mr Ivan Huff and the social worker is Mr Desmond St Vincent. Sir Parcival is represented by Bernie Blunt, solicitor, Lila Grimmly is represented by Miss Sonja Sidebottom solicitor, Naomi Grubbins is represented by Verity Timpson-Saunders, counsel, Lou Stafficoco is represented by Max Scott, solicitor and the children are represented through their Children's Guardian Mr Tim Weary by Miss Sue Rosemary. There is a slight complication. It seems that as you may be aware Waste Borough Council apply to place Blanchefleur with her maternal grandmother Mrs Tania Grimmly under an interim care order, but it was not anticipated that would be heard today. Mrs Grimmly has actually turned up and wishes to apply to be a party. She is represented by Mr Chris Ellison, counsel. Mr Huff says he is emailing statements to you from the Fire Service and the RSPCA. It seems there was a fire at the home of Sir Parcival the day before yesterday and when the Fire Service had quickly put out the fire, they called the RSCPA who deemed the house too hazardous for the family's dog and cat. The police were called but did not remove Blanchefleur on the basis her parents agreed the baby could spend a couple of nights at granny's house. He says he will be asking for the interim care order to be made today in the circumstances.

"Also, Dolores Stafficoco is here but I don't think she wants to be a party at the moment. I think her son and Miss Grubbins propose she should move in to assist with the children in the household… she says she is just there to confirm this… Oh, and Mr Huff says he has just emailed you a copy of an application filed this morning to undertake scientific testing on Lou Stafficoco… but…"

"Well," said Her Honour dela Notte. "This is a nice tangle! Alright, I think I'll have a strong coffee and then we'll get started. Please can you ask the usher to get people ready. Please ask her to bring everyone into court except Dolores Stafficoco."

Steven made sure all the equipment in court was working and arranged with Nicky the usher for everyone to be brought into court. The last person to be brought into court was Her Honour dela Notte. Steven announced the case. Ivan Huff began to address Davina. It seemed the issue of party status was not opposed for Mrs Grimmly. The issue of the interim care order was more contentious. It seemed the baby's parents did not object to her staying at her grandmother's home for the foreseeable future, but they opposed the making of the interim care order and any question of her being vaccinated.

Mr Blunt told Davina, "My client says that the Knights of the Round Table did not have their children vaccinated. He believes the ways of chivalry will protect his daughter…"

There were heated representations and the local authority's plan was supported by the grandmother and the Children's Guardian.

Her Honour dela Notte said firmly,

"I think before I proceed further I need to point out that the original Knights of the Round Table existed in a time before vaccination. Surely chivalrous ways today by their successors would be to have your children vaccinated. However, one thing which is missing from any plans is a clear indication of how much contact Blanchefleur will see of her parents and when she will see her siblings… The plans just say, 'It is hoped the grandmother will assist with supervising contact'. I am going to rise for a few minutes so further discussions can take place."

When the hearing resumed Blanchefleur's parents dropped their opposition to vaccination. They also conceded the interim care order on the basis it could be reviewed later after in-depth assessments. The contact was clearly set out, as was the sibling contact.

The hearing now focused further on Lancelot and Guinevere and Arnie. Ivan Huff stated that Lou Stafficoco agreed to move out of the family home save for one night a week pending test results and assessments. He had a room over the gym he ran and would return one night a week for contact to his baby (supervised by his mother) in addition to two mornings a week contact at a local dads' club. His mother would move into the family home to assist supervising contact and to help out generally. Matters would be reviewed speedily if it was clear he was not taking steroids.

It was agreed contact between Sir Parcival and Lancelot and Guinevere would be supervised by the local authority at a family centre. Miss Grubbins would also enrol them in after school clubs, so they had more outlets for their energy. There would be interim supervision orders on them and Arnie, but the situation would be monitored. The stumbling point was Waste Borough Council's application for hair strand tests on Mr Stafficoco for steroids. Mr Stafficoco had a completely shaved head and no beard or moustache. His face was utterly smooth as was his head which just had a small tattoo on it which read 'The Greatest'. His solicitor Max Scott addressed the court.

"Your Honour, my client has no hair."

"What about body hair?" answered Davina.

"None," said Max Scott. "None anywhere. It is all part of his body building regime…" There was a slight snigger from the lay parties.

Sue Rosemary intervened and suggested testing of nail clippings. It was agreed this would be pursued.

Ivan Huff then said, "Your Honour, I think all advocates are agreed this case should come back before you in a fortnight or so, so that assessment plans can be examined. I believe there may be applications for psychological assessments as well. Is it possible that your learned clerk can find a listing of about an hour?"

"Mr Hovell," said Davina, "please see what you can find in the diary." And, indeed Steven did as was requested.

By the time the date was fixed and Her Honour dela Notte concluded the morning's hearing by summarising the orders and stating clear reasons for each aspect the morning was gone.

Steven went to Davina's Chambers to check if she required anything further of him.

"It's a good thing nothing else was listed this morning," she said. "The afternoon does not look too bad with a couple of pleas and directions so I might get a punctual getaway."

"Indeed, Your Honour. One defendant is in custody, and I have checked the prison van has brought him. The other defendant is on bail. Everything should be good to start at 2 o'clock," replied Steven.

Her Honour responded, "You are always well organised... Now it's already 1.15 so go and get some lunch, Mr Hovell."

So that is what he did.

The afternoon proceeded effortlessly. Court sitting ended punctually at 4 o'clock which enabled Steven to undertake a number of useful admin tasks before going to pick up Scyathica. She looked rather tired but was otherwise in good spirits.

"I really fancy some chips from the fish and chip shop," she said.

Steven laughed. "This is definitely the baby talking... that's never been your sort of thing before..."

"And ginger biscuits and strawberry ice-cream," she added.

About the same time Davina dela Notte arrived back at her flat. She called out, "Frank, are you home?" as she put her key in the lock.

A deep masculine voice replied, "Who the hell is Frank?" There was her husband Jerome dela Notte Collins sitting in her living room with a face like thunder.

Davina explained, "We have told you before Flavio wants to be called Frank Nott rather than Flavio dela Notte Collins."

"I suppose you have mentioned it now I think of it, but I didn't take it seriously," said her husband calming down slightly.

"Where is he anyway?" asked Davina.

Jerome replied,

"He flew past me and went to his room and slammed the door shut."

"I suppose you called him Flavio," said Davina sighing.

"I did. It's the stupid name you chose after all when he was a new-born," he continued. "Aren't you pleased to see me? I have been really looking forward to being here. I miss you and our son, and I feel... well, very jaded," said Jerome stretching out on the armchair, one long leg dangling over the arm on one side of it. Jerome was a tall, blond man who either wore designer suits and designer shirts, or designer jeans with white or black T-shirts and skin hugging leather jackets. He was clad in the latter outfit today. His wrinkled face which had been heavily tanned by a tanning machine at the London gym he attended did not match his 'youthful' apparel.

"I am very, very pleased to see you," said Davina sounding as if she meant it. "Shall I get you a drink or a coffee or something?"

"A coffee would be fine," said Jerome. They began to have a civilised conversation about what each of them had been doing and the name issue. Jerome agreed that Flavio could call himself Frank Nott if it made him happy. They called him from his room and Jerome cleared his throat,

"Ehm, Frank… I've been talking to your mother, and I am quite happy to sign any papers so you can be known as Frank Nott. I'm sorry if I have been away so much and not much of a dad… so I promise I will visit more often."

Flavio now known as Frank said, "Thanks, Dad," without much expression.

Jerome continued, "I'm very tired tonight so as for food I'll settle for whatever your mum has in the cupboard… but in the next few days I would like to take us all out for a meal. Do you have a favourite place?"

Frank looked a little more animated. "The Harbour View pub does some really good burgers in its restaurant," he said.

Jerome raised his eyebrows but said, "Okay then."

Davina added, "It's okay their menu has many other things too!"

Davina was not much of a cook and truth be told she did not have much in store in the flat. She said tentatively, "I think maybe we'll have a takeaway tonight. There is a good Indian place by the station. I can get the menu…"

Father and son were in approval, so the evening further lightened over an Indian take-away.

Over the next few days Jerome made a better acquaintance with Waste. His previous visits had been so fleeting he had never really had time to absorb what the town had to offer. He learned about how Frank was getting on at school. He met Helal and Ali when they called in to see Frank to invite him to a sleepover to play chess. He met Aziz and Amina fleetingly. He walked around the town centre and admired the old buildings in the town square. He had a drink and lunch at the Knubb Arms. He learned about Knubb sausages (which he of course tried) and he became aware of Waste Waste.

One afternoon he walked to the town square intending to meet his wife when she finished her sittings in court. His attention was drawn to a straggly bunch of protestors with a couple of placards which read 'Save Waste Waste'. They were standing outside the Town Hall looking forlorn. He went up to them.

"I'm not from round here," he said to them, politely, "but I'm in business and I have heard the plant does good business... what is the problem?" he asked.

"Bloody typical..." started one of the bunch mouthing off about 'outsiders'.

"Hang on," said another one. "He's not from Waste... are we not trying to get people to notice? I'll explain it to him." He turned to Jerome. "It seems the plant is in danger of closing because two of its most important investors are crooks. One is a Frenchie... Xavier something who is in prison. The other is some crooked businessman Davey Scarlett who has run away," said the protestor.

"Thank you," said Jerome politely, giving nothing away.

He left swiftly and made for the alleyway leading to the court car park.

When he subsequently went out to dinner with his wife and son he mentioned the issues with Waste Waste to them and his encounter with the demonstrators.

Davina said, "The two main industries of the town are Waste Waste and the sausage and bacon factory. It would be a disaster for the town if Waste Waste went under."

Jerome responded, "I would like to do something other than just trade in the City. If I had something in Waste to keep an eye on, I might be able to do less in the City and spend more time here. I never knew what you saw in the place before, but to be honest it has grown on me. What would you think of me looking into the finances of Waste Waste and perhaps putting together a consortium to acquire it... it's a bit of a long shot... I don't know if anything would come of the idea, but I didn't even want to start looking into it, if you both did not agree. I'd have to sell some of my other investments of course. What do you think?"

Frank had been munching into a large burger. He put it down and beamed at his father. "Go for it, Dad," he said.

Davina said, "If it seems okay financially, yes, go for it."

Chapter 5

SONJA SIDEBOTTOM FOUND SHE WAS quite pleased to be given the job of going to the Circuit Court when Sir Hugo's financial dispute resolution hearing was to be heard by His Honour Judge Raymond Portentious KC. She had found Alison Oval KC very pleasant, and she also had confidence in her and Dora Smith. There was also a rapport with Sir Hugo Wentworth-Knubb and his sister Pandora. She re-read the papers in the case and as best she could studied the law on matrimonial financial proceedings. They all met at 1 Herbacious Court Chambers before going 'over the road' as counsel called it, to the Central Circuit Court. Sir Hugo and Pandora were surprised she had not asked them for a lift. Alison Oval KC took them at a brisk pace to court number 8 which stood off a gloomy hall at the back of the neo-Gothic building. An usher stood there with a clipboard waiting for them. Sonja could see Muriel Wentworth-Knubb, a fit looking man with a goatee beard (presumably her fiancé), a spindly pallid youth (presumably the solicitors' clerk) and Dr Gordon Flaughtersdough huddled in a corner at the far end of the hall. On the door of the court a sign which read 'In Chambers'.

They were soon called into court. It was resplendent in dark walnut panelling. Sonja noticed the man with the goatee had entered court with Muriel and her legal team. Dr Gordon Flaughtersdough was attired in a midnight blue velvet suit with a dark blue cravat. He must have been quite hot in the summer weather. His greying dark hair and his moustache flopped lankly. He looked like an ageing croupier. There was a stark contrast with Alison Oval KC and Dora Smith who were dressed immaculately in similar dark ladies' pinstripe suits with cream blouses.

When His Honour Judge Portentious KC came into court he scowled down from his raised dais. A man with a bulbous purple nose he looked like an old caricature of a judge.

"What's he doing here?" he boomed out looking at the man with the goatee beard.

Dr Flaughtersdough cleared his throat. "Your Honour, this is my client's intended…"

"Well, he can intend himself outside the court door," came the terse reply from the judge.

His Honour Judge Portentious KC leaned forward after goatee beard had gone. "Now outline your client's position."

Dr Flaughtersdough's summary was full of bluster and not much substance. Alison Oval KC was concise, clear and utterly relevant.

"I can give the clearest indication," said the judge. "The wife's position sounds like clap-trap... the husband's position sounds compelling. Now try to settle…"

Which is what they did. Muriel caved in and agreed to Sir Hugo's terms. They returned before the judge and explained.

"That seems appropriate," he said. "Hand me Heads of Agreement signed by both parties by 4pm today and a full signed draft minute of order within 7 days. I'll rise now."

Later in the afternoon, Sir Hugo and Pandora offered Sonja a lift but she had to decline as Alison Oval KC had left her with the task of handing in the Heads of Agreement to the court. Dr Flaughtersdough was also there when they presented the signed document to the judge's clerk. Once they had concluded this task he said with a sigh,

"One of my last cases you know. I am retiring soon... I think I am going out with a whimper rather than a bang."

"I am sure people will miss you," said Sonja diplomatically. This brought about a smile.

"I was thinking of visiting Waste after I retire… to go to the pubs and see the countryside… it's somewhere I always enjoy."

Sonja smiled. "If you come, I'll look out for you."

Somehow the world seemed a rather better place to Sonja. As she travelled back on the train her heart warmed to her hometown. She sat back contented in the railway carriage and was nodding off when a Brummy voice said,

"Hello, how are you?" It was Chris Ellison the young barrister she knew slightly who had lodged for a time at Auntie Bea's house.

"Thought I saw you at Herbacious Court t'other day…" he continued.

"Yes," she replied, "Alison Oval has been doing a case."

"She's very good," said Chris. They continued some light chit-chat and agreed they would have a drink together at the Knubb Arms when they got to Waste.

It had not, however, been such a good day for His Honour Judge Oliver Grasby KC. The case of Plinth v Spitti and Scarlett International Electric Gates Ltd had been issued and had found its way to Waste Court. The case had then found its way to District Judge Cecily Stump. She had had a brief telephone conference but had decided that there should be an attended hearing before the Circuit Judge, and she had had it listed before him, without asking him or notifying him at the time. There was a scribbled note on his desk,

'Dear Oliver,

This is about the case of the footballers and the gates. I thought you should have it as a matter of urgency rather than a Circuit Judge or High Court Judge further up the road, nearer to trial. I have done the bare minimum managing the costs and case managing it. There is an application about preserving the evidence and doing a reconstruction which sounds a bit complicated. Also, the case could attract publicity and the second defendant can't be found… Best Wishes Cecily'.

He looked at the details of the case and decided District Judge Cecily Stump had passed the buck. He would have to do something to irritate her. She was rather a nervous soul so it could not be anything too extreme. He much preferred his criminal work. Before he got to the wretched civil case, he had old Jonas Tomaltry O'Haloran up before him again on an indictment for breaking into HM Prison Waste. Give him a case like that any day! He fiddled with his phone distracted by thoughts of what he could do to irritate Cecily Stump. He scrolled down on his phone looking to play a piece of soothing music to calm himself down. An ad popped up:

"For download or CD listen to Jamson Damson and his blues band's 'Evening with Jemms Dutchland'. Listen to Jamson Damson's blues and jazz hits such as 'My little choo choo choo' and 'I got potato sadness'."

He played the sampler from the ad. It was just the sort of cacophony he was sure Cecily would hate. Her "gentleman" as she called her partner was heavily into Morris dancing and Oliver was aware Cecily was interested in traditional English folk music, so much so that she was always saying how she enjoyed listening to such music on her journeys to and from work. He had an idea. A devilish smile came across his face. He did a quick search on his phone and found a cheap compilation album entitled

'Twenty great Morris Dancing Tunes'. Making sure he made his orders on his phone not on his judicial laptop he ordered two CDs on same day delivery, one being the Jamson Damson album and the other being the Morris Dancing Tunes. Then, he got back to work.

In the first case he had to deal with seventy-year-old Jonas Tomalty O'Haloran. The magistrates had transferred the case to the Crown Court, because old Jonas was on a suspended sentence only handed out by Oliver a fortnight ago for the unsuccessful armed robbery of an off-licence. Jonas had spent the last two nights in police cells having been remanded yesterday by the magistrates after his guilty plea. Incredibly, he had been found in the prison's air venting system trying to crawl into the prison kitchens. Percy Vere had been instructed by the Crown Prosecution Service and old Jonas was represented by Verity Timpson-Saunders. However, Oliver addressed his questions straight to Jonas,

"Why on earth were you trying to break into the prison kitchens?"

"I was hungry, Your Honour," replied Jonas.

"Dear me," smiled Oliver. "Well, you must have been desperate to try and pinch the prison food."

There was laughter in court including from Scyathica who was doing some court reporting today.

Verity Timpson-Saunders addressed Oliver. "My client would not oppose a remand in custody for reports."

"I'm sure he wouldn't," Oliver grimaced. "He would be getting exactly what he wanted. Well, I'm going to see if he can be found a nice bed in a bail hostel."

After he had dealt with Jonas's remand on bail, he turned his attention to the civil case. The press had left, and Steven Hovell was clerking for him on this case. It appeared the urbane Percy Vere was representing Achille Plinth who was present in court wearing a prominent neck collar. Paulino Spitti was represented by the flustered Miss Faye Leafly and was sitting in a corner glowering. No-one was in attendance from Scarlett International Electric Gates Ltd nor was the company represented.

"Your Honour," started Percy Vere, "there is an urgent application for an order against Mr Spitti to preserve the gates and an application to have the gates reconstructed and tested…"

"One thing at a time," said Oliver. "Let's start with preservation of evidence."

Miss Leafly cleared her throat. "There is no dispute about preserving the gates. They are in a storage unit on Waste Industrial Estate."

Percy Vere retorted, "So why did the defendant post a message on social media last week 'I'll make a plinth for Plinth and have the f…ing gates melted into a statue of him to go on it if he don't bleeding shut up about his neck'?"

Miss Leafly went a funny shade of red. "I hadn't noticed that bit in the statements… My client is very upset. He is finding that messages are constantly being put up by Mr Plinth drawing attention to his alleged injuries... he certainly does not intend to destroy evidence."

Plinth called out, "Alleged...! Alleged...! My injuries are not alleged."

"See what I mean?" called out Spitti loudly and excitedly. "This is what I have to put up with."

Oliver said in a booming voice, "Gentlemen, enough. You both have counsel. If Mr Spitti is agreeable, he can give a formal undertaking to preserve the evidence. Both of you can let your counsel do their jobs, or you will find yourself dealt with for contempt."

Both football personalities looked suitably chastened.

"Turning to the issue of reconstruction, Mr Vere, why on earth would you want to reconstruct the accident? Mr Spitti does not dispute the gates were faulty and gave rise to the accident. The second defendant has not even bothered to file a defence," said Oliver.

Percy Vere responded,

"It's a question of causation, Your Honour. Mr Spitti has pleaded that the claimant is put to strict proof as to the damage to the Maserati and he has also pleaded that the banging of the doors against the car could not have caused the nature and extent of the claimant's injuries. My instructing solicitors have found an expert who can rebuild the gates on an abandoned airfield and put a test car through with a crash test dummy."

"One assumes the test car won't be a Maserati?" said Oliver acidly.

"No, Your Honour, just some old banger I think."

Oliver sighed and said, "It just seems a way of making the case more complicated than it needs to be. Surely data on Maserati cars can be obtained from the manufacturer if it's really needed? And the case will need an expert mechanical engineer for each party if the causation issues continue. Mr Plinth has already produced an orthopaedic surgeon's report. That will no doubt need updating and the court may need to consider an application from Mr Spitti to instruct a different consultant if he disputes it. The whole matter is in danger of getting blown completely out of proportion. Even the question over the preservation of evidence could have been sorted out by negotiation."

Percy Vere was persisting, "As Your Honour pleases, but can the costs be in the case?"

"No," said Oliver. "Those instructing you should learn better. Mr Spitti should have the costs of today. Granted, things may not look so good for him later down the line... The rest of the case management in this case needs to be fully sorted out with a full case management and costs' management conference. That type of hearing will not require the parties necessarily and will take about three hours. I will take the undertaking today and make orders in the terms I have discussed. I will transfer the case to the Circuit Centre Court with a request that District Judge Dattail hears the next session. I am aware he does a great deal of the multi-track case management for personal injury work in that court; you may be able to reduce costs further between now and the next hearing if you are able to agree the value of the Maserati. After all, we don't want the case to cost more than a new Maserati, do we!"

Oliver rose rather abruptly and went to his Chambers to see if his same day delivery had arrived. Steven poked his head around the door,

"Cup of tea, Your Honour?" he queried.

"Later maybe. I can make it myself," said Oliver fiddling with two small packages on his desk which had just arrived.

Steven went back to the court office. Derek Devene was absent again. He caught his colleague Julie James on the way out of a meeting of ushers which she had held in her role as usher manager.

Steven said, "The old boy's up to something. He dashed out of court at speed. I know Percy Vere wanted to tell him he wouldn't be appearing in court in future due to his involvement in politics."

"Yes," said Julie, "Judge Grasby had a same day courier delivery... something personal, he said."

They both agreed to keep an eye on His Honour.

Oliver furtively swapped the contents of each CD case with the other and put the Jamson Damson box with its new contents in his pocket. He sidled up the corridor only to bump into District Judge Eric Ercol who was hastening out of the building.

"Must dash," said Eric. "Going to see my mother in her care home."

"I hope... she's well," said Oliver. "What about your list?"

"Fortunately," said Eric, "Cecily took the long injunction trial in Court 3."

"Won't keep you then," said Oliver smiling. Eric speeded towards the backstairs.

Once Eric was out of sight, Oliver crept into Cecily's Chambers and put the CD box right in the middle of her desk. He returned to his own room and chucked an unwanted CD box and contents into his bin. He finished off some paperwork on ongoing cases and made sure he left the building well before anyone came out of Court 3.

Oliver turned the radio on as he drove away smiling to himself. The announcer said,

"And we are sorry to say we are losing Bricey for the world of politics. His last appearance on radio for the time being is a football special this evening…"

Eric Ercol and his wife Tina were pleased to find Maude Ercol in good spirits in her care-home Ivy Bank in Halfthwaite. She took them down the corridor at high speed in her walker pointing out things as if she owned the place. Pausing at the door of another resident who was asleep in her room she announced in ringing tones,

"I don't know why they keep that one. She's dead you know."

Eric found his mother's utterances both embarrassing and funny. She had eventually been unable to cope on her own in her bungalow in Gitthwaite. It was a relief to him that the staff of the home were so caring. He did Court of Protection work where relatives sometimes opposed their loved ones being admitted to homes. In his mother's case she was in the right place.

"Shhh," said Tina Ercol of the sleeping resident. "She is just having a nap, I'm sure. Let's go and sit in your room."

As they steered Maude to her room, District Judge Cecily Stump at long last finished the injunction case. On her return to her Chambers, she was surprised and pleased to see a CD box on her desk 'Twenty great Morris Dancing Tunes'. It was not a CD she had in her collection, and she was sure it was meant for her, given her musical tastes. She wondered what thoughtful person had left it there. She tidied up very quickly and left in haste for her car. She switched on the ignition and pushed the disk into the CD player as she left the court car park. She narrowly avoided running into a lorry when there was a loud blast of 'My little choo choo choo'. She found, 'I got potato sadness' even worse, but she did not want to fiddle about while driving in the Waste traffic. By the time she could pull in safely she had also had to listen to, 'I shower with bananas and trumpets' and 'The blocked plughole with hair blues'.

Needless to say, the following morning District Judge Cecily Stump was asking everyone she could who had put the disk on her desk. His Honour Judge Oliver

Grasby KC was apparently tied up, writing a judgment when he was not sitting in court, so he was one of the few people she could not ask. His door was closed with a 'do not disturb' sign.

"It was dreadful," she said. "I could have had an accident. I can't imagine who could have done such a thing."

Steven could.

When a quiet moment arose towards the end of lunch-hour Steven Hovell knocked on the closed door of His Honour Judge Grasby KC's Chambers.

"What is it, Shovell?" said Oliver. "Can't you see the sign?"

"We need to have a quiet word," said Steven, coming in, looking very serious and closing the door.

"Sit down," said Oliver. "Are you in some kind of trouble?"

"No, Your Honour," replied Steven, "but you could be. I know you left the CD on District Judge Stump's desk and I have the evidence to prove it. Right before I went home yesterday the cleaner found what looked like the box of a Jamson Damson CD in your bin, so she gave it to me in case you had thrown it away by mistake. Julie James was still there so we decided to see what the disk was inside the box and of course it was Morris Dancing Music."

"Are you going to report me to the Judicial Conduct Investigation Office?" said Oliver looking a bit sick and realizing his joke might have badly backfired.

"No... not at the moment. But you need to behave, Your Honour. District Judge Stump is a very hard-working judge. Only today she helped out District Judge Ercol."

"Where is the CD now?" said Oliver looking shaky. He hoped he could keep the incident from his wife. Annette would never let him hear the end of it as he could have been in serious trouble.

"In the safe... and hopefully that is where it will stay. I have logged it as 'Miscellaneous Judicial Music'. You have been very kind to me, Your Honour, so let us hope District Judge Stump forgets the incident quickly and we have no further such incidents."

"That's blackmail, Shovell... My how you have grown in confidence from the shy young man who came here," replied Oliver now smiling.

"Thank you for the compliment. All will be well I'm sure, if you behave, Your Honour," said Steven.

Chapter 6

NEXT MORNING STEVEN HOVELL DROPPED off Scyathica at the Newspaper and Media offices and continued into work at the Combined Court only to be faced with the not unexpected news that Derek Devene had taken early retirement to look after his husband Julian who had sadly developed Parkinson's disease. Julie James said to him,

"As soon as they advertise it you should go for the court manager's job. You've been practically running the place for the last few months anyway."

Steven said that he would think about it. In reality he probably would apply. The money would be useful with the baby coming. Last year he had trained a new judge's clerk Lindy Pinney and she had proved to be extremely competent. He would talk it over with Scyathica.

Scyathica's morning had started with a surprise. Stacey Birch sat her down.

"Right," said Stacey, "I know you've done some little bits for the radio, but the managers have a job for you. Everyone has election fever. Bricey has left us. With Nat Cartey's background it would be unfortunate if he was involved in the election coverage, so they are keeping him on light stuff for now... a pop quiz and the like. No, the managers would like you to do a ninety minute show where you interview each of the main candidates. Some will be in the studio, and some will be on the phone, so you won't have to go gallivanting about…"

Scyathica was initially a little flustered. "Me? When? … Don't you want to do it…?"

"No, not me," said Stacey, "I'm strictly a back-room manager. I do my job here. I organise people and then I'm off for a nice peaceful evening with my two ponies Smish and Smash."

Scyathica still expressed hesitation.

Stacey replied, "Well it's not until early next week so you have time to prepare."

Both Steven and Scyathica had plenty to discuss that evening.

At the same time as they returned home in the late afternoon, Penny was delighted to see a Harley-Davidson draw up at her animal shelter. She could recognise the rider instantly even before he dismounted and took off his helmet. Harley the cat appeared from nowhere, purring, and rubbed himself around Lewis Gasson's legs. Lewis took a plastic bag out of each of the motorbike's smart leather panniers.

"There," he said, "didn't I say I'd bring some meat scraps for the dogs and cats. I hope you've got freezer space for some of it?"

Penny indicated that she had.

"Would you like a tea or a coffee or a can of cold cola?" she enquired.

"Something cold would go down a treat," said Lewis.

The meat was put away and they both sat on a wooden seat outside the farmhouse in the late afternoon sun.

"Place looks great. Have you had many campers, yet?" said Lewis.

"That part of things is just taking off," replied Penny in her American drawl. Lewis could not help noticing a number of changes in Penny. In the past he might have expected her to wear a short skirt and high heels. Today she was simply dressed in a pair of old jeans and a grey T shirt. Her hair was neatly scrunched back and there was a healthy pink glow to her cheeks.

"You are looking very well," he said nervously. "How do you manage for transport these days?"

"I'm on 2 wheels too," said Penny pointing to her scooter. "But I'm also taking driving lessons."

"Look," said Lewis, "I don't want to discuss the past... I was wondering whether... I mean I won't be offended if you say 'no'... if I could get tickets for the Jamson Damson gig at the Roebuck and Hogg... would you meet me there and go to the gig with me?"

"I would love to do that," said Penny.

"That's settled then," said Lewis. "I took a gamble and got two tickets already. Jamson Damson is doing a national tour to promote his album. His main concert in this part of the country is for two nights at East Moorlands Hall. He's just doing this one small show for Waste."

Penny smiled and Harley purred. Penny and Lewis agreed when and where they would meet at the pub. Lewis also said he would drop some more meat scraps in when they were available.

"I think I best be going," he said looking as if we wished to be asked to stay.

"Alright," said Penny, with a wistful expression as if she wished he would stay. They slowly said their 'goodbyes'.

Early the next week Steven put in his application to be court manager. Scyathica found herself on air interviewing the main candidates for the by-elections in Waste.

The first candidate she interviewed was Percy Vere who was Labour's candidate for Waste East. He was suave and impeccably dressed.

"Mr Vere, many people will know you as a barrister, can you tell the listeners a little about your background?" started Scyathica.

"Well," said Percy, "my father is a motor mechanic, and my mother is a school cook. I went to a grammar school before I went to university and studied law."

Scyathica persisted, "Isn't it true your father was the motor servicing manager for a well-known chain of garages, and you went to Oxford University?"

"Yes," replied Percy. "But he wasn't always a manager."

Scyathica butted in, "Aren't some of your working-class constituents going to find you rather too middle class and posh?"

"I maintain that seeing my father coming home with oil under his fingernails makes me thoroughly entitled to emphasise my working-class roots. In my heart I am working class and I have always felt it…"

"Even when you were a member of your Oxford College's Conservative Club, and you were reputed to host dinners at the college when thousands of pounds of champagne were imbibed?"

"Just a mistake of callow youth. I'm very much a socialist now," said Percy fidgeting and sounding unconvincing.

"Moving on," said Scyathica, "is it true you would ask for the Waste plant to be nationalised?"

She was given a fair amount of waffle in reply.

Her next interview was a telephone interview with the Conservative candidate for Waste East a lady called Sally Slider. Scyathica was able to establish that this pleasant-sounding lady had originally attended Waste Grammar School and had then left Waste to attend local university in East Moorlands, where she had got a degree in Media Studies. She had her own publicity company operating from East Moorlands and central London. All was going well for Miss Slider until Scyathica said,

"Many people would say you were out of touch with matters in Waste. What are you going to do about the rumoured plant closure?"

"I did not know there was anything wrong at the sausage factory," was the surprising reply.

"But it's Waste Waste which seems to have a problem," said Scyathica. There was silence on the other end of the line and then a clicking noise.

"Oh dear," said Scyathica, we seem to have been cut-off.

Scyathica then attempted to interview the Liberal candidate, a Chemistry teacher, Dr Cardigan, but the telephone line was too bad. She could not hear him, and he could not hear her, and nothing improved when the studio tried re-dialling the call. The other candidates for Waste East had not made themselves available for interview. There was the Green Party candidate Drago Fyshe, who she understood was protesting somewhere else in the country and the Alternative Reasoning Party candidate, Mr Field Mouse who simply could not be reached.

Scyathica then had a studio interview with Bricey, the Conservative candidate for Waste West.

"Mr Brice, most people will know you as a radio presenter and DJ. Can you tell the listeners something about your background and beliefs?"

Bricey responded, "I was born and raised in Waste. I went to East Waste Technical School. I was not very academic, but I loved drama at school. My father had a TV and radio shop at a time when people still had such things. My mother, who is still around, bought and sold second-hand clothes. I believe in giving people a chance to do things for themselves... and in one Nation politics."

It was all going quite well for Bricey. Scyathica then asked him,

"Won't the voters who have revered Sir Hugo for years find you a brash replacement?"

"Well, you would say that wouldn't you? He is an uncle of yours..." was the reply. "I'm sure most voters aren't as stuck-up as you... they just want the job done."

"Aren't you more likely to get the job done if you are not rude to people?" responded Scyathica. "I mean being rude won't fix the worries over Waste Waste."

"Nor will dwelling in the past," responded Bricey. "I am sure the plant can be saved if those involved are sensible."

"Doesn't the plant need Government intervention?" probed Scyathica.

"Should I be elected, I will see what the private sector are doing and I'm sure the Department of Trade will take an interest," said Bricey, vaguely.

Stacey Birch winced as she listened to the interview. She had forgotten about Scyathica's relationship to Sir Hugo. The segment made both Scyathica and Bricey sound bad. She hoped the next interview would be better. This was also a telephone interview. It was with the Labour candidate for Waste West, Dahlia Mallinderall who it transpired was a Lecturer in Politics at the University of East Moorlands.

Scyathica asked, "How would you deal with voters' worries about the future of Waste Waste?" The answer came quickly.

"I would nationalise it. I would have the sausage and bacon factory nationalised too…"

Scyathica retorted, "I don't think it's in any trouble at the moment. I was asking about Waste Waste due to the rumours about its finances."

The answer came, "Well the sausage factory needs nationalising and making vegetarian."

"What about the farm… and the jobs…?" asked Scyathica.

"The workers will I'm sure prefer to process soya or grow lettuce," was the response. Scyathica did not press the point further.

For her next interview Scyathica had the Liberal candidate and the Green candidates for Waste West both in the studio. Dr Bobbin, a psychologist, and Teresa Frill, a marine conservationist, they got into a huge argument about who had better green credentials.

Scyathica then attempted to contact the final candidate for Waste West, the Alternative Reasoning Party's candidate Mr Ron Ratte, by telephone. All she got was a strange squeaking noise.

Once the programme was over, Scyathica went and sat down in Stacey's office and said,

"If I wasn't pregnant I'd opt for a large brandy now! That was awful."

"But it will be great listening!" said Stacey. "You can listen this evening if you want when they air the repeat. We can use some of it in the paper too. By the way, there's more political news. Norman Ryder is stepping down as Leader of the Council and Mayor…"

"Is Easy Ryder leaving the council?" asked Scyathica.

"No. He will still be a councillor, but I understand he is finding the whole Waste Waste issue and some of the other business of the council heavy going," replied Stacey. "The council is a hung council, with Labour and Tory councillors pretty well even. Then there is one Liberal, one Green and one far right councillor from the 'Super, superlative England Party'."

"Who on earth are the 'Super, superlative England Party'?" queried Scyathica.

"A far right outfit who couldn't even raise the deposit to fight in the by-election. I think their entire party may be just three grumpy racists," said Stacey. "However, the point is it is unclear who will emerge as Mayor and Leader of the Council."

As they were having the discussion Steven was hastily filling in an online form. The advertisement for court manager had yet to formally appear online, but his managers had already sought "expressions of interest" for acting as temporary court manager until the position could be filled permanently. Steven did not want to miss out on this.

Another person who was keen to advance in his work was Chris Ellison. The departure of Percy Vere for a political career meant there was a gap in the legal market. Chris had decided he would try to pick up as much good quality work as he could. He sat in the Knubb Arms waiting for Sonja. He remembered how downtrodden and dowdy she seemed when he first came to Waste. These days there was an air of confidence about her. Her eyes sparkled and she had obviously updated her wardrobe. Their relationship was developing quite fast. This was the second time they had been out to dinner together. After an initial drink, Chris intended they should drive out to the Farthwaite Arms. Members of Chambers recommended it.

Having a less sedate evening were Penny and Lewis. They met in a quiet street five minutes away on foot from the pub so they could park the motorcycle and scooter safely. Then, they together walked around the corner to the Roebuck and Hog. Penny looked like the Penny of old. She wore an extremely short, purple mini dress and a pair of thigh high patent leather look very shiny purple boots. She had purple nail varnish, purple eye shadow and what looked to be a sprig of green and purple fruit in her hair.

"Wow!" said Lewis. "You look terrific."

"It's the damson look," said Penny laughing.

When they got to the pub it was very busy. A doorman checked their tickets and when inside they squeezed into a little table in a corner. Swathes of purple red cloth hung from the ceiling over the minute stage. Eventually a soundman went to check the systems and another roady started to examine the spotlights for the stage. There was an expectant hush. The lights dimmed to near darkness in the pub. The single spotlight on the little stage shone a mauve light on a microphone. The man himself stepped out into the light towards the light clad in his damson suit with a damson trilby hat and damson tinted sunglasses.

"Than' you very much, much," Jamson said sibilantly as the small crowd applauded. "It's great to be here and play some cool music." The audience applauded enthusiastically. "I'm gonna introduce you to my band now." The audience clapped and cheered and Jamson continued, "First, let me introduce you Walnut Wippity on bass." A man stepped out from the curtains at the side carrying a double bass. The light from the spotlight expanded a little. He wore trousers and a shirt the colour of which matched Jamson's suit exactly, but he also wore a walnut brown waistcoat and a walnut brown trilby as well. Jamson went on.

"And we have Teedly Plum on drums." The light expanded a little further to show a huge man sitting with a fairly small drum kit. He wore damson shirt and silky looking damson trousers which encased the most massive thighs Penny thought she had ever seen. There was no hat over his rather full hair. He had one extremely large earring.

"Fruity toots on saxophone," continued Jamson as a saxophonist clad in a damson suit wearing an old straw hat squeezed onto the stage.

"Finally," said Jamson, "I'm pleased to announce that it is a rare privilege to have Jems Dutchland joining us on this part of the tour. He is here at the piano!"

The spotlight moved to show sitting just off stage at the pub's upright piano was indeed the renowned Jems, better known for his late-night television programme 'Late Evenings with Jems'.

Jamson Damson and his band spent the evening playing most of Jamson's repertoire. They had a huge amount of applause from their tiny audience and several encores.

Eventually Jamson said, "I love you… I love you… you have been such a special audience… You can be sure I will return to Waste one day…"

The concert was over. The audience spilled out onto the pavement. Penny and Lewis walked to their vehicles. They had only had cola to drink but the summer evening air was heady. They stopped and paused before going home.

Penny said, "Please can you take the damsons out of my hair. They feel heavy and droopy." Lewis laughed and assisted her with the wilting sprig which for some reason he put in his pocket.

"You put real damsons on your head?" he said undoing a hairclip.

"Yes," said Penny. "Although they are not quite ripe yet."

He took the sprig off her head and kissed her on the cheek.

"Please can I take you on a proper date in the near future?" said Lewis. "I will borrow a car and we can go and have dinner... maybe at the Farthwaite Arms or there is a new Thai place. What do you say?"

"I think," said Penny, "this is a proper date. But you can take me out to dinner too!"

They both laughed. They fixed the proposed date and time. Lewis kissed Penny's lips gently. Then she got on her scooter with ease despite her short skirt and made for the farm. Lewis leaned against a wall for a few seconds savouring the moment. He found he still had the damson sprig in his hand, so he put it in his pocket. Then he roared off on his bike.

When Penny got to the farm she was greeted by a bevy of creatures. Harley pushed his way to the foreground purring loudly as if approving of her evening with the man who had his namesake motorcycle.

Chapter 7

WHEN OLIVER GRASBY WENT FOR an evening stroll with Aziz Ahmed each found the other full of distraction. Oliver seemed out of sorts and kept fiddling with his pipe. Aziz kept changing hands with his cigar and twirled it. They had crossed the golf links and now sat on a bench admiring Waste Water.

"What's the matter?" they said to each other in chorus. Each told the other to go first. Eventually, Oliver cleared his throat.

"Recently, I played a joke… and it backfired."

"You mean you put a Jamson Damson disk in a Morris dancing cover on Cecily Stump's desk?" said Aziz

"How did you know?" said Oliver.

"I guessed," said Aziz. "Who else would have done it?"

"Well," continued Oliver, "Shovell being a bright spark found the evidence. He has it in the court safe and has made me promise to behave…"

Aziz roared with laughter. "Good for him. That'll teach you to play childish jokes."

"Annette does not know," continued Oliver. "I guess on reflection I could have got into a great deal of trouble… but I think I won't tell her. She'd be livid with me. It has unsettled me a bit." He then asked,

"What's the matter with you?"

"It's like this," said Aziz. "Easy Ryder is stepping down as Leader of the Council and Mayor and Amina has thrown her hat into the ring…"

"And?" said Oliver.

"Well, I don't know," sighed Aziz. "I mean we seem to be equal… but I don't want to become just her plus one…"

Now it was Oliver's turn to laugh. "You are afraid she will be more important than you!"

"I suppose so," said Aziz looking a bit sheepish.

"Well," said Oliver, "Annette is a High Court Judge, and I am just a mere Circuit Judge… albeit Recorder of Waste… but in my mind I am far more important than anyone else," he chuckled. Then he continued, "You'll manage, Aziz, old chap. You'll manage… and then your boys will grow up and consider they are far more important than anyone else…"

Aziz smiled. They started to talk about the cricket instead. They enjoyed their summer evening stroll and went home feeling better for their chat.

Early next morning Sir Hugo, Pandora, Scyathica and Steven sat having tea together in the garden.

Steven asked Sir Hugo, "Will it feel odd not being the town's MP anymore?"

"Yes and no," said Sir Hugo petting Piper the dog. "I found it very tiring going back and forth to Westminster. I'm not as young as I was. Also, I want to diversify the business a little… Now my divorce is settled I felt this might be time for a few changes... Pandora said she would help me. She has given me lots of ideas too."

"Indeed," said Pandora. "Although I spend quite a bit of time with Waste Women against Violence, I wanted to pay dear Hugo back in some way. I am aware things are very challenging for agriculture."

"What are you having in mind?" asked Scyathica.

"Just along the road from High Cliffe, just after the pig farm, there is a small farm with turkey sheds. The farmer is retiring. It is a small operation which would suit me fine," said Sir Hugo. "I am going to initially rent the turkey sheds and buy his remaining turkeys. I will take on his farmhand initially on a short-term contract. My intention is to do a bit of halal turkey bacon and a few turkeys for Christmas. Initially I will hire a halal butcher on a temporary contract and put in a little butchery room in a container next to the turkey sheds … I will keep it small scale… see how it goes."

"Brilliant," said Scyathica.

"And that's not all," continued Sir Hugo. "There's a large, abandoned greenhouse near the pig houses. It's commercial size and I think the majority of it is glass. I thought I would have it cleaned out… start growing a few tomatoes, courgettes and so on… Might have some part-time help… If there was excess produce, we might sell them on a little roadside stall and work towards having a farm shop… who knows, perhaps even a café…The pig industry is very challenging so I thought I should investigate diversifying… so there is a business for future generations." He looked at Scyathica's glowing form. "I rather think you and the next generation who is on the way will be my heir, Scyathica."

"Uncle," Scyathica replied, "I don't expect anything. The deal you did for us with the West Wing was tremendous."

"That's as maybe," said Uncle Hugo. "I sadly don't have any children living. You are the nearest thing I have to a daughter. By the way, do you know if you are having a boy or a girl yet?"

"I will know soon," said Scyathica. "I am having another scan around about the election date."

"The new plan for the business all sounds very exciting," said Steven fidgeting a bit, "but I better go to work. Scyathica do you want a lift?"

"Yes, please," was the reply. "I'm on the election campaign reporting team. I'm due to cover a speech being given by Percy Vere at 2 o'clock. He is apparently introducing his wife to the voters. It seems he was recently married to a Chinese lady Jing Ping…"

When they got to Waste, Scyathica was pleased that her morning was to be spent in the office and she would then take a taxi to the venue of Percy Vere's meeting.

When she got there, she found the hall was packed but there were a few seats left especially for the press. Percy Vere beckoned to the petite Chinese lady a few feet from him to join him on the platform.

"Ladies and gentlemen," Percy Vere said, "let me introduce you to my beautiful wife who has been supporting me on the campaign trail." His clearly nervous wife gave a little wave.

"Nice to meet everyone," she said rather quietly.

Percy then launched into a policy speech extolling the virtues of his party. The audience was getting restless.

"What about Waste Waste?" heckled Mickey Gasson.

Percy looked uncomfortable. "I will press for nationalisation… but of course we also need to make sure the plant runs in a green way with a low carbon footprint."

"But what about saving the jobs of the men and women working in the plant?" pressed Mickey.

Percy said, "I can assure you if you elect me it will be right at the top of my agenda."

Mickey was quiet so Percy was able to finish his speech.

After the meeting, Scyathica tried to interview some of the audience as they left.

"Will you be voting for Mr Vere?" she asked. The answers ranged from, "Yeah, he was terrific," to "No comment," to "Percy who?"

She took a taxi back to her office and commented to Stacey Birch that she wondered how the other candidates would get on. Stacey said,

"I'm not sending you to Bricey's meeting. I don't know why he was rude to you since I thought he got on well with your uncle. I'll send someone else. I do want you to do an interview with Amina Ahmed. They are having the vote on the council soon. Win or lose the vote it would be a good touch to have you do a short piece with her."

Scyathica looked forward to interviewing Amina. When Steven collected her from work Scyathica mentioned the assignment.

"By then," said Steven, "I might have an answer to my expression of interest to be temporary court manager, at least to get an interview or not."

"That would be quick," said Scyathica. "I thought the civil service are very slow?"

"Well they are being their normal slow selves about the permanent position," responded Steven. "They have yet to advertise it."

Aziz tidied his desk at the end of that afternoon. He had had a rather tedious trial about a fraud by a doctor's receptionist. It was clear the jury did not like the woman by the way they were glowering at her. It might be because they had had bad experiences with doctors' receptionists. He somehow thought he could not stop the trial based on the jurors' expressions alone. As he sat sorting out his papers it occurred to him that he understood why Oliver sometimes played his jokes. He had been thinking of a circular he had received, containing details of some forthcoming publications from his favourite book club. It was time he sent Oliver a little gift. There was the perfect book:

'How to tell if you have become an old fart'.

He would order it when he got home and arrange for it to be delivered anonymously. Sometimes, he now understood, it was necessary to stir things up a bit.

Amina was very late home that evening, so Aziz had plenty of time to make his order for the book delivery. The council had been voting on the positions of Leader and Mayor. Helal and Ali stayed up to see if their mother was successful.

"Did you get it? Did you get it?" they cried out with excitement.

"Yes, yes... Leader and Mayor," said a glowing Amina.

"I'm so, so proud of you," said Aziz. He really meant it.

"Will you wear a gold chain?" asked Helal. "Will there be lot of ceremonies?"

"Yes and yes," said Amina, "and I hope it will give me a platform to highlight the worries about Waste Waste. I already have an interview on radio tomorrow."

"Meanwhile," said Aziz, "I think I should order a celebration cake and other special food for a celebration meal next weekend, if you would like that, Amina?"

Amina was happy to allow Aziz to order a special meal. But first she had a clinic to run at the hospital in the morning.

The day of Amina's radio interview soon arrived.

Both Amina and Scyathica were pleased the interview would take place at the media offices, so they did not have to struggle with poor phone lines.

Scyathica began, "Mayor Ahmed, congratulations on becoming Leader of the Council and Mayor."

"Please call me Amina," was the reply.

"You are the first woman to become Mayor of Waste and the first person of Asian origins to become Mayor of Waste. Do you feel your presence at the helm will promote women's rights and racial equality?" said Scyathica.

"I did not become Leader or Mayor to promote one group or another. I am a fairly recent arrival in Waste. I found Waste to be something other than I expected… it took me to its heart, and I took it to my heart. I have a lot to do but if I can promote racial harmony and inspire some women and girls that would be a bonus," was the reply.

"Do you consider your predecessor Norman Ryder was too easy-going, leading to some of the issues we have now?" probed Scyathica.

Amina replied diplomatically, "Norman has worked very hard. He had his style and I have mine."

"What do you consider are the chief issues for the Borough of Waste?" came the next question.

"Quite obviously," replied Amina, "many people are worried about Waste Waste. The council needs to press for more information about what is going on, and if need be, call for Government help. That is not the only issue. The council needs to have an overall plan for Waste to combat issues of decline and to make sure it does not become a forgotten backwater. The town centre has some terrific old buildings so the heritage needs to be preserved. The southern approaches to the town look a bit scruffy so the council needs to consider if a regeneration plan is required. I want to make sure there are no neglected hidden corners of Waste."

"Quite a lot of ambition, then?" commented Scyathica.

"Why not!" said Amina.

"What do your family make of your latest achievements… because you are also an eye specialist too…" probed Scyathica.

"My husband and teenage sons very much support me. Unfortunately, my wider family live some distance away, but they have sent messages of congratulations too."

"One last question," said Scyathica. "There are by-elections ongoing. Do you have any ambitions to become an MP yourself?"

"Who knows?" said Amina laughing. "Let me get these new jobs done first!"

"Mayor Amina Ahmed, it has been a pleasure to talk to you," said Scyathica concluding the interview.

From Amina there was a sigh of relief. The first formal interview was over. Scyathica gave a sigh of relief; the interview had gone well.

Amina arrived home to a smiling husband. He'd heard her on the radio. He had also received a message that his parcel arrived with Oliver yesterday. They were not going on an evening walk so he would no doubt find out about the reaction later.

As it happened the delivery of the little parcel to Oliver made him smile. He knew Aziz had done it and he knew why. He would not play a joke on Aziz. He would instead show his appreciation. He went online to his cigar supplier and ordered a gift of fine Cuban Cigars with a thank you note 'To Aziz, in appreciation of the book, from the old fart Oliver'. The gift took a few days to arrive. By the time it did, Oliver and Aziz were having another evening walk. It was the day of the by-election.

"It's nice to get away from the hullabaloo of the election," said Oliver as they sat down to enjoy the view of Waste Water. There had been cars with loudspeakers going round Waste all day and several men going up and down the town square with placards. Some had got in the way of people trying to get into the court building. "Will you stay up for the count?" he continued.

"No," said Aziz. "They may not have a result until tomorrow lunchtime. But, changing the subject, thank you so much for the cigars. I shall really enjoy them."

"The pleasure is all mine," said Oliver puffing on his pipe.

Steven and Scyathica were also not staying up late for the election results; Scyathica was tired due to her pregnancy. Steven and Scyathica now knew they were to have a daughter.

"You know," said Steven, "It didn't matter to me... boy or girl... as long as we have a healthy baby, I'm fine with it." He paused. "By the way, I have an interview very soon for the temporary court manager post and they have now just published the ad for the permanent position. I understand I have an excellent chance of the temporary promotion. But I do hope I don't get competition on the permanent position. I would hate not to get it."

"Whatever happens," said Scyathica, "I know you will make the best of it as you always do, and I shall fully support you."

Another couple who were also disinterested in the media coverage of the by-election was Penny and Lewis. Lewis had booked them into the new Thai restaurant for that evening so they could have a "proper date" as he put it, although he had been round to the farm a number of times with meat for the dogs since the Jamson Damson gig at the pub.

Lewis had had his ear bent by Brother Mickey for the last few weeks all about the politics of Waste. Mickey had gone on at length about who might be the best candidate in both East Waste and West Waste to save Waste Waste. If truth be told, Lewis was more than a little sick of hearing about politics. He voted of course; he also cared about the future of the plant. He was, however, pleased to be spending the evening with Penny. He had recently acquired an old banger, in addition to his Harley, so he didn't even need to borrow Mickey's car. It was mechanically sound despite its high mileage. It was small and a bit under-powered. It was a hideous fluorescent green (mostly) with some orange bumper stickers which said randomly 'I am a Supporter' but did not say of what. Two doors were coloured dark blue but had a couple of stickers of pink flowers on each.

Mickey had said dismissively,

"That thing won't pull the skin off a rice-pudding... and you need not think I'll help you respray it." Actually, Lewis suspected Mickey would love to respray it and generally tinker with it.

However, it was a surprise to Penny when this small, ugly, little car arrived at the farm since she had had no forewarning of its acquisition. Lewis squeezed out of it, trying not to get his suit crumpled.

"Your chariot awaits," he said. "What do you think of my new car?"

Penny smiled. "It's a car," she said. "I know I like bright colours... but that is something else!"

"I want to respray it," said Lewis.

"Even I would not object... but the main thing is I hope it works!" said Penny. "I'm looking forward to this Thai meal... not an evening waiting for roadside assistance."

"Oh thee of little faith," said Lewis ushering her into the front passenger seat. "It will get us there and back... and we will have a good time," which of course they did.

Chapter 8

"DO YOU WANT TO GO to the election count?" said Stacey Birch to Scyathica Wentworth-Hovell. "It can be quite exciting, and I think we will get one result after another."

Scyathica agreed to go to the Town Hall with Stacey at 1 o'clock. They arrived a few minutes before one. There was an expectant hush and a number of persons got on the stage of the large conference room. They included Percy Vere and his wife, a middle-aged nervous looking couple who Scyathica assumed were Dr and Mrs Cardigan, a young woman with an enormous blue rosette who appeared to be Sally Slider, a crumpled looking man with his hair dyed green and a big green rosette who seemed to be Drago Fyshe and a man or woman dressed in a giant mouse outfit. An official from Waste Borough Council went to the microphone and cleared his throat.

"I, Paul Edward Bugsworth, Returning Officer for the Waste East Constituency declare that the total number of votes given to each candidate were as follows: Dr Cardigan, Liberal Party, three thousand nine hundred and two votes, Drago Fyshe, Green Party, two thousand four hundred and four votes, Mr Field Mouse, Alternative Reasoning Party, seven votes, Sally Slider, Conservative Party, fifteen thousand two hundred and twelve votes and Percy Edward Vere, Labour Party, seventeen thousand four hundred and three votes."

A roar and a cheer could be heard from Percy Vere's supporters. Mr Bugsworth could hardly be heard when he said,

"Therefore, I give public notice that Percy Edward Vere has been elected Member of Parliament for the Waste East Constituency."

The Returning Officer went on to announce the number of spoiled votes and the total cast, but he could not be heard over the din.

The clamour abated and Percy Vere came to the microphone to thank his election helpers. Everyone was shaking hands on stage except the mouse who suddenly left the stage and started jumping up and down in the body of the hall with a large yellow ball which someone handed to him. After a few minutes Percy and his wife and the other candidates left the stage, only to be replaced by Melvyn Brice, a lady with a huge red rosette who Scyathica assumed was Dahlia Mallinderall, Dr Bobbin and Teresa Frill, assorted partners and a man or woman in an enormous rat outfit complete with a tail about four feet long. The returning officer spoke into the microphone again.

"Can I have a little quiet."

The people in the conference room were quiet except the human mouse continued to bounce his ball. Paul Bugsworth ignored him and announced the results for Waste West. It appeared that Melvyn Brice had received over sixteen thousand votes with the Labour candidate on thirteen thousand or so votes, the Liberal candidate on about four thousand votes, the Green on about two thousand votes and the Alternative Reasoning candidate on twelve votes. Melvyn Brice was duly elected with a sound majority, but it was not the landslide Sir Hugo Wentworth-Knubb used to receive. Melvyn Brice attempted to thank his supporters but was rudely interrupted by the rat and the mouse who had decided to play a noisy game of catch in the hall. In the end council officials simply cleared the hall.

Stacey Birch smiled at Scyathica. "That will make a fun piece to write up."

As they attempted to extricate themselves from the Town Hall, they noticed a well-known rival national television news network had cornered both new Members of Parliament. With camera on, the TV personality from the National News network Philida Ciccofante was attempting to interview both men together. Ramming a microphone into Percy Vere's face she asked,

"Mr Vere, as a new MP, how does it feel to be upstaged by a giant mouse."

"Well," said Percy Vere, "it was plainly a publicity stunt. This is a serious country. I'm sure the public will see it for what it is."

The interviewer then thrust the microphone in Melvyn Brice's face. "Do you agree, Mr Brice?"

"No," said Melvyn. "This is a very silly country. We just have to put up with a bit of nonsense when it happens."

Despite the fact that when they had last spoken, they had had words, Scyathica was inclined to agree with him.

"It will soon be yesterday's story," said Stacey. "People will soon forget about Waste again."

In fact, she was not quite right. The national media ran a story for a whole week: 'New MP says UK is silly'. Various people also decided now was a good time to return to Waste.

The first to arrive in Waste was Dr Gordon Flaughtersdough. A few days after the election, Sonja Sidebottom was sitting in the Knubb Arms waiting for Chris Ellison who was held up in court. Her reverie was disturbed by a plummy voice.

"Hello, my dear," said Dr Gordon Flaughtersdough. "I told you I would visit Waste."

"Are you retired now?" said Sonja.

"Yes indeedee… and I am travelling about, going to old haunts. I am particularly fond of Waste, you know. It will feature in my memoirs," he said.

"Are you staying here?" asked Sonja.

"For the moment," said Gordon. "Can I buy you a drink?"

"No. It's okay," replied Sonja, "I've got one… and my boyfriend is on his way shortly."

"Well, I shall have a brandy," said Gordon and ordered one from the barmaid.

"You know," said Gordon, "it's rather too tempting having a bar and steak and kidney pud on hand… not good for my waistline or my bank balance. What I really could do with is a little room tucked away somewhere where I could write… not too expensive… and I could keep on my London flat but have a room here to visit whenever I wanted…" He looked wistful.

"My landlady has a vacant room," blurted out Sonja, immediately regretting she had told the doctor of the vacancy.

"Really, tell me more," said Gordon becoming animated. She found herself telling him all about Auntie Bea and the house in Canal Street. He asked for Auntie Bea's number which he jotted down. To her relief Chris appeared. He passed the time of day with Gordon. Then Sonja and Chris went on their way with the intention of trying the recently opened Thai restaurant.

"I think I made a mistake," said Sonja, telling Chris of her conversation with Dr Gordon Flaughtersdough.

"He may never follow it up," said Chris, but as he was speaking Gordon was already on the phone to Auntie Bea. He drove the few minutes from the centre of town in his hire car to Canal Street. Auntie Bea showed him the room and he also spent about a half an hour drinking tea with her. He said as he left,

"I am entranced and impressed and I will be back in touch."

As July began to turn to August, not only were there a series of telephone calls between Dr Gordon Flaughtersdough and Auntie Bea but there were further arrivals in Waste.

Steven Hovell's parents and his sister Denise arrived at High Cliffe in the campervan. Steven and Scyathica had each taken a few days off work to entertain them. Champ started by slapping Steven on the back, saying, "Who's going to be a daddy soon?" and Deedee gushed as to how nice the West Wing looked and wanted to be involved with planning the nursery. Denise just "ooohd" and "ahhdd" generally. Steven had arranged to have a barbecue in the garden and for Sir Hugo and Pandora to take part. A cheerful evening was had cooking Knubb sausages and bacon steaks over a large charcoal barbecue. There were salad and bread roll aplenty and slightly incongruously for dessert the speciality vegetarian chocolate Brownie from Crunchies' Vegetarian Café.

"My friend Penny used to work at the veggie café," said Scyathica. "She recently stopped to concentrate all her energies on her animal shelter. In fact, I thought we would visit her on Sunday. I was lucky to get the chocolate brownie as I believe they have been a bit shorthanded since she left."

They ate the brownie with some strawberries and cream. Both Uncle Hugo's dog Piper and Pandora's dog Kitty sat at everyone's feet, tails wagging hoping for crumbs.

Denise played with the two dogs after the meal.

"I do love dogs," she said. "Especially big ones."

"Really?" said Scyathica. "The opposite of Penny. She does not mind the small dogs but is nervous of larger ones."

Denise continued, "I think I told you in the past I can't have pets in my flat… you are so lucky being able to have animals. I think I really hate it where I am. I don't like my job either. I do lunchtime supervising and playtime supervising at a posh private school… the parents and the teachers are all snobs… In the holidays my job is to spring-clean the place except if I have holiday and the little brats make it hard by writing the rudest things you can imagine all over the toilets which I am supposed to clean…"

"Well," said Steven, "it sounds like you definitely needed a break."

When they arrived at the farm on Sunday, they were greeted by Harley the cat and Lewis Gasson. Harley sat in the centre of the farmyard. He now sported a splendid red collar with a little strip on it bearing the words 'Harley the boss'. Lewis was taking orders for teas and coffees.

Denise whispered to Scyathica, "He's quite a hunk."

Scyathica laughed and said quietly, "He's Penny's boyfriend. They split up but they have recently got back together. He has started to help her out a bit, but he can only do so much... He is Head Butcher at Knubb Sausages..."

The dogs Ronald and Roderick were yapping enthusiastically. Scyathica noticed another dog sitting in the corner of a makeshift pen on a big dog bed full of cushions. The dog looked to be a type of Labrador-Staffie cross.

"That's Scooby," said Penny. "He's a much bigger dog than I would normally take but he is old, and he was in danger of being put down."

"May I go into him?" said Denise.

"Sure," replied Penny. Denise let herself into the pen. Within seconds there were licks and wags from the dog and hugs and vigorous stroking from Denise. It was as if they had always been friends.

"He's lovely," said Denise sadly. "What a pity I don't live nearby. All he needs is a bit of love."

The visit to Penny was a success. Indeed, the visit by Champ, Deedee and Denise was an overall success. Steven's parents had only been slightly loud and embarrassing. If they had noticed, Sir Hugo and Pandora didn't show it. Steven was not sure whether his own increasing confidence in his world helped him, or whether Champ had mellowed just a little. Before the family left Denise said wistfully,

"I wish I could come to Waste too... and help Penny... but I would have to have somewhere to live and a job... and I don't want you to think I am following you, Steven."

Steven replied, "If you are serious, I'll ask around." And he meant it.

Penny herself was wishing that Denise or someone like her could help her with the dogs. The eco-glamping business had now taken off, so she had her hands full with not only animal welfare but servicing the needs of the campsite. It seemed she was forever emptying bins and making sure the eco toilets were in working order. Even the most ecological friendly campers seemed to leave large amounts of rubbish. She felt that sometimes her guests brought their rubbish with them! Things were going well with Lewis. In fact all was progressing nicely. She hoped there would not be a hiccup now her parents were visiting in a couple of days.

Senator Brad T Morton Wayney junior was keen to know how his investment not only in Penny's business but in Waste Football Club was progressing. His wife Alannah wanted to catch up with Penny and to meet Lewis Gasson about whom Penny had mentioned a little. The senator was more than a little concerned about the situation between Achille Plinth and Paulino Spitti. When her parents arrived in the large hire car they had picked up in London, the senator seemed genuinely pleased with the progress of the glamping business and Alannah also praised the comfort of their quarters in the converted farmhouse. The fly in the ointment appeared to lie at Waste Wanderers. The senator mused,

"They've got themselves into this goddamm court case... Plinth is back at work as manager, although he won't play again for a while, but Spitti is off his game due to the souring of things with Plinth... I can't even sell the great Spitti on at the moment both due to his contract and his poor form, goddammit..."

He continued grumbling to himself with a lot of "godamms" and "godammits" and then he said,

"However, on another note... can your mom and I take you and this Lewis guy out for some dinner?"

Penny nervously indicated she thought that it would be a nice idea. She suggested the Farthwaite Arms. She hoped her parents might enjoy the old-world ambience, although she was not sure what they would think of Lewis's car.

The senator continued his musing. "Also, I'm gonna meet this guy I know from business in London here... Jerome dela Notte Collins... some mouthful. He has a business idea about forming a consortium to take over the Waste Plant here... Wondered if there was any local gossip... says his wife sits as a judge here."

Penny responded, "Waste Waste is very important to the town. The locals are very worried about its future. There have been demos as the employees are worried about their jobs. It's probably the biggest employer in Waste other than maybe Waste Borough Council. I think the sausage and bacon factory is a close second." She left out any mention of Xavier Didier Le Perte, one of its owners with whom she had had a disastrous short-term relationship. "The locals are worried the people who own it are not sound... but the local talk is that the plant itself is sound and could have a very good future with recycling...The judge is Judge dela Notte. My friend Scyathica has reported on cases before her." She did not mention she had had a court hearing in the past before the judge to get an injunction against Mr Le Perte.

"Well that bears out my own enquiries," said the senator. "My people have looked at the business itself and it seems sound. But it's owned by a company, which is owned by a company, which is owned by a company... you get the picture... and it seems one shareholder is in prison and the other guy, Scarlett, is sailing around the Caribbean and seems a bit of a crook. I think there is some family connection with that media guy Coldharbour, the lord. He seems financially sound and may also be interested... It's all a bit complex but maybe..."

Penny just nodded and stroked Harley. She really did not want to think about her unpleasant interlude with Xavier, but she did hope Waste Waste could be saved. She had grown fond of the town and its inhabitants.

That evening Jerome also arrived in Waste and let himself into the flat where Davina and Frank lived to be greeted enthusiastically by both his wife and son.

"How long are you here for, Dad?" queried Frank. "Can we do some stuff together?"

"Although I am here mainly for business I would love to spend some time with you," said Jerome. "I am hoping this will not be a flying visit. If business goes well, I want to spend a great deal more time in Waste. I was also thinking we had not taken a family holiday for a long time. I was going to discuss with your mother what her commitments were for October half-term week. No promises mind... but if it's convenient to us all I would like to take us on holiday somewhere for a week."

"That would be lovely," said Davina. "I do have time off then due to it being Frank's half-term... I am sure we can all have fun choosing somewhere really good!"

Jerome did not waste much time in setting up a business meeting with the senator. Both of them had already persuaded the plant manager Ron Woodhouse to give them a tour of Waste Waste.

Next day a large, grey limousine slipped into Waste. One could not see its occupants through the smoked glass windows. A suite of rooms was taken at the Harbour View pub. The two smaller rooms were occupied by a chauffeur and an administrative assistant. The largest room was configured as an office come meeting room. Laptops and printers were on tables to the side and a large dining room table and chairs supplied by the pub had been set up in the middle of the room.

The fourth room was occupied by Lord Coldharbour.

The first thing Lord Coldharbour did was telephone his son and arrange to visit Nat, Brittany, and young granddaughter Tiffany at the bungalow in Gitthwaite. Then he sent an email to Scyathica to say he was visiting Waste. Next, he slipped discreetly into the media offices in Waste to check on the local radio station, online news platform and local paper which he owned within his media empire. Scyathica had only recently received his email and had not had time to tell Stacey Birch of his arrival. There was an audible hush as the dapper grey-haired man entered the general offices.

"Carry on," he said quietly as the staff seemed inclined to pause and look at him. He just nodded at Scyathica as he initially walked past her desk. "I will just have a quick chat with the managers," which is what he did next.

On his way out he spoke briefly to Nat who was about to broadcast a quiz show, saying that he would see him later. He then stopped briefly at Scyathica's desk and said,

"I think congratulations are in order. Does your father know?"

"I don't know," she said. "I tried to send a message, but I don't know if he got it."

"Boy or girl?" said Lord Coldharbour.

"Girl," said Scyathica. "She's due before Christmas."

"Do you mind if I communicate this to your father?" was the response.

"Not at all," said Scyathica, wondering if he had a better line of communication than she did.

Lord Coldharbour then swept out and the sleek limousine pulled away.

When she arrived home that night, Scyathica told Steven of her encounter. He was just preparing for his interview tomorrow for the role of temporary court manager. As she explained about the conversation with Lord Coldharbour and the possibility he was in touch with her father, her phone gave a sudden ping. She looked at it and saw a message from an 'unknown number'.

"Speak of the devil," she said and read out the message.

"Congratulations to my darling daughter. I look forward to having a granddaughter. My brother will keep me informed."

"Families," said Steven raising his eyebrows. "Does anyone have a satisfactory one?" Scyathica smiled so he continued. "No, don't answer that. It was a rhetorical question. I think the answer is, probably not. For all the decent relations I am sure most people have a percentage they would rather disown. That being said, I think I am sorry for people with no-one."

Chapter 9

STEVEN'S INTERVIEW FOR THE POST of temporary court manager was in many ways a big non-event. In other ways it was of great significance. He was interviewed by a video link by the Area Director and his assistant. It was evident there was no-one else in contention and at the end of the interview Steven was told the job was his. He was also urged to apply for the permanent post but obviously no promises were made. Steven immediately sent a message to Scyathica who was obviously delighted.

His Honour Judge Oliver Grasby KC was not at all in a good mood. It seemed that due to the pressure of work at the Circuit Court, Plinth v Spitti had been sent back by the Circuit Court. Granted, District Judge Dattail had recently had a case and costs management conference, but it seemed that the Circuit Court could not keep it for trial. Oliver had received a snotty email from the Designated Civil Judge at that court His Honour Judge Harold Bolton-Snodgrass. Oliver thought he would better be called 'Belt-up Snotty' but refrained from being rude when he replied to say he quite understood how overwhelmingly busy he was. He thought of saying, "I'm bloody busy too, seeing as we are a small court with few judges," but restrained himself from doing so. There was a knock on his Chambers' door. It was Steven.

"Come in, Shovell," he said with a sigh. "I know what you are going to tell me. Plinth v Spitti has come back, joy oh joy!"

"Yes," said Steven. "That's right... how did you know? It apparently needs a listing hearing or pre-trial review and then an eventual trial date. Your Honour, I can't get you out of the next short hearing, but I think we would be justified in seeking a Recorder for the trial. His Honour Judge Ahmed has no civil ticket. Her Honour dela Notte is tied up with family work when she's not doing crime. You have heavy criminal lists, and I don't think you would want to release it to the District Judges…"

Oliver smiled. "I think His Honour Judge Belt-up… I mean Bolton-Snodgrass thought I could magic up time to try it… but if we could get a Recorder that would be something. We better find a couple of hours whenever… in my list, however, in the near future." He mused for a moment. "I wonder who will represent Mr Plinth now Percy Vere has gone off to be an MP… I hope it's not that dreadful man Flaughtersdough." He pronounced it as it was spelled, rather than 'Flowerdew' which was the correct pronunciation.

"It won't be him," said Steven. "The news is the good Dr Gordon has retired to write his memoirs…"

"Well I look forward to reading that load of cobblers," said Oliver visibly cheering up. "And what of you… the court manager post?"

Steven smiled. "You've got me on that, at least as the temporary manager. By the way, are the judges doing a collection for Derek Devene's retirement, or do you want to put something in with the staff?"

"I will contribute to both," said Oliver generously. Steven smiled. They sorted out a date for Plinth v Spitti.

While this conversation was going on the senator was visiting the football club. He spent a morning looking at the physical state of the stands and the ground. He looked at the company annual accounts on the club's computers. He held conversations with Achille Plinth, Ruud Van Dijk, Paulino Spitti and some of the keen young players. He met administrative staff and groundsmen. He said very little about his intentions. At the end of the morning, he called everyone he had met into the Directors' Suite and said,

"I like this club. It has potential to be a great club and I hope we can get promotion into the next league, but we need to sort out just a few issues."

The staff and players all seemed much reassured but as they filed out of the room he said,

"Achille, Paulino can you please stay behind?"

Both of them looked at the other. They sat down at opposite ends of the room leaving the senator metres from either of them.

"Goddammit," he said, "sit closer… I am not using a loud hailer."

They moved uncomfortably so that they now sat opposite the senator but only two seats apart.

"You two sit and listen," said the senator as if he was addressing a couple of naughty schoolboys. "I don't expect you to say anything. You can go and talk to your lawyers after you have heard what I have to say."

Plinth and Spitti looked puzzled but stayed put.

"Your argument and court case is costing me money. I need you, Plinth, doing your coaching job well and managing my team. I don't mind you can't play for a while. I need you Spitti off the bench and playing your best. You're not worth anything if you don't play and just sit sulking. I've had my people look into your court case. This is how I see it. You, Spitti are not quite the golden boy you used to be. You have an expensive girlfriend and expensive tastes, so you are short of money. You bought a house, but you were conned by some shysters when it came to your gates. Your insurance company is trying to wriggle out of as much of Plinth's claim as it can because you didn't have the right consents for the gates. You are paying for lawyers yourself rather than your insurers picking up the tab, so you are reluctant to settle because you don't actually have any money to offer. The reality is the gates caused the accident. Whether anyone will catch up with the company which supplied the gates is debatable.

"As for you Plinth you are a damn good coach but realistically most of your playing days are over. You can also be a greedy bastard. Your injuries are probably being exaggerated by you. As for the Maserati you bought it off a friend of a friend, below market rate. It seems to have the right paperwork but the plate number on the engine is unaccountably missing!

"This is what I am prepared to do. I will get my lawyers to convene a 'round table' meeting. Your lawyers and your good selves will attend. My lawyer from London will chair the meeting. Anything said will be what they call 'without prejudice' so not admissible in court. You will try your darndest to reach a compromise. If you reach a compromise which is one of which I approve I will pay the money to you Plinth. However, that money will in reality be a loan to you Spitti which you will pay off by instalments. I will secure the loan on your house, second in priority to your lenders who helped you buy the house. You will also, Spitti, buy some paint and if you have to do it yourself paint those pillars at your house white and tidy it up so my investment is not wasted.

"Any compromise shall be placed before the court and made legally binding. You will then concentrate on your soccer. Do you both understand?"

Both Plinth and Spitti nodded. They then left without saying another word. The senator smiled.

Later that day Penny and Alannah asked him how he thought his business at the football club was progressing.

He replied, "I've taken the ponies to water... now I hope they goddam drink."

That evening the senator and his wife took out Penny and Lewis to dinner at the Farthwaite Arms these days a very successful establishment under the management of owner Pierre Bruele. The senator had booked and paid for taxi transport which was a relief to Penny. First the taxi picked up Lewis in town. Then it collected the senator, his wife and Penny from the farm. The taxi was booked to return at half past ten to do the journey in reverse. Lewis wore his suit and was very nervous. He need not have worried. A convivial time was had at the Farthwaite Arms due to their excellent food and good wines. If Penny saw Pierre Bruele in the distance, it no longer bothered her that he had been Xavier's assistant since she felt encouraged by Lewis's renewed interest. If the senator was aware this was Pierre Bruele who had signed the football club over to him he did not show a flicker of recognition. Lewis found he had much in common with the senator. They both liked their steaks, and it transpired the senator was interested in vintage motorbikes.

Also dining out that night were Sonja and Chris Ellison. They were having a Thai meal. As they relaxed over fragrant tea at the end of the meal Chris said,

"Sonja, I have a proposition for you."

"That sounds very serious," said Sonja.

"Just hear me out," said Chris. "We have not been going out for very long, but I think we get on very well. My flat is a small one bed-roomed flat. I would like you to move in with me to see how we got on living together. I would not want you to contribute anything at all for the first six months except towards your food. If after six months, we still wanted to be together I would propose to sell the flat and for us to buy a bigger place together. But if by six months it was 'no go' hopefully you would have a bit put aside to enable you to move out to somewhere else... Do you want to think about it?"

"What is there to think about?" said Sonja. "It's a 'yes' from me, but I think I need to allow Auntie Bea a little time to find another tenant before we give it a try... Also, are you sure about the finances for the first six months?"

"Yes of course I am," said Chris. His strong Brummy accent was accentuated when he emphasized a point.

The following day the senator said that he had to go to a meeting on his own about Waste Waste. He arrived at the Harbour View pub at the same time as Jerome dela

Notte Collins. They were ushered through to the meeting room in Lord Coldharbour's suite of rooms. The three men sat at the table in the middle of the room. There was a fresh jug of ice-water and three glasses. Notepads and pens had been placed at three places.

Lord Coldharbour started,

"I suggest we all put our cards on the table about Waste Waste. Jerome, I think you are the driving force on this so do you want to go first?"

"Yes, certainly," replied Jerome. "I would like to lead a consortium to acquire Waste Waste. I have examined the business itself and taken advice. The business itself is sound. Unfortunately, its current owners are not sound. There would be some preconditions to my involvement. First, neither of the existing owners should retain any interest at all. Second, I would wish to be a majority shareholder. Third, I would wish to be Managing Director so that I could make sure there was good financial oversight of the company. I would keep on the current manager Ron Woodhouse for day-to-day matters."

The senator joined in,

"I would like to be part of this if the price was right and I would like to have an equal stake to that of Jerome. I have been looking into the company. The business is sound. Miraculously the land on which the factory is standing does not have any loans secured on it. There are people after the ultimate owners and if we don't get a deal done fast they will go after the company and its land. My people tell me that there is a UK private limited company which purportedly owns the plant, the land and the business. That company is in turn owned by a company registered in the Cayman Islands. As far as my people are aware the company is owned jointly by Xavier Didier Le Perte and Davey Scarlett."

Lord Coldharbour commented,

"I don't mind being a minority shareholder if the two of you are in the driving seat. Obviously, price is important but if we acquire the company and the two of you own 40% each and I have 20% I would want an agreement to have first refusal on your shares if either of you want to sell any of them."

The senator responded, "Yes, I think we would all want first refusal on each other's shares."

Jerome nodded in agreement and said, "My advisors have put together a report on the book value of the company so I hope between us we would all have access to sufficient funds. The one slight concern is that some money may have gone adrift from the company's pension fund but so far, I don't think it is such a large amount to make the transaction unrealistic. On the contrary, the company could do a great more than it has been doing. I suppose the real question is how do we deal with the current owners?"

The senator responded, "I know there was a proposal to acquire land and set up Waste Paper. The reality is the plant already has unused land so there may be a future in Waste Waste Waste Paper. Certainly, with regard to dealing with Le Perte he gave his former assistant Pierre Bruele Power of Attorney and I know exactly where he is…"

"The Farthwaite Arms?" said Lord Coldharbour. "Yes, I knew that, but I do have a confession to make…"

"Davey Scarlett is your half-brother," said the senator. "My people told me this. He is currently making himself very scarce around the Caribbean. His daughter is a friend of my daughter, but I doubt she has any idea where her father is… but I take it you might know?"

"Let's just say I have a line of communication," said Lord Coldharbour looking inscrutable.

The three men discussed legal requirements, funding and stock options. They talked of Pierre Bruele's position. They gave each other the names of their lawyers and discussed in principle who would take the lead.

"So summing up," said Jerome. "The three of us can probably agree a price to offer and Le Perte or Bruele and Scarlett would have everything to gain by selling. Or at least Bruele might be persuaded to sign up and pass the money to the French authorities. We would need to move quickly, however, while the company is still a worthwhile investment. I think we all agree how the business might be owned in the future."

The senator looked at Lord Coldharbour.

"I got just one question. Jerome wants to get his teeth into something in the town. Having a controlling interest in Waste Waste fits nicely with my investment in the town's soccer club. You will be a minority shareholder so what's in it for you?"

Lord Coldharbour responded,

"A bit of guilty conscience about my brother but primarily money. I see the need to diversify from the media in terms of print papers particularly, so much is going online. Also, if Waste Waste Waste Paper works I might have a good cheap source of paper should printed newspapers survive." He turned to both his companions. "One thing I would say is that until we can make this deal happen discretion is important." He looked at the senator. "I hope your daughter can be dissuaded from talking to the locals and my niece."

The senator laughed. "The best way to deal with my daughter is if I make it all sound incredibly dull."

The meeting came to an end with the three businessmen drinking a toast. Lord Coldharbour had produced a thirty-year-old single malt from a Scottish distillery.

Another person who had a single malt that evening was His Honour Judge Oliver Grasby KC. He felt he needed to have something strong when his wife Annette informed him that they had been invited to the Circuit dinner hosted by His Honour Judge Harold Bolton-Snodgrass. He supposed they would have to attend, and he would have to be polite.

He had tried his pipe and he had tried a cigar. He had drunk some fine wine with dinner but as yet he had not got away from his seething annoyance with his colleague. He knew perfectly well that 'Belt-up Snotty' could be found on the golf course on Friday afternoons. He also knew that 'Belt-up Snotty' had a reputation for passing the buck. But he had made promises to be good. This would need the deepest of thought.

He went through all the correspondence on his desk. He found just what he had believed was amongst his heap of letters. First there was a letter from the Gitthwaite WI asking if he might be a guest speaker to talk about legal developments. There was a similar letter from the Parent Teachers' Association of Pither's Lane Junior School. Then there was a letter of invitation to attend the dinner of the Alternative Thought Party. He found three other such letters from local organisations. Usually, he would send a one line 'thank you very much but I'm not available' but this time in each letter he also said, 'You may wish to consider approaching the Designated Civil Judge at the Circuit Court His Honour Judge Harold Belton-Snodgrass who is a hugely hard-working judge'. He rubbed his hands with glee thinking of old 'Belt-up Snotty' having to deal with these invitations. No-one could accuse him of being rude. He was not sending any joke present. It was just perfect.

Chapter 10

OLIVER GRASBY KNEW NOTHING ABOUT what was going on in the background in respect of Plinth v Spitti. Had he done so he would have approved. The senator and his wife were now preparing to go home to America. Before they left the senator gave some very clear instructions to his English solicitors. The senator also took Penny to one side,

"Penny, I'm real proud of you. The business is doing great, and you are doing a fine job with the animals. Also, your young man is a keeper... I do have one favour to ask, Penny..."

"Yes, Dad anything I can do in return for all your help," said Penny.

"Please don't mention my plans about Waste Waste particularly to Scyathica... or if anyone asks because they know I've been looking at the plant, you don't know anything..."

"Well I don't know anything," said Penny laughing. "So that's not too hard."

"Things are at a delicate stage, so I want to avoid press attention," said the senator.

"I understand," said Penny.

"I hope to be back soon," said the senator.

The senator's lawyers were finding it tough going to convene the round table meeting in the case of Plinth v Spitti. First, there was agreeing a venue. Then there was the date. Eventually, everyone agreed that a neutral venue would be the Directors' Suite at Waste Wanderers Football Stadium. The fact the court listed a case management hearing before His Honour Judge Grasby KC compelled the parties to agree a date so they could see if they might reach agreement before there was another court hearing. To say the atmosphere was fraught just before the beginning of the round table meeting would be a huge understatement. However, it helped more than a little that just ten minutes before the meeting began the senator sent a text to each of Plinth and Spitti which read,

'I know the meeting is today. What I said stands but if you don't settle your future with the club will not be guaranteed'.

The meeting took a little over an hour. The two protagonists did indeed come to an agreement, although it would not have been possible without the senator's generosity. Once the two men had signed some minutes of meeting to show their intent it was like a large cloud had been lifted. There were smiles, hugs and handshakes all round.

Spitti said, "Achille, you will always be my friend," and wiped a tear from his eye.

Plinth hugged Spitti and said, "You will always be the special one, the special Spitti to me... You will return to great form... the whole world will see."

The senator was delighted when he heard the outcome of the meeting. Now, he needed the negotiations for Waste Waste to bear fruit. Hopefully the little consortium would get the plant at a 'knock-down' price. Bruele still had a valid Power of Attorney and knew that if money found its way to the account frozen for the benefit of Le Perte's creditors the French and UK police forces would not be so inclined to delve into his history. The senator likewise hoped that Lord Coldharbour could bring pressure to bear on his brother.

A few days later His Honour Judge Oliver Grasby KC also had reason to be cheerful. The summer holidays had flown by, and such time off as he had partaken had been filled with family visiting. He had done very little travelling since before the covid lockdown years. Annette had agreed they both needed a proper holiday and so she suggested that they plan to do something in January to escape the gloom of winter. She plonked down some brochures in his study. One of them really hit a chord and would be ideal if she would agree and no outside forces intervened. It was entitled 'Southern Hemisphere wine tour' and was part cruise and part fly drive. It took in vineyards in both South Africa and Chile. It was expensive but it sounded perfect. She said that while he was considering their bigger holiday, she had booked them a long weekend in late October at a luxury country house hotel; her treat to him since he had been behaving. Oliver smiled to himself. What Annette did not know would not hurt her!

Oliver was even happier after Steven Hovell imparted some news to him at court.

"You know you were due to have Plinth v Spitti before you in a couple of days, well I have a draft consent order for you to read with a request to vacate!"

Oliver carefully read the document while Steven waited in his Chambers.

"Hooray, hooray, they have settled the whole case! Thank goodness," he said to Steven.

Her Honour dela Notte was not having such a good day. She had the case of Waste Borough Council v Parcival, Grimmly, Grubbins and Stafficoco in her list today. Lindy Pinney was her clerk but as complications began to unfold even before the case began, so Steven Hovell had to be summonsed. Lindy was very red in the face and flustered.

"Just explain to Her Honour and myself, who is here and what the problems are. Just take it slowly" said Steven entering Her Honour dela Notte's Chambers.

"OK, okay," said Lindy still looking flustered. "Representing the local authority is Mr Ivan Huff and the social worker is Mr Desmond St Vincent. The dad is represented by Bernie Blunt, solicitor, but there is a problem with him... Lila Grimmly is represented by Miss Sonja Sidebottom her solicitor, Naomi Grubbins is represented by Verity Timpson-Saunders, her counsel, Lou Stafficoco is represented by Max Scott his solicitor and the children are represented through their Children's Guardian Mr Tim Weary by Miss Sue Rosemary. There is a granny, Mrs Grimmly, she has that nice Mr Ellison... It's the dad..."

"You mean, Sir Parcival?" asked Steven. "Has he turned up with his sword? I suppose security won't let him in."

"No, it's worse," said Lindy.

"How much worse can it be?" said Her Honour dela Notte.

"A lot, lot worse," said Lindy. "He is dressed in a giant squirrel outfit. Security won't let him in because he does not fit through the security arch. His head gets stuck, and his tail keeps knocking into things, and he won't take off the head for the security guards to see his face."

Steven started to laugh.

"Why has he done that, I wonder?" said Her Honour dela Notte.

Lindy replied, "I went outside to speak to him, and he has a giant mouse and a giant rat with him, he says for support. He says he is not known as Sir Parcival anymore. He has apparently joined the Alternative Reasoning Party and wishes to be known as Mr Squirrel Grey Nuts. He refuses to take off his costume. He says it would be a violation of his political rights. Alternative Reasoning Party members apparently campaign for the rights of rodents and they wear their costumes in support of this… When I suggested he might take the headpiece off to come into the court building his friends started to squeak at me in a high-pitched way… It was quite intimidating."

Lindy started to cry and sniffed dramatically.

Steven said to her, "Look I'll take over sorting out this issue for Her Honour, so you can just assist me."

Lindy stopped sniffing.

"Has anyone spoken to his solicitor?" asked Her Honour. Lindy shook her head.

"I will go and speak to him," said Steven, "but before I go, Your Honour, might I suggest that if Mr Grey Nuts wishes to stay in costume in future, he might appear by video link? That is if it is acceptable to Your Honour?"

Her Honour dela Notte said, "Yes, very good idea. I think, if at all possible, I would like the court entrance not to be clogged up by people in rodent costumes today or indeed on any other day. Speak to Mr Blunt. See what might be done…"

Some twenty minutes or so later Steven returned with the glad news that Mr Blunt had sufficient instructions to proceed today and the giant rodents had gone home. Lindy Pinney had calmed down as well and so she was able to carry on and clerk for Her Honour dela Notte.

The hearing itself was a bit of a non-event. It seemed that Mr Stafficoco had negative drug testing results. With the agreement of the local authority and approval of the children's guardian he had moved back into the family home. It appeared he and his partner were working well with the local authority. Dolores Stafficoco, baby Arnie's grandmother was felt to be a stabilising influence. She continued to live with the family in their home. Lancelot and Guinevere had engaged reasonably well in activities offered to them, although their behaviour was allegedly worse after they saw their father. They apparently ran round the house making shrill squeaking noises after contact. The local authority saw no reason why the future of these children could not be planned out in the near future, even though there were still some issues to unpick, so Mr Huff proposed there be an Issues Resolution Hearing for the next hearing.

Blanchefleur was doing well with her grandmother Mrs Grimmly. Her mother had moved out of Mr Grey Nuts' house and was embarking on some therapy recommended in the psychological assessment. Her contact was going well. The psychologist had encountered one or two problems seeing Mr Grey Nuts. She had eventually managed two video interviews, but all agreed a supplementary report would be beneficial. Contact had become a problem since Blanchefleur's father had turned up in his squirrel outfit to the contact centre on a recent occasion and had been turned away as the other children there had been either confused or alarmed by the sight of a giant squirrel. His solicitor assured the court his client would not attend dressed as a squirrel on the next occasion. However, the children's guardian was dubious bearing in mind how he had dressed for court. She pointed out his behaviour impacted on proposals for contact in respect of his older children.

The lawyers agreed that the issues relating to Blanchefleur might not be so clear-cut, but nonetheless the court should consider matters relating to her at the same hearing as for the other children. A video link would be arranged for Mr Grey Nuts if he wanted to wear his squirrel outfit. It would be a matter for his solicitor to deal with any issues arising from his costume since he would not be in the court building.

After the court cleared and the participants melted away Davina dela Notte retired to her Chambers. Lindy Pinney came to the door,

"I do apologise for panicking, Your Honour," she said.

Davina smiled and responded, "Funny old world isn't it? We can't predict the unpredictable. I shouldn't dwell on it. Something else will come along, I'm sure."

The rest of the day proceeded quietly at Waste Combined Court, but Waste was to get another resident that day. Sonja felt less guilty about her intended move to Chris Ellison's flat when she learned that Dr Gordon Flaughtersdough was to be a tenant at 3 Canal Street. As she began to make her plans and packed up some items, Gordon squeezed his car into the nearby Pither's Yard and started to bring in his possessions. There was a suit in a suit-wrapper on a hanger, a suitcase of clothes, an angle poise lamp, a laptop, a very small printer, an old-fashioned typewriter and a portrait of a very foreboding woman.

Once he had brought everything into the house and had made a good start on unpacking, Auntie Bea insisted that he sat down in her front room for a cup of tea.

"I haven't seen a typewriter like that for years… collector's item, is it?" she asked.

Gordon replied, "I find the muse comes to me with old-fashioned items. What an excellent cup of tea, my dear lady."

"Thank you," said Auntie Bea. "And the portrait, is that your mother?"

"Noo, no, no, no," said Gordon wiping a tear from his eye. "My mother, may she rest in peace, was a poor, dear, gentle soul and I always carry her picture with me in my wallet next to my heart. That is Great Aunt Gertrude. I have her picture for further inspiration… Quite a woman you know…"

"Really," said Auntie Bea, intrigued.

"She lived until she was 99 you know. She was a teacher and very strict. My father was a severe man who told me to listen to her. When I was a boy in prep school she was clear I had to work hard and be generous to others. I was about ten years old, and we had a school bazaar just before Christmas. She sent me a Christmas card and when I opened it some money dropped out. I was thrilled but then I read her note. She said, 'My dear boy here is some money to buy me something at your school fair. It should be enough to cover the purchase and the stamp'. It taught me a valuable lesson…"

Auntie Bea was not sure what it had taught him. He continued,

"She liked to write you know, but I don't think she ever had anything published. I remember her telling me how she had written a poem about asparagus. What a woman!"

Auntie Bea nodded. She hoped his other relatives had been kinder. The influence of his Great Aunt Gertrude was probably not a good one. She hoped that time in Waste would knock the edges off his apparent pomposity and make him a happier, mellow man in his retirement. She finalised his tenancy agreement and discussed meal arrangements with him. She mentioned that another new tenant would be arriving soon as Sonja was imminently moving out. He was keeping on his flat in London to enable him to go back and forth more or less at will. More tea was consumed, and she offered him a piece of her home-made cake which he gladly accepted. He felt very pleased with arrangements and after a while decided to retire to his room.

He lay on his bed. An air of calm seemed to fill his veins and pores. For reasons he had yet to understand he got off the bed for a minute and took Great Aunt Gertrude off the wall. He put the picture on the floor, and propped it up against the skirting board with her face facing the wall.

"I think you would look better back in the London flat," he said.

When Steven Hovell got home from work that day, he received a call from his sister Denise.

"Denise is moving to Waste," he told Scyathica. "You remember she wanted to help Penny with the animals? She asked me to look into a few things for her. I didn't think she was all that serious. I sent her Auntie Bea's details and details about Crunchies' Café since they were looking for staff. Well, it seems she has got herself a room and a part-time job. I wonder if Penny knows?"

"How is she going to move here? I thought your dad was back at work?" queried

Scyathica.

"Denise drives," replied Steven. "She has an old white van so I expect she will bring herself."

"I will phone Penny," said Scyathica, which of course she did.

It seemed that Penny was delighted Denise was coming and would help her with the dogs. Although she was getting used to Scooby the dog due to his loving nature, she had received several requests to take further dogs and some of the dogs were quite large. She had sensibly turned the request down until she had more help. It seemed that Denise had secured shifts at Crunchies' Café from midday to 5 o'clock Monday to Friday and three hours on Saturday 10am to 1pm so that she could come first thing to walk the dogs and for a short time in the evenings. While Lewis gave Penny as much help as he could, he of course was head butcher at Knubb Sausages and Bacon and had his own flat to maintain.

"One thing," said Scyathica. "If you were worried, she would come round here all the time, I think she will be far too busy helping Penny!"

Steven replied, "I am pleased for her. She loves dogs. Hopefully she will be able to spend plenty of time with them. Also, I am pleased Auntie Bea has her as a tenant. She had an empty room. I think they will get on well together. I am also pleased for Penny and Lewis. It may help them spend more time together."

Chapter 11

A BREEZE BLEW UP OVER Waste Water, and a flock of birds flying south wheeled and dived before they departed. The leaves in the trees had turned yellow and gold and had begun fluttering to the ground. The harvest in the fields around Waste was long over and now they had been ploughed, tilled, fertilised, and seeded.

Now and again seagulls flew down and pecked at the ground and murmurations of starlings appeared. When autumn storms did not blow in to wash the cobwebs away, it was becoming increasingly misty of a morning and evening. Wisps of smoke could be seen from farmhouse chimneys and the chimneys of the cottages in the village of Gitthwaite and the neighbouring villages. The days were shorter, and Oliver and Aziz had taken to wearing warm overcoats for their evening walk. The grass was less verdant on the golf course and even the blackberries had come and gone in the neighbouring hedgerows. Some of their usual paths squelched underfoot. The ground was muddy around Penny's farm and the people of Waste were beginning to talk of "Christmas shopping days," and, "It will soon be woolly underpants season."

Sir Hugo had settled down to a new routine which no longer involved trips to Westminster to his great relief. Percy Vere and Melvyn Brice were settling into their new routine of travelling between Waste and the Houses of Parliament. It was to them and not to Sir Hugo, constituents were now raising questions about the future of Waste Waste. Nat Cartey, East Waste's former MP had taken to having a radio show like a duck to water. His pop quiz hour was particularly popular.

Sir Hugo with the assistance of Pandora approached his business with renewed vigour. He was even able to take limited orders for turkeys for Christmas through his business as his newly acquired turkey farm had sufficient birds to fulfil some orders.

In his mind's eye he was hopeful of diversifying and passing on viable businesses for future generations. Pandora seemed to have the energy to help him and assist Waste Women against Violence. Her life in London seemed a distant memory and frankly she was much happier now. She was looking forward to being a grandmother and helped Scyathica to prepare a nursery.

Steven took being court manager well in his stride. His application to be court manager permanently was well advanced. He preferred not to think about what would happen if he did not get the permanent post.

Denise was now living at Canal Street and her battered van could be seen going back and forth out of town to Penny's animal rescue centre. The job at Crunchie's Café was not exciting but it paid the bills. It was Penny's aim that if sufficient income was derived from the glamping business and donations to her animal rescue centre, she would offer Denise a full-time job caring for the animals. At present she just helped Denise with her fuel.

Denise could not have been happier. She developed a particular rapport with Scooby the dog and soon there was additionally Tex, Rex and Mavis, a trio of playful German Shepherd pups who had been found abandoned on a roadside verge. Penny and Denise both agreed that Denise would train them sufficiently so that they could be offered to good homes.

Denise treated Auntie Bea as a mother figure and Auntie Bea pointed her in the direction of local clubs and societies so that Denise had some social life in between working at the café and caring for the animals. She was soon becoming the life and soul of a local country and western club.

Lewis continued to bring off-cuts of meat for the dogs. He took Penny out on what he said were "proper dates". He bought her dinner; he took her to the cinema and to the theatre in East Moorlands. His car was still a hideous colour scheme, but Penny didn't mind.

Jerome arrived unexpectedly in Waste. Davina and Frank were delighted.

"I will be moving here to spend most of my time in Waste he said. "Expect to see some press releases in the next few days. We pulled off the deal!"

Davina smiled. "Do you think we should sell off some of our country estate and this flat and buy a normal house?"

Frank was enthusiastic. "Maybe around Links Close or the Ridings… then I can live near Helal and Ali."

Jerome replied, "In principle, I agree. I want us to have a family life together. I also want a good base in Waste. Mind, please wait for the press release before saying anything."

The senator also arrived quietly at Penny's farm. He had messaged her just before he got on a plane, so she had a little notice. A room was ready, and she greeted him with a smile. Harley the cat rubbed against his legs and purred.

The senator explained to Penny, "This is only a quick visit because my consortium is acquiring Waste Waste. I am going to appear at a press conference after there has been a press release. Mom and I will be back for Christmas, for a proper visit."

"That's okay, I understand," said Penny. "Lewis will join us for dinner tonight. He is bringing over some pork chops. I hope you like them."

"I thought you were a vegan?" laughed the senator.

"You know very well from your recent visits I am okay if you want to eat meat," said Penny dismissing the matter.

Lord Coldharbour kept a low profile. He did not come to Waste this time. He left it to the senator and Jerome. Nat and Brittany Cartey hoped he might put in a brief appearance near Christmas to visit his granddaughter, Tiffany.

The employees of Waste were by and large delighted that the plant was saved and had been rescued by an Anglo-American consortium. Mickey Gasson was a little grumpy, however, that the development had been kept dark from the union. He expressed his dissatisfaction to his wife Maureen,

"There's no way of knowing if they'll keep the wages respectable," he said.

She replied, "Well at least people will have their jobs."

The press conference took place at the church hall near to the plant, in order to accommodate interested parties and all the media paraphernalia. There were press representatives with camera, microphones, recording equipment and television cameras. Ron Woodhouse the plant manager, the senator and Jerome all sat on the small stage smiling.

Although heavily pregnant Scyathica had been sent to cover the press conference. She was pleased to have a seat in the body of the hall. There was initially a hubbub. Then Ron Woodhouse clapped his hands.

"Can we have some quiet please. As you know the plant has just been acquired by Morton Collins Ltd. I have great pleasure in having with me two of the new owners. Some of you may know the senator from the football club," there was a small round of applause, "but I also have the new Managing Director, Jerome dela Notte Collins here as well. I am going to invite the senator to make a statement first."

The senator cleared his throat and stood up in front of a microphone. There was a sound of whirring and clicking of cameras and a number of flashes from flashlights.

"I love this town. It's a great town… so when I heard about the plant, I decided to look into it. I think it has a great future. It will need some modernisation and I also hope to see it expanding. I obviously cannot take a hands-on approach so for that you will have my dear friend and colleague Jerome Collins." He lightly slapped Jerome on the back. "He has worked in the City for years and brings plenty of business expertise."

Jerome stood up and went to the microphone.

"I appreciate you don't know me in Waste, but I can assure you I am here to stay."

There was a round of applause from some workers sitting in the back of the hall.

"I have had many years in business managing money rather than people," he continued, "so Ron will continue to do what he has been doing very well, managing the day-to-day functions of the plant and the people who work there. As a Managing Director I will be more concerned with the plant's finances. I want to see if we can get better, safer machinery, and whether some of Waste Waste's under-utilised site can be developed into Waste Waste Waste Paper. This could potentially bring further jobs to the town." There was more applause and then the senator and Jerome took questions.

There were the inevitable questions: "Can you guarantee there will be no job cuts?" and "Can you guarantee there will be no pay cuts?" Jerome and the senator finished on an upbeat note.

After the meeting ended, they sat and had a quiet drink together at the Knubb Arms.

"I can see a good future for the plant now we are getting a grip on it," said Jerome.

"Yupp," said the senator, "and hopefully it should make us some decent money too!"

He stretched in his chair. "God this town! So quaint! So individual, don't you just love it?"

Jerome agreed. He was really looking forward to not only making a big success of his investment but to also spending time in Waste with his family.

Gavin Bagshaw was not sure whether he loved his hometown or not. Next morning, he got out a suit which had been gathering dust at the back of his wardrobe. He found a shirt to wear with it. He could not find a tie, but he did not think that mattered too much. He looked at the bin bags by the front door. One contained a

Knight of the Round Table outfit and the other a squirrel costume. His home was neat and tidy, albeit a bit under furnished. He had the electricity re-connected with his first wage packet from his new job. His employers Waste Waste had been sympathetic to him having a day off in his circumstances. He had made a good start there. It was only a cleaning job for the toilets and the canteen, but his employers and new colleagues made him feel welcome. Having recently started work at the plant he was really pleased to hear of the press announcement.

When he arrived at the court, initially the security guards and the usher did not recognise him. Even Mr Blunt his solicitor was surprised to see him.

"I thought you were appearing on video link from my office? My secretary was prepared for you... she had even figured how you would best get inside wearing the squirrel outfit."

"My baby daughter is more important," said Gavin. "I just started some counselling. I don't know that what I did was all wrong, but it just made me think I had to give plain old Gavin Bagshaw a chance... a chance to do things right..."

Her Honour Davina dela Notte was delighted she did not have to deal with a squirrel on the end of a video link. She said to Bernie Blunt, "Does your client want to say anything? He has clearly gone to a lot of trouble to come today."

"I think he would," said Bernie Blunt.

Gavin rose to his feet.

"Baby Blanchefleur and Lancelot and Guinevere mean more than anything to me. I have started some counselling. I can't pretend it will deal with all my problems. However, it has made me realise I won't get anywhere by hiding behind a mask, even if I agree with the cause concerned. So, I want to at least try to be plain old Gavin Bagshaw and I want to be a father to my children."

Her Honour dela Notte said,

"Mr Bagshaw, you deserve enormous credit for coming here today as you are and making this statement."

The children's solicitor, Miss Sue Rosemary got to her feet.

"Your Honour, the Guardian and I echo your sentiments. Mr Bagshaw is on a long path which hopefully will lead to better things. He has more counselling in front of him. I understand he also has a new job, so he has all the challenges that will bring, but overall, he is doing extremely well."

By agreement the cases of Arnie, Lancelot and Guinevere were concluded. They would all remain living in Miss Grubbins' household and there would be a six month supervision order to Waste Borough Council who would continue to supervise contact with Mr Bagshaw. As for little Blanchefleur she would continue to live with her grandmother. Contact could hopefully progress quickly in her mother's case but might proceed more slowly in the case of Mr Bagshaw. There would be another hearing. By then there would be reports as to whether she should live permanently with her grandmother, or whether there was any prospect of her living with her mother. Further reports would look at Mr Bagshaw's progress, in particular whether he would be able to progress to unsupervised contact. The hearing ended on a very positive note.

It was about 20 past 12 when Her Honour Davina dela Notte rose. She indicated to Lindy Pinney who had been her clerk that Lindy could go back to the office. Afterwards, Davina slipped out of the backdoor of the court. The air was chilly, but she headed to the expensive cake shop just off the town square. There was a spring in her step. First, she bought a mixture of thirty cinnamon pastries and apple strudels for the court and security staff. Then she purchased eight mixed pastries to share amongst the judges. On her return to the court building, she handed the bag of pastries and strudels to a surprised security guard and said,

"Please take these to Mr Hovell. Tell him to distribute them to staff and security. My treat."

Then she went upstairs. As she got to the top of the stairs she almost bumped into Oliver Grasby.

"Hello," he said bearing not only his own sandwich box but a tin of biscuits. "I was just heading to the judges' dining room. Got a few choccy biccies!"

Davina responded, "I've had a morning which has restored my faith in human nature, so I've bought cake for everyone."

"My, my," said Oliver, "I think I better get my secret bottle of wine!"

Oliver and Davina took their goodies to the dining room. Aziz Ahmed appeared a few minutes later. He was holding a large plastic tub with a lid on it.

He said,

"What are we all celebrating? My wife was in such a good mood about Waste Waste being saved that she gave me a big box of samosas to share with everyone."

Davina responded, "In my case, some faith in human nature."

Oliver laughed, "Not sure about that… but my wife has been talking holidays and I'm going away for a long weekend very shortly, hooray!"

District Judge Ercol appeared. He smiled and looked at all the food.

"Gosh, this looks like a party. I have brought a bag of pears in today from the garden. Now Mum's settled I have had a chance to sort out the garden at home a bit and it seems I have a couple of lovely old pear trees."

District Judge Cecily Stump came timidly up the corridor carrying a couple of bottles containing a brown substance and a plate with some odd-looking biscuits on it.

"Well, it's the time for fruit. I thought I'd bring some of my home-made apple juice into the court for people to try. I've also brought my apple and cheese savouries too. I cooked a batch last night."

Aziz said politely, "I would love to have some."

Oliver looked more dubiously at the bottles and the biscuits but said nothing.

The judges put their food on the table. Davina found some plates in a cupboard. Oliver brought out some glasses for the wine and apple juice. Aziz, Eric, and Cecily also made some tea and coffee in the little kitchenette next to the dining room. Then, they all sat down to lunch.

The court staff were surprised and very pleased by Her Honour dela Notte's gift. While she always gave generously if there were collections, for example when Derek Devene retired, she was not known for buying people cakes. Steven thought he should go upstairs and thank her. He climbed up the backstairs and went initially to her room, but she was not there. He could hear laughter coming from the judges' dining room. He carried on along the corridor and saw that the door was slightly ajar. He stopped and hesitated about entering the room or even knocking at the door.

Sitting around the table in the judges' dining room were all his resident judges; His Honour Judge Oliver Grasby KC was at the head of the table and Her Honour Judge Davina dela Notte was seated at the other end of the table. His Honour Judge Aziz Ahmed was on one side of the table and District Judges Stump and Ercol were on the other side of the table. In the middle of the table was an open bottle of red wine of which half the contents appeared to have been poured out, two bottles of some brown liquid and a steaming pot of hot coffee. Cups and glasses were liberally placed around the table, some full, some empty. In the middle of the table were a variety of different foods.

All the judges were smiling, and Steven caught some jovial banter. His Honour Judge Ahmed was saying,

"It's always a pleasure to have such good colleagues…"

"I think so too," said District Judge Eric Ercol. "I think the friendliness of staff and judges is what sets this court apart."

"It might be something do with Waste," was Aziz Ahmed's reply.

"Maybe so," said Her Honour dela Notte.

"Whatever it is," said Oliver Grasby, "I would like to propose a toast to the court and its staff and judges… and just to be sure, to Waste too!"

Steven quietly retreated. By rights he should have objected to the bottle of wine being there; it was against the rules. He stepped back before any of the judges saw him. He heard a clinking of glasses and cups and Oliver Grasby's voice as he retreated down the corridor,

"To Waste, always Waste!"

Chapter 12

IN THE SECOND WEEK OF December the weather began to tease everyone that snow might be on the way. It was very cold.

Lord Coldharbour looked out of the window of his glass-plated Canary Wharf offices towards a chilly scene. The Thames was a dark grey under a murky sky. He considered matters. His brother was out of the picture. His son was settled in Waste, keeping out of trouble. His niece and her family were well settled in Waste. Her other uncle was retired from politics and the new Members of Parliament for Waste were inexperienced and new to the scene. Lord Coldharbour's media empire was being updated by him as was necessary for changing times. There was a good chance of making money out of Waste Waste. He straightened a pen on his large and empty desk, in his large and empty office. Everything was as it should be.

From time to time the sky over Waste Water became leaden and a few isolated flakes of snow would drift into the town of Waste from over the lake. Nothing came of these snow flurries and the longer-range prediction was for a mild wet Christmas. It was dark at tea-time and the Christmas lights had been put up around the town square. A giant Christmas tree lit with yellow lights had appeared.

Botch, Brath and Ercol were already having their Christmas party. The panelled boardroom had had the boardroom table folded down and pushed to the side so that a light buffet of canapes, mini pork pies and mince pies prepared by the chef of the Knubb Arms was available to partners, staff and invited guests. In the middle of the room there was now a small table containing several bottles of champagne, two jugs of non-alcoholic fruit punch laden with slices of fruit and a few bottles of vintage port. A couple of baskets of suitable glasses had been placed just under the table. Mr

Brath had been seated just by the table to serve out the drinks which he handed out beaming, saying, "Seasons greetings."

A small, Salvation Army band had just begun to play in the square near the Christmas tree, so the sound of the seasonal music wafted into the offices every time the front door opened. Sonja stood having a drink with Chris Ellison who was known to many of the members of the firm at the party. Seasonal greetings were being exchanged. Tina Ercol went up to the young couple and there was plenty of seasonal banter. Tina was smiling and cheerful and said,

"I never thought I would say this, Sonja, but you really have become a 'Botch' person."

Chris Ellison who did not know what she meant responded in a broad Brummy accent before Sonja could say anything,

"I should say Sonja is very much her own person, good at what she does, she doesn't bodge things at all."

Probably influenced by the champagne she was drinking, Tina just laughed his comment off, and said,

"Well, I better go and mingle quickly. I am going to a dinner with judges and partners after this." Chris looked puzzled.

Sonja grinned and as Tina moved off said to Chris, "Don't worry, I'll explain things when we get home," which she did.

As for Tina she soon wobbled off to the judges' party upstairs at the Knubb Arms where a good time was had by all. The local judiciary and their partners took in the warm atmosphere and enjoyed the excellent fair. Anyone passing the private dining room could hear laughter and from time to time there was a tinkling of glasses and a toast with a "Seasons greetings to everyone," or, "To Waste, always Waste."

Waste Waste were also having an early Christmas party. Jerome had seen to it that the company paid for celebrations to boost morale. The church hall had been hired for the evening and a barrel of beer procured. Sausages and pork pies had been obtained from Knubb Sausages and large trays of Christmas cake and mince pies had been procured from a local supermarket. The local country and western band complete with their newest member Denise Hovell on tambourine and backing vocals were due to start playing from 8 o'clock. She had promised to tell Auntie Bea all about it, and to bring her back some pork pie. Mickey and Maureen Gasson with daughter Brittany were all there tapping their feet. Nat Cartey had been left at home to baby-sit Tiffany.

Over at Knubb Sausages invitations were being handed out for a grand New Year's Eve party which was going to be thrown by Sir Hugo and Pandora. Some of the employees were going off for early Christmas drinks at the pub tonight but Lewis declined the invitation politely.

Lewis phoned Penny as he left work.

"Just to say that due to the weather I thought I wouldn't take you out, but I shall bring dinner to you. I just need to pick up a few things."

"That sounds intriguing," replied Penny as she stoked an open fire.

The farm animals were tucked up in barns with extra hay and straw. The larger dogs had been placed back into heated kennels after early evening walks given by Denise. In addition to cosy dog beds, they had been given thick dog blankets and big dog chews. The small dogs and the cats were all toasting their toes by the fire.

Lewis appeared around an hour later with a wicker basket. Inside the basket was some pasta, a large can of peeled tomatoes, fresh mushrooms and aubergines, a garlic bulb, a red onion, a pack of asparagus, a lettuce, a bottle of Chianti and a large cellophane pack of Crunchies' chocolate brownies. In the middle of the basket was a small cardboard box.

"This looks interesting," said Penny who had immediately noticed the little box. "What's in there?"

"All will be revealed shortly, but first let's get dinner sorted. By the way, before you ask, the pasta is veggie… and yes, tonight I will eat the same as you," said Lewis.

Soon, Lewis found himself surrounded by various creatures in Penny's kitchen. Harley the cat seemed particularly curious at Lewis's endeavours.

There were several "damns", "drats" and obscenities as Lewis prepared Penny a meal, insisting she should not help. Eventually she was served pasta with a tomato sauce rich in the flavour of garlic, mushrooms, and aubergines with sides of charred asparagus and a green salad washed down with the Chianti. For dessert they ate a chocolate brownie each. After the meal Penny said,

"Now, what's in the little box?"

"You stay in that chair, and all will be revealed," said Lewis who went to the kitchen and fetched the box.

He approached Penny and then went down on one knee,

"Penny," he said. "Will you marry me?" and he opened the cardboard box and took from inside it a ring box. Inside the ring box was an engagement ring with a single diamond set in a silver heart surround.

"Yes, of course," said Penny hardly drawing breath. Harley the cat purred his approval.

As Lewis was cooking dinner for Penny, Steven was explaining to Scyathica that he had now received the firm offer for the permanent job of court manager. He had been a little late home since he had been discussing his role on the telephone with his manager from the Circuit Centre. At lunchtime he had spent time making arrangements for a staff Christmas buffet next week. Julie James, the usher manager, would bring cakes and traybakes. Lindy Pinney said she would make a large quiche and a sausage plait. Waste Combined Court staff reckoned they knew how to do a good buffet.

However, when he got home with his news, Steven was initially a little surprised when a look of pain crossed her face when he gave Scyathica his good news.

"What's the matter?" he said. "Aren't you pleased?"

"I think it's time," she replied.

"Time for what?" he said.

"For the baby to arrive, you daft idiot," replied Scyathica. "I believe I have gone into labour."

"Ahh," said Steven.

Without any panic they collected Scyathica's bag which she had packed in readiness for the occasion, and they also informed Pandora and Uncle Hugo before heading for the hospital. The pets all pressed their noses to the window as they drove off. Pandora promised she would ensure everything in the nursery was ready and that the West Wing was nice and warm for their eventual return. They promised to phone her and Uncle Hugo when they could.

Steven drove carefully along the icy roads as the snow flurries continued.

It was at about 10 o'clock the following morning that Steven and Scyathica's daughter made her appearance into the world. Steven cradled her in his arms while Scyathica received attention from medical staff following the birth. Scyathica said in a weary but happy voice,

"What do you think? Is she beautiful?"

Steven replied, "Perfect of course just like her mother."

The midwife asked them, "Does she have a name yet?" Steven nodded.

"What is she called?" the midwife asked.

"Why Hope, of course," said Steven. "Hope Patience Wentworth-Hovell."

E p i l o g u e

DR GORDON FLAUGHTERSDOUGH HAD TRIED to get a grip on his memoires for several weeks. He had started three different versions only to discard each of them. The first seemed far too dull. The second version might have offended people he had met over the years to the extent he might be sued for defamation. The third version just sounded odd. It was nearly 9 o'clock and very cold but nonetheless he decided to go for a walk and clear his head.

He put on a thick overcoat and a recently acquired tweed hat. He embarked on a walk around some of the streets of Waste. There was a full moon to light his walk along the frozen, slippery pavements and snowflakes came down. After a while he found himself in front of the Combined Court. He could get no inspiration here other than a feeling it ought to appear in his book. He pressed on with his walk and found himself looking out over Waste Water. The lake shone and glinted in the moonlight as if it were winking at him. It was cold so he turned round and headed back to Canal Street.

He let himself in very quietly as it was extremely late, and he went upstairs and went straight to bed.

He awoke early in the morning, and he knew exactly what he would do. He would not write his memoires. He would write a novel. It would be an entirely fictitious work, but it would draw on his life experiences particularly in the legal profession, including the places he knew or had visited and the people he had met. He would get started that very day. He was not sure if the author in his novel would be like him in any way, whether a man or a woman, or whether they would be a rather different personality. He hoped it might be an amusing and uplifting story with what colloquially might be called a happy ending. With those thoughts he felt content.

Waste Recipes

Waste Cakes

Waste apple dumplings

Ingredients: 370-400 grammes puff pastry

4 sweet apples

30 grammes butter or buttery spread

25 grammes of summer fruit jam

Roll out the pastry and divide it into 4. The amount depends on size of apple. The pastry should be fairly thin. Peel the apples and core them. Place each apple in the middle of a square of pastry. Pull the corners of the pastry almost round each apple. Put a spoon of jam followed by a small knob of butter into the core of each apple. Pull the pastry round each apple and press together so you should have round dumpling shapes.

Place the apple dumplings on a slightly greased baking tin and place in a pre-heated oven, pre-heated to 180 centigrade. Bake for 20-30 minutes until golden brown. Can be served hot or cold. Lightly dust with icing sugar. Cream, ice-cream, custard or fresh raspberries all go well with the dumplings.

Waste almond cake with jammy lake

Ingredients: 200 grammes of butter or cooking margarine

250 grammes caster sugar

4 large eggs

150 grammes ground almonds

100 grammes self-raising flour

Small amount of grated lemon rind

350 grammes jar of summer fruit jam e.g. raspberry

Dessert spoon of icing sugar

Pre heat oven to 180 centigrade. Take 2 8-inch baking tins and either grease or line.

Cream the sugar and the butter/margarine. Beat in 2 eggs. Beat in the ground almonds. Beat in 2 more eggs. Add the flour and the lemon rind. Beat the mixture until smooth.

Divide the mixture about 2/3 to one tin and 1/3 to the other. Place the tins in the oven for about 50 minutes starting at 180 degrees. Turn down the oven to 160 degrees after 30 minutes. You may want to test the sponges after about 40 minutes with the prong of a roasting fork. The cakes are done when they are firm, and nothing is sticking to the fork.

Once removed from the oven the cakes should be left to cool on a wire tray or rack.

Once the cakes are cool take the smaller one and cut a circle out of the centre. You may want to trace a circle shape on a piece of paper to help guide you. You should now be left with a ring of cake. Use the larger cake as the base and smother with summer fruit jam. Place the circle shape of cake on top. Fill the central round circle with jam to the level of the circle of cake. From the circle of cake, you previously removed cut a couple of small triangle or wing shapes and place them in the pool of jam. Finish off your Waste cake by dusting with icing sugar.

Serve with cream, ice-cream or fresh fruit... or all 3!

Savoury Waste Cake/Dumpling

Ingredients: 370 grammes puff pastry

500 grammes sausage meat

2 small old potatoes

1 small, sweet apple (or 2 if you want a sweeter taste)

½ cup of sultanas or raisins soaked in rum

Soak raisins in advance for at least 3 hours. Peel and cook the potatoes, either boiling or microwaving and cut the peeled cooked potato into very small pieces.

Peel and core the apple and cut the flesh into very small pieces.

Pre-heat the oven to 180 centigrade. Mix the sausage-meat, the potato, the apple and the raisins together. Roll out the pastry to a large rectangular shape. Place the mixture in the middle. Press it together so it forms a ball-shape. Then fold the pastry around the ball. You should end with something which looks like a giant Cornish pasty. Prick it and place it in the oven. Cook for 35-40 minutes until golden brown.

Serve hot with a green vegetable and a chilled glass of white wine or lager. Can also be eaten cold.

NOTE; to make an entirely savoury version omit the apple and raisins and substitute with 2 large, cooked carrots cut into very small pieces.

Pigeon in Peas and sherry

Ingredients: 50 grammes of dried peas soaked overnight

250 grammes of fresh or frozen peas (adjust to taste)

Half dozen peeled shallots, or two small onions chopped roughly

4 rashers of bacon

A mug of good quality sherry

A medium potato peeled and cut into four

2 large pigeons fully plucked drawn and cleaned

Salt, pepper, 2 bay leaves

Some chicken stock.

Use a large metal casserole dish with a lid. Place the pigeons fully seasoned in the middle of the pot and drape each with 2 rashers of bacon. Add the shallots, peas and potato to the pot, making sure the pigeons and bacon are fully visible in the middle. Pour in 2/3 of the sherry and some chicken stock to a level so that the tops of the pigeons are still fully visible. Keep the rest back. Add the bay leaves to the pot.

Place in the oven initially for 20-30 minutes at 200c without the lid.

Remove from oven when pigeons and bacon seem to have browned, and liquid is beginning to reduce. Top up with rest of sherry and some chicken stock to the previous level. Put the lid on and return to the oven. Cook for a further hour at 180c. If the liquid appears to be reducing too quickly it may be necessary to reduce the heat.

Serve with crusty bread.

Sausage bunny

Ingredients: 500 grammes lean beef mince

400 grammes of sausage meat or sausages squeezed out

100 grammes sage and onion stuffing mix

1 egg (small)

A tbsp of tomato puree (optional)

2 large onions

2 large tomatoes

Potatoes (optional... see comment below)

Salt and pepper (approx. tsp of each)

Mix the mince, the sausage meat, the stuffing mix and the egg in a mixing bowl with the salt and pepper. Add the tomato puree if a hint of tomato flavour is desired. Once all the ingredients in the bowl are thoroughly mixed tip the contents out in one go onto a roasting tin and shape into a loaf shape. Cut one onion and one tomato into segments and decorate the top. Cut the other onion and tomato into rough pieces and place around the meatloaf.

It is possible too as an option to roast some new potatoes around the meat loaf.

Place in an oven and cook at 180c for about 80 minutes.

Serve hot with vegetables and potatoes and an onion gravy or with crusty bread and a hot tomato sauce.

Can also be eaten cold with potato salad.

Salmon Supper

Ingredients: 4 salmon fillets

A tub of cream cheese, for example, Philadelphia with chives

A generous handful of chives

2-250 grammes of cherry tomatoes

1 tbsp olive oil

Salt and pepper as desired

Splash bottom of deepish ovenproof dish with olive oil. Arrange salmon fillets across the bottom. Put a very generous dollop of cream cheese on top of each one. Half the cherry tomatoes and scatter them in the dish liberally. Cut the chives up finely and scatter the chives liberally. Salt and pepper as per taste.

Cook at 180c for about 25 minutes.

Serve with new potatoes and salad.

Auntie Bea's quick potato salad

Ingredients:

500 grammes of baby potatoes

250 grammes mayonnaise

Handful of chives

2-3 spring onions including stems

6-8 stoned olives

Sprig parsley to decorate

This recipe can be done the longer way or the really easy way. The long way involves making your own mayonnaise and boiling the potatoes. The very easy way is as follows.

Clean and wash your potatoes. Skin can be left on if they are small. Microwave until cooked but still firm in microwavable dish. Leave to cool a while. Wash chives and cut really fine. Wash spring onions and dice fine including stems. Chop up the olives very small indeed.

Once the potatoes are becoming cooler put them in a salad dish. Chop them smaller if you wish. They will soon cool further when you start chopping. Spoon in the mayonnaise and stir. Add the chives, the spring onions and the olives. Stir thoroughly.

If you want to decorate it pop some parsley on top.

Should serve at least 2 unless you feel greedy.

Lewis's pasta sauce

Ingredients:

1 large red onion

1 large aubergine or 2 medium aubergines

250-500 grammes of mushrooms (adjust to taste)

1 garlic clove crushed (or tbsp garlic granules)

800 grammes peeled tomatoes (chopped tinned tomato is fine)

Olive oil

A splash of red wine (optional)

Seasoning

Peel and dice the red onion. Wash/clean and lightly chop the mushrooms. Wash, slice and season the aubergines. Place large, deep, metal pot on stove and heat some oil. Place the onion, the garlic, the mushrooms, and the aubergines in the pot and soften all the vegetables. When they become slightly browned check if there is excess oil which has not been absorbed and drain it off to avoid the sauce getting fatty. Pour in the peeled tomatoes and stir everything. When the sauce is bubbling and has reduced slightly it is ready. A splash of red wine can be added optionally during the time it starts bubbling.

Serve with pasta and a green salad. For vegetarians charred asparagus is a nice accompaniment. For meat eaters lay a sirloin steak across the dish of pasta and sauce.

Author Thank You and Information about Suzanne Stephenson and her books

I WOULD LIKE TO THANK you for taking the time to read my books. If you have a moment to spare to review the book you have been reading, I would appreciate it. You may have your own thoughts about what I have written and that is fine. I was a lawyer for many years and then a District Judge. Any legal background is inspired by my long legal career although I hasten to stress the fictional nature of the humans. I am also privileged to live in the English countryside, surrounded by animals who provide a lot of inspiration, as did the bear I saw on holiday in Canada who sparked off the ideas for 'Bearswood End'. I enjoy sketching and the animal pictures are often sketches of animals around the farm.

I want to give particular thanks to Sarah Luddington from Mirador Publishing who took me and the comedic and animal inspired books under her wing.

If you want to contact me, please feel free to look at my Instagram page:
Suzanne Stephenson (@bearswood_end).
Or also www.stephensons-authors.co.uk which has further information about my books.
Email address Adventures@stephensons-authors.co.uk.

The following are books I have written:

Bearswood End

A scientist wanders out into the wilderness and finds a mysterious village populated by bears. To be accurate the bears find him. Can the secret village of the bears survive a threat from the outside world? Read the scientist's diary and the story of the woman who finds it.

Mr Perkins takes Charge

A black cat walks into a solicitors' office. Lives change of the lawyers and people who cross this cat's path, usually for the better. Is he just a stray cat and is it all a coincidence or is there something more mysterious afoot? If you like cats, you may find this intriguing. If you are just curious about the goings-on of a lawyers' office satisfy your curiosity following the trail of sunshine left by Mr Perkins' paws.

The World According to Patrick White

This is a comic tale with a pinch of satire about a lawyer who finds she has a talking pig, and we discover how he sees the human world and what he thinks of some of our habits and human foibles. Find out how the lawyer and her family cope with this pig of a situation. Needless to say, pig and human have a few adventures before the tale is over, including a court case where the pig is an expert witness and an encounter with a Royal dignitary.

Waste

This is a legal satire about activities at a combined court in a fictional northern town. Two young people arrive whose lives might otherwise have gone to waste and make fresh starts in this fictional town which boasts as main industries a waste plant and a sausage factory. Meet the judges, MPs and other local characters.

Printed in Great Britain
by Amazon

40193127R00179